Please feel free to send me an e~~mail~~
filters these emails. Good news

MW00625275

Charlotte Carol - charlotte_carol@awesomeauthors.org

Sign up for my blog for updates and freebies!
charlotte-carol.awesomeauthors.org

About the Publisher

BLVNP Incorporated, A Nevada Corporation, 340 S. Lemon #6200, Walnut CA 91789, info@blvnp.com / legal@blvnp.com

DISCLAIMER

The War of Fate

Hades' Daughter

By: Charlotte Carol

BLVNP

ISBN: 978-1-68030-930-0

Table of Contents

Praise for Hades' Daughter

It's amazing and funny. I love the suspense and danger. It's a very attractive plot for the readers.

-Amaya R.

A humorous, enjoyable yet thrilling read from beginning to end. I love the cheeky nature of the characters and the way they interact with each other. A book I would highly recommend!!

-Cath

I would definitely recommend this book to anyone. I love the drama and Hades personality that just makes me laugh so hard. Definitely a great book that was written by a great author.

-Noelle Long

I love this book so much! When I read it on Wattpad, I found it so amazing that it's very different from other books. It really is if you don't believe me. Ask other readers. Sadly, I didn't finish reading the book when the author rewrote it, so I'm rereading. I'm hoping to buy the book, when I'm able to buy an Amazon card. If you can't, ask a friend or family to buy the book for you, and tell them that you'll pay them their money back, if they don't want to. Read the sample, if you want before buying, but really, I hope none of you guys are disappointed in the book, for some parts you don't like. Deal with it!

-Jessica

Awesome book! Totally worth reading!

-Yasmyn

Hades' Daughter is a great book which I would definitely recommend to all my friends (which I did, and they're loving it too!) and family! It's definitely worth a 1000/10! Can't wait to see more of Charlotte Carol's works! <3

-Selene

To everyone who, like Scarlett, is fighting their inner demons daily.

FREE DOWNLOAD

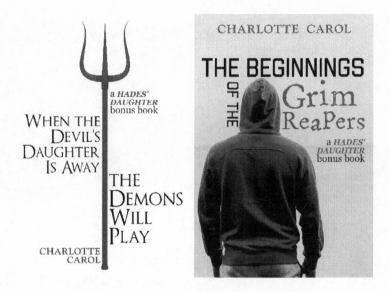

Get these freebies and MORE when you sign up for the author's mailing list!

charlotte-carol.awesomeauthors.org

Chapter 1

Welcome to Hell

Hades is known by many names in different cultures around the world—the Devil, Lord of the Underworld, and Satan. I have met the real Devil, and no, I am not dead, nor did I sell him my soul. No, I know him by a different name: Dad. My name is Scarlett Hades, and I am the daughter of the god Hades.

Lying on my back on the bed, my legs bent, I stare up at the high ceiling above me. I blow air out through my lips, resting my hands flat on my stomach. I listen to the sounds of the house: the guards patrolling, the servants going about their different duties, and Tybalt, my pet hound, padding around the house, trying to find something to eat. I ponder what to do. It's late in the "day," and I've run out of ideas. I turn my head to look at the half-finished book on the bedside table, one of the many books my dad bought me. I have been meaning to finish it for a while, so I sit up, pushing my long hair out of the way, and reach for the book. I only get halfway back to the bed with the book, however, before the silence is shattered by a deep, booming voice, and I nearly drop it. I hear this voice often, but it still gets me every time when it is unexpected.

"Scarlett Olivia Hades, come to the entrance right now!" The angry voice vibrates throughout Hell. I guess my dad decided for me then.

I return the book to the bedside table before swinging my legs over the side of the bed and strolling out of my room. I pass servants and guards as I make my way toward the big staircase leading down to the entrance hall. Every servant, all of them souls, bows their head as I pass. The guards continue with whatever they are doing. I don't get the privilege of having everyone bow their heads until I take over for my dad.

I step off the grand staircase and find Tybalt meandering down one of the hallways leading into the entrance hall. When he catches sight of me, his big, black head rises. An instant later, his dark mass is bounding toward me. I crouch down to welcome him as he skids to a halt in front of me. I scratch him behind his ear in his favorite spot, running my fingers through his thick fur. He's been in my life since he and I were newborns, and I can't imagine my life without him. I know, cliché, but it's true.

I straighten up, his big red eyes following me, silently asking me what he should do, but also pleading with me to play with him. I put my hands on my hips as I look down at him. Watching him now, you would never know how vicious he can be.

"I guess we could have one game," I tell him. I clench my hands, pointing my index fingers and thumbs out, forming a makeshift gun. I point my index fingers down at Tybalt, his tail wagging side to side in excitement, making me glad that there is nothing valuable in range, and make a sound like a gunshot.

"Pow!"

At my sound, Tybalt falls to the floor, lying on his side, his red eyes watching me to see if he did well. I loved teaching him this trick when I was younger. I chuckle, bending down to give him another scratch before walking to the front door.

With my hand on the handle, I glance back at Tybalt who is now up on all fours looking at me expectantly.

"Tybalt, stay," I command. He lies down, his head falling onto his big paws, his red eyes trained on me.

"Good boy," I say with a smile. I pull open the heavy door, and I am immediately hit by heat. I've lived here for eighteen years, and it hasn't changed a bit. I love the feeling of opening the door and being hit by the heat and breathing in the sulfuric smoke. I love the glow and color of the fire pits, and even though it seems weird, I also love the sounds. As expected, this being Hell, the main sound is the souls' screaming, but that's what I'm used to and what home sounds like to me. Any different and I would find it strange.

As soon as I step out onto the hard ground, a servant appears by my side, asking if there is anything he could do for me, offering to retrieve whatever I want. I think for a moment if I do want anything from him, maybe go and see my dad for me, but dismiss him when I decide to go for a ride. I walk past demons and souls toward the stables.

When I arrive at the stables, I nod my head at the guard posted outside the big doors. I step inside, the hay crunching under my boots. Another servant comes scurrying to my side.

"How may I help you, ma'am?" she asks. I love hearing the different voices of souls, as they come from all over Earth, but in the end, they all sound similar when they are screaming. The soul before me sounds like she comes from the south of America.

"I would like my horse. Don't bother saddling him. I'll do that," I tell her. I walk to the wall which holds the silver bridle and black saddle for my horse, Drake. I lift them up, feeling glad for my extra strength, and turn back to the middle of the stable.

I see the soul leading, with difficulty, Drake from one of the many stalls. I watch as Drake pulls his head up violently away from the soul. The strength and the height of him, which is already causing the soul to struggle, nearly pull her off her feet. I watch with amusement as the soul tries to lead an uncooperative Drake toward me.

Eventually, the soul manages to pull Drake in my direction. I take him from the soul, dismissing her afterward. As the soul rushes away, Drake tries, for the last time, to cause damage to the soul by kicking out his back leg. His massive hoof misses her by inches. I pull him down to look at me.

"Behave," I admonish him as I rub my hand down his black nose. He blows out through his nose, a lot calmer now. I place the saddle on his back, securing it around his stomach before flipping the stirrups up his back. I make sure they are at the right length and are secure.

Once I am satisfied, I then move to the bridle, securing the straps and pushing the bit between his teeth. I give him a pat on the neck as I lead him toward our exit. I halt him to get on him. Holding the reins, I place my foot in the stirrup and swing myself onto his back. I secure my other foot and place my hands correctly on the reins before kicking him with my heels. He starts to walk briskly.

"Scarlett Olivia Hades, if you are not here in one minute, there will be trouble!" my dad's voice rumbles through Hell once again.

I roll my eyes and shout back, "I'm coming. No need to go all devil on me!"

I don't get a reply, so I kick Drake again and again, and we are cantering toward the entrance to Hell, the hot air blowing my hair around my face.

As I ride, I notice a demon advancing on a little boy. I usually try to stop the demons from attacking the young children. It's very rare to get young children here, so when the demons find one, they have a field day. The souls don't age. For the rest of eternity, they stay the same age when they died. Anyone who is born here will become a demon and will age extremely slowly after the age of eighteen. Even souls can have children, but it's really rare to be done willingly. I slightly nudge Drake to the right to charge at the demon.

I get a glimpse of the demon's monstrous face as his beady, red eyes widen in surprise. A demon often looks like a human. However, when they attack, their face transforms; their eyes look like they're catching fire, and they grow fangs. The same happens to me, but I get a pair of horns too, like a tiara.

Drake knocks the demon into a pit behind him, and the fire swallows the demon's body but not his screams of discomfort, though.

I roll my eyes. He'll be fine; he's just overreacting. The fire won't kill him; it will be more of an annoyance like if you ran a bath too hot. Otherwise, half of the demons in Hell would be dead as we've all fallen in at least once. I, however, am immune to the effects of fire. To me, it's like sitting in a pleasant bath. I actually use it to tan on some days. On Earth, humans use a fireball in the sky; I use the fire in the ground.

I maneuver us back onto the main path leading to the entrance, patting Drake's neck as we ride.

As we draw nearer to the entrance and my dad, I slow Drake to a trot to control him better. I steer Drake past the demons waiting for new souls and to the winding path leading to the entrance. Drake and I climb the steep incline before emerging onto the flat piece of land at the top.

I stop Drake so I can admire the view of Hell from up here; it's one of my favorite places to sit and watch the movements of Hell, my dad's office being the other. You can see almost all the way back to the house from up here. Hell is a big place, as it needs to be able to hold everyone. The demons and souls all look the same from up here, small ant-like beings.

With a smile on my face, I turn Drake and start off at a walking pace toward where my dad is standing in a tunnel. On the other side of this cave is where the boat docks to drop off the souls from just being sorted. The demons use this as their way to get to the other side of the lake and onwards to Earth.

I stop Drake outside of the cave and tie his reins to a post that I had placed before. I give him one last stroke before I amble toward my dad.

When he hears me coming closer, he turns his angry blue eyes to me, his strong arms crossed. Before you imagine him as the universal image of the Devil—all red, horns, and a tail, holding a pitchfork—he doesn't look anything like that. Yes, like me, he grows horns and fangs if he's very angry or attacking. (The latter is rare. Not the former, he likes to blame me for all his anger.) But his normal everyday appearance is a tall, strong human. His hair is pitch black, which he likes to compare to his soul. His piercing blue eyes are one of the features I inherited from him. They say my brown hair is from my mother, but I don't remember her to know whether that is true. I also apparently got my height from my mother, as I am slightly taller than average at about 5'7", unlike my father. He looks very young, but the truth is, of course, the total opposite. He is a couple of millenniums old. If anyone were to see him walking down a dark alley, they would most likely turn and run the other way.

I shove my hands into my pants as I stop beside my dad, looking at the subject of his anger at this moment.

"What's up?" I ask cheerily.

He gives me an unamused look and then points at the wall we are standing in front of. There's not a lot for me to do down here, so I make my own fun to amuse myself. Earlier today, I painted in blood on the wall in front of us:

WELCOME TO HELL! I HOPE YOU ENJOY YOUR STAY HERE! IF YOU DON'T, TOUGH LUCK, BECAUSE YOU AIN'T LEAVING.

"Oh. That."

"Explain," he commands.

"I thought they needed a welcome. They are sorted into boats at the Styx Lake which take them to either Olympus or Hell, and in all that time, they never get a welcome," I explain with a shrug. By Olympus, I mean the place that humans call Heaven, not the mountain in Greece. However, a long time ago, my family did reside there.

The humans finding out about the existence of my family was through stories, meaning the myths that are thought to be true, are sometimes just that. Myths. Slight details can be changed or left out through time. For example, the myth about where the dead go is not entirely true. Yes, they do come to the underworld, but they also go to Olympus. The humans only heard about the underworld's problems with souls, so they assumed that here was where all the souls went. Zeus made sure it was this way, as he didn't want the souls to change the way they lived. If everyone believed they were going to the same place, no one would change their ways to better the outcome, and they would end up leading their life as the true person they are. Why make souls who have lead good lives suffer? I find that we all use Hell to describe the underworld as it fits it perfectly, and it's definitely a lot easier than saying *the underworld* each time. It's the same with my dad; people all over the world have different beliefs about who rules their version of the underworld, and as a result my dad is given different names as he is the only equivalent to their beliefs. An example, and one that I like to call my dad, is Devil.

"If you want to give them a welcome, why don't you go to the lake and throw a party saying: The Underworld isn't that bad. We have cake?"

I chuckle; you would never think that he's the god of the underworld and the dead with the way he acts.

"Hell is meant to scare the souls that come here, and if they get a welcome, we are sending the wrong message. I want you to clean this up," he says, producing a bucket and a sponge out of nowhere and handing it to me. Unfortunately, I don't have this power yet.

"What if I don't want to?" I ask, raising my eyebrow as I put my hand on my hip.

"Well, that's an entirely different story," he says sarcastically.

"Okay, then I don't want to," I tell him.

My father's caring face is gone in an instant and is replaced by the gnarled, monstrous face of a demon, his eyes red, his horns and his fangs visible.

"Are you being serious? That might scare souls and demons into doing what you want, but that doesn't work on me."

His face changes back to his normal one when he realizes that I am right. "Just do it!" he grumbles before stroking Drake and walking down the winding path.

"Great!" I mutter under my breath. I pick up the sponge, thrust it into the soapy water, and start to scrub at the wall.

***

I have been scrubbing away for five minutes when I hear the boat pull up. I grin to myself as I continue. Great, a new set of souls. After I've heard all the souls and demons disembark, and the boat making its way back to the other side of the lake, I spin around to greet them.

Demons pass by me without giving me a glance. I look at the group of souls to see if there are any children, and when I see none, I decide to scare them like my dad said we should. I allow my horns and my fangs to grow and my eyes to change color.

"Hello and welcome to Hell. My name is Scarlett, and I will be your tour guide for this lovely evening. You're a lucky bunch because, in fact, I'm actually the big guy's, Hades', Satan's, the Devil's—whatever you want to call him—daughter. So, are we all ready?"

I continue without waiting for an answer. "This is the entrance, and where all the souls arrive and the demons exit. We are currently in a state of redecoration, as you can see behind, but that should be over soon. Now, we will be heading toward the big fire pits, so choose a buddy and stick with them. Try not to fall in, but if such a thing should happen, ignore the screams, and we will continue. Any questions before we move on?" I ask, looking at each of their petrified faces.

"No? Okay, if we move on now, we can finish before it's feeding time." I start to walk toward the winding path, passing Drake who stares at the group of souls warily, a snort coming out of his nostrils. I see out of the corner of my eye one of the souls extend their hand to stroke Drake. I wait for a second, allowing the soul to get close enough, before intervening.

"Ah, I wouldn't do—"

The soul screams as Drake bites her hand. I would leave her like that to teach her a lesson, but I don't want to drag her with me when I ride back. I let out an exasperated sigh as I walk past the souls who are following me and back to Drake. I pry the horse's mouth apart, allowing the soul to take her hand out.

"Learned your lesson? Don't touch things down here," I tell her before walking back to the head of the pack. I continue to walk down the winding path, and we eventually get to the bottom where the demons are waiting eagerly for the new arrivals.

"Here is your first look at demons. You will be seeing a lot of them while you are here. Unfortunately, you will not be seeing what they are capable of yet, but I'm sure you will later. Try to keep up," I call back at the souls.

"Back off. You can have the next batch," I tell the demons. They look like they want to argue, but most of them keep their mouths shut. The ones that do argue don't act on their complaints. As we walk through the group of demons, I can sense the souls starting to get scared; I would be too if I were in their situation. The demons are looking at them like they're food, and this is true.

A short walk later, we arrive at Tártaros, where the souls live near the biggest fire pits of Hell. Again, I am glad that I'm not in their situation, as they have to live with five others in small mud huts. The demons live closer to the mansion, in much nicer accommodation.

I turn to address the group again. "This is where you will be staying for the rest of eternity." I push open the door to the closest hut and show them the inside, which is empty apart from the souls staring up at us with scared looks on their faces. The things that are needed on Earth to survive are not needed here. They survive off nothing; after all, they are dead.

"If you have any problems, feel free to suffer. Do you have any questions?" I ask the group.

A man raises his hand, obviously more confident.

"Yes?"

"Two things: who are you and what the hell is feeding time? Do we get food?"

"One, I told you earlier I am Hades' daughter—" I start counting the points with my fingers—" and two, feeding time is my favorite time of the day when the demons feed on the souls. It's kind of like a big hunt that we all take part in. That doesn't mean you're safe during the other times of the day, though. Demons can feed whenever they want. It's just a fun thing for us to do together. Also, I don't appreciate you using my home's name in that way." I end with a quick, sweet smile.

"Oh," the man says, losing his confidence.

"Is everything clear? Are there any other questions?" I ask, looking around at their faces.

"Yes, I have one. What do you think you're doing?" my dad asks from behind me in a low voice.

I scream and jump around to face him. "Shit!"

"Missy, watch your language! If I don't see you back by the writing, cleaning it off in ten seconds, there will be consequences," he advises before disappearing.

When I don't move straight away, his voice resounds all around us as he uses his "Devil voice," as I like to call it. "Five seconds!"

I groan.

"Okay! Keep your hair on. I'm going!" I shout back in the same way.

"Sorry about that. It looks like our little tour has been cut short. I hope you enjoy your stay here, or preferably don't," I say to the group of souls in my normal voice with an apologetic smile.

Thunder echoes around Hell before lightning flashes through the air. My dad has a flair for theatrics. Zeus, dad's brother and my uncle, gave the power to my dad as a "thank you for taking the underworld" gift many years ago, and when I was born, I was also given this power.

"Here we go again," I mutter. I turn to my dad who suddenly appears beside me. I look at him with an innocent smile.

"What did I say?" he asks in a fed-up tone.

"A lot of things. You have to be a bit clearer," I respond, lifting my hand to show him the small gap between my thumb and my index finger.

When his nostril flare, accompanied by a look in his eyes that says, "Don't play with me." I quickly amend my statement. "Sorry, Sir!" I shout with a salute. "I was just trying to have fun with the new souls. They were going to be my dinner." I whine and pout.

Like the demons, my dad and I have to drink blood to survive. My dad tried to explain it to me when I was younger, but I never really got it. It has something to do with us being, technically, not alive, and the blood helping our body to function as if it was. Along with the blood, we can also eat what is considered normal food on Earth. The souls have an endless supply of blood in their "bodies." They wouldn't be of any use if they didn't. However, fresh blood from a living human tastes much better.

"Get back to work, Scar." My dad sighs.

"Fine," I groan. After waving at the souls watching us curiously, I run back up the winding path, past Drake, and to the half-cleaned wall. I pick up the soaking sponge and press it against the wall. I watch as the water drips, turning red from the blood as it goes.

***

After one last scrub over the wall, I step back to admire my hard work. *Dad will probably get me to clean everywhere else now*, I think to myself as I drop the sponge into the bucket.

Wiping my hands on my pants, I walk to Drake who is patiently waiting for me. He makes a sound when he sees me, obviously glad to be getting away from all the souls walking past. I detach his reins from the post and put them in my left hand as I lift myself onto the saddle. Drake takes a couple of steps forward, eager for us to move.

"Come on then. Let's go home," I tell Drake as I kick his sides. I steer him down the steep path at a slow pace and kick him again when we get to the bottom, starting home at a fast speed. I close my eyes, listening to the rhythmic pounding of Drake's hooves on the hard ground, trying to get the courage to ask my dad again.

I love living down here, and I would never change it, but I've always been curious about Earth. Lately, I've been trying to persuade my dad to let me go and live up there for a year so I can see what it's all about. It's not like I've never been up there before; my dad had taken me along countless times when he had to go up, but they were never long enough for me. I've never experienced Earth fully.

My dad, however, was good enough to teach me how to drive when I asked. He also makes sure that I have all the things I need to keep up to date with the current events and the lingo in most languages up there so I wouldn't sound out of place. It's always through books and newspapers he finds on his visits.

So far, all I have received from my dad in response to my constant pleas are the different variations of the word *no*. I am determined tonight for him to change his mind.

I open my eyes and find the stables almost right in front of us. I pull back the reins, slowing Drake down to a walk before stopping outside the doors. The guards have changed, and I meet a new one outside the doors.

"Nice ride?" she asks.

I smile, moving my head from shoulder to shoulder. "Yeah, what met me at the destination wasn't so nice, though," I tell her.

She's bound to have heard what happened. She chuckles, not engaging in any more small talk.

As we walk past the wall, holding all the equipment, I pause Drake and remove his gear before picking up one of the many brushes. I run it down his back, smoothing out his hairs.

The same servant from earlier scurries up to me and curtsies. As I place the loose straps over Drake's head, I look the soul over.

Her face is slightly red, tears pooling in her green eyes. She tries to give me a smile, but it comes out more as a grimace. Her messy, light blonde hair is made darker by the blood matting it to the side of her face. I look her clothes over and see that her clothes are dirty, blood-stained, tattered, and crumpled. The souls don't just stay the same age they are when they die, but they also stay in the same state. If they die brutally, you will see it.

"You alright?" I ask, turning my attention back to Drake, clipping a rope to his harness.

"Yes, ma'am," she says quietly, looking down, extending her hand to take the rope from me.

I purse my lips slightly as I look at her.

"You know that demon earlier outside, did he, by any chance, have anything to do with this?" I ask, still holding the rope attached to Drake.

"I don't know if I should say, ma'am. After all, I am in Hell, and I deserve it after what I did," she mumbles. Her young face stares at me, waiting for my command. She looks fragile and innocent, and I feel slightly sorry for her. I am always told that I get my compassionate side from my mother, as she was once human before my dad changed her.

"How old are you?" I ask.

"Um, I died when I was seventeen, but that was in 1965."

What did she do? She must have noticed my eyes widening because she continued, "I killed four people and was shot dead by the police in a high-speed chase."

Suddenly, I don't feel so sorry for her anymore; I thought she was going to say something totally different.

"Where were you from?" I inquire.

"Miami, Florida. Ma'am, I'll take your horse now." She bows her head.

Happier now that she is rightly suffering, I pass over the rope to her, leaving her to battle with Drake.

***

I step through the front doors of the main house to find Tybalt exactly where I left him. He raises his big head from his paws when I enter.

"Come here, boy," I tell him.

He jumps up and comes toward me. At the sound of Tybalt's paws hitting the tiled floor, my dad pokes his head out of the door of his study. When he confirms that it's me, he exits and walks into the entrance hall to meet me. He smiles at the ecstatic Tybalt, whose body is swaying with his tail.

"He wouldn't move, even when I told him to," my dad says.

"You know who your master is, don't you?" I look down at Tybalt, holding his face in my hands.

I look back up at my dad, whose smile has faded from his face, his strong arms crossed.

"Why did you feel the need to act out?" my dad asks.

"I was trying to have some fun until *someone* came and spoiled it. I was going eat out tonight with them being my dinner. The new souls are my one source of fun down here. There is really nothing else that I can do. I keep asking if I can get out of here for a year before I start helping more down here to run Hell, but you say no. So, I'm going to ask again, and this time, remember what I just did and how you felt about it. Ready? Can I have a year on Earth?" I whine and pout.

As always, he rolls his eyes and shakes his head. I'm breaking him.

"Alright, I didn't want to do this, but you leave me no choice," I warn him. I deepen my pout and throw in my puppy dog eyes.

His eyes quickly avert from mine, letting me know that he's cracking even more.

"What about a year in Olympus with your aunts and uncles? I can sort that out. They'd love to have you!" My dad tries to compromise.

I put my hand on my hip, cocking my head to the side with an eyebrow raised. "Dad—" I smile "—I love them and all, but can you imagine me in Olympus for a year? I would drive them, you, and the souls there mad. I need a break from this life."

I see his teeth grind together. I internally jump up and down, throwing my hands around. I've got him. He only gives me that look when he knows I'm right. He exhales.

"I can't believe I'm saying this, but alright, you can go." He finally breaks fully, relenting. I shriek in delight, letting my excitement finally show. "Someone else can deal with all the trouble you cause," he mutters.

"Yay!" I exclaim, running to hug him with Tybalt following me, not exactly sure what is going on. Before I can make contact, my dad puts his hand up, and I skid to a halt.

"There are conditions," he tells me.

"Of course, there are."

"One, you will come home every other month for a week. And two, you will go for exactly a year from the date you arrive, no longer."

"Whatever. Thank you!" I skip the rest of the way to my dad, and he pulls me into one of his big hugs that I love.

"Alright, decide when you want to go, and I'll sort everything out. I need to deal with something now, but I'll see you for breakfast tomorrow," he says as he pulls back.

I nod before he walks around me and out the way I came in. I bend down to hug Tybalt as well, knowing I won't be able to take him.

"I'm finally going!" I squeal.

Feeling upbeat, I straighten up and make my way to the kitchen, dancing as I sing a tune in my head. The only times I was able to listen to music were when I went up to Earth with my dad, and now that I'm going up for a year, I can't wait to know more about it.

I enter the modern stainless-steel kitchen and walk to one of the big fridges. I love to cook, so my dad makes sure that it's stocked with everything that I may need, keeping it up to date with everything on Earth, including appliances. I pull open the heavy door to one of the fridges, retrieving a bag of blood, which has been taken from one of the many souls by torturous means. One fridge is set to a cooler temperature, whereas the one we use for the blood is set at a higher temperature (at 98.6°F or 37°C). If we were to leave the blood outside, it would be at boiling temperature after a couple of seconds. Satisfying my hunger, for now, I dance back out of the kitchen and up to my room, looking forward to what's to come.

Chapter 2

A Day in the Life of Hades

When I enter the dining room the next morning, I find my dad already sitting there waiting for me.

"What's for breakfast?" I ask, sliding into one of the many chairs.

"Waffles sound good to you?" he asks, amusement shining in his blue eyes as he looks up from his writing.

"Of course," I respond. He knows I would never turn down waffles.

Curious as to what he's doing, I pull the papers away from him and turn them to me. I look down at them and chuckle. They were all contracts. I push the papers back to him.

He produces his pen that he uses to sign all the contracts, making them unbreakable, as the servants walk in with plates piled high with waffles and a jug full of blood from the souls. Once the jug and waffles are placed in the middle of the table, the servants bow their heads and walk out of the room.

I reach for the jug and pour myself a glass as my dad spears a couple of waffles from the plate in the middle, having signed the contracts.

"So, what do you have planned for today?" he asks, making conversation, as I reach for my own waffles.

"I'm thinking about repainting the message," I joke but quickly amend my statement when I see his furious look. "I actually don't have a lot planned. I was going to start packing, as I've decided that I want to go up to Earth in the next couple of days." I cut a triangle of the waffles topped with cream and chocolate sauce and shove it eagerly into my mouth.

"I'll sort that out when I'm up there today, distributing these. Where do you want to go?" he asks.

There are so many places on Earth that I can go to. I think back to the servant working in the stable.

"Miami, Florida, USA," I tell him. Whenever I visited with my dad, America was my favorite destination.

"Okay, as I'm not here, I need you to go to the Styx Lake and supervise," he requests.

I swallow my mouthful before groaning playfully.

"Ugh. Fine, if I have to. But you have to get me a car and motorbike when I go up," I negotiate.

He ponders it for a moment and then adds onto my clause.

"Yes, but you also have to help at the lake tomorrow."

I grin, extending my hand to him. "Deal, but only if they are both day shifts."

He takes my hand in his and gives it a firm shake.

We finish the rest of our breakfast in silence, and while the plates are being cleared, I go back upstairs to get dressed. I open the door to my room and look around this familiar room that

I love. My big comfy bed sits against the wall to the right of the door.

I walk into my walk-in closet and flick the switch. Fire lights up in niches in the closet's walls. I decide to wear all black to look more intimidating, so I walk to one of the many drawers, pick out a pair of black ripped jeans, and throw them onto the cushioned stool behind me.

I walk further into the closet, past another door, hunting down a black vest. Once I find it and my leather jacket, I move to my shoe collection and grab a pair of black boots.

After finding all my clothes, I step out of my closet, turning the fire off as I go, and step into my bathroom. I am instantly met with hundreds of reflections of myself looking back at me from all angles. I move past the sunken bath and put my clothes on the counter next to the sink. I then take my pajamas off as I walk to the shower.

***

Once I am clean and dressed, I walk back into the main room. Being the daughter of the lord of the underworld has it perks, like inheriting some of his powers, as is expected. Along with the superhuman senses, strength, and speed that all demons have, and the power over storms, I have also gained the ability to teleport in the blink of an eye and compel any human, dead or alive. I usually use teleportation to get around, and today, I also decide to use my power over thunder for extra effect.

I picture the Styx Lake with my eyes closed, visualizing myself standing there. I feel my feet hit the ground, which is softer than the one in Hell, and summon thunder and lightning.

I survey the familiar terrain. The actual lake is massive; you won't see the other side where the lake meets the dark sky because it is blurred by fog. The ornate gate where all the souls enter the afterlife and all the demons and angels enter the human world is far away from the hubbub where the boats pull up at the docks to pick the souls up.

The demons must have permission to move from the lake to the human world. Someone works at the gate constantly to allow people through. Souls are physically unable to leave once they come through the gate. I don't know how the demons and angels come back through the gates once they are out, but I believe it has something to do with a certain grave in every graveyard. They need a way of coming back; otherwise, Earth would be overrun with them.

I turn my attention back to the souls standing like statues on the dark sand, waiting to be taken to their different destinations, watching me in fear.

"You can officially start the party now I'm here," I tell them with a grin.

When they continue to stare at me, I sigh. "Take a picture. It lasts longer. Oh wait, you can't! Hearing me, Dad? You should have looked at that!"

I wait a moment for my dad to reply. I don't know if he has left yet. I get my answer when thunder reverberates through the place. I smile.

"Always know how to make an entrance, don't you, Scar?" someone says behind me.

I spin around, my smile turning sarcastic. A boy my age meets my eyes. His blonde hair is bright and almost luminescent even though we are standing in the dark. His hazel eyes look down at me as he stands tall above me. I feel even more dwarfed by his strong build.

"Jack! What a lovely surprise!" My sarcasm leaks into my tone as I look around for a way out.

"I hear Hell's still Hell, probably because you're still there."

My mind goes to what my dad said.

"Hell's meant to be scary, but I was actually going to ask you whether Uncle P, your dad, has had enough of you yet. Is he sending you back with me? Is that why you are here? Oh, wait, I would probably kill you before the first day is over, so it looks like your dad is stuck with you, unfortunately. Now, if you excuse me, I have souls to sort."

I turn on my heel and walk towards the gates where the lines of souls are waiting to be sorted. I turn back before I get too far and call back to Jack, "Say hey to the Olympus family for me."

As you have probably guessed, Jack, Poseidon's son, and I don't get along. It's not that I don't like my family; it's just Jack's personality. I turn back and approach the guards who are sorting the souls. I walk to the closest and tap him on the shoulder. When I recognize him, I address him by name.

"Brian," I greet him with a nod.

My hand extends for the only device that works down here. It's a sort of electronic tablet which has an ever-updating list of the dead souls that have not been sorted. Once you have a name, the device shows you information about the soul and tells you whether they should be in Olympus or the Underworld. It's only programmed to do that and nothing else.

I turn on the device once Brian passes me one. A message pops up asking for authorization and proof that I'm not a soul. I type in my unique password—my mother's name, Candice— before pricking my finger. The device scans my blood for demon or angel qualities and any signs of duress; souls heading toward Hell will do anything to get on the other boat. After the device is happy that I'm rightfully in charge of the tablet, a list of dead souls appears on the screen, my name in the upper corner. Being the daughter of one of the many gods, I have administrative access. Now logged in, I move to the end of the line of waiting souls.

"Next!" I command.

A kind-looking old lady toddles toward me, a smile on her face even though she is dead.

"Excuse me, dear, would you mind telling me where I am?" she asks. That explains why she's so happy.

"The afterlife, the promise land, whatever you want to call it." I try to be as gentle as I can; after all, I'm telling her she's dead.

"Oh. I hope my daughter is alright," she comments with a sad smile.

I admire her for being frank and selfless about it. I return her smile as I ask for her name.

"Beatrice Moore," she answers.

I type her name into the search bar; otherwise, I would be here all day searching through the hundreds of names manually. Luckily, this time, she is the only Beatrice Moore to have died recently. I click on her name and scan her information. She's ninety-six, and she died from old age.

"Congrats, you're going to Heaven." I motion to the line of patiently waiting souls at one of the docks. I look down at the tablet as she thanks me and walks off. I press the "sorted" button, and Beatrice's page disappears. The screen shows the list of names again.

"Next! I command again.

A man in his late twenties saunters to me, giving me a once-over, a smirk on his lips. Creep! I have a feeling what line he'll be in.

"Name?"

"Bradley Davis," he replies cockily. "What's yours, sugar?"

I ignore him as I enter his name, getting three results back. I click through them, looking up from the tablet every so often. One Bradley was sixty, so I know it isn't him, unless he aged really well, which I doubt. The other two are closer in age. The device doesn't tell you any physical features, only the age, the way they died, and where they are heading, along with the reason why. One Bradley died from cancer, and the other from an overdose. Both are heading to Hell.

I sigh when I look him over, trying to find a clue, but he could have died either way. Not wanting to encourage any more conversation with him, I force myself to open my mouth anyway.

"Put your hand on here," I say in a bored tone, trying to let him know I'm not interested in him. I turn the tablet around, allowing him to place his hand on the screen.

I wait for five seconds before the device beeps. I pull the tablet back to me and see the Bradley who died from the overdose is standing in front of me. He had killed and raped two people. What a surprise! We only use the hand scan as the very last resort to stop the souls from having a chance to steal it. I press the sorted button and look back at Bradley, motioning with my thumb to the unruly line behind me.

"Oh, you have been a naughty boy, haven't you, Bradley? You're in my line. Get ready for an eternity of pain and torture."

He looks from the line to me. I give him a smile, my eyebrows raised. A groan leaves his lips before he reluctantly walks toward his Hell-filled future.

***

I carry on helping until I get bored of interacting with all the souls, so I decide to stand back and supervise. I keep the tablet just in case I need to use my admin. I am looking around at the souls huddled on the shore when I see a boy around the age of six wandering around, looking lost and confused. I don't see anyone helping him, not even the angels standing around, so I decide to.

I step into his path, and he looks up at me his eyes filled with fear. I give him a reassuring smile and ask for his name, which he hesitantly gives.

"Well, Tim, it says here that you should go to Hell for gang activity. It says you stole." I raise my eyebrows in shock. He's only six!

"I didn't want to do what I did," he tells me on the verge of tears.

"If you understand that what you did was wrong, then I think I can make an exception. Don't repeat your actions, okay?" I explain with a caring smile as I use my admin access to change his course. There are enough souls for the demons to torment that they will be able to go with one less soul today. That's why the tablet searches for signs of duress; souls have been known to demand to go to Heaven when they're meant to go to Hell.

I point Tim in the right direction, wishing him luck. Once he has started in the right direction, I go to stand back where I was but am stopped when I hear a commotion behind me.

I turn to find that a soul from the line for Hell has made a break for it, trying to get to the line leading to Olympus. Some of them are just stupid enough to try running to the other line. Luckily, the guards have been able to stop him from getting very far, but that doesn't stop some of the others from trying. The guards struggle with them, pushing the mob back.

I grunt angrily, as this happens a lot, before shouting in my devil voice. "Enough!"

Everyone stops. I storm to where my line is frozen. "The boat will be here any second! Just wait patiently until then, if you know what *patient* means! You're giving me a headache!"

Nearly all of them listen and return to an orderly line. I say nearly because one of them still thinks he can make a run for it. I run at high speed until I am standing in their way.

"Thought you could make a run for it?" I ask. He has the decency to look to the floor when I am talking to him. "You'll have to be punished."

I let my fangs descend and sink them into his neck. His pained screams fill the cavernous space. If there is malicious intent, if a demon wants to hurt the person they're biting, then—I was told—that the pain is unbearable. Otherwise, a bite is usually pleasurable. His blood is alright; I've tasted better.

Once I've made my point, I remove my fangs, seal the wound with a lick, and drag him by the arm back to the line.

"Now, does anyone else want to try their luck? Feel free. I'm still hungry." I get shouts of protest and denial. "Good. Now, shut up!"

I massage my temple; the heightened hearing can be a curse sometimes. But other times, it's very useful, like now, as I can hear the boats making their way to the shore. I move past the now calm line, some of them moving out of the way and nearly falling into the murky, turbulent waters below.

I get to the end of the pier and tap my foot as I wait for the boat to pull up. The person at the front of the line watches me warily. I flash them a quick smile before I look over at the other pier.

I see Jack similarly standing at the end of the pier talking to the souls near the front. I envy how calm and nice his line is, but I would never swap jobs for the world. As if he can sense me watching him, he looks over to me and smirks. I narrow my eyes and stick my tongue out at him.

Before I realize what is happening, a wave comes crashing down on me, soaking my clothes through. Jack's loud chuckle carries over the water. Of course, he would use his powers!

I contemplate throwing fire back, but I think against it, knowing I would be told off for going against the whole reason of Olympus. Spoil sports.

I groan and light a fire in my hand (another inherited power). I move it over my body to dry my clothes. The fire I create is different to the one in the ground; this one is much more harmful to demons. It doesn't kill them, though.

I look up and see that the souls are watching me curiously. "What? You've never seen someone dry their clothes before?"

I put the fire out and turn to the boat which is now making its way past the pier. I examine what I can see of it, which is the bottom of the side of the ship. The metal seems rusty and grimy as if it will fall apart, but this is just a facade for the souls, as under the rust and grime, it is made of a strong metal that is as good as new. The deck holds a cabin where Charon controls the boat, while the outside is patrolled by guards. Charon looks like a stereotypical pirate from Earth, a scraggly beard clinging to a scarred, dirty face, his body clothed in a filthy, dark cloak. However, unlike a stereotypical pirate, his eyes flicker with fire.

The inside of the boat, where the many souls will be placed, is just as bad as the outside. The floor is rotting, and the whole space has the most disgusting smell. This is the reason why I never use the boat; however, the demons crossing never mix with the souls below; they always stay on the deck.

The boat making its way to Olympus is the extreme opposite. My dad describes it as a palace on a boat, and I agree.

Eventually, the boat stops, and one of the guards on patrol jumps down to open the latch for the souls. Black boots thud as they hit the wood. I look past the black uniform of a guard, which is stretched by the normal tall, broad build of most guards, and my eyes finally land on a familiar face.

I smile. He may be muscular and taller than me, but I've kicked his ass many times. Adrian is one of my closest friends; he has been there for me my whole life. The skin around his blue eyes wrinkles as he returns my grin. Adrian moves out of the way of the demons and stands beside me.

"Scar, I haven't seen you here in a while," he says, pulling me into a side hug. I watch the demons walk down the pier, leering and snarling at the souls as they go.

"Yeah, my dad finally allowed me up to Earth for the year, after I have worked here for two days as a clause of the deal."

"You made a deal with the Devil. You know that's dangerous," he says with a wink.

I chuckle; I'm going to miss him and his jokes.

"Oh, well, I'll just have to deal with the consequences whatever they are. I can't wait to go up!"

"Cool. Bring me a souvenir back?"

"Of course, I will," I tell him, reaching up and ruffling his blonde hair.

The last demon jumps down from the boat, letting us know it's time to board the souls.

"All aboard. Next stop: Hell," I say and make a train noise.

Adrian laughs at me and at the souls' expressions.

The one at the front looks from me to the top of the boat. "You're not expecting us to jump like they did, are you?"

Adrian is about to respond, but I stomp on his foot before he can get anything out.

"Yep. All the souls have done it in the past, so it's possible." I lie. The soul's eyes widen, and he gulps. "Go on. We don't have all day. There are more souls to board after you."

The soul closes his eyes before he runs and does a feeble jump, not even getting close to the deck. I sigh, pretending to be annoyed.

"Well, I guess you're going to be difficult. You'll have to go the other way. You're the first one who couldn't do it, by the way," I tell him and let down the ramp on the side of the boat. I stand by the opening, letting him and the rest pass, snarling at them every so often, causing them to flinch away. Once they are all in the boat, I turn to Adrian who is looking at me.

"What did you do now?" he asks amusedly.

"I may or may not have bitten one of them." I return with a sheepish smile. His amused smile becomes bigger.

"Been up to any other trouble lately?" he asks, already knowing the answer. I usually do, and sometimes, it's even with him. I explain to him about painting the sign.

"My dad didn't like it, so he gave me a lecture on how Hell is meant to be scary, and if I wanted to welcome them, I may as well throw a party here and say, 'Hell's not that bad. We have cake,' which we do…" I realize I am rambling, and Adrian chuckles.

"Well, I should go. I have to get these back," he tells me, indicating the boat with his thumb. "Have a great time gallivanting around Earth without me, if I don't see you before."

I nod, telling him I'll see him soon. I move back down the pier a bit, watching as Adrian jumps back onto the boat. Seconds later, the engine starts, and the boat sputters toward its destination over the rocky waves. I look over to the other pier and see that the boat for Olympus has started as well, moving over the calm water. It's almost like the lake is two separate bodies of water.

Once both boats have disappeared, I turn around and get back to work (standing around and doing nothing is more like it). I don't see Adrian again today when the boats continue to travel back and forth.

It's a couple more hours until I decide to go home. I am just picturing my room when I hear the boats coming back, the voices of the demons and angels working the "night" shift floating toward me just as I disappear.

Chapter 3

Don't Miss Me Too Much

The following days fly by without any more trouble than usual. It's the night before I go to Earth, and my dad has called me down to his office to talk to me.

I enter to find that he is sitting behind his desk, his hands clasped together in front of him. The room is big enough to hold all his furniture and him comfortably. A bookshelf stands by the wall to the side of his big desk, holding an assortment of books. A reasonably sized filing cabinet sits in the opposite corner by the door. Although the room is not huge, it seems like it is because of the glass wall behind my dad and the desk. The view is of the whole of Hell, the demons and souls walking about below. This was my favorite place to come when I was a kid, and it still is. It's the only place where you can watch the movements of Hell in peace. I would press my face up against the glass and imagine what it will be like when I take over. It's hardly changed.

I sit down in the chair opposite my dad, leaning my elbows on the table, and resting my head atop my hands.

"I wanted to go over the accommodation and details of your trip," he says.

"Cool."

"I have been able to acquire you a house for the year, on the beach just outside of Miami. Like promised, I have also been able to obtain you a black Yamaha R15 and a white Aston Martin Vanquish for you to use. You are enrolled in the local school in grade 12, and I expect you to attend. You wanted the whole experience," he quickly adds when I start to protest.

I grumble but allow him to continue. I should have known; there's always a clause you don't know about with my dad. "When you arrive, it will be Sunday, meaning you will have school the next day. You will have all the correct documentation that you will possibly need at your new address. Your house will also have everything that you may need. There is a bank account that you can access with this card, but I don't want you spending it all straight away and on trash, got it?" He hands me a card.

"Yes," I respond, snatching the card from his hold and examining it.

"You have wanted one your entire life, so I have found you a phone. I have been able to get reception down here for a phone for me so we can contact each other, but don't expect it to be a permanent feature. It will stop as soon as you come back."

"Where is it?" I ask eagerly.

"It's at your new house. My number will be in it when you get there. Finally, don't get into any trouble. The demons that I have allowed on Earth know not to disrupt you, but if you find any that are there illegally, send them back down. Also, try not to let anyone find out who or what you are. That means do not use any powers unless you're in a situation where they will save you. Actually, even try and find something else to use then."

I give him an innocent smile. "Like I'm going to do that…"

He gives me the look that I am used to getting from him. It's the one that says that it's not a joke.

"Okay, okay." I relent, putting my hands up in surrender. The look disappears as he stands up along with me. He walks around the desk and to where I am standing.

"I'm going to miss you, even all the trouble you cause," he tells me, pulling me in for a hug.

"You too," I mumble into his chest.

My dad tries to hide the tears in his eyes as he pulls back. He hardly ever cries.

"Everything packed?" he asks after clearing his throat.

"Yep." I confirm. "I'll come and find you before I leave."

He gives me a grateful smile as he walks with me to the door, moving to the filing cabinet. I open the door and look at him when he's not watching me. He may be annoying sometimes, but I'm going to miss that and him. I leave the office and see Tybalt at the end of the corridor. He raises his head and looks at me.

"Come on, boy. Let's go for a walk." I walk past him and to the front door. This will be the last time I see the whole of Hell for a while.

***

After a very bad night's sleep and barely eating breakfast, I go to find my dad with all my bags in hand. I say goodbye to Tybalt who is none the wiser as I walk to the office. I enter his office to find my dad looking over some papers. I've never been able to get my head around why he has to do paperwork, but he does it when he's not signing contracts or his other duties. I clear my throat to let him know that I am here.

"I'm off now," I tell him when he looks up.

He immediately places the papers down on the desk and stands up, walking around the desk.

"Be safe. I expect to see you in two months. If you are not here, I will be sending someone up to find you."

"Why? Why do I have to come back down?"

"To check in. No matter what happens, I want you down here when we agree."

"Okay, what's the address of my new house?" I ask, suddenly feeling nervous. I don't know why; I've gone up before with my dad, but it's never been just me.

My dad reaches for a piece of paper, allowing me to visualize the address in my mind for the teleportation. Once I have read it and committed it to memory, my dad destroys it with fire from his hand and passes me the front door key.

I say a final long goodbye to my dad and get ready to leave. I am just closing my eyes when we hear a loud bang outside. My eyes fly open, and I go to look out of the window to see what the commotion is, but my dad stops me.

"Don't worry about it. I'll go and sort it out," he promises me.

I look at him hesitantly; I don't want to leave if there is trouble.

"Go on. You've wanted this for ages," he says as he walks toward the door.

The look on his face worries me as I close my eyes. I quickly push the thought of how he looks scared to the back of my mind and decide to leave with my own bang.

"Goodbye, Hell! Don't miss me too much!" I shout in my devil voice so everyone in Hell and by the lake can hear me before I disappear. My dad's laughter is the last thing I hear.

***

When I feel my feet hit the ground, I open my eyes to find myself standing in front of a large, modern-looking, white house. I am nearly blinded with the drastic change in brightness. Goosebumps erupt over my skin at the considerable difference in temperature even though the sun is out. I look around the deserted street of similar houses to see if anyone saw me pop out of nowhere.

I'm safe. I take a deep breath before stepping onto the driveway of my house for the next year. I continue up the drive and pause and admire the bike and the car waiting for me before walking to the front door. I juggle the bags I am carrying so I can place the key in the lock. I twist it before pushing the door open.

I enter into a bright, small entrance room. In a bowl on the table beside the door, I place the key with two others, which I assume to be for the car and the bike on the drive. I drop my bags to the other side and step through the second door and into the house. My first thought is how bright it is. The light streaming into the big room is courtesy of the wall of glass, only broken by the sliding doors, looking out over the hot tub on the deck, the pool below it, and the beach at the bottom. Stairs connect every level. The resemblance to my dad's office reassures and calms me slightly, bringing a fond smile to my face.

The living room is massive, furnished with white couches, chairs, and a TV hanging on the opposite wall. Not having one at home, I would always hope whenever I came up with my dad that I would have the chance to watch one.

I continue through the living room and see that the kitchen is only separated from the living room by a breakfast bar. I give the fridge a quick glance and see that it's stocked full of everything that I may need. The breakfast bar holds a basket which is full of blood bags wrapped in a ribbon. A card is amongst them, so I pull it out and open it.

Welcome to your new home.

Enjoy your time on Earth.

Dad.

xxx

My smile broadens at my dad's playfulness. I walk back out into the main area and to the front door, picking up the bags before walking up the stairs to the side of the room. When I arrive on the landing of the second floor, I see five rooms. One of them is a bathroom with a big sunken tub similar to mine at home. Behind the tub is a wet room holding the shower.

The three other rooms are all similarly furnished bedrooms. They are all modern and stylish. The last room that I enter has its own short corridor leading to it. I push the door open and see that this one is obviously the master. It faces the ocean, and the glass wall from downstairs carries on up. Also like downstairs, the wall has a pair of sliding doors; these ones lead out onto a balcony.

I look back to the room and see a big bed covered in white sheets. A black rectangle sits in the middle. I rush toward it, place my bags on the bed, and pick it up.

I wipe my thumb over the smooth glass screen. I turn it over in my hands, trying to find how to turn it on. I find a button on the side. I press it, and the glass lights up, showing me the time and date.

Once I have followed the instructions on the screen which allows me to unlock it, I look at its different features. My eyes fall on a small square which says that it holds the contacts. I press it and see my dad's name at the top. I didn't expect anyone else's.

I fiddle with it a bit more, looking at the different apps, quickly understanding what everything does and how to use it. Once I am satisfied, I lock my phone again, putting it into my pants' pocket.

Noticing two other doors in the room, I walk to the closest and open it. I reach on the wall beside the door for the light switch, flicking it on. I let out a gasp when a spacious bathroom, not too dissimilar to the main one, greets me.

Now even more eager to see what's behind the second, I walk quickly over to it, pulling it open. I walk through the big door, entering a generous closet. I let out a low whistle as I walk back out into the main room.

"You outdid yourself this time, Dad," I announce out loud as I walk to the bags on my bed. I unzip them and take out the clothes I have packed, telling myself that at the closest possible time, I'll go and buy more. I chuckle knowing that it's exactly what my dad doesn't want. Can you blame me? I haven't gone shopping without a time and money restriction before. I finally have free rein, and I can buy anything that I want.

I am just stashing the now empty bags in the back of the closet when I hear a two-tone electronic beep throughout the house. Looking cautiously around, I ponder what it can be. It sounds like it's coming from downstairs. It beeps again. I walk out of the closet and my room, going to the top of the stairs.

I see a middle age woman standing on the other side of the door. I realize then what the beeping is. It's a doorbell; however, I don't know why it's called a bell because it doesn't sound like one at all. Whenever we had to call at anyone's house on Earth, we would always knock and ignore the button beside us. I had only heard an actual bell at home. "Knocking sounds more ominous, especially if you put some force behind it," my dad explained to me when I asked why we knocked.

I make my way down at a human pace, opening the door when I get there. The woman greets me with a cheery smile on her face, her gray eyes reflecting that. With one hand, she tucks a piece of her mousy hair behind her ear while the other is holding a container. The warm, chocolaty smell wafts toward me, letting me know that there are probably brownies hiding under the lid.

"Hi, can I help you?" I ask, returning her smile with my warmest.

"Hi, I'm Rosie. I live a couple of houses down across the street," she says, motioning to her house. "I just wanted to come over and welcome you to the neighborhood. I hope you like brownies. My welcome gift to you." She thrusts the tub into my hands.

"Um…thank you," I tell her, placing them on the table by the door. "I'm Scar."

"What an unusual name."

"Yes, my full name is Scarlett, but my dad liked the idea of Scar," I tell her honestly with a fond smile. My mom wanted a real name for me, as she was once human before my dad changed her, but my dad thought that it wasn't scary enough, so they compromised.

"Are they in?" she asks, looking into the house behind me.

I move so I'm blocking her sight of the kitchen. It would be hard to explain why there are blood bags on my counter.

"No. I live by myself," I tell her.

"Oh, I'm sorry." I don't bother correcting her; she doesn't need to know. "When did you move in? I didn't see you arrive." She fires another question at me. What's with all the questions? Are all humans like this when they meet each other?

"I arrived early this morning, and I'm just unpacking," I answer, hoping she'll get the message to leave me to it.

"It was nice to meet you, Scar," she tells me brightly.

"You too," I respond, matching her tone, closing the door behind her once she has left.

For the remainder of the day, I sit beside the pool, my feet dipped in it, until the sun goes down. As I turn the light off in my room, I let out a contented sound. I hope all my days on Earth are like this.

Chapter 4

Slut #1

The next morning, I wake disgruntled to my mobile ringing shrilly.

"Hi, Dad," I say sleepily, knowing it can only be one person, as I try and adjust my blurry sight to look at the clock on the bedside table.

"Can you hear me?" my dad asks.

"Yes, coming through crystal clear," I answer, resting my head back down on the pillow.

"Great, it works. Remember your first day of school is today, and I expect you to be on time," he reminds me.

I groan. I don't need a wake-up call.

"I won't. It's only 6:20, and school doesn't start for about an hour."

"Enjoy your day, but not so much that you get into trouble," my dad tells me, ignoring my comment completely before hanging up.

I chuckle at him.

"Bye," I say into the silent phone with a sigh before returning it to my bedside table. I roll onto my other side. I'll just close my eyes for a second. I have plenty of time to get ready.

I blink away the sleep in my eyes as I sit up. I yawn, stretching before I look at the clock on the bedside table. Shit! I overslept. It's 7:23. School starts in seven minutes. I fling the covers back and tumble out of bed, trying to stay on my feet. I run to my closet and pick out a pair of shorts and vest. While I'm there, I also grab a bag, filling it with pens and notebooks (what I think I may need).

I rush through my morning routine before I go flying down the stairs. I grab a bag of blood from the stock in my kitchen. I forgot to eat last night, but today, I know I will need it. I won't be able to sit around humans with fresh blood running through their veins for eight hours.

I grab an apple as well as I quickly walk to the door. I hop around, trying to put my boots on with the apple in my mouth. Once I have stopped jumping around, I grab the car keys from the bowl.

I will drink the blood and eat the apple on the way. I pull open the door, turning to lock it when I realize that I left my bag. With a groan, I reopen the door, reaching in for my bag on the floor before closing and locking it.

I run down to my car and slide into it. I push the key in before setting the GPS to the school. It says that it will take twenty-five minutes. I look at the clock on the dashboard and see that school has just started. Proud of myself for getting ready in seven minutes, I press down on the accelerator. My dad should just be happy that I'm going; does it matter if I arrive twenty-five minutes late?

Once I am on the main road, I have finished the apple, throwing the core out of the window. I reach for the blood bag, tearing it open with my teeth. I take gulps of the nectar in intervals, aware that people may be able to see into the car. I squeeze the last of the liquid out of the bag and into my mouth as I turn into the school parking lot.

I put the car in park, shove the empty bag into the glove compartment, and check myself over in the rearview mirror. It will be a bad first impression if I enter with blood-stained teeth and cheeks. Satisfied that I am clean, I reach for my bag as I exit the car.

I stroll leisurely until I find the main office, needing to get my timetable. I push open one of the doors and find a small space. A desk sits in front of a corridor, facing the doors I am entering through. I turn to see chairs to the side of the room where a couple of students are sitting. I turn back to the desk where a woman is waiting with a warm smile on her face.

"Can I help you, dear?" she asks.

I inwardly cringe at the endearment as I walk closer.

"I don't know. Can you, Miss—" I look down to her name tag "—Williams? I'm new, and I need my schedule."

She looks at me, her jaw going slack.

"Name?" she asks in a daze.

"Scarlett Hades," I say.

She looks at me weirdly for a moment before she shakes it off and begins to type into her computer. I just give her a smile, tapping my fingernails on the desktop.

I'm used to getting weird looks. It's either for my last name or my actions. Humans can also sense demons. They don't know what the feeling means, or why they have it, but it's a result of what we are—predators who are higher in the food chain. When you see a wild, predatory animal, your body reacts by getting ready to flee or fight.

The sound of paper passing through a printer starts, and the woman turns her back on me to collect the papers. I see her shoulders relax, but as soon as she turns around, her shoulders tighten again. Some people are more susceptible to us than others. She passes the papers to me, and I notice her hand is as far away from mine as possible.

"Here is your locker assignment and combination and schedule. I hope you enjoy your time here at Aspen Valley High School."

I take them from her.

"Thanks, but I doubt it," I quickly say before I turn and leave. I pause and look down at the schedule.

Homeroom – Room 212 – Mr. Matthews

AP World History – Room 124 – Mr. Ward

AP English – Room 139 – Mrs. Hale

Gym – Gymnasium – Coach Karmen

Algebra – Room 106 – Mrs. Smith

Lunch

AP Psychology – Room 217 – Mr. Jeff

French – Room 230 – M. Francis

Physics – Room 226 – Mrs. Jackson

I sigh. Eight classes! What has my dad got me into? What's the point of coming to Earth if I'm going to be stuck in the same building each day? I force myself to make my way to room 124 and World History, which I am five minutes late to.

I eventually find the correct room, pushing the door open. As soon as I step into the class, a pair of watery, beady, blue eyes hidden behind a pair of glasses move to look at me. The owner is a balding, slightly overweight, older man. I look from them to the students to my left. They are all watching me curiously. I flash them a smile before looking back to the teacher.

"May I help you?" he asks, his voice grating.

"I should hope so. My name is Scarlett. I'm new."

"Ah, yes, Scarlett Hades, correct?" He checks, looking down at his papers.

"Yep, that's me."

"What a unique name…" he comments, his eyes meeting mine, his thin lips pulling up into an uncomfortable smile.

"Thanks. It runs in the family."

A few students chuckle.

"Well, you joined us at the right time, Ms. Hades, as today we will be learning about your namesake. Take a seat."

I move through the tables until I get to an empty one near the back. Mr. Ward turns to the board and writes two words: Ancient Greeks. I groan.

"To get us started, can anyone tell me any facts about the Ancient Greeks and their beliefs?" he asks the class, turning back to look at us.

"They believed in myths which included gods," a boy from the front shouts out. I want to shout at him, 'Do I look like a myth to you?' but I shut my mouth knowing my dad won't be happy if I were found out on the first day of my time here.

"Correct. Can anyone name any of their gods?"

"Hades," a girl answers, shooting a quick glance at me.

I roll my eyes when a few of the other students also take a quick look at me. I shift in my seat when I feel Mr. Ward's gaze also falling on me. The moment passes, however, as students continue to call out some names of my more well-known family members and family friends. I haven't seen any of them recently, except for Jack. Do they know that I'm down here?

"Zeus."

"Poseidon."

"Hermes."

"Aphrodite."

Not liking that my other family members and friends have not been mentioned, I pipe up, finishing off the list. "Hera, Hestia, Demeter, Chiron, Ares, Apollo, Hephaestus, Artemis, Dionysus, and Athena. Want me to name any of the Titans?" I ask innocently.

They all stare at me baffled.

"That won't be needed, but yes…that is a correct list of the main ones." Mr. Ward stutters. "But to start off with, we will only be looking at each of them separately. Hades is the first god we are going to be looking at. So, can anyone tell me any facts or myths surrounding him?"

I want to jump up and shout at them if they want to know anything, just ask his daughter who is sitting right there, but I stay silent, wanting to see what people think of us. I don't have to wait long as people start to call out answers again.

"He is the lord and god of the underworld and the god of wealth and the dead."

"He kidnapped Persephone from Earth to be his wife."

"He has a three-headed guard dog called Cerberus."

The last time I checked, Tybalt only had one.

"Anything else? No, okay. Please take notes. We will go more in depth in the next couple of lessons," he says before going into his lecture. "Hades, son of Rhea and Cronus, has three sisters and two brothers. His sisters are Hestia, Hera, and Demeter. His brothers are Poseidon, Zeus, and Chiron, his half-brother…"

"Wasn't there, like, a lot of incest back then?" A boy cuts Mr. Ward off.

I roll my eyes as I shake my head. I'm not going to say that it's a lie because it isn't. It happened ages ago when it was probably more acceptable, and since then, they have all moved on to different partners. I find it weird, and it makes my skin crawl whenever I think about it, knowing my dad was the product of incest.

"Uh—yes." The students show their disgust. "Let's get back to Hades. He and his brothers all overthrew their titan parents after a ten-year war. When it came to deciding on who ruled which realms, they all drew lots. Hades was unhappy with his choice of the underworld, and this caused a rift between Hades and Zeus.

"Hades' wife *is* Persephone. You are correct. She is the daughter of Demeter and Zeus and is the goddess of nature. He acquired her by abducting her from the field of Nysa where she was picking flowers. He tricked her to eat pomegranate seeds. As she tasted food from the underworld, she was obliged to spend a third of her year there. They do not have any children…"

I look around incredulous. My dad may have had a short fling with Persephone, but he was no abductor. Is that what she's telling everyone? And as for having no children, hello! Living proof right here. Not able to stay silent any longer, I pipe up again.

"That's a lie," I mutter, getting fed up.

"Excuse me, what did you just say?" Mr. Ward asks.

"I said you don't know your facts. Hades was happy to take the role of lord of the underworld and even offered to take it if Zeus or Poseidon drew it, and the fact that they don't get along is utter bullshit. They get along fine. Hell may be filled with souls and demons, but they visit each other regularly, along with their other siblings.

"I don't get why Hades is seen as evil. He was the one to maintain relative balance and was more selfless than evil," I tell him, getting heated. I always do when I defend my family. I quickly go back over what I said, trying to see if I gave anything away.

"And how do you know this? I think I would know the correct facts as I am a history teacher," Mr. Ward replies in the same tone as me, bristling.

"I'm really into Greek mythology?" I respond as more of a question, deflating slightly. Technically, I am replying truthfully.

"As you are so into Greek mythology, then you can all write me a paper about Hades and the myths surrounding him. 5,000 words please," he tells us smugly. He does *not* like being told he's wrong.

I groan along with the students, although it's for a different reason. I'm just writing about my family.

As soon as I hear the bell ring, I jump up out of my seat and head to the door. I push myself out into the busy corridor. Thinking I will have to fight my way through, I'm surprised when people stop walking and move out of my way, allowing me a clear path. I feel stares on me as I walk and realize whispered rumors are circulating about me. I listen in on them, wondering what facts I don't know about myself.

"That's the new girl." *Obviously.*

"She was the one to correct Mr. Ward." Wow, news travels fast in this school.

"She looks like a slut," a girl comments to her friends.

I stop in my tracks and stare at the girl. I see people start to move away from her as I walk closer. I look her over. I start at the top of her head, moving past her dyed, bleach blonde hair and brown eyes to look at her clothes. I don't know if I can even call them clothes. The fabric covered only a quarter of her body. I look to either side of her and see that she is accompanied by three clones. I watch as her eyes move from me to a passing boy, her shoulders going back slightly, before moving onto another. I raise my eyebrow.

"I'm sorry. I don't think I remember you...Have we met?"

Her eyes fly back to me, giving me a narrowed glare. "No."

"Then don't make assumptions, because it makes an ass out of you and me. Anyway, have you seen yourself in the mirror lately? At least I don't feel the need to dress up—well, down—and dye my hair to get men's attention, honey."

"How do you know I didn't dye my hair because I felt like it?" she responds, a smug grin coming on her lips. However, her heartbeat quickening tells me I'm right.

"Oh, loads of people dye their hair just for themselves, but you don't. You do it because you think it will gain you more attention from men, so if anyone is the slut here, I'm looking at her. How many of the school population have you fucked? I'm sure I could find out," I say bluntly, raising an eyebrow.

She glares at me before she turns around and storms off, her clones following closely behind. I turn to see everyone is staring at me, some in admiration but mostly in shock.

"What?" I shout. Everyone looks away, and I nod in approval before I continue onto English.

When I enter the classroom, I get a similar response to World History. Everyone looks at me as if I were an alien. I turn to the lady at the front and see that she is in her early fifties, her brown hair put back into a bun. Her warm smile deepens the wrinkles around her gray eyes.

"You must be the new girl. Everyone, this is Scarlett Hades. Please make her feel welcome," she says, turning to the class. "Would you like to introduce yourself?" She looks back to me.

"No. I think you already have," I tell her as I walk to the back, slumping into a seat.

She looks flustered for a moment, not quite knowing what to do, before she clasps her hands together.

"Well, um, welcome to Aspen Valley High," she manages to say before turning to the board, writing our lesson material up there. She places the pen down before turning back to us, calmer now.

She opens her mouth to start the lesson when someone flings the door open. A tall, well-toned figure stands in the doorway. The longer brown hair on the top of his head is styled to keep away from his caramel eyes. His thick, pink lips are pulled up into a small smile as he watches Mrs. Hale sigh in exasperation. His gray shirt allows everyone to see that he looks after his body. A leather jacket stretches over his strong shoulders. If I didn't know differently, I would have guessed that he was a demon who worked with my dad from the sheer size of him. My dad makes sure that the guards keep fit.

"Hunter, late again. What is your excuse this time?" Mrs. Hale expectantly asks Hunter, her hand placed on her hip.

"I was kidnapped by the devil," he answers simply as if it were a normal thing.

"And why did he do that?" Mrs. Hale responds in disbelief.

"You can ask him in person soon. He said that Hell was meant to be hellish and asked if I knew anything or anyone whom I thought was Hell as he needed something extra. I thought straight away of this class and your teaching. I think he purposefully allowed me to escape, as he asked me to request that you go down there now, instead of a couple of years. I'm just relaying a message. Don't shoot the messenger." Hunter finishes with a shrug.

I can't contain my laughter anymore. Thinking of Hunter's and Mrs. Hale's faces, the discussion I had with my dad, and the irony of all this, I let out loud laugh. I laugh so hard that I find it hard to breathe and tears start to stream down my face. I know I'm laughing louder than the students' quiet chuckling, but I don't care.

"What is so funny, Ms. Hades?" Mrs. Hale asks in a clipped tone.

"Nothing, Miss. I'm just remembering something my dad told me."

"Well, Hunter, next time the devil kidnaps you, tell him to do it when it's not school time. Now, go and sit down, and stop wasting my time." Mrs. Hale gets louder with each word. She takes a couple of deep breaths before shuffling a couple of papers on her desk.

I watch Hunter smirking as he walks to a desk rows away from mine.

Finally composed, Mrs. Hale looks back to us with a forced smile on her face. I see her open her mouth but tune out what comes out of it. I rest my chin on my arms and wait for the fifty-five-minute lesson to be over.

I watch as the hand of the clock moves past the three, groaning at the prospect of another thirty minutes sitting in this boring lesson. I can understand where Hunter is coming from now.

Someone nudges my shoulder, and I sit up. I look over to my right and see a girl holding out a folded piece of paper. She points at Hunter. I crane my neck to look at him and see him wink at me. I roll my eyes, take the piece of paper from the girl, and open it.

What's your name, newbie?

I lean forward and give him my best glare, putting the paper on the corner of the desk. I rest my head back on my arms, only to be nudged again five minutes later. He obviously didn't get the message. I open it to see what another paper says.

Is it hard or embarrassing? I'll tell you mine, and then you tell me yours. Hunter Stone and you are.

I scribble out a reply before handing it to the girl.

No, it's not. Maybe it's because I don't want to tell you.

Two minutes later, instead of going through the chain, a piece of paper flies through the air. I catch it and pull it open.

I know your last name is Hades...all I need now is your first name. Pretty please. :(

I groan knowing he won't give up.

Scarlett.

I glance at Mrs. Hale before throwing the paper at him. It misses his desk, landing on the floor. Hunter bends down to pick it up before smiling. He shoots me a look before responding.

Well, that wasn't hard. Nice to meet you, Scarlett.

I am about to write out my response when I am stopped by a shadow standing over my desk. I look up to see Mrs. Hale.

"How can I help you, Miss?" I ask, giving her a sweet smile.

"What are these?" she asks, picking the pieces of paper up.

"That? That is a piece of paper," I tell her in a patronizing tone.

"Very clever. What is on the piece of paper?" she asks, matching my tone.

"Writing," I respond. I bite my lip, trying to stop myself from laughing.

Hunter gives up hiding his amusement and is sniggering noticeably.

"I will not tolerate note passing and people talking back at me in my class," she tells us sternly. She opens the papers, reading each note out.

I shrug, not feeling embarrassed like she hoped.

"Ms. Hades and Mr. Stone, leave my classroom right now. I will not be disrespected."

"Finally!" Hunter shouts, getting up with his bag. I chuckle and join him standing up.

"Can I have them back?" I ask, pressing my lips together to suppress a grin when I see her irate reaction.

"I'll take that as a no," I say, picking my bag up and following behind Hunter.

When we both enter the hallway, I turn and walk the opposite way to him. I only get halfway down the corridor, however, as he stops me.

"Hey, Newbie!"

I turn around, looking expectant.

"What?" I say.

He holds up a pack of cigarettes. "Do you smoke? If so, do you want one?"

I look at the pack in his hand. If I were mortal, I would tell him no; they can kill you, but as I am not and I need a reminder of home right now, I agree.

He waits for me to catch up with him before he starts walking with me out to a small grassy area behind the school. We sit under a tree. We can see through the doors and the whole school.

He flips the pack open and offers it to me. I take one, and he offers his lighter. I press down on the lever, letting my thumb closer to the flame than normal, feeling the familiar flicker of warmth. I bring the lighter up to the cigarette, lighting it, before letting the lever go and passing it to Hunter. I bring it to my lips and breathe in. The warm smoke fills my mouth, moving down into my lungs. I let out a sigh of relief as I look over to Hunter who I see is looking at me curiously. The silence stays for a while before Hunter musters the courage to say something.

"You don't have a noticeable accent. Where are you originally from?" Hunter asks.

"Greece, but we move around," I tell him.

"Really? That's cool. So, why are you here?"

"I wanted to get away before I take over the family business," I reply telling him a version of the truth.

"What is it your family does?"

"Look after people, sort stuff," I answer vaguely.

"Are you here with your parents?"

"No. I don't know where my mom is. I never met her. It's just been my dad and me. He stayed behind at home, looking after the business. So, I'm living by myself for a year," I say and blow a smoke.

"So, have you stopped moving around? Where was home before you moved here?" he asks.

I take one last drag from the cigarette before standing up. I brush my pants before walking back toward the school, stepping on the cigarette on the way.

"We should go back," I call over my shoulder.

"You're bringing them next time!" he shouts after me, referring to the cigarettes.

"Who says there is going to be a next time?" I shoot back at him as I pull the door open.

I enter the school to hear the bell for the next period ringing. It only takes a couple of seconds for the doors in the hallway to open and all of the students to exit their different classes.

I ignore all the stares that are sent my way again and force my way through them until I arrive outside the gym. I see two doors on either side of the gym's entrance, one signed 'Boys' and the other 'Girls.' Not knowing what I should do, I enter the girl's locker room hoping to find a teacher. Luckily, I find Mrs. Karmen talking to one of the students just inside.

"I'm sorry, Laura, but you'll have to participate."

I hear the girl groan before walking further into the room. The young blonde woman turns around, jumping back slightly when she sees me standing there. A small smile appears on my lips when I see her shocked, green eyes travel up to mine. She quickly pushes her shock away as she clears her throat.

"Ah, yes, you must be Scarlett Hades," she states, looking down at the clipboard in her hands. I confirm with a nod. "Do you have the gym clothes on you?" I shake my head, and she sighs.

"We have some that you will be able to use for today, but I expect you to have them tomorrow. We're out on the track today, so get changed and join us out there." She motions to the back of the changing room.

As she moves around me to the door, she runs her fingers through her hair, pushing it away from her face before giving a smile to the girls entering the locker room.

"Hi girls, we will be out on…"

I move through the lockers and the girls changing until I find the bin of clothes. My nose wrinkles as I smell the unwashed clothes next to the clean ones. I rifle through the white and maroon mass. I find one white vest in my size and put it over my shoulder as I search for a pair of maroon shorts. My bag falls off my shoulder as I continue to search. I only find ones in sizes too big or too small for me. I groan and pick one of the small shorts; at least they will stay on my hips.

***

I look at the sun, closing my eyes, as I stroll toward the gaggle of girls standing near the track. The heat of the Miami sun does not compare to the heat of Hell, but it's nice to feel the rays on my skin. My eyelids flutter when I open them as they adjust to the onslaught of light. That's one thing that accompanies the heat that I'm not used to: the brightness.

I bring my hair up into a messy bun, securing it with the hairband from my bag as I join the class. Mrs. Karmen stands at the front, her hands on her hips as she waits for the class to gather.

I hear the voices of the boys' class walking onto the football field in the middle of the track.

Mrs. Karmen claps her hands together loudly, bringing our attention to what she has to say next.

"Okay, everyone, today, we will be doing running…" She gets groans in response from my classmates, and I notice that the loudest groan is coming from the girl who I had the exchange with in the hallway earlier.

"Quiet! We'll start with some stretches before moving onto a warm-up run," she commands before leading us. I follow her orders, going from lunges to stretching my arms.

"And touch your toes for ten seconds." She finishes. I bend down, my fingers clasping around the trainers I found. I count the seconds in my head. One. Two. Three. Four.

Loud wolf whistles sound through the air.

"Nice ass, Newbie," Hunter calls over to me.

I roll my eyes and stand up, looking over my shoulder.

"I understand why you like it. You see a version every time you look in the mirror," I call back before I move back to doing the stretch.

Guys jeer and chuckle at Hunter. I finish the stretch and stand back up to look back at Hunter. His mouth has fallen open, and a slight blush tints his cheeks.

"Shut your mouth. You're catching flies," I shout to him when he still doesn't move. His mouth quickly shuts, and he smirks.

I turn back to the group as Mrs. Karmen instructs us to run a lap on the track. I smooth down the vest as I walk to the starting line. The whistle blows after we have all congregated, and we move as a group.

My legs easily fall into a rhythm; I move at a fast human pace, allowing me to complete the lap quickly and with ease. I slow to a walk as I cross the line. I look back and see the group behind me is just turning around the last corner of the track. Mrs. Karmen looks surprised when she sees me cross the line.

"Wow, Hades, how long have you been running?"

"Ever since I could walk…" I answer confused.

She chuckles slightly before clarifying. "Have you ever competed or thought about it?"

"No," I answer simply, moving to the other side of the track as I wait for them all to finish.

I watch the field, looking at the boys running as they throw a football around. Hunter draws his arm back and uses his strong muscles to throw a fastball at a boy across the field. Before he runs, he looks back over his shoulder and catches that I am watching him.

He wiggles his eyebrows suggestively as he flexes his arm. I shake my head at him, a small smile on my lips as I hear most of the girls run over the line.

I turn to see that one of the last people over the line is the girl from the hallway, whom I have decided to call Slut #1. Her breaths are short and irregular as she pushes a piece of her bleached blonde hair off her red face. I press my lips together to suppress a laugh. I thought she would have better stamina.

Mrs. Karmen tells us to catch our breath for a moment before we do hurdles.

The rest of the lesson goes by, a few people tripping over the hurdles to my amusement, and eventually, we have ten minutes left before we go and change.

"Okay, everyone, line up. Let's see how many laps you can do in the ten minutes left. *Remember,* if you do not complete four laps within the ten minutes, then you will be given a detention," she orders after a couple of minutes.

Once we are all lined up, Mrs. Karmen blows her whistle, and we all set off again. I keep a steady pace with the main group, but they quickly fall behind as my legs push me to go slightly faster. I don't keep track of the time, and it passes by quickly.

When Mrs. Karmen shouts that we have been running for half of the time, I am just coming around the last bend on my sixth lap. I look to the bleachers and see that people are slowly struggling their way up the steps. I look at the faces and see that Slut #2 and #3 are two of the people who have given up. I look behind me and see that Slut #4 and their leader are gaining on me, their faces red and sweat dripping down them. Slut #4 is looking worse than her leader. She looks longingly at the bleachers but then back to the girl running determinedly beside her. She eventually gives up and slows to a walk, and Slut #4 takes this as them giving up and starts toward the bleachers happily. However, a glare has her returning to Slut #1's side.

I stay at the same pace until Mrs. Karmen tells us to speed up for the last minute. I kick the notch up a bit and run the lap, passing Slut #1 and her clone who are both still walking. I hear the beat of their feet hitting the floor start to quicken, and they force themselves so they can try and pass me. I slow down, giving it to them.

I see it before it happens; Slut #1 sticks her foot out, waiting for me. I step over her leg, moving to the side, slightly sticking my leg out in return. When she starts off, thinking she has to catch up with me, she doesn't notice my foot in her way and trips over it, her head flying back as she zooms toward the floor.

A satisfied smirk makes its way to my lips as I start off again, seeing the finish line is around the next corner. Holding my breath, I run the rest of the way and over the line. When I let myself breathe again, I draw in deep breaths, panting, giving the illusion of me losing my breath to the exercise. I bend down, resting my hands on my knees for extra effect. Mrs. Karmen walks up beside me.

"Wow, Hades, you should really think about trying out for the track team. Twelve laps, that's the best I have seen," she comments. Straightening up, I put my hands on my hips.

"Maybe," I say to please her.

"However, I did see you trip Tiffany. We do not tolerate that sort of behavior," she points out, an amused edge to her voice. So, Slut #1 is called Tiffany. I nod, letting her know I understand.

Mrs. Karmen walks away when Tiffany joins us, and Tiffany calls the coach. A snigger leaves me as I take in the girl in front of me. Her hand is upon her face, hovering over her nose. Blood trickles from it, smearing at the bottom of her hand. At the sight of blood, I panic momentarily, wondering if it will trigger my hunger. It doesn't, thankfully. I had no appeal to her blood; if anything, it made my nose scrunch up. Her usually nasal and whiny voice is dimmed as if she had a clogged nose. I laugh.

"Mrs. Karmen, did you see what she did to me? You should put her in detention or something," she exclaims.

Mrs. Karmen closes her eyes and sighs before responding,

"Tiffany, if I were to do that, then you would need to join her, as you went to trip her first. Do you still want to complain?"

Tiffany grumbles but doesn't argue any further.

"Okay, you can all go in and change now!" she calls back to the group of girls behind us. There are a few weak cheers as we join the boys in making our way back into the main building. I trail behind them, hoping people will not start a conversation with me.

It doesn't work, as moments later I see a male figure stop in front of me, allowing me to catch up with him. I turn to see it is Hunter. Rolling my eyes, I start to walk quicker.

"You're very welcoming," he says sarcastically.

"Thanks. I'm glad you noticed," I reply dryly, looking ahead. I don't need a relationship; I'll be gone in a year, and how do I explain to them why they will never see me again? It will never work out with humans anyway unless I change them like my dad did; they grow old and die, and I would never entertain the idea of having a relationship with a soul.

My way into the building is blocked when Hunter stands in front of me. My eyes find a sweat-soaked shirt in front of me. I force the thoughts that it provokes out of my head as I look up into his chocolate eyes. A drop of sweat falls from his brown hair over his eyes; his hair is matted with sweat also. I would have imagined that he stinks, and he does slightly, but the overwhelming manly smell that comes with it has me backing up. The muskiness and slight spiciness seem to encircle me. I breathe in and hold it there, going to move around him, but he steps with me.

I groan, my jaw clenching. I give him a false smile.

"Let's get this over with. No," I tell him, going the other way, but he steps in front of me again. I cross my arms as I cock my head, glaring at him.

"What?" Hunter asks confused.

"No, I will not go out with you. You have your answer. Now, let me past," I tell him irritably, trying to move past him. I throw my hands up in exasperation when he doesn't let me pass again.

He chuckles, stepping toward me.

"That wasn't what I wanted to talk to you about. That question will come another day." His hand reaches out for my face, and I grab it, bending his fingers back slightly.

"I'll break your fingers if you try that again," I threaten him, dropping them. A glint comes into his eyes.

"You like it rough? Good to know." I roll my eyes, shaking my head. He does not give up. "You're a violent little thing…"

My mouth falls open. Did he just call me *little*? I'm not a kid. I poke him in the chest, hard.

"Watch what you say about me, because I may just break your fingers anyway," I warn him.

He chuckles, thinking it's a joke. I will; I don't like being called little. I'm short in comparison to all the demons back home, and I get teased about it endlessly by the friends that I have, mostly Adrian. I know they mean it all good-heartedly, but I don't need it pointed out.

"Anyway, I saw you trip Tiffany."

"And you've come to defend her? Are you her boyfriend or something?" I ask, crossing my arms again as I raise an eyebrow. "She deserved it."

"No, I just wanted to let you know it was pretty funny."

"That's it? You annoyed me just to say you thought that it was funny that I tripped Tiffany?"

He shrugs. "You made it longer than it needed to be. Maybe you like me after all," he adds cheekily before turning and continuing into the building.

I scoff at him as I reach up into my hair, untangling the band there, running my hands through it to try and make it presentable. Tiffany shoves my shoulder as she walks past.

"Hunter's mine, bitch," she sneers.

"Does he know that? He just told me he found it funny that you were hurt," I call after her with a slight chuckle.

She spins around before storming back to me.

"You're just jealous."

"Jealous? Have at him. I have no interest in him whatsoever, so back off," I tell her firmly before going around her and into the building.

Chapter 5

Blood Bags Instead of Sandwiches

I enter Algebra to find that the lesson has started with the teacher at the board, writing up a couple of problems. I look at what she's writing, and my brain hurts just thinking about trying to solve them. I was given basic training by my dad at a young age, including most languages and simple math, but nothing to this extent; I didn't need it.

Mrs. Smith pauses and turns to look at me in the doorway. She looks at me expectantly.

"Can I help you?" I think about turning and walking out of the school, but the image of my dad has me opening my mouth.

"Yes. I'm Scarlett Hades. I'm new."

"Okay, well, take a seat, and we can continue," she says with a kind smile.

I look at the rows of students and find an empty seat at the back, next to a girl with her blond hair up in a ponytail. I weave through the students and slide into the seat. I pull out a notebook, and I sit back up to see that the girl's brown eyes are trained on me, looking me over. I return a questioning look.

"You're the new girl who confronted Tiffany in the corridor," she states quietly.

I internally groan, looking around for a different seat. I don't want to have to deal with Tiffany in every class.

"Is there any other new girl? You're not friends with them, are you?"

"What you mean Tiffany, Brittany, Cindy, and…"

"Wait! Don't tell me. Barbie?" I say with a slight smile.

"No. Courtney," she replies. I look her over, not able to figure out if she thought I was being funny or a bitch. Wow, tough crowd.

"So, are you?" I prompt her.

"God, no, I can't stand them. Tiffany is head cheerleader and ultimately feels like she's the head of the school but only comes across as a bitch. Someone needed to stand up to her, but everyone was scared of being ruined."

My smile grows bigger at her explanation. I think I'm going to like this girl.

"A bit cliché isn't it that the head cheerleader is a bitch? I bet you she couldn't even ruin anyone." The girl giggles as she agrees.

Mrs. Smith notices us talking and calls back to us.

"Ms. Hades, I don't know what school you came from recently, but I'm sure they had a no-talking policy also."

I hold back a facetious remark that in fact, it didn't, as my dad never stopped me from talking, although he sometimes got sick of it. I only wait until Mrs. Smith tells us that we should work through the problems before I turn back to the girl.

"I'm Scarlett, but you can call me Scar," I tell her quietly.

"Lily," she responds. "Do you want to sit with us at lunch?"

"Who are us?"

***

We enter the bustling cafeteria, the smell of the food causing my stomach to growl. I noticed that ever since gym, where I exerted myself, my hunger has made itself known. I usually receive blood whenever I want and always have it three times a day. I'm sure it's only hunger for normal food. I had hoped that I would be able to go the whole day without blood and have some when I get home.

Pushing the thoughts to the back of my mind, so I don't make it worse, I follow Lily to get our food and then to a table near the doors into a courtyard. I look at the clear blue sky and see the sun shining brightly. I place the food down on the table before giving my attention to the people already sitting there.

"This is Lottie, and her boyfriend Max, and this is Tasha." Lily points to them individually. "Guys, this is Scar."

I look at Lottie and see that her skin is fairer than mine, which contrasts her black hair. Her green eyes are welcoming as she gives me a cursory once-over. Her figure is dwarfed by the fair boy next to her. He runs his hand, the one that is not resting behind Lottie, through his brown hair as his hazel eyes meet mine. Like his girlfriend's, they are welcoming and kind.

I turn to the last person at the table and am met with a girl who's about the same size as me. She's the most tanned at the table with blond hair and blue eyes that remind me of a surfer. I greet them with a smile as I sit down next to Tasha, facing the entrance to the cafeteria. They all return the greeting in their own ways.

I answer most of the same questions that Hunter asked me, like "Where are you originally from?" and "Why did you move?" When I see my earlier interrogator walk in with four other boys, I cock my head as I watch them, trying to figure out something. Something is confusing me about the scene.

Hunter looks around the room before his eyes land on me, and he smirks. I look away from him when I see he's making his way to where we are sitting, the four other boys following him. I rest my head on my hand as I look away from him.

When Hunter addresses me, I turn and force a smile on my face.

"Newbie, I heard you and Tiffany fought over me after I left. I wish I was there."

"Yeah, you wish, Oldie. You would have not seen anything because all I did was tell her that I was *not* interested in you."

"Now, we both know that's not true," he says with a smug smirk.

"I would only be interested in you if... if..." At that moment, the door swings open, causing a slight breeze to blow into the cafeteria. The overwhelming smell of hundreds of bodies flowing with fresh blood hits me. I gulp as I feel the hunger take over.

Losing control, my body thinks that I'm going to attack, and this causes my features to change. My fangs grow, and I feel my face start to transform. My horns begin to push through my hair, and I know my eyes have turned red. Not on the first day of school! I can't be found out; my dad would kill me and then never let me go anywhere again.

I immediately act, bending my head down and running my hands up through my hair, pushing it back over my horns, the hands resting on them for another protection, the sharp points digging into my hands the more they grow. My longer fingernails are hidden in the tangle of hair. My face is hidden my arms. I breathe a couple of breaths, not caring how weird I look for cutting off mid-sentence and ignoring all the concerned questions being shot my way. After a couple of breaths, my horns slowly recede, along with my fangs. My face begins to smooth out, letting me know that my eyes have also changed back to the normal blue. I clear my throat before slowly straightening.

"I'll be back. Sorry," I mutter before getting up and running out of the cafeteria. Great! Now everyone thinks I'm a freak.

I rub my face as I bring my phone up to my ear. Only one person can help with this. I'm not willing to risk teleporting, and drinking from someone here is out of the question. I wouldn't even drink from Tiffany.

"Dad, I need you to send *something to eat* up to school. It's too risky for me to change places," I plead with him, hoping he'll catch on to what I'm asking.

"Hello to you too. Isn't there food in the cafeteria?" he asks, but he understands perfectly, as it's followed by a chuckle.

"Not the kind I'm talking about. Now, are you going to help or not?" I ask irritably.

"Of course, I was just playing with you. Someone is on their way up. What I don't get is why you didn't take any with you."

"Thanks," I tell him before continuing in a sarcastic whisper. "Yeah, that would be totally normal. While everyone has their sandwiches, I take out a blood bag. I wouldn't get any weird looks at all!"

"You could tell them it is soup or something." He laughs.

"Fine, I dare you to do that. Tell me how it goes," I say before hanging up. Not wanting another disaster like before, I breathe in and hold it there, hoping that the demon won't take long.

I arrive back at the table to find it's silent. When they see me coming, they all look at me worried.

"Are you okay?" Tasha asks. I nod, knowing if I talk, it will come out rushed as I try not to breathe in.

"You sure?" Lottie asks, biting her lip.

I give her a reassuring smile as I nod again. I look around the cafeteria to find where Hunter went. I meet his concerned gaze across the room; I give him the same smile before I sit back down in my seat. I listen as they start to talk around me, sending me glances every so often to check I've not freaked out again.

I am beginning to wonder where the person with my blood is when I hear the sound I've been waiting for. Silence in the corridor, followed by a few screams. Immediately the cafeteria goes silent as they wait to see what the threat is. A few people stand up, including Hunter and his friends, ready for whatever happens next. I watch them all curiously with a small smile on my face. They wouldn't be able to take down whoever was in the corridor, even if they tried.

The door opens, and people back away from it. A blonde head pokes in, surveying the room. The blue eyes fall on me, crinkling at the sides as the face stretches with a smile. The door flies open, and the person walks in, arms outstretched.

"Scar!" he shouts. Everyone fearfully looks at me. I can understand the fear; he's big, tattooed, and from the underworld. The blonde hair and blue eyes and his smile do nothing to help ease it.

I stand up, letting my breath out.

"Adrian!" I shout back in the same way. I run at him with my arms open, catching him in a tight hug which he happily returns. "You couldn't go without me for two days and came to find me? That's so sweet." I tease him.

"Then you don't want what I have…" he responds.

I send him my best glare.

"You know I do. Follow me." I grab his hand before moving around him and opening the door. Before I can step out, Adrian opens his mouth.

"What are you all staring at? Never seen someone go to make out with his girlfriend before?"

I turn back and punch him in the arm.

"Ow, babe, that hurt." He yelps, continuing the charade.

I raise my eyebrows and lift my fist again—a challenge for him to continue. However, he's smart and mutters an apology with a chuckle. I pat his arm with a smile before grabbing his hand again and pulling him out into the corridor.

We pass the students standing like statues on either side of the hall before I find a door and push Adrian into the cupboard behind it. I pull the door forcefully close behind me, turning to Adrian.

"Why… Did… You… Do… That?" I exclaim, hitting him with every word.

"You should have seen their faces and yours. It's not you like you care what these people think anyway, right?"

"Of course, I don't. I'm hungry which is making me grumpy, so give it to me," I retort.

He grins, producing the bag of deep red liquid out of his jacket. I snatch it from his hands, ripping the top of it. I let out a content sound when I feel the familiar ambrosia slide down my throat. It only takes a couple of gulps for me to finish the bag. I throw the empty plastic at Adrian's chest before licking my teeth, trying to clean them. I do a quick check around my mouth as Adrian returns the bag to his pocket.

"Do you think you could stay for a couple of minutes?" I ask as I twist the handle to open the door.

"I'm sure your dad can go without me for a while."

I smile as we re-enter the hallway, finding that the students are a bit louder than they were before. In the hallway and the cafeteria, ignoring the silence that falls when they see us again, I go back to the table, Adrian close behind.

"Guys, this is Adrian, a close friend from home," I introduce him as I take a seat. Adrian reaches to a table next to us, turning the empty chair around so he can sit next to me. Everyone at the table gives him a skeptical glance with a hesitant smile before their eyes move to my face. When their eyes don't move from me and they shoot each other questioning glances, I begin to get paranoid. I pretend to scratch the back of my head as I look at Adrian.

"Do I have anything on my face?" I murmur.

His eyes widen, and he gulps as he points to my cheek.

I instantly bring my finger up to wipe any blood that I missed away. I feel nothing, and thinking I have the wrong place, I prod my cheek, trying to find any smudges. When I realize that there is nothing, I shove Adrian's shoulder.

"Idiot." He rights himself and gives me a grin.

Our interaction seems to relax everyone else, and they replace their hesitant smiles with proper ones.

"So, Adrian, have any embarrassing stories about Scar?" Tasha asks.

I snort, looking at Adrian. The question isn't whether he has them; it's which one he should tell. I watch him, curious as to the answer.

"If I tell you them all, we would most likely be here all week, so let's start with the most embarrassing. The year is 2009. Now, the thing you need to know about eleven-year-old Scarlett Hades is…" he starts off dramatically.

I absentmindedly pay attention to the rest, knowing what he's going to tell them. It was not my finest moment; let's just say that. He's not stupid enough to mention anything paranormal, so I don't have to worry about that. I reach for the unopened bag of chips on the table, slowly eating them as I watch the table laughing at my misfortune.

I crumple up the now empty bag and throw it in the closest trash can. I watch as it falls short, and I sigh in disappointment. I turn back to the table tuning back in at the end of the story.

"And that's why her uncle always locks away the marshmallows whenever she visits," Adrian says. This causes raucous laughter from the whole table.

"If I remember it correctly, you were…" I start but am cut off when a crumpled packet is thrust in front of my face.

"I believe this is yours," Tiffany says sweetly.

I breathe in deeply, trying to force myself to deal with her without punching her.

"Look at you, following one rule," I remark. "Why don't you *go*, and on your way, put the packet in the trash. You know, where you get your clothes from," I say, pointing to the aforementioned container.

Her eyes narrow, but she doesn't move and instead turns her attention to Adrian beside me. I roll my eyes as she places her hand on his shoulder, rubbing his arm slightly. Adrian looks her over; however, I can tell if he likes what he sees. Hopefully, he understood that I don't like her.

"Hi, I'm Tiffany, and you are?" she asks, her voice lowering.

"Not interested, and seriously, leave before I break it," I tell her, nodding to her blue and black nose, which she unsuccessfully tried to cover with her makeup.

She returns her glare to me before looking each side of her at her clones. One of them looks to be holding back her laughter. Tiffany grunts loudly, clenching her fist. She drops the bag on the table before turning and stomping off in her heels.

"You were the one that did that to her?" Lottie asks me. I nod. She grins, leaning over the table for a high five, which I happily give.

"She had that coming."

I stand up and throw the packet back toward the trash can. It falls in this time.

"Nice throw, Newbie."

"One annoying person to another," I mutter before turning to Hunter. "What do you want now, Oldie?"

"An introduction," he says, looking at Adrian. I can't quite decipher what his feelings are. I smell his adrenalin is pumping, but I don't know whether he is angry or scared.

"This is Adrian. He works for my dad, but he's been there my whole life. He was just dropping something off for me."

"We're best friends," Adrian says in a child's voice, pulling me closer to him. I push him away as best I can. I give up waiting for him to tire. I give an awkward smile as the hug goes on. I pat his arm as I look at Hunter's friends.

"Sorry I ran out on you earlier. I'm Scarlett Hades, but you can call me Scar depending on how well we get along," I tell them with a wink.

"Hades? Like the devil?" a tanned boy asks. His dirty blonde hair is shorter at the sides, only slightly longer on the top, and pushed up away from his dark eyebrows and green eyes underneath.

"Yeah, like the devil," I confirm trying to suppress a smile. Adrian pulls away from me, and I sigh in relief.

"I'm Jake, by the way."

I nod in greeting and acknowledgment before turning to the next guy. He is about the same size as Jake, so slightly shorter than Hunter. He pushes his brown hair, which is swept across his forehead, away from his blue eyes before he reaches for a handshake.

"Liam," he introduces. I squeeze his hand firmly as I shake it. "Wow, you have a strong handshake. I think you broke my hand," he complains.

"Aw, you can't handle a girl shaking your hand?" the next guy teases. "I'm Leo and the only one of these idiots that you should know. They all have sticks up their asses. I'm the most fun," he finishes with a whisper.

I let out a small chuckle. Leo is blond like Jake, but his hair is styled more like Liam's. His gray eyes are cheeky. He winks at me.

The fourth boy has been standing at the back of them this whole time, and when he pushes through them to introduce himself, I understand why. I think back to what was confusing me earlier and realize that it was me sensing a demon. I didn't understand why I thought one was close.

His dark eyes meet mine before sliding to Adrian beside me. He looks around the room, his heartbeat rising. Obviously, my dad didn't allow him to come up.

Adrian stiffens next to me as he senses the same thing, his head turning to me silently, asking me what I would like to do. I turn back to the demon and give him a smile and a chance to explain himself.

"What are you doing here?" I ask.

When he doesn't answer, I feel myself getting angrier. He wouldn't dare disobey my father by not answering him, so why does he feel he can do it with me? He's now going to see that I'm no different from my father.

"I asked you a fucking question. Now, what are you doing here?" I shout at him, thunder rolling uncontrollably. I feel the sun hit my back as if telling me that I made a mistake. Adrian's hand falls onto my arm, warning me to calm down. Hunter looks from me to the demon, confused.

"What do you think you're doing?" Lily asks lowly. I ignore her as I wait for the demon's response.

"I was bored and needed something different from the normal stuff," he answers, thankfully, cryptically.

"Go back. Adrian will escort you," I tell him, causing more confused expressions to come our way. I can get why; they've just seen a girl flip out on something she apparently just met. I'm used to this sort of thing at home, and I deal with it every day, so this is normal for me. I guess it'll take a while for me to get used to the different ways.

"No," he replies defiantly with a smug smile marking his face.

I slam my hand down on the table, getting even angrier.

"Go back! Don't make me make you, or worse tell my dad that you're here!" I shout. How dare he defy me? Another roll of thunder resounds, causing murmurs of bewilderment.

"Scar, don't worry. I'll go now and take him with me. Your dad will be glad to know you're settling in well," Adrian assures me, standing up. He marches forward and grabs the demon by the arm before dragging him out of the cafeteria, passing Mr. Ward on the way.

"Hey, you, what are you doing here?" he calls, following them out again. The bell rings overhead to let us know that it's the end of lunch; however, I ignore it as I turn to Hunter.

"You still have the cigarettes?" I ask, needing a reminder of home and my dad right now.

"Yes, but what's the magic word?" he taunts.

"Don't mess with me right now! Just give me the pack!" I yell, causing another roll of thunder to sound. I close my eyes as I try to calm down. I need to keep my emotions in check. "Please," I add, gritting my teeth.

He smirks before reaching into his leather jacket and passing me the pack and his lighter. Before anyone can ask me any questions, I walk out. I have had a very stressful day so far, and it's only my first! Gods help me!

Chapter 6

Demon Teacher

When I finally collapse into the chair in room 217 for Psychology, between Tasha and Lottie, I feel much calmer. I swap the cigarettes and lighter for a notebook and pen as I look up and around the room realizing that it's louder than it should be. Narrowing my eyes, I look from Lottie to Tasha.

"Where's Mr. Jeff?" I ask.

Lottie shrugs as Tasha chooses the verbal option. "We don't know."

I rest my forearms on the table and my head on top of it, waiting for the teacher to arrive. It only takes a couple of seconds before the door flies open, and someone comes striding in. I hear them writing on the board before turning to the class, throwing his bag onto the table. The class instantly goes quiet.

"Ms. Hades, look lively," a deep voice commands with a slight edge of amusement.

I shoot up, looking at the teacher, not because of his command, but because of his voice. I recognize it as belonging to one of my dad's most trusted guards. My dad has a soft spot for him—well, as soft a spot that Hades' can have—and thinks of him as a son. My dad brought him up since he was a baby, and he's been around me my whole life, so he's like a brother. He's older than me by around forty years, and ever since I was a kid, I've looked up to him as a role model, along with my dad. I should have guessed my dad would do something like this. Can't he trust me? I didn't really give much thought to him not being around the last couple of days when I was in Hell, as I was busy getting ready to leave.

I groan, making my feelings clear. "Are you serious? I don't need a babysitter."

He hears my comment, as I see one side of his lips pull up in a smirk, but he continues as if he hadn't.

"You will address me by my first name, which is Kyle, nothing else. I will be taking over from Mr. Jeff, who unfortunately as a result of health issues, consequently decided to take this year off to work on getting better," he explains. Of course, he has; my dad must have had something to do with it. I wonder what he gave to him. It's very rare for a demon to have a last name unless they are born from souls.

Kyle crosses his strong, tattooed arms as his dark eyes survey the class. I see all the girls perk up, pushing their hair over their shoulders. I roll my eyes; of course, all the girls will be falling over him.

"Do you know him?" Tasha whispers to me. I ponder whether to admit it or not. I look from Kyle back to Tasha.

"No," I say with a shake of my head.

"Oh, it looked like you did."

I give her a smile before turning back to Kyle. His dark eyes meet mine with his head slightly cocked. I shake my head minutely. *No one is to know.*

"I am not usually a teacher of psychology, so we will mainly be working out of books." He twists back to his desk and the pile of books there. He picks them up, giving a portion of the books to each of the desks at the front. "Take one before passing the pile back. We will be looking at page 35 today."

When the book lands on my desk, I slowly flick to page 35 and push it back on my desk as I take out a notebook. Kyle starts his lesson, every so often asking people to read a paragraph, ignoring me. I do the same, focusing on the doodles I am doing in my book. Kyle wouldn't fail me. He might mention something to my dad but would never fail me.

"Ms. Hades!"

I look up at Kyle who is still standing at the front.

"Can you please read the next paragraph before we all leave?"

I sigh, rolling my eyes, before putting on a smile.

"Of course: We communicate additional information through the gestures we make. Some of them are deliberate to emphasize what we are saying, or affect the behavior of another person, whereas others are unconscious, and we do not realize we are communicating information. An example of this is nervously tapping your fingers, or raising an eyebrow," I read aloud. I know what gesture I want to give to my dad for sending me to this school.

"Thank you, Ms. Hades. If you could stay behind, I would like to talk to you before you go onto your next lesson," he says. The bell rings, and everyone starts to talk and gets up. "Read the rest of the chapter by next lesson!" Kyle calls over the din of the students.

I move toward the front of the class, leaning against one of the desks there.

"We'll wait for you outside," Lottie tells me as she continues out of the class.

I wait for Kyle to finish bidding farewell to every girl going out of their way to walk past him to say goodbye. I find myself tapping my fingers on the desk, like the excerpt from the textbook said, but this time, as a result of impatience.

Finally, Kyle closes the door and turns back to look at me. I raise my eyebrows at him expectantly. He plunges into an explanation without me asking the question I've been burning to.

"Your dad sent me up, Scar, because he wanted someone to make sure that you didn't do anything stupid and be found out."

"Were those his words? Stupid?" I ask, getting offended.

"That's not what..." He takes a step toward me. I cross my arms. I should have known they were up to something. I hadn't seen Kyle for about a week before I came up to Earth, and I usually see him every day. Well, now I know why.

"I'm not stupid. I don't need to be looked after. I can take care of myself. You both should now that and trust me," I rant, uncrossing my arms and throwing them around me with my words to vent my frustration even more. "Is there anyone else up here?"

"No. It's just me."

I let out a small sigh of relief at this.

"Okay," I reply shortly before moving to the door. I go to push the handle down, but Kyle calls to me.

"Scar, I'm not just here because your dad ordered me to keep you out of trouble. I wanted to be up here with you too."

I nod to let him know I heard but don't look back as I push the door open. Still breathing heavily from the hurt and anger I feel toward my dad and Kyle, I storm out of the room almost missing Lottie and Tasha waiting for me leaning against the lockers opposite. They push off and come to walk beside me.

"What happened?" Lottie asks as she walks quickly to keep up with me.

I stop when I realize they are with me. "It was nothing," I tell them even though my tone is still slightly irritated.

They exchange a skeptical look before turning back to me.

"At lunch, with Hunter's friend..." Tasha begins.

"I know him. He's trouble and shouldn't have been here," I answer the question I knew was coming. They exchange another look, probably asking themselves, *Who is this girl standing in front of them who overreacts to almost everything and knows people who are trouble?*

"What's your next class?" Lottie asks.

"French," I say.

"Cool. I have that too!" Tasha exclaims.

Lottie tells us that she'll see us later and goes toward the stairs. A short walk down the hallway later, we stop outside room 230. As we enter, Tasha apologizes to Mr. Francois for being late as I go to the back of the class, passing Hunter on the way.

"Thanks," I mutter to him, flashing him a quick smile, as I chuck the pack of cigarettes and lighter at him. He smirks at me but doesn't say anything. I take a seat, placing my bag at my feet.

For the lesson, I zone out, knowing I won't fall behind, as I'm fluent in most languages. My mind starts to go over everything that happened earlier. I think about my dad sending Kyle up and how I overreacted to my dad just wanting me to be safe; I think about Hunter's friend, the demon; and I think about what Mr. Ward said about my family. The more I think about it, the more I start to doubt what I was told by my family. Did my dad abduct Persephone? Did my dad and Zeus not get along at one point? All the questions start to play on my mind, and they won't leave me alone until I get reassurance. I resolve to ask Kyle about it when I hear Tasha's voice break through the fog.

"Class is over," she says to me when I look up to where she is standing next to my desk. I look around the rest of the class and see the last students are slowly trickling out.

"Sorry, I wasn't paying attention," I admit.

She chuckles. "You can say that again. What's your next class?"

"Physics," I tell her.

"I think Lily has Physics now. I'll see you tomorrow," she replies.

"Oh," I reply distractedly, knowing I won't be attending. It's the last lesson of the day, and once I've got my answers from Kyle, I may as well go home.

Tasha and I split ways in the hall, going to our different destinations, me making my way back to Kyle's classroom. I don't care if he is teaching; I'm not going to rest until I have reassurance or the truth. I look through the glass in the door to find that he is teaching.

I steel myself for a couple of minutes, my hand resting on the handle, convincing myself that my view of, and everything I know about my family, is going to change. My reasoning has gone out of the window, probably as a result of being away from my dad for the first time in somewhere I'm unfamiliar with. I know the doubts are irrational, but they are still there. Telling myself I'm being stupid, I finally push the door open.

"So today I thought we would…Scar, what are you doing?" Kyle asks, surprised.

"I need answers," I reply, ignoring everyone who is staring at me.

"Can't you see that I have a class?" he asks me pointedly.

"Yes. I do have eyes. Hello!" I say as I look to the right and see that the students are all looking at me with the same curious gaze as Kyle. I give them a small finger wave and a smile before turning my attention back to Kyle.

"We can talk later," he says through his teeth, just low enough that a human ear can't hear it.

"We can, but no, we talk now," I reply at the same level, putting a slight assertion in my tone.

He sighs, agreeing. "Okay, out into the corridor."

I turn back to the students, giving them another wave before turning around and pulling the door open. I chuckle as I see the awe and horror on the students' faces.

A minute later, the sound of the door closing makes me look up and find Kyle standing before me, his hands in his pockets.

"What answers do you need?" he asks.

"Earlier, when I was in World History, we were doing about my family and their origins. In the lecture, Mr. Ward said something about my dad abducting Persephone and that Zeus and my dad didn't get along at one point. Is any of it true? I don't really want to think of my dad as an abductor."

His shoulders fall as if he expected something worse, and his worried face softens into a smile.

"None of that is true. You know about your dad and Zeus' relationship and the fact that some facts are twisted for the humans."

I listen to his heartbeat, seeing if he's lying. He causes me to relax slightly when I hear that it's steady.

Why do demons have a heart? We need something to pump blood, ours and any other we drink, around our body; otherwise, our body would be unable to function. The blood is different to a human's because it has healing qualities. If I were to plunge my hand into Kyle's chest and rip his heart out, it wouldn't kill him; it would hurt, but the blood in the body, with help from the brain using other muscles to push the blood to where it is needed, would slowly start to form the heart again with blood that would also start pooling in the cavity where the heart was. The blood's healing qualities keep the body alive long enough for it to repair the missing piece (unfortunately, our body cannot repair anything outside of our body, so if we lose a limb, we lose a limb). It apparently feels like you are unconscious. If I were to cut the brain's connection to the rest of his body, meaning it would not be able to send a message to the kidneys to alert the bone marrow to make more blood to help in the healing, I would kill him.

"Yes, I just doubted myself," I explain. "What about Persephone?"

"She's a jealous bitch," Kyle says with a shrug. "It was when your dad was younger, before your mom, and he got sick of the possessiveness, so he dumped her. It was also the period when your dad and your family started to realize that the incest was weird and wrong. Persephone was unhappy and started to spread rumors on Earth." His heartbeat continues to stay steady.

"What about the pomegranate seeds? Is that true?" I ask.

He shakes his head with a smile. "She was obsessed and wanted an excuse. I thought your dad would have told you."

I sigh, bringing my hand up to my hair, pushing it back from my face.

"He did. I wish I had listened." I chuckle. "I'm sorry for interrupting. I feel like an idiot. I've just had a very stressful day, and you know how stress gets to me."

He laughs. "It's okay. I was bored anyway," he assures me. I give a small smile, bringing my hand down from the back of my head. "However, you shouldn't be out of class," he admonishes playfully.

"So? Are you going to do anything about it?"

"No, of course not, you saved me from boredom, and for that, I'll be ever grateful," he jokes, placing his hand over his heart. I've missed Kyle, and I didn't realize until now. "Didn't you want to come up to Earth? I thought you would be more eager about it."

"I did. I just don't care about doing the whole school thing. I wanted a change of scenery, not go to another Hell. I'm only here for a year, and it's not like my future depends on what happens at school."

He lets out a loud laugh before changing the subject with a sigh.

"Well, I should get back to class, even though I don't want to. Be good," he orders, pointing his finger at me.

"When have I ever been bad?"

"Should I remind you of that time when you went to visit your uncles and aunts?"

"I did a lot. You'll need to be more specific," I joke, even though I know what he's talking about. It's the time that always gets brought up.

"Two words. Showers. Blue. I'm not even sure if they have been able to get it all out of the showers."

I laugh at the memory. Jack was blue like the water he can control for at least a month. That is by far one of my best pranks.

"I learned from the best," I say, pushing Kyle's shoulder with a wink. He's always been, and always will be, my partner in crime. He doesn't disagree.

"I never knew you would do it so well when I taught you."
He laughs. We both reminisce for a bit longer before Kyle says
with finality that he has to get back to his class.

As the door closes behind him, I can still hear his
chuckles. I smile and decide to make my way home. It may not be
that bad at this school if I have Kyle by my side.

Chapter 7

What Are We? Toddlers?

I sigh as I rest my head on my hand, tapping the pen with the other. I thought the homework that Mr. Ward has set to spite me would be easier. After all, I am writing about my family. If I weren't worried about saying too much, or something that the humans don't know, I would be able to complete this easily. My dad made sure I knew every legend surrounding us, but I would never listen, thinking that I didn't need it.

After talking to Kyle, I realized that school is part of the experience of Earth and I may as well give it a go, even if I do it reluctantly.

I have found an electronic device with a screen and a detached rectangle with the alphabet jumbled up on it, which I recognize as a computer, in a room on the ground floor. This is where I am sitting now, trying to write the paper. I quickly learned how to use it, finding an app that would allow me to type it and then send it to a printer in the same room. My dad had taught me on a high level how to use all inventions on Earth, but I never actually used some of them.

I stop fiddling with the pen, putting it down, and wiggling the mouse to wake the screen up. I look at the word count and see that I have just over seven hundred words. I'm not used to writing essays or reports, so I doubt this is going to be good anyway.

I start to type out a sentence when the doorbell goes. Thankful for the distraction, I get up and walk out of the small room and through the open living room to the entrance hall and the door. I look through the window beside the door and groan, beginning to walk back to the computer.

The doorbell rings again, but this time, repeatedly. I try to ignore it, thinking they'll stop, but when it continues, I spin on my heel, pulling the door open forcibly.

"What?" I snap at Hunter who has a goofy grin on his face as if it was normal for him to be here. "How do you even know where I live?"

"I followed you home," he says as if it were not a big deal.

"And you do this often? Are you my stalker now? I left before school was even over."

"So did I. I'm interested in where the new bad girl lives," he tells me, ignoring my other questions as he looks past me and into the house.

I put my hand up on the door, blocking his view. He returns his gaze to me with an amused smile.

"So you *are* my stalker," I tell him, bringing my hand down from the door and crossing them in front of me. "What do you mean by 'bad girl?'"

When he goes to look past me again, I replace my hand with my whole body as I lean against the open door, giving him a raised eyebrow.

"You know, when a girl is seen as dangerous, or scary, and troublesome, they are usually given the bad girl label," he states like he's reading it from the dictionary.

"I know what it means, but where did you hear it about me?"

"It's the big thing going around the school, and seeing as though I am the 'bad boy,' I thought I would come and get to know more about you, and the first thing is seeing where you live. I was also curious," he explains, leaning back and looking through the window.

"And why does everyone think I'm the bad girl?" I ask.

Hunter stops peeking into my house and looks at me straight on.

"You don't know? You're bitchy with Tiffany and the teachers. You have scary friends, and there is something about you which is threatening," he tells me, looking me over for effect.

A smirk touches my lips; I would be disappointed if I didn't make people frightened.

"Is there anything else I can do for you?" I ask him pointedly. "You've seen where I live like you wanted."

"Can I come in?"

"Nope."

"I've only seen the outside, and I won't leave until I see the inside," he says with a pout.

I make a noise which is halfway between a sigh and a groan.

"Fine, five minutes." I relent, opening the door wider as I move out of the way. I shake my head when I see his triumphant smile as he swaggers past me.

"Wow, Newbie, what did you do to get this place?" he asks almost breathily in awe.

I was born the daughter of Hades.

"I know the right people," I answer vaguely but truthfully.

This causes his eyes to widen before they trail over my body again and turn back to the living room.

"This would be a great house to hold a party in," he comments, looking out the through the glass to the hot tub, pool, and beach below.

"It would, wouldn't it?" I wonder aloud as I look around, trying to see it from his perspective.

"Yes, you should throw one this weekend. You know to welcome you to the school," Hunter suggests.

I let out a loud laugh.

"Let me get this straight. *I* throw a party to welcome *myself* to the school?"

"Yep."

I scoff at him in disbelief, pursing my lips as I think about it. Although the way he suggested it was silly, I decided to do it anyway. I like a good party, and it'd be nice to go to one which doesn't end in death. Well, hopefully. Usually, demons leave Hell to bring a human down so that they can play with them before killing them at the end of the night. It's strictly against the rules, but my dad can't always stop them, and I usually ignore it.

"Okay," I agree but add on a condition, "Only if you supply the drinks."

He looks indignant. "What? No!"

"Why not? You wanted me to have this party. It's only fair you bring the drinks," I counter with my hand on my hip.

He lets out a huffy sigh before relenting. "Fine."

This time, I'm the one with the triumphant smile. I let my hand fall from my hip and walk toward him, turning him around.

"Your time's up," I tell him as I push against his back, and he stumbles toward the door.

"Jeez, I'm going, woman. Stop pushing me," he exclaims, looking over his shoulder.

I stop, allowing him to open the door.

"Bring the drinks on Friday," I request as he walks out.

"Sure!" he calls back as he starts to walk down the drive. "Nice car and bike, by the way, Newbie." He pauses next to them to get a better look.

"Goodbye, Oldie," I shout, hoping he'll get the message. I watch his black leather jacket disappear around the corner before I turn and re-enter my house.

I lean against the door as I look around the living room. *The party will be fun,* I try to convince myself. If anything, it's an excuse to get drunk. Adrian and I would always smuggle alcohol into Hell. We had to be careful, however, as it was a hazard with all the fire around.

I chuckle at the images of how we found out. Adrian's face was priceless.

I reach into the bowl on the side table, taking out my keys to lock the door. I move through the white furniture and back to my small study, steeling myself to write the rest of the paper.

I fall down into the chair, swiveling it slightly. When I face the monitor and wake it up with the mouse, I read what I was doing last. Where was I going with that? I groan, not thankful for the distraction anymore as I delete the beginnings of a sentence. It's going to be a long night.

***

The next morning, my alarm's screaming wakes me up. Without thinking, I roll over blindly, throwing a ball of fire toward it. That should shut it up.

When it eventually stops, I roll back over and hug my pillow closer to me. It takes me a moment to realize that the room is warmer than usual. It's not unbearable; it's almost normal, but my tired brain slowly realizes that I'm not in Hell anymore.

I open my eyes and see the wall I am facing has an orange glow to it. I roll over, sitting up as I go, to find the alarm is now alight. I kick myself mentally; the appliances aren't fireproof.

"Shit!" I shout. I grab the fire like it's a blanket off the alarm and run into my bathroom, placing it in the sink before I turn the tap on. If it were still attached to my hand, only I could extinguish it, but once it loses contact with my body, it's almost like normal fire. The only difference is that I can pick it up, move it around, and control it.

I amble back into my room, checking the time on my phone. 7:00. Crap, I need to get ready! I run into my closet, searching through the racks and drawers of clothes. I pick out a pair of tan ankle boots and a tank top a couple of shades lighter. I slide a pair of denim shorts on under my tank top before making my way out of the closet, picking up a long necklace on the way. I do a quick layer of makeup before making my way down the stairs and to the kitchen.

I lean down to the cupboard under the sink, grabbing two bags of blood this time. That should keep me satisfied for the day. I don't want another episode like yesterday's. I wolf down the first before taking slow sips of the second. After finishing, I check for any remnants on my face before I realize I should get to school.

Deciding to take my bike today, as it's faster, I run back up the stairs to get my helmet and my leather jacket. I take a moment to admire the sunrise over my balcony, the colors reminding me of the fire of Hell. I don't get this at home.

I jog back down the steps, picking up my sunglasses, my keys, and my bag which holds the essay I finally finished late last night. Most of it ended up being drabble and me repeating myself over and over.

I lock the door behind me and make my way down to my bike. I open the storage compartment, stuffing my bag into it.

I arrive at the school, earlier than yesterday, with a short amount of time until the first bell goes. I clamber off the bike, pulling the helmet off my head. As I neaten up my hair, I notice that everyone is staring. Again.

"Are we really doing this again? I'm not exactly new!" I shout, annoyance ringing through my tone. Everyone suddenly finds the floor interesting or finds something else to do.

"Thank you!" I shout, pleased. I move past and through the students who are avoiding my gaze and into the school building. I walk down the crowded hallway, hearing gossip about me that I didn't even know about myself. I stop at my locker and find that Tasha, Lottie, Max, and Lily are all waiting for me there. I give them a smile in greeting as I enter my combination.

"Hey, where did you disappear to yesterday?" Lily asks as I place my helmet and some things that I don't need now into the locker.

"Um…I needed to get some answers from a friend," I reply, keeping it vague, but at the same time, giving enough information so they don't ask any more questions.

"I hear you're throwing a party this weekend," Tasha excitedly changes the subject.

"Wow, news travels fast here. Yes, you heard correctly," I tell her as I close the locker door. "I have homeroom with Mr. Matthews. Do you know anyone else who has it?"

"Yay! Yes, I have it too," Lottie exclaims as she hugs me to her.

I stand awkwardly, not knowing what to do. Max chuckles at my face.

"She's a hugger," he says.

"I can see that."

Lottie pulls back and looks at my face, apologizing. "Don't worry. I just wasn't expecting it. Who else has homeroom with us?"

"Hunter, Tiffany, and their friends," she says, and I groan.

"Really? I have to deal with them this early in the day? Do you hate me that much?" I exclaim dramatically into the air, looking up at the ceiling. I chuckle internally: I did make sure they were blue for a while.

"Let's get this over with," I tell Lottie as I hear the bell ring above us. I bid farewell to the group as Lottie hugs and kisses Max goodbye before she comes to walk next to me and toward the hell I don't want to be in.

We arrive at homeroom to find Tiffany and her friends already huddled together at the back, a couple of other students sitting closer to the front. I ignore them all as I walk to a seat in between the two groups of students, near the window. I look up to see why Lottie hasn't sat down yet and see she is giving the door a worried glance. I get my answer as to why when she looks back to me.

"You can't sit there!"

"Why can't I?" I ask, giving her a confused look.

"That's where Hunter sits, and he gets annoyed when someone else sits here," she explains but doesn't give me a satisfactory answer as to why I can't.

"And? What's so special about this seat? There are other seats, aren't there? It's not like his name is specifically on this seat," I ask, looking around at the other empty seats. She sighs with a shrug; however, her worried expression is still present on her face.

"Fine, sit there. Don't say I didn't warn you."

I think for a moment before ripping out a piece of paper from my notebook and write a message on it for Hunter. I then look around before getting up and out of my seat and walking to the wall in between the two windows, where a poster is up.

I take the poster off the wall, grabbing the putty-like substance off the back before returning to my seat. I attach the putty to the back of my note and stick it to the back of my seat.

Lottie shoots me a confused look, and I motion for her to look at it. She leans out of her chair to look at the back of mine, letting out a laugh at what she sees there. After seeing my little note, she relaxes more and begins to talk freely and easily. I listen to her, piping up when I need to, but never taking my eyes off the door.

A couple of minutes later, Hunter and his friends walk through the open door, his eyes moving over the class before they come to rest on me.

I raise my eyebrow at him questioningly, giving him an innocent smile. His eyes narrow as he marches toward me, stopping in front of the desk. Jake moves behind me to what I assume to be his seat, Leo and Liam joining him.

"That's my seat, Newbie. What are you doing in it?"

"Oh, I'm sorry. I didn't see your name on it. There are a lot of other seats, so go and sit your ass down," I tell him as I hear raucous laughter from behind me, letting me know Hunter's friends have found my message.

"But I always sit here," Hunter complains.

"Stop acting like a two-year-old, and go and sit down in another one. It is not your chair. It doesn't have your name on," I tell him, pointing to the empty seats around us.

"She's right there," Leo says with a chuckle.

Hunter looks at me weirdly before looking at Leo. He motions to the back of my chair, and my message there—If it's anyone's chair, it's mine because it has my name on it: Scarlett Hades.

Hunter moves around and reads the message on the back, letting out a grumble of frustration. I look over my shoulder at him with a smug smirk. He glares at me for a moment, but a small smile twitches at the sides of his mouth. He turns his back on us as he falls into the seat in front of me. Liam comes around me, muttering to me that he thought it was hilarious before sitting down in the seat next to Hunter.

After the fifteen minutes of Homeroom are up and the bell has gone, indicating that we can leave for out next class, I jump out of my seat and make my way out into the hallway. I start on my way to my first lesson but am stopped when a blonde army of clones step in front of me.

"I hear you're having a party this weekend," Tiffany declares.

"I am, but I don't know why you're worried about it because you're not welcome."

"I wouldn't want to come to your party even if you were the last person on Earth," she tells me in a rush, her heartbeat rising, letting me know that she is lying.

"Sweetie, if we were the last people on Earth, I would kill you so I wouldn't have to endure you," I tell her. I go to walk around her, but Tiffany steps in front of me, continuing our "conversation."

"Don't expect anyone at your party because I'm going to hold my own," she says petulantly.

"Oh my God, Tiffany, you're such a bitch!" I tell her, putting on a high pitch voice while faking anger before laughing and continuing seriously, "I don't care what childish things you do for attention."

Her brown eyes narrow into a glare before she stomps her foot and storms past me. I let out a slight laugh at her antics. First, Hunter, and now, Tiffany. What are we? Toddlers?

Chapter 8

Nothing Says Party Like a Red Cup!

The bell rings seconds after I step into World History. Mr. Ward's watery blue eyes meet mine as I walk to my seat.

"Ms. Hades, are you going to allow me to teach today's lesson without any interruption?"

"It depends. Do I need to correct you again?"

He flashes me a quick, forced smile before turning to look at the board. I travel through the desks until I get to the one I was sitting in yesterday. I swing the bag down under the desk as Mr. Ward claps his hands together loudly getting our attention.

"We will be continuing with what we were doing yesterday and will be focusing more on the myth about Hades and Persephone."

I let my head fall onto my arms which are crossed in front of me. I don't want to know what other rumors Persephone spread about my dad.

The bell rings, finally, causing the classroom to become a flurry of activity. Mr. Ward shouts to us all over the commotion to leave our essays on his desk as we leave.

I reach into my bag as I walk, bringing out the pages of paper. When I pass Mr. Ward's desk, his eyes meet mine, a disconcerting smirk pulling at his lips. I drop the essay onto his desk with a flourish, giving him a sarcastic smile. I don't get to see his reaction, as I continue to walk out of the nearly empty class. I pass Tiffany at the door, who gives me a glare, and continue to my next class, carefree.

***

The feeling stays with me all week, as I start to get into a routine and get to know the people at the school better. I have grown closer with Lily and her friends, and I even started to like Hunter and his friends' company. Overall, it was uneventful and boring, which was good. I don't know how long I can handle being on Earth if all the days were like my first. I want a change, and if all the days were like that, then I may as well have stayed at home.

It's Friday, and I am slouching in front of the TV, watching a show that I found on one of the many channels, trying to decide what to do this weekend after the party tonight. I found one of my few sweatshirts that I own and put it on with a pair of yoga pants. The difference in temperature from home and here is obvious, and when I'm sitting still, it starts to get to me. It'll take some time to get used to.

The commercials start to run again as I hear someone walking up the drive and toward the front door. Confused as to who could be here before the party is due to start, I listen closely to see if I can get any more clues. There is a clinking akin to a glass object hitting another, and by the sound of the footfall and the speed of the heart, which is slower than a female's on account of having a bigger heart, it's a male. I have got used to hearing the difference, and I like to play guess what gender sometimes when I'm bored.

I count down in my head the time it will take before the doorbell goes off. I stand up and make my way to the door, sneaking a glance out of the window, seeing that it's Hunter. I roll my eyes when I see him juggle the bottles in his hands and reach for the doorbell. I pull the door open before he can press it, earning me a shocked expression from him. It's quickly changed into a smile as he lifts the bottles up.

"The party is here!" he hollers.

"The party's later, come back then," I grumble before going to close the door again. His foot shoots out, stopping the door in its tracks.

"But I'm here now," he counters.

"Yes," I start patronizingly, "but the party's later."

"If you don't let me in through the front door, I'll find another way in," he promises. I contemplate forcing the door close, not caring about what's in the way; however, I pull the door back.

"Yet another piece of evidence that you're my creepy stalker. I'll make sure to have it where the police can find it when they find my body in a ditch," I tell him dryly as I move out of the way so he can enter.

He lets out a loud laugh which fills the space as he moves past me. With a flick of my wrist, the door slams after Hunter.

"What did you get?" I ask Hunter as I follow him into the kitchen and the breakfast bar. As I go, I reach over the back of the couch for the TV remote, turning it off.

"Anything you can drink without killing yourself and red cups. Nothing says party like a red cup!" he announces like a narrator of a commercial as I lean against the breakfast bar and look him over.

His dark blue, button-down shirt clings to him, his muscles in his arms bulging against the rolled-up sleeves of his shirt and his leather jacket. The dark gray pants he wears stick to his legs as if they were a second skin. I move my eyes back up him and see his eyes are on me, a smirk present.

He shrugs off his jacket, throwing it on the couch. He pushes his sleeves back up his arms, re-exposing his tattoos. I drag my eyes off him and look at the three bottles of vodka on the breakfast bar.

"Is that all you can drink without killing yourself?" I ask with a laugh.

He replies with a fake laugh. "There's more in the car."

"Well, go and get them then," I encourage.

As he makes the journeys back and forth from the car, I decide to go up to my room and get ready. I go immediately into my closet and to the section holding some of the dresses I brought up with me. I slide them across the rail, casting an eye over each of them. I stop my search, looking at a short black dress. The bodice would cling to my curves, and my shoulders and arms would be covered by black lace which made up the top quarter of the dress, with a cutout where my cleavage would be. I take it off the hanger, putting it over my arm before moving to my shoes and grabbing a pair of five-inch pumps.

Closing the closet door behind me, I listen to Hunter downstairs. I hear something heavy being put down before footsteps move back out of the house. He wasn't lying when he said that there was more in the car. I listen as he makes a couple more trips before deciding that I should get changed. I slip out of my casual clothes and shimmy the dress up my body before moving to start my makeup and hair.

Back home, to stop the makeup that I would acquire when I went up with my dad from melting, I have a refrigerated room in my closet. It's useful when I just want to experiment with makeup, but as soon as I step out of the room, it starts to melt off my face, so I rarely use it and keep it on. Now that I'm on Earth, I'm going to use it whenever I can.

After I have finished applying my red lipstick, I systematically start to curl my hair. Once I have finished and checked myself over in the mirror, I slide the pumps on, glancing at the clock as I leave the room. The advertised time for the party to start was ten minutes ago; however, I don't expect people to start arriving for another twenty minutes.

When I step off the last step, I find that the breakfast bar is covered with all types of different drinks from alcohol to soda. Hunter is fiddling with his phone, trying to get the music to play through the speakers. Once the music is blaring, Hunter turns to see me.

"Wow, Newbie, you look hot!" he exclaims, his eyes raking over my body.

"You don't look too bad yourself, Oldie," I reply honestly. I see a satisfied smirk touch his lips, but before his ego can revel in the compliment any longer, I change the subject. "Help me move the couches."

He moves to one end of the couch as I move to the other. He nods behind me, indicating where we should go, so I start to pull them. I could probably do this by myself, even in the heels, but it would probably look suspicious that I am able to do it so easily. Hunter was obviously not expecting it to move so quickly and far because he stumbles forward. This time, I'm the one with the satisfied smirk on my lips.

Once all the couches have been moved, creating a makeshift dance floor, I move to the kitchen and more specifically, the drinks.

"How about we get this party started?" I suggest, reaching for one of the many bottles of vodka.

Hunter grins, joining me at the counter, agreeing enthusiastically. "Hell yeah!"

I reach for the shot glasses and pour us each one. I lift it to him before bringing it to my lips and swallowing the liquid down in one. I grimace slightly as it goes down but put the plastic shot glass back down on the counter next to Hunter's, ready for another one to be poured. After gulping that one down and before our third could be poured, there is a knock at the door.

"The door's open!" I call to the people outside. I look to the door as it is swinging open to see that Leo, Jake, and Liam are standing on the other side, all with matching grins. They look between us and then around what they can see of the house, their jaws falling open slightly in awe. Jake lets out a low whistle.

"Wow, little devil..." He trails off, unable to put his amazement into words. His nickname for me has me snorting. If only he knows how true it is.

"Come on, you can explore later. We're starting the party already," Hunter says, lifting the bottle up for them to see.

I raise an eyebrow at him and his invitation for them to explore *my* house, but I roll my eyes and take the glass that he pushes toward me. I bring it to my lips, but Leo stops me.

"Wait, shouldn't we do a toast or something?" I look around and see that they all are nodding.

"Alright then. To Scar, hopefully, a new friend, and to an amazing party," Liam toasts, bringing his glass to the middle of where we are standing.

I smile and lift my glass toward the collection in the middle, trying not to slosh the liquid as I clink it against them.

"Hear, hear," Hunter says, shooting me a wink.

I bring the glass back up to my lips, gulping it down. I place the glass back down onto the counter as the doorbell goes again. This time, I walk to the door and find Lily and her friends on the other side. As they follow me back into the house, I leave the door open, allowing the onslaught of people arriving afterward to stream in.

***

Bodies push at me from all angles as I dance on the makeshift dance floor with Lily, Lottie, and Tasha. I throw my head from side to side as I dance to the fast-paced music. As the hair whips out of my eyes, I stop abruptly when I see someone watching me through the dancers. I narrow my eyes and shout to the girls that I am going to get a drink. I push through the closely packed bodies and toward the person who continues to watch me. I stop in front of them, crossing my arms.

"What are you doing here, Kyle?" I ask lowly, the music masking my voice to any human.

"I'm here to make sure you don't do anything stupid. How much have you had to drink?" he asks, lifting my head up by my chin so he can look into my eyes. I pull away from his grip as I answer.

"Not enough to affect me but enough to have a good time, *Dad*." As our blood heals our body and the body sees alcohol as a type of poison, it takes a lot to get demons drunk.

"Hm, I'll be watching," he says before turning and disappearing into the crowd.

"You know how ominous that sounds, right?" I call after him, earning a chuckle. I try to follow him with my eyes but quickly lose him. I throw my hands up into the air. They may say they do, but they don't trust me. Why allow me to come up if my dad's just going to send someone up to dampen my fun?

I spin on my heel and make my way to the kitchen and to get the drink I told the girls I was going to.

I enter the kitchen to find that most of the drinks that Hunter bought are still standing on the counter. I reach for a bottle of light amber liquor, not looking at the label, and pour it into a cup with some 7-Up. How much will Kyle let go before he comes and intervenes? I smirk as I bring the cup to my lips and gulp it down. I'm going to put it to the test. I place the cup back down and pour another, bringing it to my lips, and gulping that one down too. I am just pouring a third, feeling the alcohol starting to affect me more, when I see Hunter walking toward me.

"Whoa, Newbie, slow down there. You'll be flat on the floor," he jokes, leaning on his hands placed on the counter opposite me.

"I'm not a lightweight, Oldie," I retort before gulping down the one I just poured. I place the cup back down on the counter and reach for the bottles again. I twist the top off and go to pour it into the cup, slowing down as the alcohol starts to make the room sway.

My throat begins to dry out as my fangs descend. The only downside to alcohol is it causes my thirst for blood to heighten, and with the blood pumping in the people who are dancing, it becomes overwhelming for me.

I drop the bottle down onto the counter with a clunk and bring a hand up to my mouth to cover my fangs. I force myself to hold back the horns, hoping people won't see the changes on my face and my eyes. I immediately turn. Hunter chuckles and calls after me.

"Not a lightweight, huh?"

I lift my hand up to him, showing him my middle finger as I walk through the throng of students by the counter, talking. I force my way through, keeping my head down. I make my way between the dancers in the middle of the floor as I try to get to the stairs.

Hands fall onto my hips, and I spin around going to shout at whoever it was but stop when I realize that the boy in front of me will see my fangs and that will be hard to explain. Taking me looking at him as a good thing, he pulls me closer, allowing me to smell the alcohol on his breath.

His green eyes look me over as he starts to move us to the music. My bloodlust grows, and I take a couple of breaths, trying to decide what to do. I let out a small groan, knowing deep down that I shouldn't be doing this. This'll give Kyle something to think about. Almost as if my body knows that it'll be satisfied in a minute, my fangs retract, allowing me to go through with my plan.

I begin to move my hips on my own accord against him, and this causes the boy's grin to widen. I return his grin, showing him my now straight teeth. When he pushes himself toward me and I feel how aroused he is, I have to force myself to not step away from him. Think of the end game, Scar. I say it over and over in my head like a mantra.

The next song starts up, and I brush my lips against his ear. "Why don't we take this upstairs?"

His eyes widen, but whatever he is thinking doesn't stop him from nodding his head vigorously. My hand finds his, gripping it tightly as I drag him off the dance floor and to the stairs going up the wall near the front door.

The boy struggles to keep up as I march up the stairs. I glance over my shoulder to see if Kyle is going to stop me, but he's nowhere in sight; instead, my eyes meet Hunters. I can't tell what he's thinking from here, but I see him turn his back just before we disappear upstairs.

I look back to the boy who is going to be my snack and see that his face in slightly pained. I let go of his hand, noticing that his fingers are almost purple as well as being squashed together. His face relaxes slightly as he pulls his hand closer to his body.

A hand, which is not purple, attaches itself to my hip. I spin around to find his mouth is traveling toward me. I lift my hand and place it on his face, pushing so he goes stumbling back into the wall. The boy gets a fearful look on his face. My fingers trail down his face before resting on his neck, right above his jugular.

"If I place a bite here," I say, pressing against it, "you'll most likely survive…"

"What the—" he starts scared, but I stop him with my other hand over his mouth.

"But if I were to move to here," I add, trailing my fingers to his carotid artery, "you would be dead in minutes."

He mumbles into my hand, his eyes frantic. "What sort of freak are you?"

I flash him a smile, showing him my fangs.

"One with fangs. And I wouldn't move. If I were to nick your windpipe, you would drown in your own blood, and that wouldn't fun for either of us," I warn as I step toward him. He goes to step back, but being already up against a wall, he has nowhere to go.

"You're crazy!"

I ignore his exclamation as I continue to step forward.

"Now, before we start, we have to set a few rules. So, if you wouldn't look into my eyes," I request, knowing that he wouldn't do what I wanted if I just asked him straight.

No matter how hard a human tries, they will eventually want to look into our eyes. Humans are curious creatures by nature, and if you plant something in their mind, they'll want to do it eventually. If I were to say, "Don't think of a pink elephant," what's the first thing your mind goes to?

When I was first learning how to compel, my dad tried to explain to me what happened to a human to make them do what we ask. Demons have to get the person to look into their eyes to establish some sort of connection, and once you have the connection into the person's mind, the demon will automatically, without any prompting and knowledge, form the human/soul's dream person.

The human brain will then do anything that the demon says, afraid of upsetting the image of their dream. The demon will also take the voice in the person's head, telling them what they should do. If the demon says jump off a cliff, dazed from what they are seeing and the constant voice of the demon in their head telling them to, they'll comply. If the demon tells the person to forget what is about to happen, the brain will have temporary anterograde amnesia. It can be really useful sometimes. I've never experienced the feeling because compulsion doesn't work on demons.

It takes a moment before finally the boy looks up and into my eyes. I smile, starting the process of a connection. I imagine entering the boy's mind, and only when the boy gets a dazed look on his face do I know that it's working. If every time someone looks into our eyes, they were compelled, it would cause a lot of trouble.

"You will forget everything that happened tonight when you wake up tomorrow. You will think it's as a result of drinking too much," I compel him.

I break the connection by blinking and then leaning down to his neck and trailing my fangs over the jugular vein which I pointed out to him earlier. I'm not worried about being caught because if anyone were to come up the stairs, it would be just like we couldn't wait until we got to my room.

I let my fangs pierce the skin and then feel the blood starting to pool into my mouth. It's tainted by alcohol, and so it's less sweet than it usually would be. If I weren't drunk myself, I probably would have chosen someone who is soberer.

The boy's moans fill the upstairs as I continue to gulp down his blood. A vein is smaller than an artery, so it takes longer for me to be satisfied.

As more of his blood enters my system, the more the alcohol in it affects me. My barometer of when to stop isn't as good, so I continue drinking when I should really be stopping.

The boy's moans grow weaker until he finally slumps against me. Still not wanting to stop, I catch him and continue to suck the blood down.

Through the haze of alcohol over my mind I register that I am not alone. The muffled sound of my name being called reaches my ears, but I still do not stop, only getting blood matters to me at the moment. Hands come down onto my shoulders.

"Scar, stop!" This time the voice cuts through the fog of alcohol and blood-lust. I detach my fangs from the boy's neck and turn to the person who dared to interrupt, baring my blood-covered fangs.

Kyle's calm face stares back at me, and only then do I understand what I have done.

What if Kyle were Hunter instead? Have I killed the boy? I turn back to find the boy has fallen to the floor. I go down next to him, shaking his shoulder. *Please don't be dead!* I will it over and over again as I pat his cheek. My dad would kill *me*.

I listen for a heartbeat, and over my own pounding one and Kyle's, I hear a faint one. I breathe a sigh of relief as I fall onto my butt. I use my hand to wipe away the blood on my chin and my tongue to wipe my teeth clean. I've not lost control like that in a long time, and it scared me.

"You have to get him out of here," I plead with Kyle.

He nods. "On it, you compelled him, right?" he asks, knowing exactly what I am thinking.

"Yeah, of course, I did." I push myself to my feet, using the wall for support, as the alcohol is starting to make me unbalanced on my feet.

Kyle picks the unconscious boy up and starts down the stairs, turning back to me at the last minute.

"Don't worry about it. He's going to be okay." He continues down the stairs, calling to the people at the bottom to move out of the way. Hopefully, no one is going to look closely at the boy, and they will assume that he's just drunk.

I run my hand through my hair. I'm getting sick of this party and just want my house back. I follow Kyle's path and walk back downstairs. The pounding music is still going, and it's giving me a headache.

I shove people out of the way as I go to where Hunter's phone is still sitting and turn the music off. Shouts of complaint start up, but I shout over them.

"Everyone, get out. The party's over!" They all stare at me, not moving, and I begin to get angry.

"I mean it! Get out of my house!" I give each of them my most threatening look and am pleased when it causes everyone to race out of the house. I move through the house and open doors, telling the people in the rooms behind them to leave before I make my way to my room.

I lie in my bed and listen as the house slowly becomes silent again, only a few people trailing behind. Tired and too comfy to get out of the bed to see if everyone has left, I fall asleep in my dress to the sound of the front door closing.

Chapter 9

A Normal Day

I wake the next morning to a fuzzy memory of what happened the night before and a splitting headache. One of the downsides to being a demon is the morning after you've consumed alcohol, the hangover is much worse than what a human experiences. I groan and pull the duvet up to cover my sensitive eyes. I yearn for the darker surroundings of Hell right now.

Slowly, memories start to trickle back to me: Kyle being there, biting that boy, and then forcing everyone to leave. I let out another groan when I think of the mess that is most likely downstairs waiting for me.

I roll over in my bed and hug the pillow to me, hoping that sleep will claim me again. When it doesn't come and I only become more awake and less likely to fall back asleep, I peek at the time through squinted eyes.

I fall onto my back, my hand going to my forehead. I don't want to get up. I want to lie in my bed for the rest of the day, but my throat is scratchy and dry, and I need the toilet. I begrudgingly get out of the bed and stumble toward my bathroom, relieving my bladder.

I have all the same bodily functions as a human, as the anatomies of our bodies are both the same. The only differences between human and demon are the blood and the fact that we are technically not alive.

To change from human to demon, you have to drink the blood of a demon and then six humans before dying. The demon blood in the human system starts to fight the blood already there, and as if you were a demon all along, you start to get cravings for blood. The rationale behind drinking the six human's blood is that you will have enough different human blood in you to keep you in a limbo state when you die. Not quite dead, but not quite alive.

It's only once you die and drink the blood of a soul that you fully change. The blood of a soul is the third and final kind of blood there is. The combination causes your body to replace the blood you already have in your veins by copying the strongest of the three and the one that can handle it—demon blood. This helps you survive having the other blood in your system. Your soul will then return to your body on Earth, and your body will stay with the blood you drank in the process.

The whole process makes you partly already dead (which means you can't die again) and also minutely human but mainly demon. The technicality of you being already dead, along with the demon blood, helps the aging process slow down and the healing process speed up. The blood we drink has all the nutrients and things in it to keep us looking human. If we were to stop drinking the blood, our demon features would take over.

It's long and complicated, and my brain hurts from just thinking about it, so it's rarely done. The end result isn't as good either. You are much better off being born a demon, as that way, you don't have to go through the hassle and are a much stronger demon.

I leave my bathroom and stroll past the wall where I fed on the boy, noticing the bloodstain on the carpet. That's going to be a pain to get out. I move down the stairs, stopping when I see a body on the couch amidst all the trash from last night.

I lean on the banister, trying to get a better look. Are they dead? I shake the thought away when I notice that it's Hunter and his chest is rising and falling with his breaths. I continue down the stairs and walk to the couch, leaning over the back. I extend a finger and poke Hunter's bicep which is covering his eyes.

"Oldie."

He stirs slightly, rolling over, but doesn't wake up.

I poke him again this time in the back. He grumbles in his sleep but still doesn't wake up.

I walk past all the trash covering the floor and counter and go to the sink. I grab a glass and fill it with water, taking a quick gulp to try and alleviate the dryness somewhat; however, I know that only blood is going to help fully. I'll kick Hunter out and then have the blood I desperately want.

I pad back to Hunter and empty the contents of the glass over him. He sits up in a start, spluttering through the water.

"What the—"

"Get up, Oldie," I say as I walk back into the kitchen, placing the glass on the counter near the sink. I hear Hunter getting up from the couch and sit on a stool behind the counter where the empty bottles of alcohol are strewn across.

"What are you doing here?" I ask him as I fill the glass again.

"There was a party last night, lightweight…Remember?"

"Yes, but that doesn't explain why you are still here," I tell him as I reach for an apple. I bite into it as I raise an eyebrow at him, waiting for his response.

"The guys and I decided to stay over."

"Well, you can go and wake the guys up and then leave."

He grumbles but slides down for the seat and begins to walk up the stairs. I wait for the confusion and scream when he sees the blood, but it never comes.

Moving quickly, I bend down and open the cupboard under the sink and take out a bag of blood. I rip the top off and gulp down the liquid.

Once the bag is drained, I open the trash can and shove the empty bag to the bottom. I wipe my mouth, burping slightly. I lift the apple back up to my mouth and take another bite when I hear Hunter and his friends making their way back down the stairs. I expect them to continue out the front door, but they all come grumbling and groaning into the kitchen, sitting on the stools. I finish the apple in a couple more bites before throwing the core into the trash.

"What are you doing?"

"Waiting for breakfast," Jake answers, his head resting on his arms on the counter. "What are we having, little devil?"

"My foot up your asses if you don't leave right now," I tell them, crossing my arms.

Jake lifts his head up, a pout gracing his face. I look to Liam who looks like he's fallen asleep again and to Leo who is getting down from his stool, shrugging.

"I would have preferred you to cook us a nice meal, but I guess it has to do." Leo turns around, his ass out in the air in my direction. He wiggles it side to side.

I groan, rubbing my hands over my face. I can't deal with them this early in the morning, especially with a hangover as well.

"Ugh! Fine, what do you want?"

"Pancakes and lots of coffee!" Jake says, his head resting back on his folded arms.

I kick Leo in the ass, just for the hell of it, before turning my back to them. Leo yelps before going back to sit with his friends.

I yawn as I put the coffee on, wanting it and needing it as well as them.

"You expect me to make it all?" I ask as I take out mugs.

"You are a woman," Hunter points out.

I scoff and place the mug down on the counter before turning to him. I may be a woman, but I could kill him in seconds and run the worst place in the universe at the same time.

"And you are a misogynistic asshole," I retort. An amused and almost proud smirk touches his lips as the others laugh. "Now, get off your fat behind and come and help." I turn back to the coffee, pouring it into the mugs.

"You think I have a fat ass?" Hunter asks, faking sadness as he goes to the fridge.

"I would have to look at it to make that judgment," I comment, placing the full mugs in front of Leo, Liam, and Jake.

"You've looked at my ass? I didn't know you cared," Hunter jokes, placing the ingredients on the counter.

I pick my own mug up and walk past the guys drinking their coffee, trying to wake up. I look back as I get to where the kitchen and living room meet.

"No. I took a guess." I take a sip of my second favorite liquid as I turn and continue to the stairs.

"Hey, where are you going?" Hunter calls after me, walking out into the living room to come after me.

"Upstairs, to get ready for the day, while you make them breakfast," I call back as I get to the landing. I hear the guys still in the kitchen let out hoots of laughter. "After all, if you expect me to clean the house as well, I thought I could get a head-start, being a woman and all," I add on a sarcastically.

I step past the bloodstain, noticing that it's dry and relatively small. The boy was only down there for a short while; it could have been worse. I take another sip of my coffee as I push the door to my bedroom open, going directly to my closet to grab a pair of white cut-off shorts and a blue tank top.

I shove my feet into a pair of sandals, slipping a long necklace over my head as I exit my room with my empty mug of coffee. Knowing that I will forget to do it later, I decide to clean the blood up before I leave for the day.

I lightly run down the stairs, and walk into the kitchen where Hunter, Leo, Liam, and Jake are eating pancakes. When they see me, they all wear matching grins.

I look at them suspiciously as I walk to the closet, grabbing a brush, bucket, and detergent. I fill the bucket, still watching them cautiously. They continue to eat, but the grins don't go. I shake my head at them as I walk back out of the kitchen and upstairs. I will never understand them.

Careful not to get any of the blood on my clothes, I start to brush the patch before adding the detergent to the water and working at washing the stain away. My mind goes back to Hell and the last time I was cleaning blood away. I wonder what my dad is up to now. Probably happily relaxing, knowing I'm not there to cause trouble. How long will it take him before he gets bored?

I exhale as I stand up, looking down at the patch where the blood was. Right now, it's damp, but when it dries, it shouldn't be obvious that someone was bleeding there. Needing to get rid of the bloody water before I go back down, I walk into the bathroom and tip it down the drain. I don't feel up to making excuses this morning; the magic of caffeine hasn't started working on my hangover yet.

Returning back downstairs, I find that they have all moved from the kitchen to the living room and in front of the television. *Make yourselves at home, why don't you?*

"I'm going out. I better find the house in the same state as I left it!" I warn them.

They grunt in response, their eyes not leaving the screen. I look around and see that the remnants of the party are still scattered around the house. *They would have to destroy it for it to be majorly different,* I think to myself as I pick up the keys to my bike and helmet. Albeit, I can't believe that I'm leaving these boys alone in my house! I only hope that I don't come back to ruins.

***

I decide to drive to Miami and go to one of the beaches. I need a nice and relaxing day on the beach after all the long days at school and last night. I've not had the chance to explore and experience the different things to do on Earth like I wanted to. Has my dad done that on purpose? Is he afraid that I'll leave him for Earth, or that something will happen to me? If so, he has nothing to worry about. I may fall in love with Earth, but it would never stop me from going back to Hell. Hell's my destiny, and the love is much stronger for there than it ever could be for Earth.

I pull the bike into a space on the side of the road and clamber off. Pulling the helmet off, I shake my hair out, using my fingers to try and neaten it out and get rid of the tangles caused by the wind.

I turn back to the bike, placing the helmet in the compartment. I look around and see that families are here together, as well as groups of friends. My eyes linger shortly on a group of men standing by a van, looking expectant. They look too different to be family, and they don't look close enough to be friends. I wonder why they're here. I love people-watching, as humans are all so different from each other. I turn back to the beach and see the turquoise ocean sparkling in the bright sun, the light sand peppered with people enjoying their days out.

I join them, walking on the warm sand, finding a patch of sand where I can sit down and soak up the sun. I lay back, an arm going up to cover my eyes. The comfort from the higher heat, which is more similar to what I am used to, starts to make me feel drowsy. The white noise given by the people around me talking and the sound of the waves have me drifting off.

The peace is shattered by a scream. I jolt upright, half-annoyed at my relaxation being ruined and half-annoyed as it seems I never get a day off. I would have left it, but it was a young girl who had screamed. Thinking the worst, that a demon is here wreaking havoc, I jump up and turn in the direction I heard it come from.

Chapter 10

Game On

An interesting thing I have come to realize about humans is that if an event where help is needed doesn't concern them, they will bury their head in the sand and do nothing to help, as they don't want to get involved. Whether it be fear stopping them, or uncertainty with how to help, they will ignore whatever is going on. The onlooking crowd has a pack mentality. If no one else is going to help the person in need, they won't be the first to move.

Take for example what is happening right now. A girl, who could only be ten, is being kidnapped by the group of men I saw when I first arrived. Is anyone going to help her? No. They are all avoiding and ignoring the situation. People are even moving out of the way of the kidnappers, not wanting to be in the middle. Some people's faces are unsure, and they look like they want to help, but the underlying fear of what could happen to them stops them from acting. Demons are no better, though; if anything, our kind is worse. We would be the ones to stop and help them abduct the girl.

Keeping my eyes on the slowly moving group of men struggling with the girl, I ruffle my hair before pulling the tank top down to expose more of my cleavage. I start to saunter toward their direction, aiming to walk through their path to the van, as to get their attention.

Swaying my hips, I block their path as I walk past. I give a quick look to see if I have their attention and am pleased to find that I do. As I continue, some even start to shout out lame pick-up lines and whistle loudly. I wait a moment longer, making sure I don't go too far, so they don't lose interest.

"Hey, hottie, are you wearing space pants because your ass is out of this world?"

I hold back from giving a sarcastic response as I turn around, my eyelashes fluttering as I bite my lip. I saunter back and put my hand on the chest of the closest man. I let my lip go as I look up at him through my eyelashes.

His blond hair is greasy, and his blue eyes are glinting with something that would have me shifting uncomfortably if I weren't the daughter of Hades. He shows me his yellow, crooked teeth when he leers down at me. His face is marred by scars, and the scent coming off him surrounding me has me holding back bile. I force a smile on my lips and continue with the charade.

I let out a low whistle, holding back a laugh as I talk, knowing if I do, it'll ruin everything.

"Hello, sexy," I say seductively, making my voice husky and low. "Why don't you and your friends come with me, and we can have some fun?"

I see the man's eyes light up but dim slightly as he looks over my shoulder. I trail my fingers over his chest to encourage him. I'm not losing his interest!

"Can't you tell we're busy?" a deep voice, which has me shivering, asks. The slight gruffness and gravelly quality of his voice screams danger at me, and I like me a bit of danger.

I let my hand fall from the tubby chest in front of me and turn to come face to face with a god. In the figurative sense, not the literal of course, as I know and have met all the real gods. However, the man standing in front of me could be worshiped. He's the youngest of the group, probably by half their ages, but even so, he seems to be the one in charge.

The man I was talking to looked to him when I suggested they deviate from what they were doing with the girl, and he just has the feeling of power emanating from every pore of his body.

His light brown hair is messy and looks like it's waiting for someone to run their hands through it. *I'll happily volunteer,* I think as I continue my inspection. His piercing, ice-blue eyes are hard and guarded as they return the inspection, traveling over my face.

My eyes move down his plump lips waiting to be kissed— over the stubble scattered over his tanned skin on his strong, defined jaw—and to his body. His arms are crossed, causing his biceps to bulge against the cropped sleeves. The skin which is exposed is tattooed.

At some point when I am ogling him, my lip ends up between my teeth. I let my lip go as I move my attention back to the situation at hand and off the man standing in front of me.

"What is it you are doing?" I ask, faking obliviousness and innocence, twirling a piece of hair between my fingers. I internally roll my eyes; the dumb girl is my least favorite persona I use.

His eyes seem to burrow into me, seeing my every thought and feeling. His eyes become amused, telling me my act didn't work on him.

"Huh," I let out quietly. No human has ever been able to see past my charade. This makes me even more intrigued by him. Not trusting my first appraisal, I smell the air discreetly, wondering if maybe I was wrong and he is a demon. He has the dangerous feeling coming off him, but his blood is fully human and intoxicating.

"It's none of your business what we're up to," he replies.

I like a challenge; he's not going to let up easily. I step toward him, resting my hand on his hard chest. The smell coming from him overwhelms me, and the smell of the earlier man is pushed out of my mind as the intoxicating musky smell consumes my whole thoughts. My breaths start to quicken as hunger rears its head, eager to taste whether he's as good as he smells.

A throat being cleared has me jolting out of the hunger. I need to gather myself. He's only a human, so this should have been easy and completed already.

"Are you sure you can't do it another time?" I ask with a pout, taking a step back from him, thankful for the reprieve. I stretch my arms behind me, joining my hands at the back, letting out a groan as if I am tired, my eyes trained on the man the whole time.

A satisfied smile comes to my lips when I see him look down at my breasts which are now pushing against the material of my vest, his jaw clenching before he looks away. Men are so easy to manipulate.

"Oh well, your loss," I continue before turning and walking slowly away.

The other men in the group start to protest, trying to get their leader to change his mind.

Five.

Four.

Three.

Two.

"Wait!"

I pause.

"What did you have in mind?"

I grin and spin around.

"Ditch the girl," I sneer as I look at her, trying to communicate with my eyes to run as soon as they let her go. "And you'll find out." I just hope that she understands what I'm trying to tell her. If I were her, I wouldn't think twice about it when I got a chance to escape.

After a long minute, the leader nods at the man holding the girl. Without hesitation, he lets the girl go.

She runs off, not giving a look back, and I exhale in relief. Triumph has my sneer turning into a grin again as I watch the girl grow smaller.

My attention is brought back to the group of men who are all now looking at me with a hungry look in their eyes.

"So, what was your idea?" the leader asks with a smirk. What throws me about the smirk is that it's not malicious or expecting anything; instead, he almost looks amused.

"I don't even know your name…" I say, not taking my eyes off him. I have no interest in the others.

"Reid Brice." He looks like he's waiting for a reaction of sorts. Should I know who he is? He looks pleased before continuing by introducing the others. I don't need to know their names, so I tune him out. So who is the illustrious Reid Brice who kidnaps ten-year-olds and is known by people?

"Name?"

It takes my brain a moment to piece together what he is asking. Name. *He wants to know my name,* I think, pulling myself together.

"Scarlett, but you can call me Scar," I answer with a wink. The eye contact I have kept with the leader is broken when one of the men starts advancing toward me, gripping my arm so I'm looking at him instead.

"Well, I know what I want to do with you Scar," the man tells me with a sadistic and lust-filled grin.

I step back from him, tearing my arm out of his grip. I had set the girl free and had found out the hot guy's name. My work here is done. The man takes a step forward only to falter when I stop his train of thoughts, a false smile on my face.

"Yeah? Well, whatever it is, it's not going to happen."

His smile falls as anger takes over. "What?" he demands.

"You heard me."

He steps forward to get to me, his face clouding over with the fury. His hand shoots out and grabs my arm tightly.

I tut at him as I wave my finger from side to side.

"Uh, uh, uh, you don't want to hurt me," I warn him.

"And why not?" he asks cockily. I love when they think they know everything.

"Because you don't want to make me angry. I have seen my fair share of dead bodies in my life, shall we say. So, my suggestion to you if you want to keep that hand and your dick is to let go of me and never try to kidnap a girl again and then lose her when a girl more than half your age comes along that you want to fuck. Okay? Trust me, I will find out if you do something like this again," I advise bluntly, yanking my arm out of his grip. I move away from the group and back toward my bike.

"You do realize that I'm probably only about five years older than you," Reid mutters to me as I pass him, brushing him on purpose, a light smirk on his lips.

"I know. I wasn't talking to you. See you around," I respond, looking him up and down one last time, knowing it will be unlikely I will see him again. I carry on to my bike, feeling eyes following me until I'm out of sight.

I straddle the bike, pushing my helmet down onto my head, and set off back to the house.

I turn onto the main road, noticing that it's relatively busy. Looking in the mirror to see if I can change lanes, I spot the van from the beach following me a couple of cars back.

I decide to put it to the test, wondering if they are just leaving the beach to go back. Instead of changing lanes, I turn left, keeping an eye on one of my mirrors.

Soon enough, the van turns as well. I turn right this time, speeding up slightly. Yet again, the van follows closely behind.

I snort; they're not very good at tailing someone, as they are now nearly directly behind me. I could lose them if I wanted to; however, I decide to have a bit of fun with them.

I notice that the street is a dead end but has an alleyway that the van could fit down. I turn into it, skidding to a halt. I look around the alley and see that it holds dumpsters for garbage, but that hasn't stopped the floor being scattered with articles of trash.

As expected, seconds later, the van turns into the alley, coming to an abrupt stop when they see me standing halfway down. The doors simultaneously open as the group of men exits the van. I am slightly disappointed and glad at the same time that I do not see Reid among them.

"We're here to collect our 'fun,' as you called it," one of the men says as he pushes the doors shut, causing a slamming sound to resonate off the grubby walls of the alley.

"You didn't get it, did you?" I ask rhetorically, my hands going up to my helmet still on my head. "Maybe this will help." I pull the helmet off my head, allowing them to see my red eyes, demonic features, and, of course, my tiara of horns. I flash them a toothy grin, showing them my fangs.

"You wanted fun, so why don't we play a game?" I suggest. "You run, and I'll catch you and make you my dinner."

They are frozen, staring at me in shock and terror.

Internally, I laugh; I love when they look scared and vulnerable. "I'll take that as a yes. Well then, game on!"

Once the last word has left my lips, the men begin to shove each other, trying to get back to the van before the others. I wait a moment until they have bundled each other back into the van before I act.

I run at my fastest pace, stopping abruptly inches away from the van. Their eyes widen even further, and I see a couple of them swallow. The man in the passenger seat and the one that called the lame pick-up line to me shouts at the driver.

"She's a demon. Run her down!"

I raise an eyebrow as I move my gaze to the driver, waiting to see what he's going to do. I can see when he decides because his face hardens. The engine rumbles to life, and a smirk comes to my lips.

Deciding to play with them, I push my demon side back and return back to my normal face, but if they wanted to change their mind now, it's too late. The van jolts forward, and I take a couple of steps back, forcing a scared expression onto my face.

The van picks up speed, and I force myself to hold back a smile when I continue backing away, my hands going up.

Just before I feel the impact, I stutter out a word, pretending to plead with them. "S-stop!"

The pain of the van hitting me spreads throughout my body, but I don't have time to think about it as I go flying back through the air. I get a glimpse of the men recoiling from the glass. My attention, however, is centered on something else—a male voice shouting.

"What the fuck?"

I hit the ground, knowing that if I were human, I would be knocked out, rolling a couple of times before coming to a stop. I bite my lip to stop the pain leaving my lips in a cry. I need to stay "knocked out," so I close my eyes and regulate my breathing.

The pain begins to lessen gradually as my blood starts to heal the injuries I suffered. If only we didn't get hurt. I hear footsteps come rushing to my side and turn me onto my back. I fight the urge to open my eyes so I can see the face looming over me.

I recognized the voice, and it's only now I remember where I heard it before. The beach. It is Reid, the leader of the men who rammed me. Where was he, and why show up now?

"Shit! Why did you do that?" he shouts.

The sound of the doors slamming for the third time echoes around the alley, and I feel Reid's eyes move from my face. His rough hands stay on my face, holding it.

"She's a demon or something! She has horns, fangs, and her eyes change color," one of the men explains.

I try to relax when I feel myself start to stiffen as I wait for Reid's response. Will he believe them? He doesn't know me; he knows his men more. Does he trust them enough to believe even the most ridiculous of stories?

His eyes return to my face, and I feel the intensity in them.

"Does she look like one? What did you take?"

"Well, she doesn't now!" another tells him, almost patronizingly. I feel Reid's grip tighten before leaving my face.

"We didn't take anything. We all saw her." He's just digging himself into a bigger hole, maybe even his grave. It seems like Reid is getting angry at his men. This feels like the perfect time for me to become "conscious" again.

I stir slightly, trying to get Reid's attention, before I open my eyes, fluttering my eyelashes slightly. I groan, bringing a hand up to my head where a headache is almost completely gone.

"Ugh. What happened?"

Reid's ice blue eyes stare back at me, softer than I saw them earlier, concern shining from them.

"You were hit by a van," he responds, his deep voice quiet, anger leaking into it.

"What?" I ask, making my voice tremble by shaking my lower lip as I speak quietly, breathing out. I look around the alley, pretending to try and remember. I try to keep a smile off my lips as my eyes fall on the group of men crowding around the van. I stare in false fright at it before turning back to Reid. "Oh."

When I see Reid turn his back, I quickly flash my demon features at the men watching us fearfully, winking. I see Reid begin to turn back, and I quickly school my features back to the usual façade. I force tears into my eyes, biting my cheek as I imagine chocolate being banned from Hell. What can I say? Chocolate is almost as good as blood to eat. It's up there with coffee.

I feel the tears start to trail down my face.

"They followed me, and when I came down here to get home, they cornered me. I said no and started to fight back, but they pushed me to the floor and got back into the van. I got up and saw that they were coming toward me..." I trail off as if it pained me to remember it, stuttering over my words.

When I see that I have Reid's full attention, I breathe in, my lip poking out slightly to make it tremble.

"She's lying! She's a demon," one of the men calls over.

I furrow my eyebrows as I watch Reid shoot a look to the man who called out. "A what?"

"Their story is that you are a demon," he clarifies for me, disbelief clear in his voice.

"Like in books?" I ask, and Reid laughs, agreeing with me. I laugh as well. If only he knew!

"That's what they're saying," he tells me with a shrug of his strong-looking shoulders.

I try and pull a demon-like face on my normal one, earning another chuckle from Reid.

"Do I look like one?" I ask, relaxing my face.

"No. Quite the contrary," he answers with a wink.

A small smile comes to my lips. So the attraction is not only one way.

Before I can go any further with the conversation, Reid's face turns hard and looks to the men still standing and watching us both.

"You are dismissed. Actually, make that fired. I don't want to see you again," he commands them all, giving them each a serious stare. He *is* the leader of them all, but he must be the leader of a much larger organization if he doesn't care about getting rid of four men.

He turns back to look at me, his eyes finding mine. His look reminds me of my dad's when he has given orders to a demon. He knows that they will follow what he says and will do something about it if they don't. The men start to complain.

"You're going to believe a girl you just met over us, boss?"

"This is bullshit!"

However, all their clamoring is cut off by Reid with one glare. Just like my dad, again. The men all grumble under their breaths but do as Reid says, getting back into the van and backing out of the alley.

"So, who are you? The godfather's son?" I quip, wondering if I will be able to gather any information from his answer.

"Grandson?"

He laughs, but his answer has me intrigued. "Not quite."

***

I push the door to my house open, throwing the keys into the bowl on the side. I pull my vest out, trying to see the damage. Tears from where it caught on stones when I was rolling across the floor have ruined it. I sigh, wanting a long bath to relax my still sore body and wanting to forget about the whole day. Well, except for one particular man.

Speaking of Reid, he was sweet, making sure that I was okay before I left. I've survived much worse, and I wonder what he would think if he found out. He thought it was ridiculous what his men were saying; would he still find it ridiculous if I were to see him again and show him?

I am halfway to the stairs when I notice that something feels off.

The house is clean; that's what it is. I look to the couches and let out a startled shriek when I see Hunter and his friends sitting there watching the TV, which is currently muted. I forgot that they were here.

"Gods," I exclaim, raising a hand up to my erratically beating heart. I'm much better at being aware of my surroundings usually. They all turn to look at me, their faces bored. "What are you all still doing here?"

"Gods?" Hunter asks.

"Yes, it's an exclamation," I snap.

"To answer your question, little devil, we were too comfortable and didn't want to leave," Jake says over his shoulder before turning back to the muted TV, picking the controller up and un-muting it.

"You didn't break anything, did you?" I ask, walking through the downstairs and into the attached kitchen, searching for any damage or differences.

"I'm hurt that you would think that, Newbie," Hunter says with mock offense. "What happened to you?"

I wave it off as I walk back into the living room portion.

"I was hit by a van."

They all stop watching the TV, and turn to me, looking me over for injuries.

"Are you…"

"I'm fine, but I would feel even better if I had my house back," I tell them all pointedly, my hands on my hips.

"I'll give you a massage," Hunter offers, suppressing a grin.

"And I'll give you a kick in the balls if you don't leave now," I reply.

His face contorts as he imagines the pain that I could cause him.

"I should get going," Leo rushes as he scrambles to his feet and out of the door.

"Me too," Liam and Jake both call as they quickly follow their friend. I turn back to Hunter who is still sitting on my couch.

"Are you so desperate to have some sort of girl's contact with your balls that you're going to stay there?" I ask.

He looks like he's actually pondering it for a moment before standing up.

"You just have to ask if you want to touch them," he retorts.

I roll my eyes and shoo him out of my house, pushing him to help him on his way. We finally get to the door, and I give him one last shove, and he's out of the house. I give him a smile as I move to shut the door. Before the door closes, I see Hunter's face move to the gap, calling into the house.

"Great party last night, Newbie. Let's do it again sometime!"

I rest my back against the door and listen as Hunter's steps fade as they walk down the drive. Once I hear an engine start and then the vehicle moves off, I bound up the stairs and into my bathroom. I turn the taps on and get to work on filling the big tub.

Chapter 11

The Grim Reapers

I walk into the kitchen, my muscles relaxed after the long bath and feeling better as a whole. I grab a bag of blood, emptying it into a mug so I don't have to worry about drinking it all at once or it spilling out onto the surface I placed it on. I hold the mug in my hands as I look around the house.

Hunter and his friends did a good job of clearing up, I think as I walk through the house and into the room holding my computer. I fall down in the desk chair, spinning in it before maneuvering myself to look at the screen. I place the mug down and turn it on. I don't exactly know what I want to do, but I'm bored and think that it might be able to entertain me in some way.

The desktop stares at me, and I stare back, trying to think of something. Leaning back in my chair, I take a sip of my blood as my mind wonders to earlier. Who is Reid Brice? I sit up, putting my mug down and opening the app that will take me to the internet.

Eventually, I used this with Mr. Ward's homework. What's better than getting what humans believe right from their own words?

I enter his name into the search bar—Reid Brice—and press the enter button. I don't expect to get many responses; usually, someone like him will want to keep a low profile. I'm surprised when I get hundreds of results, and most of them news articles. I click the first one that is the most recent, leaning forward, and start to read:

The Man Behind the Name

The Grim Reaper. The name alone strikes fear into our hearts. Rightly so, as throughout the whole world, it has the same meaning—Death. Imagine the fear you feel at the one personification being multiplied by hundreds, maybe even a thousand. That feeling is present in the hearts of the people of South East America. Hundreds of Grim Reapers are roaming the streets of Florida, and they are all under the order of one man. Reid Brice.

Mr. Brice, now aged 24, didn't have the best of upbringings. Born into poverty, and to a mother who either couldn't care for him or didn't want him, Reid was quickly placed into an orphanage and stayed there for most of his childhood. We spoke to one of the people who worked there when Mr. Brice was living with them, a Suzie Brown, and she was able to give us some insight into young Reid Brice:

"He was troublesome from the word go. He was quiet, not socializing with any of the other children, but when he did, he would regularly get into fights. I think it was when he was twelve that we first started to see just how dangerous he would grow to be. He started to mix

with a group of children who were into narcotics and criminal activities. The first time he was dropped back at the orphanage by a cop car, he held a smug grin with a glint in his eyes, and I knew we would have the same situation recurring over and over again. We tried to get him adopted, but the prospective families found him to be too much of a handful. He was fourteen when he left us. I still shiver at the memory of that night."

We tried to ask her about the events that took place but were unable to learn anything else. The charges that Suzie talks of mounted up over the years, and ended up coming to a total of forty-three cases against him which were all promptly dropped, by the time he was fifteen.

It was at that time, nine years ago, that Reid and a couple of his friends started the beginnings of the gang which would become the notorious Grim Reapers. We do not have specifics or much documentation on them, but we do have crime figures going up by nearly double the first year that they were on the scene, and they have not been resting since, having the figures continuously rising ever since.

The police have issued warnings telling anyone who sees suspected Grim Reaper activity to keep away, and call 911 immediately to report it. Only names have been able to be acquired, coming to a total of over 300 members, but it is suspected to have many more. Their reach is far, but the police have been unable to find any evidence or catch them. Everything they have done is so well executed, or covered up, that the crimes supposedly committed by them are all speculation.

Some of the older Grim Reapers can be recognized by their telltale tattoos of a scythe and skull on their wrist. Newer members are said to have gone without. No photographic proof or examples have been found, but the source of the information is said to be reliable.

The police stress constant vigilance and have released photos that have been captured of Mr. Brice and some of his colleagues (as seen below).

Below the article, a grainy, unclear CCTV shot of Reid and some other men walking out of a store can be seen.

I am about to close the page, happy that I have found my answer (that Reid is a leader of a gang) when a popup appears on my screen, telling me of a breaking story. I click through when I see the headline:

Four Members of the Infamous Grim Reapers Gang Have Been Captured.

The story tells of an anonymous tip, which let on the whereabouts of the men who were captured. I scroll through the rest, which gives some background on the gang, most of it the same as I just read. At the bottom are the photos of the men.

The four men who tried to run me over stare back at me, all wearing scowls, with their names printed underneath. I grin. Was Reid the anonymous tip? Would he have risked it? He seemed pretty angry earlier, but would he risk getting recognized to get revenge on his members? It was most likely a member of the public.

I turn the screen off and rub my hands over my face. I knew Reid was somewhat dangerous and he was a leader, but to get confirmation of my theory is different. I now am certain that bad people gravitate toward me. The Devil's daughter doesn't get a day off!

Chapter 12

The Incredibly Hot Leader

When Monday finally comes around, the rest of the weekend seemed boring in comparison to Saturday.

I roll over in my bed, stretching out. My alarm has stayed silent, which I am thankful for. I don't want something going off loudly at this time in the morning. What time is it?

I fumble on the bedside table, feeling for my phone, bringing it above my face. I squint at the onslaught of light and manage to find the time through it. 09:05. I sit upright abruptly, throwing the covers off. Shit! I'm late.

Although I am thankful for not having an alarm screaming at me to get up, I need it. As I rush around my room, gathering everything that I need, I set an alarm for tomorrow. I nearly trip as I try to get my shorts on, all the while still trying to move. After jumping around my room, I am fully dressed and ready to leave.

Stopping shortly at the kitchen to wolf down two bags of blood, I run out of the front door. I glance at my phone as I shove my bag into the compartment on my bike, noting that it took me just over fifteen minutes to get out of the door.

I straddle the bike, shoving my helmet down on my head before pulling out of my driveway at a fast speed. I zoom in between the cars on the road, running a couple of red lights and going over double the speed limit. Luckily, I don't see any cop cars; otherwise, I would have been delayed even further.

I eventually pull into the parking lot of the school and jump off my bike, running into the building at a human pace.

I burst into room 139, causing Mrs. Hale to stop talking and the whole class to look at me. Hunter's face stands out amongst the rest, holding an amused expression. I give him a sarcastic smile before turning to Mrs. Hale at the front.

"Ah, Ms. Hades, I see you have finally decided to grace us with your presence! How kind of you."

"Got to make a big entrance," I tell her as I make my way through the desks and to mine. "Well, don't keep us waiting for more of your enlightening teachings."

She looks like she wants to say something back but thinks better of it and looks down at her desk and carries on from where she left off.

Murmurs of the party on Friday fill the hallways as I walk to the gym. The people that were there were talking about how great it was even though it finished early, and the people who weren't there were talking about disappointed they were that they missed it. I try and fight it, but I can't help a smug grin making its way onto my face.

Gym is uneventful, apart from the glares I am getting from Tiffany and her followers. I shrug it off, getting an explanation from Lily in Algebra. Apparently, Tiffany's party wasn't as big of a success as mine, rumor being that only she and her followers attended.

***

I walk through the buzzing cafeteria and to the table to find everyone even Hunter and his friends already sitting there apart from Lily and me. I take a seat at one of the tables which have been pushed together, putting my sandwich down on the table in front of me. I pick it apart, eating it slowly as I listen to the conversations.

"What did you do over the weekend?" Tasha asks me.

I laugh, brushing my hands together.

"I woke on Saturday to find that some idiots had stayed behind from the night before," I say.

"Hey!" Leo interrupts, fake hurt in his voice.

"I then went to the beach, saved a little girl from being abducted by the Grim Reapers gang, met their incredibly hot leader, got hit by a van holding some of the members who were angry at me, and then got saved by the same smoking hot leader. The next day wasn't as eventful. Oh no, wait, I stubbed my toe, so you could say it was up there with the Saturday," I say and smile.

They all stare at me some with fright and some with amazed shock.

"Huh," Hunter lets out.

It takes me a moment to realize that cafeteria has gone deathly silent and that everyone's eyes have gone behind me.

"You wouldn't happen to be talking about me, would you?" I hear a low voice say from behind me.

I let out a squeak in shock and turn around.

The school seriously needs to work on their security; anyone can just walk in. And it seems that they do. First, Adrian, and now, Reid.

I turn and give a sheepish smile to Reid, who is standing there flanked by three men.

"Hi," I greet awkwardly.

"Well?" he asks.

"Well, what?" I retort.

"Well, am I the incredibly hot leader?" he asks.

"Well, that depends if you are the leader of the gang called Grim Reapers," I tell him, raising an eyebrow.

"Well, that would be telling, wouldn't it? Your life would be at stake as well if you were to know," he says.

"Can we all stop saying *well*? It's getting on my nerves!" Lottie interjects.

I laugh.

"Well, we could…" I remark.

"Ha ha, very funny," she responds drily.

I grin at her, and she does the same. I turn back to Reid to see what he wants.

"What are you doing here? How did you find me?"

"I have my ways of finding people," he responds mysteriously. "I came here to ask you a question."

"Me? Don't I feel privileged? Oh, hang on. Is it where babies come from? Because if it is…"

Reid's loud laugh fills the cafeteria, and the men standing either side of him jump, looking shocked at hearing it.

"No, it's not, but you could show me if you wanted," he responds with a wink. I smirk. "Go on a date with me?"

"Are you asking or telling me?"

"Asking," he replies uncertainly.

"Then no," I let him know, looking away. I can feel the confusion rolling off him. I need someone to challenge me and maybe take control of some situations.

"What if I was telling? What then?"

I stand up, ready to go to Psychology, and turn to look at him properly.

"I wouldn't have any choice then, would I? So, I would say send me the time and place." I pat him on the shoulder as I walk past him and toward the doors leading out into the hallway, the bell ringing overhead.

"I don't have your number. How am I meant to do that?" he calls over the noise of the students making their way to the next class.

"Surprise me. I thought you had your ways."

"You know my name. I don't know yours," he shouts after me again.

I look over my shoulder at him. "I gave it to you when we first met."

"I don't have your last name, Scar," he recalls.

"How did you find me then?"

"I didn't. I just got your location from one of my people," he calls, standing up straighter so he can still see me.

"Hades," I call back as I walk out of the cafeteria.

Chapter 13

Hey, Dead Man!

It's Thursday, and I still haven't heard from Reid. I have come to the conclusion that he isn't being serious about our date and isn't going to determine a place and time.

Sitting in the fifth class of the day, I listen to Kyle reading out a passage from the textbook, trying not to fall asleep.

"This is commonly—"

Screams from down the corridor have everyone in the room straightening, and the smell of fear slowly rises.

I share a look with Kyle, both of us trying to determine how much we should do. We both seem to come to the same conclusion—it depends on what the threat is.

As the threat grows closer to the room, the screams and shouts become louder and move with it.

The door handle rattles, everyone in the class stands up and prepares themselves for what is behind it. I step toward the door, getting ready to attack whoever is behind it, and by the looks of it, so is Kyle.

The door flies open to reveal Reid holding a man to his chest, a gun up to the man's temple who is already covered in something red. Blood?

The whole class let out a collective scream as they stumble, trying to get away from the danger. I falter and take a step back, my hand discreetly telling Kyle to hold off his attack. His heartbeat is too strong, and the man is too calm, for someone who has lost that amount of blood. I get even more suspicious as it doesn't look like blood either; it's too bright. I sniff the air, and tomatoes hit me instead of the scent of blood.

I bite my lip to stop myself from laughing, as I listen to what Reid has to say.

"Let me have Scarlett Hades, or I will kill anyone who gets in the way. You will deliver her to the address that is written on the corridor's walls at the specified time. If not, there will be consequences," he warns in a threatening tone. "See you then," he adds, winking in my direction.

I clap my hands together in front of me discreetly, causing Reid's grin to become bigger. He drops the man before turning and making his hasty exit. The security is seriously lacking; this is the second time that Reid, a dangerous gang leader, has entered the school, and this time he even had a gun.

I wonder for a moment if Reid has some sort of connection to the school, which makes them look the other way, but I'm jolted out of it by a high-pitched voice.

"Oh my God, we have to call 911," a girl shrieks, looking faint as she looks at the man on the floor who is pretending to be dead. Kyle ignores the traumatized class as he walks closer to me.

"We need to tell your dad that you were threatened," he mutters, concerned.

"No. We don't. He was asking me on a date. Can't you smell that it's ketchup?"

Kyle discreetly smells the air, like I did, and relaxes when he verifies that the man is not hurt.

"So, that's how humans ask each other. Weird," he mutters, making me laugh as I walk toward the "corpse" deciding to play with my classmates a bit more.

I examine the man who is now pretending to be dead and note the small movements he is making. I shake my head; he's not very good at being dead. I lean down and scoop some of the ketchup on his chest, up, bringing it to my mouth. I lick it, turning back to the class.

"Mm. Tastes good, want some?" I ask, extending my hand out to them. They scream in horror and step back even further if they can. I laugh, shaking my head at them.

"Relax, it's just ketchup," I tell them, licking the rest of the "blood" off my finger. The best thing about that is that I just showed them the real me, and they thought that it was a joke.

I crouch down on my haunches next to the man so I can talk to him quietly.

"How much is he paying you?"

"Enough," he replies, moving his mouth as little as possible.

I beam and stand up, deciding to see where and when the date is. I step over the "dead man" and exit into the hallway. The wall, as promised, has writing on it, also in something red. It drips down the wall, causing it to look even more horrific.

Now will you go on a date with me?

Aspen Valley Park, 11 a.m.?

The students look at the wall, confusion clear on their faces. It doesn't add up with what they saw.

A boy grins at his friends before making his way to the wall, his hand outstretched. He scrapes some of the liquid off the wall and moves it to his mouth.

Something feels off and different, so I sniff the air. I throw my hands out in front of me as I take a step back trying to calm down from the overpowering smell of fresh blood.

"Wait! That's not ketchup this time!" I shout, stopping the boy in his tracks.

A second passes where the corridor is still, almost like someone pressed pause on a remote.

The boy who went to the wall suddenly crumples and falls to the floor having fainted. This seems to start the scene playing again as everyone shouts and screams.

"We need to call 911!" someone screams again. Sobs come from some of the students, but I focus on Kyle who is silently asking me what we should do.

I shrug; we need to get them to calm down. I look around for something that will do the trick. I spot the fire alarm on the wall and push through the chaos to it. I smash the glass, causing the alarm to start blaring throughout the school.

I light a fire on my fingertips. The smoke detectors catch it, and the sprinklers try to put it out. Hopefully, it will shock them enough to forget about the blood and maybe even clean it off somewhat. The screams change to ones of shock, and the teachers in the hallway shout over them to get their attention.

"Everyone, make their way out of the building in an orderly fashion!"

I move back to stand with Tasha and Lottie, seeing that they are rolling their eyes at the screamers.

"How did you know that it was ketchup on the man and the writing wasn't?" Tasha calls over the alarms and terror.

"The man looked too calm for it to be real blood, and the writing looked different to the ketchup on the man," I tell them truthfully.

"You're very observant," Lottie comments as we start to push through the people still in the corridor.

As we walk, I notice that the man who pretended to be dead is now making his way out of the building, through the confusion. I follow him with my eyes but quickly lose him in the crowd.

"I need to go back to the class," I shout to Lottie and Tasha before making my way back against the tide and toward the man sneaking out.

I hear Lottie and Tasha call to me, their shouts getting fainter the further I get away from them. I finally make it to the back of the crowd and step out into an empty corridor.

I notice the man walking quickly toward a back entrance and follow him, staying quite distant behind him, not worried about losing him in the empty halls. He pulls the door open, slipping through, and I catch the door before it closes.

"Hey, dead man!" I shout to get his attention, walking across the grass.

The man stops and spins with a grin on his face.

"I do have a name."

"Everyone does, but I don't know yours so..." I stop inches in front of him.

"Danny," he responds, his hand out.

I take it. "Scar."

"What can I do for you, Scar?" he asks.

"I want you to tell your boss something."

"I'm listening."

"Tell him I'll go on the date, but next time, I would have preferred an actual dead body as my gift," I tell him seriously.

His smirk drops, turning into a grimace. I pat him on the arm before turning to make my way to the front of the building.

"See you around," I call back as I take a cigarette out and light it. I bring it down from my lips as I make my way along the outside of the building, looking at the cigarette. Who knew that something so small could have deadly effects? I chuckle at myself. My second week on earth and I'm already addicted to them, albeit for a different reason to mortals. It's my little piece of home on Earth.

I pause on the way to dry my clothes off, as I was getting cold from the colder air than I am used to touching my wet clothes and skin.

Once I am dry, I turn the corner and walk to the front entrance of the building, seeing that all the school has crowded there.

Mr. Ward's watery gaze meets mine, his eyes narrowing.

"Ms. Hades, do you care to explain to me why you did not exit the building with the rest of us? And please put that out."

I take one last drag from the cigarette before dropping it to the floor, standing on it.

"I was having a cigarette around the back while talking to a dead guy," I tell him.

Mr. Ward looks surprised for a moment, opening his mouth in what I'm sure would have been him insisting for the truth. Kyle cuts in before he can say anything.

"Excuse me, Mr. Ward, but as it's been said, it is safe to go in now. I will be taking Ms. Hades to my classroom so I can talk to her about the homework." Kyle motions for me to start walking into the school, but we are stopped by Mr. Ward.

"Mr…" Mr. Ward starts, looking for Kyle's surname.

I chuckle, knowing he'll be there for a long time, waiting for that. Kyle doesn't even know his last name. I raise an eyebrow at Kyle, mocking Mr. Ward. *What's your last name, Kyle?* I mouth. He shoots me a look, trying not to laugh.

"Call me Kyle," he insists.

"No, that would be improper. Your last name is what I am looking for," Mr. Ward replies impatiently.

"You're not going to get it. So if you would just say what you have to tell Ms. Hades, then I can discuss her work with her," Kyle tells him with a forced smile.

"I…I'll talk to you later, Ms. Hades," Mr. Ward states before walking off in the other direction.

"It would be improper," I mock Mr. Ward with a laugh, nudging Kyle in the side. He pushes me back playfully, a grin on his face as well as he pulls the door open for me. I fake hurt as I walk in after him, our laughs filling the empty hallway.

Chapter 14

Surprise Gifts

Kyle leans against the desk in his classroom as he looks me over, his arms crossed.

"Want to further explain to me what just happened before I tell your dad?" he asks.

I consider the situation for a moment. Kyle already knows that I was being asked on a date, but do I want my dad to know? Can I get Kyle on my side? My dad would just interfere, and I wouldn't hear the end of it.

"Nope, you already know all there is," I tell him, leaning back on my hands as I sit atop a desk.

"Hm." Kyle steps forward, his hands going to either side of my thighs. His eyes meet mine, and I feel a slight tug at the back of my mind as Kyle asks, "Are you sure?"

I raise an eyebrow; Kyle knows better than to try and compel me. I relay my thoughts to him. He lets out a breathy laugh.

"Oh well, it was worth a try," he responds.

"Even though you knew it wouldn't work?" I ask.

"I thought you would tell me anyway," he admits.

"You can be really stupid sometimes, Kyle." I laugh. He rolls his eyes.

"Your dad will want to hear about it, so if you give me a story to tell him—" He gets cut off by the sound of the handle turning.

Wanting to prank whoever is behind the door, as a result of them barging in, I reach for Kyle's face and bring it the short distance to my own. His still lips fall on my own, his eyes widening. I implore silently for him to go along with it as the door opens.

Being used to my pranks, Kyle reaches for my thighs, sliding me closer to him on the table. I hold back from cringing when our lips start to move. It feels like I am kissing a family member. I can't get how my family used to be able to do this. It feels so wrong, and I am barely able to do it for a short while.

My heels pull him closer as my hands go to his hair. He groans in frustration but continues to go along with the charade. I hear the door swing open, but I don't stop until a cough breaks the silence. I turn to see who we pranked, Kyle's lips staying on my face.

Mr. Ward stares back at us, his own clothes and his hair slightly disheveled. A slow, sardonic grin touches his lips as he looks at us. When Kyle notices it is Mr. Ward, he jumps back from me.

"Mr. Ward..." Kyle starts, faking fear of Mr. Ward telling someone. If need be, we can always compel him, but I doubt that we will need to do that.

"Mr. Kyle, I'm going to have to tell the principal." Mr. Ward all but sings.

Kyle stares back at him with an amused look as I try and hide the laugh that is threatening to leave my lips. I was expecting him to drop the "Mr." and by the looks of it, so is Kyle.

"I don't think that is necessary, or even wise," I tell Mr. Ward as I jump off the desk, trailing my hand over Kyle's chest as I walk toward the door. Thinking that I could use his disheveled appearance to get out of this, I sniff the air, and my suspicions are confirmed with the smell of sweat and sex. Mixed in with the smell is Tiffany's scent. My eyes light up with amusement.

"Why is that?" he retorts smugly.

"You don't want to because if you tell the principal about us, you'll also have to tell her about your little fling with Tiffany. How long have you been fucking her, and does your wife know?" I ask, looking down at the glint of gold on his left hand.

Mr. Ward's smug look quickly fades and is replaced with an angry one. His furious eyes meet mine, but I notice that his right hand is now covering his fingers on his left.

"How dare you—"

I cut off what I am sure would have been a threat which had me quaking in my boots. "It's been nice to talk to you, as always, Mr. Ward." I step around him and through the open door, going out into the corridor.

As I step off the last step of the stairs, I notice Tiffany still in the hallway. I look her over and see that she is in the same state as Mr. Ward.

"Your lipstick's smudged," I say as I continue to the exit only to stop and turn back to her.

She rubs below her lip at the smudge as she glares at me.

"You know the only reason I can think of as to why you keep going back to Mr. Ward is that he's a good fuck because it's certainly not for his looks. Is it?"

Her eyes are still narrowed at me in a glare as she opens her move before closing it again. Eventually, she thinks of a comeback as I am turning to leave again.

"At least people want to fuck me."

"You must have a really good rate then," I retort as I pull the door open.

I walk through the parking lot, stopping at my bike. I clamber on, starting it up, and start on my way home. I've had enough of the school for one day. I didn't get a chance to talk to Kyle about my date with Reid, so most likely he will tell my dad about it. But what day? Reid gave me a time but not a day. Maybe I'll get around my dad finding out and as a result, interfering.

I pull onto the road leading to my house, smelling the saltiness from the sea in the air. Something else, which is somewhat familiar, underlies it also. I pull onto the drive, stopping the bike abruptly when I see that the door is ajar.

Turning the engine off, I slide my leg off and look around for a sign that the intruder is still here. I cautiously walk forward, sniffing the air again. The smell of Reid and blood hit me, causing me to speed up.

The blood doesn't smell like Reid's, but worry starts to go through me. Is there another reason for him finding me again, which isn't for a date?

I step up to the side of the door, pushing it open further, casting an eye over the space. It looks normal, except for a trail of blood. The house is silent, letting me know that I am alone. I step into the doorway, now able to see the room fully.

The trail of blood leads to a wall, which is covered in writing in something red, exactly like one the corridor walls of the school.

I forgot to say that the date is this Saturday.

Well, that answers my question, I think as my eyes move down the wall and to where the trail of blood ends. A dead body of a man I do not recognize lies on the floor of my living room. I wonder what he did to get the privilege of being my gift.

I step closer and inspect the body, finding that the body is relatively fresh. The blood pooling around the body has my hunger poking its head up. *Nice of Reid to get me dinner,* I think as I start to clear up the mess.

Chapter 15

Boredom

The last bell rings, prompting everyone to jump out of their seats and for Mrs. Jackson to, with no avail, call over the tumult for us all to sit down.

As I walk to the door with Lily, my shoulder is pushed forward as Tiffany barges past to get to the door. She shoots me a look over her shoulder, causing me to roll my eyes. All day Mr. Ward and Tiffany have been shooting me looks of contempt as if it is my fault that they have been fucking. All I did was find them out.

"So, have you got anything planned for this weekend?" Lily asks as we walk out of the school.

"It won't be as eventful as last weekend. I have a date tomorrow," I say. "What about you?"

"I have a date with my laptop and a ton of junk food. Who's your date with? Anyone I know?" she responds as we walk out into the afternoon sunshine.

"I would say you know them but not personally, or well."
I continue to my car, unlocking it, leaving her to ponder the possibilities.

I start the engine up and pull out of my space and join the groups of people trying to get out of the lot. I tap my hand on the steering wheel along with the beat of the song on the radio as I rest my arm on the door and my head on top of my hand.

Earth isn't what I expected it to be. All I see all day every day are the same walls, and I am bored already. I would never admit it to my dad, or even Kyle, as they would take it that I don't want to continue with my time up here. For the first week I was up here, the idea of school, and finding what it was all about, was appealing and interesting; however, its repetitive nature has me wanting to get out and do something else.

I can finally pull out of the parking lot and onto the road, making me sit up straighter and press down on the accelerator, wanting to get home.

***

I stand in front of the standing mirror, looking at the outfit I have on. I decided that I would choose my outfit for tomorrow this evening, as I can't be bothered to get up early tomorrow to do it. My eyes travel over my reflection again, deciding against this one.

I walk through the open door to my closet, sifting through the rest of my clothes. I find a white, lace Cami which crosses at the back, and I pair it with ripped jeans. I put them on before searching through the mess of shoes covering my floor for a pair of white heeled pumps. I slip them on and walk back out to check the finished product in the mirror for the third time.

However, before I can get to the mirror, I am scared shitless to find someone sitting on my bed. My first instinct is to attack the threat. I run over and pull the threat, who happens to be Hunter, up by his neck. Once I register it's him, I loosen my grip.

"How did you get in here?" I shout.

"The door was unlocked. That's not a safe thing to do. Any creep could come in Newbie," he chastises with a shrug.

"It looks like they have, yet another thing to add to my stalker file," I mutter, letting go of him and stepping back. I don't bother locking the door because I could take on whoever decided to try their luck.

"Wow, you're strong and fast," he comments, rubbing his neck. His hand slows to a stop, his eyes traveling over me. "You're hot as well."

I turn and go to my previous destination. I look at my reflection again, and a smirk comes to my lips. I have to admit that I agree with Hunter; I do look pretty hot in this. I've found my outfit for tomorrow. I walk to the dressing table near my closet and pick out a pair of silver hoops and a long necklace, laying them out.

"What are you doing here, Oldie?" I ask Hunter as I walk back into my closet to change into something comfier. I push the door closed as I kick the shoes off.

"I was bored," he answers.

"So you decided to come and annoy me," I state sarcastically.

"Yep," he responds as I hear a drawer being opened.

I roll my eyes.

"I don't know what you think I will do to help with that boredom." I walk back out of the closet, now in much more casual clothes. I see that Hunter is still looking through drawers.

"Make out with me?" he suggests as he opens yet another drawer, looking up at me.

"Buddy, if you come within an inch of me, I will make sure that no woman wants to make out with you ever again," I tell him, moving to close the drawer he has opened.

"Okay, no to the making out."

"Good choice. What about a film?" I counter, moving to the selection of DVDs my dad supplied, under the TV in my room.

Hunter moves until he is standing behind me, looking over my shoulder. I pick a random one, which looks good, waiting to see if Hunter has anything to say about the choice. When he doesn't complain, I put the disc in.

"Want popcorn?" I ask as I walk to the door leading out of my room. I hear his confirmation as I walk out of the room. I put the popcorn on to cook, drinking a bag of blood while I wait.

I am just putting the popcorn in a bowl when I hear the theme music of the film starting. I wipe my mouth and my teeth once more as I rush up the stairs.

I launch onto the bed next to Hunter, passing the popcorn to him. I turn my attention to the screen to see a street of houses at night. I quickly get immersed in the story, every so often reaching for a handful of popcorn. When I do, I get a glance of Hunter. Sometimes he is focusing on the film, but for most of the time, he is watching me. His expression is guarded, meaning I can't work out what he is thinking.

Halfway through the film and after the hundredth time I caught him watching me, I finally decide to ask him.

"What?" I ask, placing a kernel in my mouth. He looks like he's thinking of something before asking me seriously.

"What are you?"

The piece of popcorn nearly falls out of my mouth as I process what he is saying. I was stupid to attack him; he witnessed something that no normal human could do—run at speed in heels. Luckily, I wasn't the fastest I could be.

"Pardon?" I choke out.

"You're super fast and strong, like inhumanly so," he says.

I tense up and wait for him to start screaming at me that I am a monster, an abomination, but it doesn't come. I gulp, going to respond, but he beats me to it. "Are you a vampire, or something?"

I close my eyes as I look away from him.

"Yeah, or something…"

He laughs, but when I don't join in, he asks for clarification.

"Wait, what—you're being serious? I was just joking. No, wait you can't be something like that. They don't exist, do they? What's the or something?" he rambles.

I slump, the tension leaving my body. He was only joking.

"No, they don't, you idiot. The or something being *a human*," I tell him, stressing the last two words.

Hunter guffaws, resuming stuffing popcorn into his mouth.

Someone is only going to find out if you tell them. They can have all the theories they want, but unless you confirm them, they are just that—theories. If they were to tell someone their theories, no one would believe them. Humans would find it hard to believe a story about a real supernatural being.

"You had me going there," he says, nudging my side.

So did you, I think as I try and get my focus back on the film in front of us, my mind running from what just happened. I let out a laugh at the stupidity of the situation. I relax back into the bed, my heavy breathing from the nerves of someone finding out calming down. I need to be more careful and think about my actions now that I am on Earth. I dodged a bullet there, but I may not be so lucky next time.

Chapter 16

The Date

I place the necklace over my head, completing the outfit for my date today. I had to drag myself out of bed this morning, as my mind kept going over what happened with Hunter last night, after he left. Luckily, the rest of the film went by without any more awkward questions, and he promptly left when it ended.

I glance at the clock and see that it's 10:30. I bring my flat-iron out, working on straightening my hair before pulling it up into a sleek ponytail. I put light makeup on and make my way downstairs to have something to eat before I leave.

Once I have finished the blood and had something normal to eat, it is time for me to make my way to the park to meet Reid.

When I pull into the parking lot, I check myself over again in the rearview mirror before opening my door and exiting into the bright sunshine. The clock on the dashboard of my car tells me that it's just gone eleven o' clock, the time that Reid said he would meet me. After locking my own car, I walk through the others and past smiling families sitting and playing on the grass, enjoying their day at the park. I stop under a tree, leaning against the trunk as I look for Reid.

My phone begins to ring. Wondering if Reid has tracked down my number using his ways, I take it out of my pocket only to let out a disappointed and confused sigh. My dad's contact photo, a baby devil with a pacifier in its mouth, glares back at me. I answer it, bringing it up to my ear.

"Daddy!" I exclaim, faking brightness, hoping he doesn't know about the date.

"Don't 'daddy' me. What is this I hear about you going on a date?" he asks.

I groan. I'm going to kill Kyle.

"I have no idea what you're talking about," I answer innocently, still looking for Reid as I talk.

"Where are you now?" he asks, seeing through my act.

"At the park."

"Doing what?" he asks.

I look around and see the nearest family throwing a disk to each other.

"Playing Frisbee with a nice family I met."

"Mm," he hums as if he doesn't believe me. "Dressed like that, I don't think so."

My mouth falls open as my hand loosens around my phone, causing it to slip out and fall to the floor. I look frantically around the park, knowing he must be here.

I find him standing near the swing set, his phone on his ear, and a hand in the air waving at me. I can see the smug grin he is wearing from here. I snatch my phone up from the ground before stomping toward him.

"What are you doing here?" I whisper harshly.

"I have come to see my lovely daughter," he tells me with his stupid grin still on his face.

I let out a laugh.

"Ha. Yeah, and I'm the queen of England," I respond sarcastically.

He eventually gives me the truth. "Kyle told me about my daughter going on a date, so I have come to check that he is worthy of her," he explains as if he were talking to someone else.

I shake my head at him.

"Dad, he's the leader of a gang. I hardly think you'll disapprove."

His eyes light up as he pats me on the cheek. "That's my girl."

"See. So, now that you approve, can you go? He'll be here soon."

"Oh," he says with a pout, "but I want to meet him..."

"Scar?" Reid asks from behind me, and I spin to face him. I motion to my dad to leave with my hand hidden from Reid by my body.

"Hi!" I greet him as I hear my dad chuckle before leaving. I'm surprised that it's easier than I expected. I thought my dad would complain and insist on being introduced.

I bring my attention back to Reid, who is wearing a dark gray shirt which doesn't fail to hide his muscles, a pair of dark jeans, and a pair of aviators covering his blue eyes. I see that he is returning the appreciative look.

"Like what you see?" I ask, smirking.

"Very much," he replies, his lip turning up slightly at the edge.

"What do you have planned for us then?" I ask.

He lets out a chuckle, sounding like it doesn't escape his lips often. I guess you have to be serious if you are a gang leader of one of the most notorious gangs around.

"I want to show you something," he says as he reaches for my hand, pulling me behind him and back toward the parking lot.

"What?" I ask as he maneuvers us between the cars until we come to a stop by a black bike.

"You'll have to wait and see," he replies, a smile in his voice as he picks up the helmet on the back. He turns, passing it to me. I look down at it and then up to Reid who is now straddling the bike, watching me expectantly.

"Shouldn't you have a helmet as well?" I ask.

"Nah, I'll be alright. We need to keep your pretty face pretty anyway." He taps me under the chin, and I scoff at him as I bring the helmet up.

"You would be surprised at what this 'pretty face' can take," I mutter snidely as I shove the helmet down onto my head.

He snorts as he extends his hand for me. I roll my eyes as I push his hand away, gripping onto his shoulders instead as I kick a leg over the machine. I edge forward, wrapping my arms around his waist. He shakes his head as he kicks down on a lever to start the bike.

"Hold on," he calls over the roar of the bike as we pull out of our space and the parking lot.

I turn my head to look through the visor at what we are zooming past. We stay on the main roads, leading us to a highway which we ride on for about twenty minutes before turning off onto a quieter road, which leads to a dirt track. We ride down the dirt track, following it through trees until we finally stop at a dead end.

"We're here," Reid says. I sit back from him, placing my feet down onto the dusty track. Maybe white shoes weren't the best idea.

I look around, my eyebrows rising involuntarily.

"This is what you wanted to show me? Was this just all a ploy to get me alone so you can kill me?" I joke.

Reid gets off the bike, causing me to balance it as I watch him. He lets out a dark chuckle before turning around, his gun now in his hand inches away from my face.

"Shit. You're too good for me," he mutters.

I can feel how intense his gaze is even though I am unable to see it.

I contemplate for a moment if I would be able to steal his bike, but he seems like a good aim and quick on the trigger. I know that I am probably being stupid to even try and take the gun from him, but if I were to be shot, it's not the end of my life.

I act quickly, turning the gun and the situation around, so I am now the person aiming the gun. My finger twitches over the trigger, waiting for him to do something that would allow me to shoot him.

"Whoa, don't shoot!" he tries to placate me. "I was just playing along."

My grip on the gun goes slack, allowing Reid to take it back. He was kidding! It was all part of the joke.

"Don't be so serious next time! I was ready to kill you," I chastise, hitting him on the arm.

He lets out a laugh.

"I'm going to keep you. You didn't react badly to a gun being pointed at you."

"Does that happen a lot around you?" I quip, half curious to the answer as I accept his hand to help me off the bike. His palm warms mine as he begins to rub his thumb over the back of my hand.

"I hope you don't mind, but it's a little walk until we get to our destination," Reid comments as he begins to pull me after him.

"I'll survive." I sigh jokingly.

He pulls me through two trees and onto a path that I missed when we first arrived. To be honest, I was preoccupied with the gun being aimed at me.

After a short walk, like Reid said, we come to the top of a hill that slopes to a secluded beach below.

The turquoise sea is sparkling in the bright sun, the waves lapping at the light sand. I look around and see that we are the only living things in sight. I don't have a lot to call beautiful and rarely use the word, but this is stunningly beautiful. I turn to Reid, a grin on my face.

"Wow. How did you find this?"

"We were once on the run from the cops, and this is where we ended up." He starts looking at the scenery. "Now, whenever I need somewhere to escape to, this is where I come."

I move my eyes off Reid's handsome face and look back around. I can see why he does; it's so peaceful here. You could be here without fear of anything or anyone finding you.

"Do you trust me?" he asks.

I press my lips together, watching him. Do I? He threatened to shoot me, even though it later turned out to be a joke, and I know nothing about him. However, my gut has me nodding.

"Okay, close your eyes. No peeking," he instructs.

I hesitantly let my eyes flutter close as I feel Reid take my other hand in his. He tugs gently, letting me know he wants me to walk forward. We move down the gentle incline of the small hill until I feel my feet sink into something soft. My mind wanders back to the Styx Lake at home at the familiar feeling.

I stumble through the sand in my heels, Reid righting me every so often when I lose my balance. A small smile comes to my lips as he makes us turn around something. A few steps later, we stop. He releases my hands, and I feel him step back.

"Open your eyes."

I do so, blinking at the onslaught from the sun. Through squinting eyes, I see what Reid has led me to. A few feet away from a big rock is a blanket lying on the sand, a wicker basket on top. "I know it's corny, but what else can you do at a beach…" Reid says, worry creeping into his tone.

My eyes zoom to him, trying to hide the surprise that I feel at the insecurities I see on his face.

"It's perfect," I tell him, giving him another big grin.

I have never been on a date before. Yes, I had been with other demons as I grew up but never actually went on a date. There is not really much that you can do in Hell date-wise. Maybe joint hunts, but that's not really date material. It warms my usually cold heart to know that someone has gone to this extent to do this for me.

I bite my lip as I watch Reid bend down to open the basket. I know that this date will be memorable.

Chapter 17

You're a Weird Chick

I stare into Reid's eyes, a slow smile forming on my lips when I see that Reid is struggling.

After Reid has emptied the basket of the food it held, we both sit down and start to work our way through the feast silently. At some point, an unannounced and unplanned staring contest starts.

I giggle when I see Reid's eyelid twitch as his eyes begin to water. I feel sorry for him because I have an advantage, as I can go for a long time without needing to blink. I continue to stare him down, and I am surprised to find that it takes another minute before he finally gives up with a groan as he looks away to blink rapidly.

"I win," I sing.

"You had to be cheating," he rationalizes, trying to comfort his bruised ego. I bet he doesn't get beaten by girls very often.

"How can you even cheat at a staring contest?" I ask.

"I don't know. You'll have to tell me because you were the one doing whatever you do to cheat."

I laugh and tear off a bit of my sandwich to throw at him.

"Hey!" he shouts in objection, tearing his own piece of sandwich off to throw back at me. I giggle, taking a bite of my own. His eyes glint in amusement as he watches me.

"So...did you like my invitation?" he asks with a smirk gracing his lips.

"Yes. May I ask who was lying dead on my floor?"

"You're a weird chick," he says, ignoring my last question.

"And you're a gang leader, so what?"

"A normal girl would have screamed or fainted if they found a dead body, but you didn't care," he comments.

"How do you know I didn't?" I challenge, raising an eyebrow.

"You wouldn't have accepted," he states simply.

"What I said when I first met you was true—I've seen a lot of dead bodies in my lifetime," I supply as an explanation.

He looks at me closely as if to try and work something out before shrugging.

"So have I," he adds.

"Why crime? Why start a gang?" I ask, firing other questions off at him.

"Whoa, those are big questions," he remarks, clearing his throat.

I shrug. "The big ones usually have more interesting answers."

I wait for his answer, noticing how he is less comfortable. I know I've hit a nerve with this question, and confirmation comes when Reid rubs his now empty hands over his face. When his face reappears, vulnerable eyes stare back at me.

"Ask another question, please..." he says quietly.

Shocked at seeing and hearing him that way, I relent and ask another question.

Reid sips some of his beer, his mask coming back into place. Whatever wall he has built up—I just knocked it down with that one question, and now he is slowly placing the bricks back into place. I guess no one really asks him that question. They're probably too afraid to.

"Okay...Why are you called the Grim Reapers?" I ask.

Instantly, a smile comes onto Reid's lips, his vulnerable moment forgotten.

"Easy. Because we bring death and destruction wherever we go, and people fear the name," he answers. "Want to see the infamous tattoo?" he asks with a wiggle of his eyebrows.

I laugh and nod. He moves his arm so his wrist is facing up. A skull with a scythe in the background is the main part of the tattoo; however, the two seem to be entwined with a vine. On one of the leaves are the initials G.R. I trace it, marveling at the artistic excellence. Although it is in black, it looks so lifelike.

"I also have one on my neck to show my rank. Want to see it?" he asks, moving his head so his neck is exposed. I lean forward to have a closer look, balancing myself on his knees.

"I can't..." I start, pulling back slightly to look at him puzzled but am cut off by Reid's lips on my mine. My fingers clutch his thighs tighter as the taste and smell of him touch my senses. His soft lips move once over my lips before he pulls back. I lick my lips as I fall away from him, trying to get over the sudden bloodlust I am starting to feel. I take a couple of breaths, trying to focus on his words.

"I don't have one to show my rank," he admits.

"I kind of guessed that when I couldn't see it, and you kissed me. Nice move," I tell him with a slight laugh, my bloodlust dampening slightly. The next four words that fill the silence has my bloodlust being extinguished completely.

"Nice day, isn't it?" a familiar voice asks from above us.

I let out a low growl so only the newcomer can hear as I look up to see his shadow blocking the sun. I should have guessed that he would pull something like this when he allowed me to shoo him away.

"Yes, it is," I grit out to my dad who is grinning down at us.

"Do you mind if I join?" he asks, already sitting down.

I scoff. "Yes, actually."

"Sorry, I didn't catch that. I'm sure you wouldn't have said no. You look like nice people."

I scratch my head as it goes silent and as a result, awkward.

"So..." I say.

My dad turns to look at Reid, his expression going confused and then thoughtful.

"I've seen you before," my dad says slowly.

I see Reid's chest puff out slightly as he waits for my dad to say he's the leader of the Grim Reapers, but my dad, true to form, doesn't miss the chance to embarrass. He clicks his fingers as his face lights up. "That's it! You were the guy that served me McDonald's earlier. Thanks for that!"

I have to hold in my laughter at Reid's smug expression falling and being replaced with a murderous one.

"Are you being fucking serious?" Reid asks, his fist clenching at his side, looking like he's ready to punch my dad. I'm not sorry to admit that if he did, I wouldn't be quick to stop Reid. I would allow him to get in a few punches.

"Yes. Why wouldn't I be?" my dad answers seriously.

"Do you know who I am?" Reid asks my dad who is now holding a shit-eating grin on his face. I bite my lip as I watch their interaction. This is not technically how I thought my dad and my potential boyfriend would be getting on.

"Father Christmas?" my dad asks, not missing a beat.

"Ha ha, very funny," Reid answers sarcastically before continuing proudly, "No, I'm the Grim Reaper."

"Believe me, you're not..." He chuckles as he gets up, brushing the sand off his pants.

"It was nice talking to you," my dad calls over his shoulder as he walks off down the beach, his hands in his pockets. I look back to Reid who is staring off at the sea before his eyes fly to me.

"He was the guy you were talking to at the park, wasn't he?"

I nod. "I think he's stalking me," I reply, not showing any inclination that I am joking. I watch his reaction, testing to see if it came to it whether he would protect me.

Reid jumps up, his eyes furious again, scanning the beach for signs of my dad. I know he would have teleported home by now.

"Where did that bastard go? He was here a minute ago," Reid says loudly, going to walk away from the blanket before stopping. His shoulders rise and fall with his heavy breathing from his anger.

He turns back to me, his eyes a lot softer than they were now but still holding the steeliness that was there the first day I met him. I shrug at him, hiding my smile with my drink. He kneels in front of me, concern shining in his blue eyes. He takes my hands.

"Please, if you see him again, let me know?" he pleads.

"Okay," I agree.

Silence returns to us again, and as Reid moves back beside me, my eyes fix on the clear, inviting water. I stand up, looking down at Reid.

"Are you coming?" I ask, reaching for the hem of my shirt. His eyebrows rise for a moment before he responds.

"Where?"

"The sea," I reply, pulling the shirt over my head and moving to my jeans. I drop them both to the floor and take my necklace off, putting it on top. Reid's eyes move over my underwear-clad body. I bite my lip as I see a smirk tug at the corner of his lips.

"You don't need to have an excuse to take your clothes off around me," he tells me.

I roll my eyes at him as I kick some sand toward him. Before I can see his reaction, I am off running to the waves at a human pace. I giggle when I hear the thud of clothes hitting the sand.

I enter the waves, gasping at the shock of the coolness against my skin. I shiver but continue on. I continue walking until I can no longer stand, kicking my legs to stay afloat. I turn back around to find Reid but don't see him.

I furrow my eyebrows before feeling something encircle my ankle. I struggle against it as it pulls me down and into the cold water. I continue to fight until the bubbles clear, and I see Reid's face smiling back at me. I pretend to stick my tongue out at him, not actually doing as I don't feel like swallowing salty water.

He lets go of my ankle, allowing me to swim back up to the surface.

As I watch him swim back up, I wait until he breaks the surface before resting my hands on his shoulders. He leans forward, but I use my extra strength to dunk him under. He grabs my hips, meaning I go down with him.

I grin at him as I feel his hands go up to my waist. His fingers trace lightly there. He's tickling me! I fight against his grip as he continues. I hate being tickled. I open my mouth, swallowing water as I laugh. I choke on the water, swimming back to the surface, letting out a giggle through my coughing when I know I won't swallow any more water. This is the most fun that I have had in a while.

Reid's hands find me again, holding me up from drowning. My laughter dies down, and my smile lessens when he begins to pull me through the water. I cling onto his shoulders as our chest press together, our eyes meeting in an intense gaze. I lean closer to him, and that's when everything from earlier, the bloodlust I felt, comes rushing back in full force, and my demon instincts kick in.

My fangs descend; my eyes change color; my face transforms until my horns sit on top of a demonic face. I just get a glimpse of Reid's face before I bury my face in his neck, biting into his soft flesh there. Blood starts to pool into my mouth instantly, and I begin to swallow down the blood.

I gasp and begin to swallow it down faster when the shock of the taste hits me. I clutch Reid's shoulders even tighter as the ambrosia-like liquid enters my body, trying to keep my long, sharp fingernails from piercing his skin. I let out a moan into Reid's neck when he grabs my legs and brings them around him, allowing me to feel just how much I am affecting him with my bite.

"Scar…" he moans. Reid's voice is the thing that cuts through the haze of lust. If he hadn't have said anything, I wouldn't have stopped until he was sucked dry. His blood is addicting.

I pull away, detaching my legs from his hips. I look away from his eyes, which are reminders of what I just did, with the haze that is blurring them. I look down at his neck and see the wound. Blood begins to trail down from it, so I lick the red river and then the puncture wounds on his neck, healing them.

"Sorry…" I mutter, moving my gaze from him completely to look at the beach.

"Don't apologize," Reid says, and I hear the waves break around his body as he moves closer to me.

"No, I shouldn't have lost control like that," I respond, moving further back from him, not trusting myself. What must he be thinking of me?

"I liked it. Is that weird?" he asks. Finally deciding to look him in the eyes, I only see lust and curiosity. No fear. No resentment.

"No, it's not weird." My head is spinning at how well he is taking it; he hasn't even mentioned anything about what happened. He hasn't even known me for long, and I'm already showing him that I'm not human. He's not showing that he's the least bit scared as he moves closer to me. His hands move up to my face, cupping it.

"Stop with that look, please," he implores, staring into my eyes. "You look like I'm going to go running off screaming."

"Aren't you? It would be a natural reaction."

"No."

I sigh, closing my eyes. I only have one choice. I promised my dad that I wouldn't let anyone find out, and I don't want to give my dad an excuse to bring me back down to Hell.

"Look into my eyes, please," I mutter reluctantly; I don't want to hide from him. I want him to know, and like, the real me, not an image I have to show the world.

His piercing blue eyes meet mine, and for a moment I forget what I am doing. I swallow.

"You are going to forget what just happened with the bite. Instead, you will think that we were playing around in the waves and ended up making out."

His eyes stay trained on me for a moment before he blinks and he raises his eyebrows as if waiting for something.

"Is that a trick of yours?" he asks after another minute.

I stare at him puzzled. He hasn't forgotten?

"Wait, what? You can remember?" I ask.

He nods slowly. "Yeah, was I not meant to?"

"Obviously. Did you think I just did that for fun? *Hey, why don't I ask him nicely to forget about me! That will work!*" I say harsher than I intended.

My compulsion has never not worked. It can't just stop working; I need it for moments like this! I decide to see if maybe I had done something wrong the first time and try and compel Reid again. However, the same thing happens as before. Is there something wrong with me, or is it Reid?

Not giving him time to ask any more questions, I grab his arm and drag him after me to the beach. When my feet hit the dry sand, I pull him to the blanket and basket.

"Put your clothes on," I tell him sharply, shoving them into his chest before pulling my own on.

"Are you mad at me?"

"No, I just don't understand why it didn't work. It's never happened before," I say, pulling the elastic out of my hair and combing my fingers through it.

I search for my phone and pick it up, hitting my dad's contact. I pace the patch of sand, watching Reid pull his shirt over his head, waiting for the phone to connect. When it does, I don't allow him to talk.

"I'm coming down with Reid. Clear the house and surrounding area of anyone who can't control their hunger," I say simply before hanging up. Shoving the phone into my pocket, I grab Reid's arm again.

"Wha—"

"Hold on and don't let go. I don't feel like searching for you. If you do, it can guarantee that it wouldn't be any fun for you to find yourself lost," I tell him, already closing my eyes.

"What are we doing?" he asks as his hand comes down onto my arm holding his other.

"We're going home," I say, gripping his arm more firmly, picturing the ornate front doors breaking up the stone wall of the front of my house back in Hell. *Who thought I would be back there so soon?* I think as I feel the familiar pull on my body, dragging me down to my destination.

Chapter 18

Fun and Games

I feel my feet hit the hard floor, and when I open my eyes, I see the ornate doors in real life. I look around and see that my dad followed what I asked by getting rid of everyone, meaning the part of Hell we are now standing in is empty. I let my head fall back and the heat encompass my body. It feels good to be home. I look to Reid, who is still holding onto me in a vice-like grip. Beads of sweat roll down his red face.

"We're here," I let him know.

"Jesus, it's hot!"

"We won't be here long," I say.

Reid opens his eyes and looks around. "Where is here?" he asks, his eyes wide.

"Home."

"Where is home?"

"Hell," I answer as if it isn't a big deal; it's not for me.

"No, really…"

"Yes, really…" I answer with a laugh.

His grip on me seems to get even tighter.

"Come on, Grim Reaper, you can let go of me now, or are you scared?"

"I'm not scared," he insists defiantly, letting go of me.

"Yeah…" I say as I begin to walk to the doors.

Someone screams nearby, and I hear Reid gulp and take a step toward me. I chuckle as I push the heavy doors open, going to take a step in. However, I don't get very far because as soon as I step over the threshold, I am thrown through the air, landing with a thump on the hard ground ten feet away from where I was. What just happened?

I groan, rolling onto my side and pushing myself to my feet. I gingerly walk back to Reid, wary of anything else that could potentially happen. When I get back to him with, thankfully, nothing else happening, Reid asks what I was thinking, "What was that? Are you okay?"

I survey the door and know that only one person could be behind this. He may not like to admit it, but I get my prankster side from him.

"Yes, I think my dad is playing a joke on me," I answer Reid's question, glaring at the open doorway. "Cover your ears." I wait until Reid has placed his hands over his ears before calling for my dad.

"Dad, you sneaky devil, where are you?"

Reid turns to me once I've stopped shouting, a smirk on his lips.

"Wow."

"I'm full of surprises," I tell him with a wink. I look back to the door and see that my dad has decided to join our date for the second time. A big grin stretches across his face as he looks me over and then Reid.

I turn to see that Reid is sending him a glare, looking like he's ready to charge at him. I have to hold back a happy smile at Reid being protective of me. He looks like he would kill my dad, whom I told him was my stalker.

"I'd watch how you look at me. You may be stuck here if you don't stop glaring at me like that," my "stalker" threatens menacingly.

"Be nice," I chastise. I ignore the curious look that Reid is sending my way. He seems to have put two (my stalker on the beach) and two (him showing up when I called for my dad) together and got to four (that my "stalker" is my dad, and I lied to him).

"But he started it!" my dad objects, pointing toward Reid.

I raise an eyebrow at his childish actions. Sometimes it feels like I'm the one raising him and not the other way around.

"I assume you had something to do with this," I say, waving my hand at the doorway, against which my dad is leaning.

"You know me too well. How do you like it?" he asks gleefully. I swear he doesn't care about hurting me.

"Well, it works," I tell him, rubbing my sore butt. "Can I come in now you've had your fun?"

He pretends to think about it for a moment.

"Hm. No," he answers with a smile.

"Why not?"

"You can't control your bloodlust, by the looks of things," my dad says, motioning to where there is now dry blood on Reid's neck, "and you asked me to rid the house of anyone like that, so that is why this thing has been put up." After he has finished his explanation, he turns on his heel and walks back into the house.

I stomp my foot, letting out a sound of frustration, just like a petulant child not getting her way.

I take a deep breath and turn to Reid and then back to the door. My dad didn't say anything about humans not being able to get through.

"You try," I suggest.

"Pardon?" he asks, slightly scared, his gaze going to the door. I raise my eyebrows at him.

"I thought you were a gang leader, but as soon as you face something that is 'scary,' you become a wimp." I goad him.

He stands up straighter, his face hardening. "That's not true," he tells me.

"Prove it," I say, waving my hand toward the door.

He smirks at me and walks through the doorway. I see his muscles lose some of their tension when he doesn't go flying back like I did. However, instead, an alarm starts to blare and the sound of my loud voice fills the air. Shit! I forgot I set that up!

"Fresh blood!" my voice repeats. I set this alarm up when I was younger and wanted to taste live human blood. It would start to blare whenever a live soul stepped into the house so I could feast on them. It quickly annoyed my dad as he would have to sometimes talk to humans from Earth, and it wasn't for always making deals.

"Shit! Stay there," I order Reid, putting my hand up to him when he looks concerned and confused, moving toward me. If I was thrown into the air trying to get through the door, hopefully, any demons who will try their luck to feast on the human that they have been alerted to will meet the same fate. I look away from Reid and see demons have started to crowd around the front door and me, all leering at Reid who is standing just in the doorway.

"Sorry, guys, you're going to have to go without fresh blood today," I tell the demons surrounding us.

They close in, and some of them even lick their lips. I sigh.

"You're not getting past me, or even into the house, so back off." One of the demons tries to run past me, and I let him, hoping my conclusion was correct.

I'm wrong, though, as the demon is able to step over the threshold, his hand reaching out for Reid. I don't let him have any chance to get any further, meaning I won't be able to get to him, as I pull him back by the collar of his shirt, throwing him back and sending him toward a group, knocking them all over.

"Back off!" I shout in my devil voice. They don't listen. Unlike when my dad uses it, using that voice doesn't force anyone to do what I say. I can't wait until I take over for my dad and get that quality and don't have to scare them into doing what I say.

"Oi, bastards, I swear if you come within an inch of me, I will shoot you in the head," Reid threatens, coming out of his scared phase. Nice try, Reid, but bullets won't affect them.

The alarm is still running, and for this once, I agree with my dad: I'm getting tired of hearing my own voice. I create a ball of fire, holding it over my shoulder, getting ready to throw it.

"Don't make me use it."

The demons eye the ball warily before they all begin to slowly turn and find another soul to satisfy their hunger.

Once they have all cleared, I breathe a sigh of relief.

"Very funny, dad. Joke's over. Now, let me in."

My dad appears next to Reid, causing him to jump and his fist to go flying through the air toward my dad, who easily closes his hand around it, stopping it.

"Hm. What do you think, McDonald's boy? Should we let her in? Do you think she's learned her lesson?" he asks, dropping Reid's hand, my dad's arm going around his shoulders instead.

"Don't touch me," Reid forces through his teeth, his eyes narrowed in a glare.

My dad chuckles at him and allows his arm to drop off Reid's shoulders when Reid shrugs it off. My dad moves from beside him and to the door, where he presses a button. My dad smiles at me.

"You can come in now," he tells me.

I go to step over the threshold and instead of being thrown back, I am met with a wall of electricity. I fall to the floor, my muscles unable to hold me up. I match Reid's glare at my dad from the floor.

"I'm meant to be related to you, and you keep trying to hurt me! It's abuse!" I say, pushing myself to my feet again.

My dad's eyes widen innocently as his hand reaches out and he presses another button. I cross my arms.

"If this is another trick, I will disown you."

A smirk comes onto his lips as he tries to stop the laughter leaving him and his hand comes up to rest on his heart.

"I promise that nothing will happen to you."

I watch him cautiously as I take a tentative step forward. When my foot hits the tiled floor on the other side of the door, I don't hesitate and rush through and to my dad, who I hit.

"You say I'm the one abusing you, but who's the one hitting me?" he asks smugly, his blue eyes lit up with amusement.

I mimic him as I cross my arms forcefully.

"I know you said dad earlier, but did your brother come down instead?" Reid asks me, looking at us.

"No, can't you see how old he is?" I ask incredulously, uncrossing my arms to point at my dad.

"Old? Old? I'm not old!" my dad says his voice getting louder and higher as he mocks offense and outrage.

"You act like siblings," Reid comments.

"And look like it, right?" my dad asks as he pulls me into his side. I shove him off me as I hear the padding of paws on the tiled floor. I grin and look up for Tybalt. I've missed him and wish that I could take him up with me. I watch as he turns a corner and bounds toward us, his tongue lolling out the side of his face in a wolfish grin.

I bend down to welcome him, but his gaze, as well as his course, shifts to Reid. A loud growl rolls through the air as he knocks Reid off his feet, his head leaning down so he can bare his teeth in Reid's face. He barks loudly, causing Reid's ice blue eyes to widen in surprise and fear. I rush toward them, clutching Tybalt's collar to pull him off Reid.

"Tybalt, down. Friend," I command.

He growls once more before he walks back without my help. I let go of his collar, allowing Tybalt to turn and nudge my hand with his nose, licking it in greeting.

"Sorry about that. He'll get used to you," I tell Reid. I look up to see he is running his hand through his brown hair, his eyebrows raised.

"Yeah...I think I'll be staying away from him in the future."

I shrug as I continue to stroke my hand through Tybalt's thick fur.

"He's missed you," my dad says as he watches us. I smile sadly as I look down at Tybalt who has plastered his body to my leg, his red eyes trained on my face.

"You obviously have a reason for you coming down here. This place is not exactly date-worthy. What do you want?" he continues, looking between both of us.

"Why do you think I have to have a reason to visit?" I ask innocently, looking back down at Tybalt. I was preoccupied with my dad's antics and the demons that I forgot the true reason for the visit. Now remembering, I feel all the worries come rushing back. My dad ignores me, knowing me too well.

"So?"

"Well, um, we had a problem…"

"What sort of problem?" my dad questions warily, concern obvious in his tone.

"It's not a *huge* one," I say, buying for more time.

"Scar…just tell me."

I sigh before mumbling in a rush, "I-couldn't-make-Reid-forget-me-biting-him."

"What?" my dad asks, confusion now replacing the concern.

"I bit Reid," I say. A smug look appears on my dad's face as if to say, 'What did I say?' and I stick my tongue out at him, my eyes narrowed. "And then when I tried to compel him to forget, I couldn't."

"What do you mean you couldn't? You tried to, but when you got 'round to it, you couldn't because you got lost in his eyes, or it didn't work?"

I shoot him a look of contempt. "It's not funny. It didn't work."

"Hm. That's new to me."

My jaw drops as I throw my hands up into the air.

"I thought I would get something more than 'That's new to me!'" I exclaim, mimicking him.

"What can I do? Tell you some bullshit? It's not from lack of blood as you had some before you tried, so I don't know any more than you do," he responds, his dark eyebrows rising.

"Are you sure you're not siblings?" Reid pipes up, looking away from where he was watching Tybalt warily and up to look at my dad and me.

"Yes," I answer, still watching my dad. He has not eased my worries at all. I thought he would be able to give me a reason to reassure me that it's not me, and all I got was something that made my worries heighten. Am I a freak? My dad would have heard about something like this if it had happened before.

"Yeah, she was the result of..." my dad starts, a cheeky grin on his face.

"Dad!" I shout, interrupting him as I throw my hands over my ears to stop myself from being scarred for life.

He lets out a loud, booming laugh at my reaction before he furthers his earlier answer. "It's most likely that the answer to our problem will be in one of the books in the library. I'll also ask your uncles and aunts to see whether they have heard of this happening before. Have you experienced this problem before with anyone else?" he asks.

I shake my head. "I was able to make someone else forget on Earth."

He opens his mouth before thinking better of it.

"I'm not even going to ask," he mutters, shaking his head. "In the meantime, I will see if I can make Reid forget. If not, we'll work something out, and it'll give us some more information to go on."

"What? No. Why?" Reid says, taking a step back from my dad. "I can keep a secret, and anyway, I like this side of Scar."

I hold back a smile at what Reid said when my dad's eyes narrow at the wink Reid sends my way.

"Because I don't trust you and that's my daughter you're talking about. So, if you would, look into my eyes..." my dad says, putting force behind his words, which has Reid doing what he says.

I tune out, knowing the drill, as I walk through the doors on the search for something to do while I wait.

***

Two minutes pass until I hear my dad's booming voice calling me back to the house, "Scarlett Hades, to the entrance hall, please. Scarlett Hades, to the entrance hall!"

I shoot one last ball of fire at a soul before counting the ones that are alight and now running around in panic. Thirty-two: a high score!

I lift my feet up from where I was dangling them over the edge of a pit and run back to the house. I cautiously open the doors again, waiting for one of my dad's booby-traps to be set.

Thankfully, I arrive at Reid's unconscious side unhurt. I look down at Reid and then to my dad.

"You compelled him like that, right? You didn't knock him out?" I ask.

He chuckles. "Not this time. I made him think that you guys fell asleep, forgetting about the bite and trip down here."

"And what else did you do?" I ask him, knowing he wouldn't pass up on an opportunity to play a joke on me.

"Nothing," he says all too innocently for my liking.

"Mmhm," I let out in disbelief.

"You'll have to wait and see, won't you?" he taunts gleefully.

"Weirdo," I mutter, bending down next to Reid, picking him up easily.

"It's in the genes," he responds.

I snort. "Bye," I say, looking down to Tybalt who followed me and watched my game with the souls, stroking the black fur on his head. I step back from him so I don't take him with me, even though I want to.

"Bye." I picture the blanket behind the rock on the beach, focusing on the white sand.

When I feel my heels sink into something soft and feel the breeze in my hair, I open my eyes. Looking down, I see that the blanket is still where we left it, with the basket and food still lying on it. I lay Reid down next to it all, sitting beside him as I wait for him to wake up. I kick my heels off, staring out at the ocean.

The knots in my stomach from the worry lessen slightly as I force myself to forget about it. It's out of my hands now. All I can do is wait until my dad is able to find an answer; in the meantime, there is nothing I can do.

When I hear Reid's breathing start to become lighter and feel his body start to stir, I curl up next to him, resting my head on his chest. I relish in the comfort and body heat coming from him, listening to his strong heartbeat under my ear which is being pushed up and down with every breath. I almost forget what I am meant to be doing as I feel myself slowly drifting off to sleep. I am jolted awake, however, when I feel Reid move under me, trying to reach for his drink without waking me. I open my eyes slowly, pretending to be coming out of a deep sleep.

I've done a lot of pretending around Reid, first, with the van attack, and now, here. I just wish I don't have to keep doing it.

"Sorry, I didn't mean to wake you. I'm really thirsty for some reason," he says, his voice raspy, as I bring my head up from his chest.

That'll be you visiting Hell, the hottest place imaginable.

He gulps down the water.

"You look really peaceful when you are asleep," he comments. I inwardly chuckle; he's going to be in for a real shock when he sees me truly asleep. As he looks down at his watch, I inspect him for any differences that my dad could have caused, but he seems perfectly normal. I furrow my eyebrows; my dad must have done something. I quickly smooth my expression out when Reid looks back up.

"We should go. I need to get back soon," he says.

"Oh, okay," I respond, not wanting the date to end so soon.

"But first..." He leans in to place a kiss on my lips. I smile, moving forward to meet him halfway.

Before his lips can touch mine, he pulls back, starting to cluck loudly like a chicken. I turn my head away from Reid, letting out a laugh.

Thanks, dad!

"You said you needed to get back?" I prompt wanting to change the focus off what just happened, taking my phone out. I type a message to my dad: Ha ha, you're hilarious. How long will it last?

Almost instantly, I get a response: Will what last sugar?

"Do I amuse you?" Reid asks, annoyance creeping into his tone. I look up at him after typing out a reply to my dad: Don't try and sweet talk your way out of this. The clucking!

"No," I answer him, still smiling. I look back down at my phone when it buzzes.

You found out already? You haven't even been gone 10 minutes.

I roll my eyes before responding, Answer the damn question!

Reid makes a harrumphing noise, standing up. He extends his hand to me, pulling me up off the blanket. When I am on my feet, I look down at my phone to see my dad's message.

It will last the day. :) Have fun! xx

I groan, returning my phone to my pocket. I look up to find that Reid is smiling at our proximity. He goes to lean in for another kiss, but before he gets close enough to start clucking, I slip out of his grip, moving around him.

"Oh, look," I say, feigning shock to try and give an excuse for me moving away from his kiss.

"What?" he asks, his tone getting more annoyed. I bite my lip, trying to think of a valid excuse. I didn't think this through very well.

"Oh, um…I thought I saw a blue turtle," I explain. His annoyance turns to confusion and amusement.

"A blue turtle, huh?" he asks, his disbelief clear.

"Yes, but it was just a rock," I say, giving him a reassuring smile. He shakes his head at me, his annoyance gone completely now.

"Okay, I think you've had enough sun for today. Let's go, sweet cheeks," he says, tapping the end of my nose and I scrunch it up. He chuckles, taking my hand in his. I bend down to grab my shoes, halting when I stand back up.

"Shouldn't we take the blanket and basket?" I ask.

"No, a Grim Reaper will come and collect them," he says as he starts off again, and I jog slightly to catch up with him. We both round the rock and start up the hill. I pause halfway to look back at the beach and to where I had a date that was definitely memorable.

Chapter 19

Meredith

Once we arrive back at Reid's bike, we have a little incident. That sounds like one of us wet ourselves (we didn't). Instead, Reid tries to kiss me again, causing him to let out loud clucks. After I reassure Reid I am not laughing at him again, he finally starts on our way back to the park and my car.

We have been driving for fifteen minutes, and for the last five, Reid has periodically glanced over his shoulder.

"Shit!" Reid swears.

"What?" I ask him over the roar of the bike.

"We're being tailed," he calls back.

I try to look over my shoulder, but without turning my whole body and risking falling off the bike, I am not able to see much.

"Hang on!" he shouts as the bike speeds up, moving between the cars.

I grip on tighter as he suddenly swerves the bike into an alley. I get an eerie sense of déjà vu to the last time I went to the beach.

"Get off!" he commands.

I do so, pulling the helmet off as well. He puts the stand down before he swings his leg off the bike, watching the entrance intently. "Stay behind me."

I roll my eyes at him; I've faced bigger threats than someone who is tailing us.

"Hey!" I say getting his attention as I poke Reid's back. A black sedan pulls into the alley, and Reid raises his gun, not taking his gaze off the slowing car.

"Not now," Reid responds.

I poke him again, this time, harder.

"What?" he snaps, finally turning from the still slowing car.

"Do you have an extra gun?" I ask him, raising an eyebrow at his tone. Whoever is in that car has Reid rattled.

"Yeah, it's in the compartment of my bike..."

I ignore his following question of why I am asking as I move to his bike, opening the compartment. I smile when I find a black gun lying there. I grab it, checking the cartridge for the number of bullets, finding that it's full. I run back to Reid, stopping beside him. He turns to look at me, his eyes going to the gun in my hands.

"What are you doing with that?" he asks loudly, going to take it out of my hands.

"I'm protecting myself from an unknown danger," I reply, moving the gun further away from his reach.

"You can't..."

I'm obviously going to have to show him that I'm not going to shoot myself in the foot with it. I bring the gun up, flick the safety off and aim it at one of the cans sitting atop a trash can. I pull the trigger, watching as the bullet flies through the air and hits its mark in the center. I turn to Reid, who is watching me with a mixture of lust and admiration, and I give him a smug smile and a wink.

"I can handle a gun," I tell him. I turn to look at the car which has now stopped. I want to ask Reid who they are, but the sound of the doors opening and then slamming close stops me.

Standing next to the passenger side, flanked by three men in casual clothes, is a woman. Her long, blond hair is down, flowing around her in the breeze. One of her cold, hard, gray eyes is marred by a long scar running through it and onto her cheek. She wears a short, dark gray dress with pockets, which she has her hands in. Her red heels, which have spikes on the tips and down the heels, click against the concrete as she saunters toward us. A crop denim jacket hangs tops her outfit.

"Darling! Why are you pointing that gun at me?" the woman asks with an Australian accent, pouting her lips which are painted a bright red.

Reid's aim doesn't waver from the woman's forehead. I keep my gun down by my side, knowing it will only take me a split second to aim and fire.

Her gray eyes go to me, giving me a once-over. "Who's the whore?" she asks.

"Your worst nightmare," I say as I pull my gun up and fire a bullet so it barely scratches her ear. She narrows her eyes at me as she lifts a hand up to touch the cut that has formed.

I give her an innocent smile. She scrutinizes me for a moment before she looks to Reid and back to me. A grin comes to her face as she takes a couple of steps toward Reid, making him rest the gun where he has been aiming. She raises her eyebrows as if she was surprised.

"Go on then. Shoot me," she taunts.

Reid doesn't do anything and grimaces when she cackles and knocks the gun away from her head.

"You would have done it by now if you really wanted too," she tells him, patting his chest.

Reid grunts and backs away from her. "What do you want, Meredith?" he asks her.

"You," she says simply, leaning in and kissing Reid passionately.

I suddenly feel a surge of anger and maybe even jealousy. Reid goes to pull his gun up, but I'm quicker, lifting my gun up again, pressing it against her temple.

"He may not shoot you, but I will," I threaten as I see her tense up before pulling back. She laughs, looking me over again.

"I knew it," she exclaims gleefully, clapping her hands together. I narrow my eyes at her as she pushes my gun down, clicking her fingers at one of her men who walks toward me. He pushes me back and away from the woman, Meredith, until I am forced up against a wall. He rips the gun out of my grip.

I don't do anything, as my dad would be extremely unhappy with me if we have to go back down today. I look directly into the man's eyes, and he looks away and shifts in discomfort. A triumphant smile comes to my lips.

"Hey! Don't you fucking hurt her," Reid yells, stepping forward. Meredith pushes Reid back forcefully.

"We won't hurt her if you comply with our demands," she explains.

Reid glowers at her and spits in her face. The man holding me sees this and takes it as Reid won't go along with what they want. The man reaches into his pocket and pulls out a knife; he brings it up to my neck, pressing it against my skin. Reid doesn't even think and reacts immediately, lifting his gun up and shooting the man's head. He falls to the floor like a bag of rocks, finally resting in his own pool of blood.

I let out a small laugh. It's nice to get proof that he'll protect me. The remaining men step toward me, expecting me to attack their leader.

Meredith, however, doesn't feel the same way as me as she pushes Reid back violently, using her leg to swipe at Reid's legs. Reid falls onto his back. She's fuming as she lifts one of her heels, resting it on Reid's chest.

"You're going to pay for that," she grits out at Reid as she brings her gun out of a holster on her thigh, pointing it at me.

Chapter 20

The Gates of Hell and Fallen Angels

"Have you got any last words?" she asks, cocking her head to the side as she watches me.

I bring my hand up to my chin, holding it as if I am thinking.

"Hm. Let me think…Roses are red. Violets are blue. I have five fingers, and the middle one is for you," I say, showing her the finger in question with a smile.

"Anything else?" she asks, not amused.

"Oh yes, there is."

"What?" she asks impatiently.

"Shoot me," I challenge, extending my arms out from my body giving her an easy shot.

Reid shouts out, struggling against Meredith.

"Happily," Meredith says as her finger curls closer to the handle of the gun and she pulls the trigger. *Click.* Meredith pulls it again. *Click. Click. Click.* Meredith groans, forgetting Reid on the floor, allowing him to move out from under her foot. I walk up to Meredith, putting my head right to her ear.

"Next time you leave to shoot someone, *darling*, make sure you are prepared and have the bullets and magazine to do so," I advise.

She looks down at the gun, and sure enough, the magazine is not there. Surely, she would have noticed that they were missing, as it would have been lighter than usual, so maybe she's not as smart as she thinks. She storms past me and to the two men of hers which are remaining.

"You guys are fucking idiots. I don't even know why I employ you because you don't do your bloody job…" she starts on a rant, shouting at them as she hits them both over the head.

I laugh and reach down for Reid, pulling him up.

"I think that is our cue to leave. Sorry that I lost your spare gun," I tell him. His smile is admiring as we walk the short distance to his bike.

"Don't worry about it. It was worth it." He chuckles. I snag the helmet up off the floor and push it down onto my head.

"I need to stop off on the way back to the park. Is that okay?" he asks, sitting on his bike.

"Where are we going?" I ask, getting onto the back of his bike.

"I hope you're ready to meet some Grim Reapers," he says, starting the bike up.

Over the roar of the engine, we are still able to hear Meredith's voice ranting at her men. Just as Reid is pulling out the other end of the alley, two gunshots ring through the air, and as Reid is turning, I get a glimpse of Meredith holding a different gun, standing in an alley with all three of her men she arrived with, dead around her.

It only takes us a short ride to get to our destination—a set of iron gates. I look through the visor of the helmet and see at the top of each rung of the gates is a curved piece of metal. I smile at the scythes that they form. The scythes are all held together by curving metal in the shape of vines. Where the gates meet is a solid skull, half on each gate. Where the eyes should have been are the letters G and R.

"Ooh! Are we at the gates of Hell?" I ask, trying to hold in my laugh at the irony of us actually being in Hell earlier. They're not exactly hiding.

"Yeah," Reid replies, playing along, reaching into his pocket. Seconds later, the gates are opening, and Reid is pulling through them. The drive curves up in front of the house before turning in a circle to go back down. On either side of the tarmac is a garden where people are lounging in the sun. The house, which is a sandy yellow, sprawls out either side of the front door and looks to be more than two stories high.

"You live here all by yourself?" I joke.

He chuckles. "No, some of my members are unable to be down on record of where their accommodation is, so they stay here, along with some others who can't afford their own place. It's handy having them here, as it's safe for all of us. It's harder for them to be caught. There's plenty of space, as you can see," he explains.

"How come no one has been able to find you. The gates are kind of a big clue," I ask as I get off the bike, looking up and around.

"Oh, they have. They're just dealt with," he answers lightly. I think back to the dead body in my house.

"Was my present one of those people?"

"No, but I can give you one next time if you want," he answers, looking at me out the side of his eye.

I laugh. He reaches for my hand, pulling me after him to the open doors. When we enter the entrance hall, I am surprised to find that it is spacious and seems to be the epicenter of the house. A staircase is the main feature splitting and going up to different parts of the house. An archway leads to what I assume is the living room, and all the other rooms leading off it are hidden by doors or are down corridors. Men and women are walking through, opening doors to go to different rooms, or walking up the stairs. The splashing of water hits my ears, letting me know that a pool is outside, and judging by where people are walking, it's out the back. Reid whistles loudly, catching everyone's attention.

"Meeting!" he calls simply before dragging me through the people and to an archway leading into one of the corridors. I stumble after him, trying to get any sounds coming from any of the rooms we pass, but it's silent. We eventually stop outside a door, which Reid opens.

Behind the door is a spacious room with rows and rows of seats. Reid leads me through the middle of them, stopping at the front.

"This won't take long," he assures me as we watch people begin to trickle into the room, taking seats.

"What are we doing?" I ask him.

"We're having a meeting," he replies, stating the obvious.

"No shit, Sherlock. Why is the meeting taking place?"

"I need to talk to them about the encounter we had, and it's best if we do it now when we know their most recent sighting. We could get to them if we act fast," he explains.

"Okay, but you haven't explained who *they* are."

"All will be explained in the meeting," he tells me unhelpfully.

I mimic him, shaking my head afterward. "You're so helpful."

He looks away from the slowly filling room and at me, letting out a laugh. When I look back at the now sea of people, I see that they are all watching me warily like I am the threat. As the last people file in at the back, I move off to the side, leaning against the wall. Reid clears his throat, and the minimal chatter in the room goes silent.

"There was an incident," he starts, his voice powerful and full of authority, holding the room's attention.

"No shit, Sherlock," I mutter under my breath again, however, obviously I wasn't quiet enough, as everyone in the room, including Reid, looks to where I am standing. A ripple of chuckles goes through the room. Reid raises an eyebrow, silently challenging me to interrupt again.

"That's the Scar everyone knows and loves," says a voice coming from someone standing next to me. I let out a yelp, jumping into the air.

"Holy shit on a stick!" I shout, lifting a hand to my erratically beating heart. I'm usually aware of my surroundings, but I didn't even know someone was standing next to me just now. I lash out at the person next to me, catching them on the arm with my hand.

"What the fuck are you doing here, Hunter?" I shout.

"I could ask you the same thing," he counters, an amused smile on his lips. Reid clears his throat again, looking between the two of us.

"Have you finished?" he asks.

I send Reid an encouraging smile for him to continue before muttering to Hunter, "This isn't over."

"Let's try and continue without any more interruptions," Reid announces, sending a pointed look in my direction.

I stick my tongue out at him, causing more chuckles to bounce around the room. "But before we do, I should really introduce someone first. Everyone, this is my girlfriend, Scarlett."

My head shoots up in surprise, but I gather myself enough, trying not to embarrass either of us, to step forward and give a salute to the room.

"What's up?" I ask as I start to scan the rest of the room. If Hunter is here, Leo, Liam, and Jake are most likely somewhere nearby also. Sure enough, I see the three faces sitting at the back of the room, with varying shades of boredom on their faces. When they see me looking at them, they grin and nod at me in greeting. I let out a breathy laugh and step back to the wall.

"Let's get back to the whole reason for the meeting. As I said, there was an incident including Meredith and a couple of members from the Fallen Angels," he says, gaining everyone's attention again. The Fallen Angels? Really? Does every gang in this area have a name to do with death? I clear my throat, trying to cover up my laughter. But a few indications slip through.

"Something amusing you?" Hunter whispers in my ear, his eyes still on Reid at the front.

"Are all the gang names to do with death or Hell?" I whisper back.

He laughs himself. "No. Not all of them. There is a history between ours and the Fallen Angels. The Fallen Angels were created by an ex-member of the Grim Reapers who had gone rogue. That's Meredith. She named her gang the Fallen Angels to piss Reid off. You know the scar running down her face…"

"Yes, it was kind of hard to miss it."

"Yeah," he says, laughing. "Well, she received it in a fight between her and Reid. It happened just before she left. Reid has his own scars from the fight, but you wouldn't be able to see them now. He likes to keep them hidden. Meredith went rogue about two years ago, but there was always a rift between them before then. Ever since she left, she has been hell-bent on destroying the Grim Reapers and Reid."

"When did you join then?"

"*That* is a story for another time," he says as Reid is just rounding off the meeting.

"I want to know straight away of any Fallen Angels activity. If you see anyone who is not here now, let them know about the things said today as always. Okay? Everyone is dismissed," he tells them before moving to the side and to me. I quickly say a goodbye to Hunter before meeting him.

"Are you okay with sticking around here for a bit longer? I'm waiting on people to return," he asks, pulling me closer to his body.

I wrap my arms around his neck. "Hm. I guess."

His gaze moves off my face and around the room; his face shows that he thinks that this isn't the best place to be doing this. I unwrap my arms from around his neck, taking a step back, understanding completely why. I wouldn't want any demons to see me being affectionate with anyone. You need to come across as a leader with no emotions, especially in his job.

"Come on," he says, taking my hand and leading me to a door opposite the entrance to the meeting room. He reaches into his pocket, bringing out a key. He inserts it, twisting it with the handle.

When he allows it to swing open, it shows an office on the other side. A big desk is the main feature in the middle of the room, a bookcase on one of the walls next to it. I look around and see that this is one of three doors. One looks as if it leads back into the hallway.

He pulls me past the couch next to the bookcase and into the middle of the room, to the desk. I try and glance around the room some more, but I am only able to see a potted plant in the corner before my gaze is obscured by Reid standing in front of me.

He lifts me up by the hips and places me down on the solid wood of the desk. He walks forward, nudging my knees apart to stand between them. I wrap my legs around him, resting my arms on his strong shoulders.

"There's a perfectly good couch over there," I tell him, motioning to where it sits.

He smiles. "I know. I wouldn't be able to get this close to you there though," he says.

"I'm your girlfriend, huh?" I ask.

"Yeah," he replies smugly.

"The funny thing is I don't recall you asking," I remark, putting on a fake somber face. "I'm sorry, but it's not official."

"We can't have that, can we?" he says, playing along. "Scarlett?"

"Yes, Reid?"

"Will you do me the honor of being my girlfriend?" he asks.

I pretend to gasp in shock. "It's all so fast. I didn't expect this *at all,*" I joke.

I pretend to contemplate it for a moment. "Hm. Why not?" I say with a shrug.

"You've made me the happiest man alive with your 'Why not?'" he says sarcastically, still playing along with our act.

He and I laugh.

"I like your laugh," he says, moving forward. Sensing the incoming kiss, I lean back, looking around for something to use as a distraction, not wanting another clucking incident. I snatch the closest thing, which happened to be a photo frame holding a picture of a young boy.

"Who's this?" I ask, examining the picture. The boy looked like what I expect a young Reid to look like. I hear Reid let out a low, annoyed groan but still answers.

"That's my brother."

"I thought you were in care for most of your life," I say, remembering the article I read about him. I freeze as soon as I let it slip that I had looked him up.

"How did you know that?" he asks defensively. He admitted he got one of his people to look me up after we met, so how is this any different? Maybe it's a touchy subject. I place the frame back down and try and think of a response.

I, however, am saved from answering him when there is a knock on the door. Reid lets out another groan.

"Who is it?" Reid calls out.

The door opens a crack, and Hunter pokes his head in. He looks to where Reid is standing and down to where my legs are wrapped around him. His jaw clenches along with his fist.

"What do you want, Stone?" Reid snaps.

"I need to talk to you. Alone," Hunter says.

I let my legs fall from around Reid and cross them, leaning back on my hands. Now free, Reid turns fully to look at Hunter.

"Whatever you need to tell me, you can say in front of Scar," Reid says with a tone that suggests no argument, but it doesn't seem to reach Hunter because he goes to open his mouth in objection. Sensing that this could cause an argument and not really feeling like I want to see another fight today, I intervene.

"Nah, I'm not really interested in what you guys have to say. Anyway, I want to go and look around and cause havoc somewhere else," I tell them, jumping down from the desk. I walk past them both, ignoring them staring each other down. I guess Meredith isn't only one with a history with Reid.

I open the door leading to the hallway, calling over my shoulder as I exit, "Play nice."

I just hear Reid telling me he'll come and find me when they're done before the door closes behind me.

Chapter 21

Which One of You Am I Shooting?

I walk down the empty corridor, the clicking of my heels the only sound. When I emerge into the entrance hall, like when we arrived, it holds a scattering of people going their own ways. Unlike earlier, I find that there are children amongst the men and women. My mind flashes back to the boy that I let go to Olympus before I left. The device said that he would be going to Hell for gang activity. Did he have anything to do with this one?

I look around, trying to decide where to go. Thinking it would be best to start from the top and work my way down, I amble to the stairs. I take the steps up until they split, wondering which way to take first. Purely because I was standing closer to it, I decide the left side is the wing I am going to be nosy around first.

I don't see any more steps leading up, so I assume that they will be at the end of the hall. I start to wander down the hall, listening to the rooms behind the doors, trying to find something interesting and snoop-worthy. I walk past countless people having conversations which don't pique my fancy until I get to something that does.

Leo, Liam, and Jake are talking quite heatedly on the other side of a door nearing the corridor turning to the right. I pause in my wanderings and listen closer. What can I say? I've always been nosy. I always listen into people's conversations at home; you never know what kind of information you could glean from it. My favorite kind is an argument, and it seems that Jake, Leo, and Liam are debating about something.

"I wonder if that's what Hunter's talking to Reid about," Liam ponders.

"I don't think so…Hunter would get his balls chopped off and shoved up his ass if he told him," Leo counters.

I have to hold in a laugh. What would cause Reid to be so angry? I think for a second about compelling them to tell me, but a mixture of doubts about my compulsion working, and it being no fun, makes me push the idea out of my mind.

I now regret not staying behind and seeing what Hunter had to tell Reid. I walk slightly closer to the door involuntarily, wanting to hear more. Unfortunately, they move onto a new topic: yours truly.

"I wonder how little devil and Reid met," Jake says.

"She told us about meeting Reid after the party, remember?"

"Oh yeah."

"Did you see her face when Reid said about her being his girlfriend?" Liam asks.

"Yeah, she looked as if it was new to her as well," Leo answers. I must have not been quick enough to hide the shock. But is that such a bad thing? What they say next confuses me and has me rethinking my last statement. "Do you think?" Leo continues.

"No. Let's not go there," Liam says, putting an end to that conversation.

I sigh when they move onto something more boring. It was more interesting when they were talking about Hunter and Reid. I turn, deciding to see if I can catch the end of Reid and Hunter's conversation when the door that I was just listening at opens. I jump down the corridor, landing ungracefully on my heels. My hands fly out and press against the walls, holding myself up.

"Little devil?" Jake asks, mirth in his tone.

I straighten up and turn, giving them an innocent smile.

"I was just coming to find you three," I say, telling them a half-truth. Liam looks unconvinced as he raises an eyebrow.

"Well, here we are," he says. Leo claps his hands loudly. He strides toward me, taking my arm, and dragging me down the hall after him.

"You are going to come with me. I want to see if you are worthy."

I shoot him a confused look and then a pleading one to Liam and Jake behind us. They just chuckle.

"I'm not going to miss this," Jake says, Liam agreeing with him.

"Worthy of what?" I ask.

"Worthy to be Reid's girlfriend," he explains as he continues to drag me.

"I'm coming willingly. You don't need to abduct me," I tell him, ripping my arm out his grip.

"Aw, and I had the blindfold all ready," Leo says with a pout, shooting me a wink over his shoulder.

Leo leads our group down the stairs I came up, through the entrance hall, and to a door hiding another set of stairs going down into the basement. We all tread down them, going through the open door at the bottom and into a gym-like area.

Lying in the middle of the room is a mat, where two men are currently fighting. Weight and exercise machines are placed around the edges of the room, interspersed with punching bags. Running along one wall are different types of weapons and training implements.

"What do I have to do show I'm 'worthy?'" I ask, surveying the room, noting the different things. Whatever they want me to do, I'll be able to do with ease. My dad, with help from Kyle, has been training me ever since I was able to walk.

"Oh, we're not using this room," Leo says as he continues past the men on the mat, who are ducking each other's swings, and to a door on the other side of the room. He pushes it open, and we enter a long, narrow room only holding a trunk next to the door.

I look around puzzled, finding my answer when I see the four doors flush to the opposite wall, painted the same color as the rest of the wall to disguise them. I listen closely and hear muffled gunshots. You can't trick a demon with soundproofing. I realize what they want me to do; they've brought me to a firing range in their basement.

I raise my eyebrows, extending my hands out from my body.

"Is this it?" I ask, not letting on what I've seen or heard. Jake chuckles and shakes his head. Liam opens the trunk next to the door, grabbing four noise-cancelling ear protectors and protective glasses.

"*Wow*, that makes things *so* much better," I say sarcastically as I take the pairs that Liam is holding out for me.

"Right?" Leo agrees, putting his pair of ear protectors on. "Now, we won't be able to hear each other!"

I snort as Leo pulls them off his ears with a grin.

"I'm sure you've worked out what we want you to do," he says.

I nod. "So, which one of you am I shooting?" I ask, looking at them with a serious look on my face.

"What? No!" Liam says loudly, looking slightly scared. "There are targets behind that wall." He motions to the wall I noticed when we arrived.

"Oh," I say, acting disappointed. "You should make that clearer next time. Don't get a girl's hopes up like that."

"It's meant to be hidden so if anyone were to enter the house and come snooping, say a police officer, they wouldn't find them," Liam explains.

"You don't want them to find the shooting range, but you have weapons on show in that room," I say incredulously, motioning back to the gym.

"It's always covered whenever the room's not being used. There's a sliding partition," Liam explains as Jake begins to walk down the room, opening the hidden doors quietly to check if it's occupied. When he hears gunshots, he closes it and moves onto the next one.

"Have you ever shot a gun before?" Jake asks as he leaves the door to the third open, turning back to me.

"Of course!"

"How stupid of us! Of course, you have!" Leo says, mimicking my tone.

I laugh as I walk past him and to Jake who is holding his gun in his hand, pointing the grip in my direction.

"Come on then, little devil. Show us what you're made of."

I take the gun off Jake and enter the shooting range. Like the room holding the secret entrance, this one is long and narrow.

The walls on either side of me are thin, allowing me to hear the others occupying the cubicles. I walk to the counter, resting the gun down on it. I hear Leo, Liam, and Jake enter behind me, and it holds us all comfortably.

As Leo gets the mechanical track to pull in the target paper which has already been shot, I check the gun for bullets. Happy that's it's loaded; I slam the magazine back into the gun. I look up and see that Leo has placed a clean target at the end of the space.

"Whenever you're ready," he tells me as he steps back behind me.

Placing my ear and eye protectors on, I lift the gun back up. I pull the slide back, loading the gun before flicking the safety off. I lift it up and aim it at the first point marked on the target.

I take a deep breath as I move my feet apart and lift my other hand to hold the gun also. I let it out as I pull the trigger; I watch the bullet making its way to mark, piercing the paper in the middle of the target on the head of the drawing. I move my aim, hitting my mark with each pull of the trigger. Once the cartridge is empty, I push the ear protectors off; I place the gun down and turn to Liam, Leo, and Jake whose jaws are all hanging slack.

"I told you I can shoot a gun," I tell them, putting one hand on the counter and the other on my hip.

Liam nods in amazement and approval. I smile.

"Okay, little devil, how are you with moving targets?" Jake questions.

I turn back to the counter. "Set it up," I instruct him. I reach into the box of bullets that one of them placed beside me, refilling the magazine.

"It'll start in two minutes," he tells me.

I push the ear protectors back down over my ears and lift the gun again, waiting for the first target to appear.

The first one comes from the right and moves slowly into the space using tracks on the floor. I don't let it get far as I shoot the picture of the man in the head. As I shoot each one, they begin to get faster, and I'm thankful for my quick reflexes.

As I see the fifth one appearing from the gap in the wall, I feel the air shift and smell that Hunter and Reid have joined us. I feel the heat radiating off Reid as he moves up behind me. I fire off the last bullet, placing the gun down on the counter.

Hands fall to my hips, resting there as I feel a pair of lips touch my neck. I smile; at least my dad didn't stop Reid from doing that. I turn around in his arms, meeting a pair of piercing blue eyes which are full of admiration. I press my lips together as he leans forward, whispering so only I can hear, "You're sexy when you're shooting things." His lips go to fall onto mine, and before I can pull away, Reid lets out a loud cluck. I groan, silently cursing my dad.

The room stays silent for what feels like an age as they try and work out what just happened. When they finally come to the conclusion that it did actually happen, they all start to laugh loudly. I press my lips together again, trying my best to suppress my laugh which is threatening to bubble up and out of my lips. Tears start to form in my eyes at the suppressed laughter.

"Did something happen that I missed?" Reid asks, looking down at me confused.

I am about to deny that anything happened, but Hunter beats me to it.

"Dude? You were clucking like a fucking chicken," Hunter says and continues to laugh. I look over Reid's shoulder, at Hunter. He looks like he still has his balls in the right place;

maybe he didn't tell Reid what his friends thought he would. I look back to Reid who has a furious look on his face.

"No, I was not!" he grits out.

I squeeze Reid in a hug, trying to calm him down.

"So, how did I do? Am I worthy?" I ask, trying to change the subject and get the attention of Reid who looks ready to kill someone.

"Yes. You did better than Leo and Jake," Liam replies, his laughter dying down now.

Once the laughter has died down completely, the atmosphere in the room starts to get tense. I can feel Reid's grip is tightening on me, and when I look up at him, I see that he and Hunter are avoiding each other's gazes, annoyed looks on their faces. Now I really regret not being there for their conversation.

"Who pissed in your cereal?" I ask.

"What the hell are you going on about?" Hunter asks, giving me a weird look.

"You and Reid both look like someone pissed in your cereal. What were you talking about?"

"We were talking about the…weather," Hunter answers.

I don't even need to have my extra hearing and sight to know he's lying about that one.

"The weather? You wanted to talk to Reid about the weather without me there?"

"Yeah," Hunter says, sounding unsure about it himself.

"Okay, so what did you guys think about the weather that got you so annoyed?" I ask Reid.

He balks at the question but answers, "We thought that it was… um…too hot."

"Right," I say, patting his chest as I step back. "I think it's time that I go home."

"I'll take you," Reid tells me.

I smile at him in thanks.

"Bye, boys. I'll see you on Monday," I call back over my shoulder as I walk out of the small room. Reid follows closely behind. I just catch Hunter talking to the others before I enter the gym area.

"Was it just me who thought that she was extremely hot when she was shooting the gun?"

Chapter 22

I'm Clucking Mad About You!

Reid drives me back on his bike to where I parked my car at the beginning of the day. As we ride, the sky gets gradually darker. It's a phenomenon that I am not used to. At home, the light barely changes; it's just constantly a glowing red from the fire pits being the only light source. The only time that Earth is like Hell is at sunset. The sky then can go the same color of the sky at home.

The sun has set fully when Reid finally pulls into the parking lot. I am happy to find that my car is still where I left it. I push down on Reid's shoulders as I get off. Standing next to his bike, I pass my helmet to Reid, who is still on his bike.

Thinking back over the day, I let a smile come to my lips. When I think about Jake, Leo, and Liam, the question which was nagging at me resurfaces. Who was the girl, and what were they going to do to her?

"Do you remember how we met?" I ask him.

He places the helmet down on the bike between his legs.

"Yeah, it wasn't that long ago," he responds.

"You were kidnapping a girl…What were you going to do with her?

'   "Oh," he says, his hands resting on the top of his helmet. I can see that he is realizing what I am referring to. I don't mind most things, but when it comes to hurting children, I am hesitant.

"We weren't going to rape or sell her if that's what you mean. She was a daughter of one of the members of the gang, and she has run away," he says. For the first bit, his heart stayed steady, but for the last, his heart sped up. I cross my arms.

"Did the leader and a group of men have to go and get her, causing her to be scared?" I ask sarcastically.

He looks hesitant, but the next time he talks, his heart is steady.

"Her mom is Meredith. We were going to use her as bait," Reid relents.

"She was ten!" I exclaim.

"She wasn't going to be hurt…I wouldn't let that happen. I would never hurt a child," he says, trying to reassure me. "I turned the men in who were helping me that day, as they let the girl go for you, but I don't regret them doing that. I'm actually thankful."

"Well, I'll see you soon," I say, turning to walk to my car. Before I can get very far, Reid pulls my arm. I spin, stumbling toward where he is still on the bike. He goes to kiss me, and I unhappily pull away. I really hate my dad right now.

"Why won't you kiss me? What have I done?" he asks, his voice full of hurt. I close my eyes.

"Nothing, you're just clucking mad," I tell him, leaning down to kiss him on the cheek. I pause, not knowing if he will react, but when he doesn't, I continue to his cheek, letting my lips touch the stubble.

"Goodnight," I mutter before straightening and stepping back. Reid, now with a satisfied smile, lifts the helmet to his head. Once his face is covered, he kicks down, starting the bike, and pulls back out of the parking lot.

As I walk to my car, I bring out my keys and click the button to unlock it. I pull the handle, pulling the door open before sliding down onto the seat. I let out an annoyed sound as I hit my head against the headrest and my hand against the steering wheel repeatedly. Why is my dad such a pain sometimes?

"Finally!" someone says.

I scream, and the person screams too. Without thinking, I let my demon features take over, my horns extending as well as my fangs, my eyes changing to the red flickering with the fire inside me. I grab the person in the passenger seat by the neck.

Meredith

I've seen that girl before, but where? I know I have. I turn on my pacing route again, ignoring the curious eyes of my daughter. I groan, deciding I need to get out of here and clear my head. I think better in the night air.

"I'm going out!" I call, knowing one of my members will look after my daughter.

I don't know how long I have been walking when I find myself going through a park. The roar of a bike's engine fills the quiet night air. I look up and recognize the black bike as being Reid's immediately.

My eyes light up when I see the girl is sitting on the back. Maybe if I get a glimpse of her face again, it will jog my memory. I step behind the closest tree, not wanting to be seen by them.

I watch the girl get off the bike. A conversation, or a small argument, follows. Reid tries to kiss her, but she pulls back. Interesting. Instead, she kisses him on the cheek. Maybe their relationship isn't strong.

After Reid rides off, the girl turns and starts toward a white car a couple of spaces away from me. I study her face, trying to get my memory to start working, but nothing. I move my attention to the car, noticing that someone is in the car already, waiting for her. Is she cheating on Reid?

I watch closely as she gets into the car, the safety lights coming on, and she slams her head against her seat. I look to the man who is waiting for her and see that he is an attractive blond. His mouth starts to move, and the girl screams. This has the man screaming as well.

She turns to the man, grabbing him by the throat. Her face, however, isn't the pretty one from earlier; it's an ugly, gnarled face of a demon. From my hiding spot, I have a great angle. I know exactly where I have seen her before now. I quickly snap a photo of her with my phone before finding my second-in-command's number. I bring it up to my ear, waiting for the rings to end.

"Things just got interesting."

Chapter 23

I Thought We Could Have a Little Talk

"Scar, it's only me," Adrian says. What is he doing on Earth and more specifically, in my car? The reason for his last visit was because my dad sent him up with some blood. Is my dad the reason behind his visit this time?

"Gods, Adrian, what are you doing here?" I ask, letting go of his neck, pushing him back.

"Um...Well," he starts hesitantly as he looks around anxiously. I watch him, getting more and more concerned. I've never seen him like this before; something must definitely be wrong.

He lets out a shaky breath; rubbing his hands over his face and up into his blond hair. He bunches it between his hands as he looks at me. I swallow when I see the scared look there. Is he scared of the thing he seems to be running from, or of my reaction?

"What is it?" I ask him forcefully.

"First of all, I want you to know that I didn't do what I'm accused of..." he starts. My eyes widen. Accused? What is going on? If he's not down in Hell, probably in fear of his life, then it must be bad. I close my eyes.

"Shit, should you be talking to me?"

Adrian lets his hands fall from his hair, looking out into the dark, empty parking lot. My phone starts to ring, breaking the silence. I jump, pulling it out of my pocket. Whoever is calling now has the worst timing. I look down at my phone and see my dad's contact photo, an image of a cartoon devil with a pacifier in his mouth. I look up to Adrian, turning it so he can see.

"Do I tell him you're here?"

"No, you should answer it, though. He'll suspect something if you don't," Adrian responds, looking out of the window again.

I survey him, deciding whether whatever is going on with him is worth me lying to my dad. I finally decide to hear him out before deciding whether to turn him in to my dad. If he says he's not guilty, then I believe him. He's innocent until proven otherwise. My phone's rings continue to fill the car.

"Okay, wait here. He'll hear you if I stay in the car." I open the car door and step out of my car, hitting the answer button as I go.

"Hey, dad, what's up?" I ask, trying to keep my voice steady to sound normal as I answer the phone. I move away from my car, putting some distance between the phone and any noises Adrian could make. I start to walk into the park.

I love night on Earth. After the sun has set, it brings out all kinds, and not all of them are human. At home, there are no stars, but looking up now, I can see the black canvas is spotted with white flecks and swirls of blue. This is one of the times that I am thankful for my enhanced eyesight.

"Scar? You there?" my dad asks.

"Yes, sorry. What can I do for you?"

"You're friends with Adrian, right?" he asks, his voice serious.

I clear my throat, my worry heightening. What did he do to get even my dad worried?

"Yeah, what about him?"

"Have you seen him recently?"

I let my fingernails grow and pierce the skin of my hand, taking my attention off the lie I am about to tell, hoping that it will calm me down enough so my dad can't tell I am lying to him. I grit my teeth but keep my voice steady and light.

"No…Why?"

"I just want to speak with him…Let me know if you see him," he instructs.

"I will," I tell him, my fingernails still embedded in my palm. "Why do you want to speak to him?" I ask, finally flexing my hand after letting my fingernails shrink. I bring my hand up, watching as the crescents heal before my eyes.

"Don't worry about it," he comments, sounding distant as if he's listening to someone else.

I turn and walk back toward my car. I stop just short of being able to hear the radio that Adrian is fiddling with. I watch him for a moment, wondering if the Adrian I know is still the same person as I hear my dad mumbling incoherently to someone.

A movement from behind a tree catches my eye. I step to the side, trying to work out what I saw. A blond woman, with a scar running down her face, has her phone to her ear as she keeps sending quick glances to my car. I narrow my eyes. What is she up to?

"Dad, I have to go," I mutter into the phone, hanging up after. He sounds like he is busy anyway.

I stroll back to my car, bending down as I rap my fingers on the glass in the window of the passenger side. Adrian looks up from the radio.

"I'll be back in a minute, and then I can take you home where you'll explain your reason for being here," I say. He nods, although I can see his blue eyes are silently asking me what I'm going to do.

I straighten, looking to where I saw Meredith finding that she is still there talking animatedly on the phone. I contemplate for a minute on how to approach her. I quietly tiptoe until I am standing by her, waiting for the perfect moment to act.

"I'm being serious. This could be our chance. I knew that I had seen her before. I knew I wasn't crazy…" she says.

"Chance for what?" I ask.

She leaps into the air, spinning around, with her phone now down by her chest. Her gray eyes are wide as she looks me over, her expression scared.

"I thought we could have a little talk," I tell her, flashing a quick smile before nodding down to where she is clasping her phone like it's a weapon. "Wrap it up."

She hesitantly brings the phone back up to her ear.

"I should go. I'll be able to tell you more than I know now, later," she says quickly into the phone, ending the call afterward. I check the screen just to be sure.

"How long have you been here?" I ask, thinking back to when I first found Adrian in my car. If she was looking at my car, she could have seen me turn into a demon. Her scared expression now has nerves thrown in there too.

"Why?"

"Just wondering," I reply lightly.

"I was here when you arrived with Reid," she says, looking expectantly at me, waiting for some kind of reaction. Dread starts to run through my veins. However, I try and keep my feelings off my face. I obviously didn't keep it all hidden, as Meredith begins to smirk. "Oh, I saw, and I have proof," she continues, getting more confident. She unlocks her phone, tapping on the screen a couple of times, turning it to me when she's done.

I look down at the screen and see that it's holding a photo of me with my demon features present on my face, holding a shocked Adrian by the throat. I've never really seen myself like that. Yes, I've seen my demon features on my face before in the mirror but never when I'm attacking. I don't look as bad as I thought I would.

"Oh, come on, you could have got a better angle. That is *so* not my best side," I tell her.

"Wh—" she starts, surprised and confused at my reaction. She looks back down at her phone and then up to me.

"Sweetie, if you did show anyone that photo, which you won't, they would think that it was Photoshopped," I tell her, faking sympathy. "Anyway, like I said, you won't get the chance to show anyone." I grab her by the neck, slamming her into the tree behind her.

"I sent it to my second-in-command. They've already seen it," she chokes out, her head lifting to try and alleviate the pressure on her windpipe.

I tilt my head with an amused smirk on my lips, knowing that she's lying. "You're lying."

"Try me," she says cockily. She's being bold for someone in her situation.

"I will," I respond, slamming her head back into the tree again, this time, harder than the first. Her head lolls forward, and a trickle of blood makes its way onto my hand from the wound on the back of her head. I lift her up, slinging her over my shoulder. Her heartbeat is still there, letting me know she's not dead.

Yet.

I look around the park to make sure no one saw as I lift my hand to my lips, licking her blood off my hand.

When I am satisfied that we were the only people around, I make my way back to the car, going to the trunk. I am not getting blood in my car. I open it, stuffing Meredith's unconscious body in the space. I slam the lid down, but it doesn't go down all the way. I push down on the top, only to realize that one of Meredith's arms is sticking out.

"Oops," I say, not caring as I open the trunk again. I push her arm in, quickly closing the lid after to hold all of her in there. I walk to the driver's side and get in. I let out a sigh as I slip the key into the ignition.

"So, let me show you my house," I say to Adrian as if nothing just happened.

***

I turn the car onto my driveway, putting the roof up as I drive the short distance. Adrian wants it down, even though the sun isn't out. I put the car in park and get out of the car. When I see Adrian's head pop up over the car, I throw him the keys.

"Go and let yourself in. I'll go and get our package."

I hear Adrian unlocking the front door as I walk to the back of the car again. I open the trunk, causing an arm to flop out. When I see that her eyes are still closed, I check for a heartbeat again. She's still not dead, just unconscious. I didn't mean to hit her *that* hard.

"Come on then," I say as I hoist Meredith onto my shoulder again. I turn around as I slam the trunk close again, meeting eyes with Rosie's gray ones. She's standing at the end of her own drive, her mouth agape as she takes in the sight of me carrying a body.

"Hi. Lovely night, isn't?" I call out to her. Her look turns to horror as she turns and rushes up the drive.

I chuckle as I make my way up my own drive, pushing the door open. I find Adrian already sitting on one of my couches as I nudge the door close with my foot.

"Have you eaten recently?" I ask as I grab the blanket lying on the back of my couch.

"Is she my dinner?" he asks, nodding to Meredith still on my shoulder. I shake my head as I unfold the blanket.

"There's blood in the cupboard under the sink," I tell him, lifting the blanket into the air, letting it float down to the floor.

"What is she for then?"

"She took a photo of me," I reply simply.

He shakes his head at me, muttering under his breath something to the effect of 'I will never understand you.'

I let Meredith drop down onto the blanket now covering my floor to stop the blood from staining it. A blanket is a lot easier to clean than a carpet. Once my work is done, I take Meredith's phone out of her grasp and plop down onto the couch, grabbing the TV remote and switching the TV on.

"Grab me one as well?" I shout to Adrian who is bending down to collect some blood. He appears beside me in a second after running from the kitchen. He passes me a bag before sitting down with his own. I rip the top off and sip at it as I turn Meredith's phone on.

Noticing that it has no passcode, I enter the phone and go to messages, checking them to see if she was telling the truth earlier. Even though her body told me she wasn't, I still want to check. You can never be too sure.

"Mm, this is good stuff," Adrian comments as he takes a gulp of his own. I look up and notice how quickly he is drinking it. How long has he been without blood?

"So...why have you come to me?" I ask as I move onto the mail app.

"I need a place to stay," he admits.

"Why?"

"Some demons have been causing trouble by trying to rally forces to join them in a plan to overthrow your dad. Your dad thinks I am the one that is leading them."

A revolution? This is serious. How did I not know this was going on? How bad is it? Hundreds of questions run through my mind, but Adrian is not the one to ask them to. My dad should be the one to answer my questions about it all, especially if Adrian *is* the one behind it all.

"What? Why didn't he tell me?" I exclaim, moving my gaze from the phone, which is clear of messages with my photo in.

"He thinks he can handle it."

Of course, he does! He will rarely tell me things unless it's a life or death situation.

"Why does he think it's you?" I ask, looking back down at the phone. I go to the photos and clear all the ones she has of me as a demon.

"Gossip," he simply replies. Sucking the last bits out of the bag of blood, I throw it over the back of the couch. Not knowing what other evidence my dad has, I decide to believe what Adrian is telling me. He has been my friend my whole life, and if he's risking his life by coming to me, then he's either insane or innocent.

"Okay. I believe you, but if I ever find out that you do have something to do with all of this, I will personally be the one to kill you, got it?" I ask, poking him in the chest.

He nods quickly, agreeing to my terms. I just hope that I don't have to sharpen my sword.

"You can stay here until my dad is able to find the culprit." Either my dad will find someone else to blame, or he will come for Adrian; either way, he can stay until then. It will be nice to have someone from home staying with me. It might even begin to feel normal.

"Thanks, Scar," he says sincerely. I give him a forced smile.

Meredith starts to come back to awareness, so I turn the TV off. I throw the phone back down, as I am quick enough; if she tries to reach for it, I can stop her.

I run into the kitchen, grabbing a knife and a chair. I walk back into the living area, sticking my tongue out at Adrian who is rolling his eyes at me. I turn the chair around, the back facing Meredith, and straddle it, waiting for her to wake fully.

When Meredith's eyes finally flutter open, they flick around the room before her face contorts to show her pain. She groans and clutches her arm which has a deep blue line.

"What the fuck happened?" Her eyes finally fall onto me and Adrian, realization dawning on her face.

"Hi," I greet her, waving the knife in my hand. Her eyes fall onto the moving blade, her eyes widening in fright.

"What did you do to me?" she asks, her eyes going to Adrian before continuing. "Am I like you?"

"What? A demon?" I ask, amused.

She nods.

I burst out laughing, Adrian joining in with me.

"What?" she snaps.

"The transition process is long and complex. It involves drinking the blood of a demon, which you haven't. You then need to drink the blood of six humans in six days, so you have it in your system when you die. After you have died, you complete the process by drinking a soul's blood. If you don't drink the soul's blood, you'll be stuck in a limbo place, and apparently, it's not so nice there. If you drink too little blood before you die, it doesn't work, and it's the same if you don't die, at all or in the six days," I explain to her. "See? Complicated."

Some demons make humans go through the process without them knowing; they put the demon and human blood in their food or drink, and they never know that they've had it. The demon then kills them, and the human then does the rest because they don't want to go to limbo.

"Oh," Meredith says.

I smile, pointing the knife down at her.

"Now, I have a knife, as you can see, and I don't really want to dispose of a body. Are you going to cooperate and make this easier for me so I don't have to kill you and worry about getting rid of your body?" I ask her.

"What do you want to know?" she asks shakily.

"How do you know me?"

"You're Reid's girlfriend," she replies.

"Hm. Not going to cut it. Well, it might your carotid artery," I tell her, reaching down to pull her up to face me. I press the knife against the skin of her neck. Her eyes widen, looking to Adrian frantically for help.

"Don't look at me. I can't stop her. Scar can't be stopped when she has a goal," he tells her matter-of-factly.

"Okay, okay," she pleads, a tremor in her voice as I press harder with the knife. I pull the knife back gradually, taking it off her skin.

"When I was still in the Grim Reapers, I was going to deal with a payment issue. When I arrived, I saw you and a man talking to the person I needed to talk to. I waited a minute, and things started to get more heated. You grabbed him by the neck with the same face as earlier, and then all three of you disappeared. Nobody believed me when I told them, and after that, people thought I was crazy. Reid was angry because I hadn't retrieved the payment and didn't trust me after that. You were younger then, but I recognized your face all the same," she explains.

I must have been helping my dad. A tip: never break a deal with Hades. I look over my shoulder, sending Adrian a sweet smile.

"Adrian, would you be a dear and leave?" I ask.

He sends me a quizzical look. I drop Meredith to the floor and turn more.

"You thought that the bagged stuff that has been in my cupboard for a while was good...It's much stronger from the source," I say. Adrian narrows his eyes at me.

"Just don't kill her."

"Aw, why not?" I pout.

Meredith lets out an eardrum-piercing scream as she tries to scramble away from me with her injured arm. I get up from the chair and step into her path. I grab a handful of her hair, bringing her to her knees. I look back up to Adrian, motioning to the stairs with the knife. He sighs but leaves. I turn back to Meredith.

"Listen here, bitch. If you tell anyone about our little conversation or what you saw, I will personally hunt you down and finish what I have started," I threaten.

I don't compel her yet, wanting the fear to sit with her for a while longer. She nods vigorously, telling me silently she'll go along with it. I lift the knife up, dragging it down her face on the side of her face which is scar-free. Now she will have an identical scar on the other side of her face. Her screams fill the room as blood erupts from the fresh wound.

"A constant reminder of what I told you today," I tell her before dropping her back to the floor into a crumpled, sobbing mess.

Chapter 24

No One Likes a Snitch

I rub my temple as Meredith's cries still fill the room. She has been like this for the past five minutes, and I am getting bored of it.

"Gods, pull yourself together," I tell her. "You're meant to be a gang leader."

She glares up at me through the blood, the best she can, but her sobs slowly ebb away. She hiccups as I hear heavy footsteps making their way up the drive. I walk to Meredith, holding my hand over her mouth, silently telling her to stay quiet. I had already cleaned and returned the knife, so I have nothing to threaten with her. All the same, Meredith seems to comply. I listen closely, hearing them stop outside the door. I cock my head to the side, wondering who could be out there.

"Adrian," I call. Almost immediately, he is standing at the top of the stairs. The doorbell rings followed by knocking. "Look after her while I deal with whoever is at the door," I request.

He runs down the stairs and takes my place. I go to the entrance hall but realize that it could look a bit weird if I were covered in blood. I quickly sprint up the stairs, taking them two at a time. I enter my room, grabbing up a dressing gown on my way to the bathroom. I take my clothes off, scrubbing at the blood stains all over my body, getting rid of any traces of blood.

Another ring of the bell sounds impatiently, followed by knocking, again. I run my hair under the water before running back down the stairs, shouting as I go, "I'm coming!"

I enter the entrance hall, closing the door I usually keep open behind me. I pull the front door open, balking slightly when I see two male cops standing there. "Can I help you?" I ask, slight surprise in my tone.

"Sorry, Miss, but are your parents home?" the older of the two asks.

"I live alone," I tell them. Both of their eyes travel over my body in the flimsy gown before looking to each other, obviously uncomfortable.

"We received some complaints about screaming coming from this house, and one person reports seeing you carrying a body into the house," the younger of the two tells me, his eyes trailing to my bare legs before returning to my face.

The only person who saw me with Meredith was Rosie. I force a confused expression to my face, pursing my lips. My act falters, however, when Meredith shouts out.

"Help me!" I try not to flinch and keep my expression calm; however, on the inside, I am silently cursing at Adrian, shouting at him to keep her quiet.

"What was that?" the older of the two asks, his hand going to the gun on his hip. I quickly think of an excuse, forcing yet another fake expression onto my face.

"Ugh, sorry, my brother is visiting and he's watching a horror film currently. That probably explains the screams being heard. I'll tell him to turn it down," I say, the fake annoyance seeping into my tone. Their body language is still guarded and tense.

"Why didn't he come and answer the door?" the young cop questions.

I sigh, getting irritated at all the questions, but I still keep my tone pleasant.

"Because he's lazy," I tell them. They both let out a chuckle, letting their body relax.

"Miss, would we be able to come in and have a look around? I'm sure there is nothing, but it's standard procedure." I look over the cops' shoulders and to Rosie's house, wondering if my suspicion on her calling the cops is true. I catch the curtains on the top floor twitching and a glimpse of Rosie peeking through them. I smirk, looking back to the men on my doorstep.

"Yeah, sure," I say, pulling the door open wider, hoping that Adrian has been listening and is ready for us. I turn, opening the door to the rest of the house and walk in confidently. They follow after me, looking around the open-plan living room and kitchen. I mimic their actions. There is no sign of Meredith or any evidence of what has been happening. Adrian, who is now slouching on the couch, watching a horror movie on full blare, looks up when he sees us. My shoulders sag. What would I do without him?

"Adrian, turn it down. The neighbors think we are torturing someone," I chastise.

"Ugh. Fine," he says reluctantly, playing the role of a lazy brother, picking the remote up and turning it back to a more manageable volume.

"We'll only be a minute," the cops tell me before starting their search of the house.

"Take your time," I tell them, happy that they won't find anything. Although, I keep an eye on them when they're in the kitchen, but luckily, they skip over the cupboard under the sink before moving on.

I flop down on the couch next to Adrian, resting my head on the back.

"That was a close call." Looking over the back of the couch, I see that Adrian even thought to pick up the blood bag that I flung there.

"I don't think I've moved so fast in my life," he tells me.

I laugh and poke him in the side.

"You did it, though...Where is she?" I ask, looking around for any signs. A blood trail, an arm, anything.

"I knocked her out and put her under the cushions," he tells me, nodding to the couch we are sitting on. That explains Adrian sprawling out on top of it; he is trying to hide the bulge. I laugh, watching the movie that Adrian has put on.

Like the cops said, it only takes them a couple of minutes to conclude that there is nothing suspicious. I turn on my seat, leaning over the back.

"Everything okay?" I ask.

They nod, and I smile at them.

"Do you mind me asking which house reported the body sighting?" I ask.

"I'm sorry, but we can't supply you that information."

"That's okay. I'm just wondering because I think the house over the road and a couple down has something fishy going on there," I tell them, referring to Rosie's house. They exchange a significant look before they turn back to me.

"Like what?"

"Narcotics. When I first moved here, they gave me these brownies, and I'm sure they were 'special' brownies if you know what I meant...I threw them away, scared to eat them," I lie (I ate them, and they were delicious), putting emphasis on the word *special.* "If it was that house, they were probably hallucinating when I came home," I add.

"We'll go and check it out," they promise.

I stand up and round the couch. I walk to the door with them, opening it. "That's the house," I tell them, pointing at Rosie's house. They exchange another significant look before turning back to me when they have exited my house.

"Thank you, Miss. Have a good night."

I breathe another sigh of relief when I close the door behind them.

"Right, I'm going to dry my hair and change, and then I'm going to deal with Meredith," I tell Adrian as I enter the open plan area.

"Why did you say that?" Adrian asks, looking over the back of the couch, the horror movie still playing on the TV.

"Why did I say what?" I ask.

"The stuff about the brownies."

"Why do you care? She was being nosy, and it will teach her a lesson to mind her own business and not to snitch. Anyway, she won't get arrested if she didn't do anything wrong, will she?" I say, stopping on the stairs.

"I thought it was unnecessary, and you're right," he says with a shrug.

After I dry my hair and change into something more comfortable, I walk back downstairs to find that Adrian has retrieved Meredith from her hiding place and has sat her up in an armchair, her head flopped forward. I step in front of her, leaning her head back so I can slap her a couple of times to wake her.

She jolts awake, her eyes going around the room. Like last time, when she sees she's in the same place with Adrian and me still here, she slumps.

"Come on then, I'm going to take you to the hospital," I tell her, walking into the entrance hall, retrieving my car keys.

"Why are you being nice to me all of a sudden?" she asks warily as if at any moment I could attack her again. I ignore her question as I come back into the living area.

"Are you coming? If you try anything at all, I *will* kill you without any hesitation," I tell her, gripping her arm tightly, causing a cry of pain. I look down and see that I am holding the injured one. I yank her up and to the front door. I open it, peeking out to see if there are any witnesses, especially the cops. I see that they are still on the street somewhere but not in sight.

I quickly lead her to my car, bundling her in it. As I walk around the back to get the driver's side, I glance at Rosie's house to find a man being escorted out of the house in handcuffs by the two police officers who visited me earlier. I wasn't expecting that.

Reversing out of the drive, I see that Rosie is standing in her open door, her arms crossed with a worried expression on her face. I send her a small wave as I go past her.

"Look into my eyes," I say, looking away from the road and at Meredith. I don't know if this will work with both of her eyes being wounded and me not being able to compel Reid earlier, but it's worth a shot. She turns her stained red face to me, the blood starting to dry.

"When we get to the hospital, you will not be able to remember what happened to you tonight. If someone asks you what happened to you tonight, you will lie. After leaving the hospital, the memory of tonight will come back and stay with you as long as you live. If you go to tell someone, or they ask what happened, the pain you felt tonight will come back to you, and you will be unable to tell them. After death, this will not apply. Do you understand?" I tell her, covering all my bases and making sure when she eventually comes to Hell she will fear me.

"Yes," she replies in a sort of daze. It sounds like it has worked, but I will check at the hospital just to be sure.

I look back on the road, resting my head against the window; it's been a long day.

When I eventually pull into the hospital dropping-off bay ten minutes later, I turn to Meredith.

"Oh gods! What happened to you?" I ask faking shock and concern. A quizzical expression comes onto her face before she replies in a slightly robotic voice.

"I fell down some stairs and cut my face on a piece of glass at the bottom."

"Go and get yourself sorted out," I tell her, satisfied that the compulsion worked. She clambers out of the car, and as soon as the door is closed, I drive off, not wanting any witnesses of me arriving with Meredith.

***

On Monday, when my alarm goes off, I groan, not wanting to go back to school after the weekend. Yesterday felt like I was back home again with Adrian and I messing around in the house. It felt even more like home when Adrian tried to bake some cookies and set the kitchen alight.

"Shut up that fucking thing already!" Adrian shouts from the other side of the house. I turn it off and roll out of bed reluctantly, landing on the floor with a thud. I let out another groan, this time from the pain, and push myself up. I stumble into the closet, picking out the first outfit that I see.

After I am dressed and have consumed two bags of blood, I call up to Adrian.

"I'm going now. Don't do anything I wouldn't do!" I pick up my bag as I make my way to the front door.

"I don't care!" I hear Adrian call back.

"Love you too!" I snigger as I make my way out of the house. Adrian hates waking up more than I do.

Getting to my bike, I stow my bag into the compartment, straddling the bike as I go to push the helmet over my head. I stop however when I hear a text come into my phone. I shift, pulling the phone from my pocket.

Reid: Are you free later? - The incredibly hot leader.

I smile at Reid's text message, replying.

Scar: That depends...

Reid: On what?

Scar: On what we're going to do – I don't think I can deal with another gang war. One is enough for me.

Reid: I only want to spend time with my extremely sexy girlfriend. We don't even need to go out. We could get hot and sweaty together.

I raise my eyebrows at his response.

Scar: I don't sleep with someone that I've known for a short while.

Reid: I didn't mean that, but now that you mention it... ;)

Scar: Right! I believe you, many wouldn't. So what did you have in mind?

Reid: We could train together.

Scar: OK. I'll come over after school. Get ready to have you ass kicked. :)

I put my phone away and start the engine of my bike to get to school.

***

I walk through the doors to the bell ringing. I make my way to homeroom slowly, thinking about the weekend and wondering what happened to Meredith as I walk through the empty corridors. I'm about to go into room 212 when I hear Hunter call my name. I turn to find him, Leo, Liam, and Jake standing down the hallway, looking as if they were waiting for me.

"Want to ditch?" Hunter asks. "I'll even supply the cigarettes."

"How can I turn down that offer?" I joke, turning to walk down the stairs again and out of the building to the tree where Hunter and I sat on my first day.

When we are all sitting under the shade of the leaves, Hunter passes the pack to me, holding the lighter out ready. I take one, holding it out for him to light as I pass the pack on. I thank him as I bring the cigarette to my lips.

"So, how did you all become part of the Grim Reapers?" I ask.

They exchange glances before Leo answers.

"We were all 'head hunted,' if you could call it that, by Reid."

"Were you all friends before?" I ask.

They nod. "Since childhood," Liam adds.

I look at the glowing end of the cigarette as it goes quiet again.

"Where did you learn to shoot like that?" Liam asks.

I press my lips, needing to be careful on how I answer. I can't give too much away.

"My dad taught me," I say, telling them the truth.

"What did your mother think when she found out?" Jake asks.

I clear my throat, taking another drag of the cigarette. I rarely talk about my mother, as I don't get the chance. My dad doesn't like talking about her. I meet Hunter's eyes, which are sending me a sympathetic look.

"Um, she doesn't know," I tell them with a sad smile. "I've never met her." I consider her as dead, as I don't know better; my dad has never said what happened to her. The only things I know about her are her name (Candice) and that she was once human before my dad turned her before she had me.

Sensing the discomfort I am feeling about the topic, Liam intervenes, changing the topic.

"We had a couple of Fallen Angels at the house this morning," he comments. This grabs my attention.

"What did they want?" I ask, thinking back to last night and my compulsion. Did it wear off?

"Meredith had gone missing and then returned with a fresh cut on her face, a broken wrist, and a wound to the back of her head. They were there because she was last heard from by her second-in-command talking about you," Liam explains.

"Did they say anything else?" I ask, worried.

"Nope, they just wanted to know if you were responsible and if the orders came from Reid. Apparently, she kept insisting that she fell down some stairs, but they don't believe her...Did you see her on Saturday?" Jakes says.

"Uh—yeah, I did actually," I tell them, feeling relieved that the compulsion is still firmly in place.

"Did you do it to her?" Leo asks.

"No, I didn't really talk to her. She wasn't hurt when I saw her," I lie.

"I didn't think you did. They are probably just looking for a reason to start something and pinned it on you as you happened to be the last person she was talking about," Hunter speaks up.

I agree with him, but I can tell that they know that I haven't told them the whole truth.

Chapter 25

Wanted

When I walk into Psychology, I am surprised that nothing extraordinary has happened yet. I expected Reid, or someone else, to show up, which seems easy to do, or Tiffany to start something, but no. It's been a normal, boring school day.

I sit down behind the desk, between Tasha and Lottie, waiting for Kyle to arrive. When he walks in, I can feel his gaze on me. I look up and meet his penetrating, dark eyes. He breaks the connection as he turns to the board, writing out something. I notice that the muscles in his shoulders are tense, letting me know that he's worried about something. I narrow my eyes at him when he addresses us.

"Hello, class. Instead of a lesson today, the principal has asked us all to collect in the hall, so I have written a homework assignment on the board for you to do to hand in next lesson."

I listen as the scratches of pen on paper fills the room, but I don't move, still watching Kyle. Something's up with him. Did my dad tell him about Adrian?

When there is silence once again in the room, Kyle tells us all to make our way to the hall for the assembly. As the whole class leaves, with Kyle leading the way, I try and catch up with him to ask him what's wrong. Whenever he hears me closing in on him, he speeds up, and soon, I lose him in the crowd. Why is he avoiding me? I give up going after him and walk back to Tasha and Lottie.

"I wonder why the principal is going to talk to us," Tasha ponders aloud. I shrug as we enter the hall, keeping an eye out for Kyle, but I don't see him.

"Lottie!" Max calls, standing up from where he is sitting with Lily. Behind them both are Hunter, Leo, Jake, and Liam. Lottie runs up to Max, hugging him with a kiss. Tasha and I follow behind, meeting an exasperated-looking Lily.

"Finally! I couldn't take sitting with them alone any longer," she says, looking back at where Hunter and his friends are. I look behind her as well, where they are all grinning.

"They are pretty annoying," I say loud enough to catch their attention.

"Oi!" Leo complains.

"Everyone, settle down!" the principal, an African-American woman in her late twenties, commands loudly from where she is standing in front of a screen. Her hair is wild and curly, and her eyes are hidden behind a pair of glasses. I sit down in front of Jake and Hunter, and next to Tasha. Jake lets out a loud wolf-whistle, causing chuckles. The principal clears her throat before continuing,

"Some of you may know the new teacher, who has replaced Mr. Jeff, Mr... Kyle. He has an important matter to talk to you all about today, so please give your attention to him."

My eyes fly around the space, trying to find Kyle. My eyes rest on him, and he seems to feel them as he avoids meeting my gaze. I watch as he swallows noticeably. What does he want to talk to us about? Is that why he's been avoiding me?

"Thank you, Principal Kimberly," Kyle says, stepping forward. The principal's heartbeat rises as blood rushes to her cheeks. I raise an eyebrow at the principal's reaction and at what Kyle is doing.

"I have been asked by the school and the police..." A murmur goes around the hall at the mention of the police. Why would Kyle be talking on behalf of the police? "...to let you all know about a situation which you may hear about in the news."

I narrow my eyes as he clicks a button. A situation that the police want us to know about is not going to anger me, and Kyle knows that. He clicks a button on the remote in his hand, turning slightly so he can look at his audience and the screen.

I take my gaze off Kyle and look at the screen, only to let out a gasp when I see a face there. What the hell is he doing? Finally, Kyle meets my gaze to gauge my reaction. I show him a blank expression. I was wrong. The police have nothing to do with this.

I feel Jake lean down to whisper to me, still staring at the screen shocked. "Hey, little devil, isn't that the guy you know?" he asks.

I nod, not able to get anything out as I continue to stare at Adrian's face. How the fuck did Kyle get this photo anyway? Adrian was giving the camera a sadistic smile, and it looks as if this photo has been taken from a long distance away. This is all my dad's doing.

"The police are looking for this man, who they believe is going by the name Adrian. However, they believe this to be an alias. I cannot stress enough how dangerous this man is, so if anyone of you so much as encounter someone looking like him, you are to tell the police or any of us. We believe he may have reason to come to the school," he tells us, looking directly at me as he talks. He ignores the murmurs traveling through the hall again as he carries on, "So, for the meantime, until he is caught, there will be security officers situated around the school."

I cross my arms. My dad won't let me know what is going on, but he'll have security placed around the school to make sure that I am safe.

"What has this guy done?" I call out, not able to stay silent any longer, feeling the need to defend Adrian. Shouts of agreement come from other students. Kyle looks mildly surprised at me but answers my question in human-safe words.

"He was arrested for first-degree murder and escaped last week."

An audible gasp sounds from the students.

"There is no reason to be scared. This guy will be caught," Kyle says loudly, his eyes traveling over the room before resting back on me. "The advice is to stay in…"

"Why didn't we hear about it in the news yet?" I ask, wanting to pick at the holes in his story, standing up. I don't get why my dad has to include humans in on the search.

"Ms. Hades, please sit down. The police did not want unnecessary panic. They are making it public knowledge tomorrow," Principal Kimberly says.

"Why are you telling us then?" I ask, putting my hands on my hips and staying standing.

"So you don't get scared if you see any of the security around the school, which will be put in place tomorrow," she replies with a sigh.

I fall back down onto the seat, a smile now on my face, happy that I'm not making it too easy for them.

"Continue," I tell them, waving my hand at them. But before they can say another word, someone else shouts out.

"Who is this person after? You said that he had reason to come to this school. He was here the other day," she says.

Kyle's posture shifts and he raises an eyebrow in false interest, already knowing the reason. "Really?"

"Yeah, so who is this guy after?" the person asks again.

"Who was he talking to the other day?" the principal asks, stepping forward, showing her concern.

I stand up slightly, looking for the person who is talking. When I find them, I give them my scariest glare, tilting my head to the side slightly as if to say, 'Try it.'

She squeaks and answers in a little voice, "I don't know."

"We can't supply the details of the interested party, for their safety, but the security is just a precaution put in by the police. The person is aware and can take care of her—themselves."

By *police*, Kyle means my dad. I sit back, trying to take everything in. My dad must really want Adrian, and he must have something to go off if he's willing to make it public. I feel a tap on my shoulder and shift to see Hunter's face by mine.

"Hey, is he staying with you?"

"No," I snap defensively. "Why?"

"Because if he was, I'm sure Reid would be able to sort something out for him. But as he's not…"

I turn to look at him fully, getting a knowing look.

"Ask him later. You have a date tonight, right?"

***

As I drive home, I think about how my dad is getting what I assume to be some of his guards to come up and protect me, risking exposure, all for one person—Adrian. Doubts about my decision to harbor him run through my mind as I pull onto the drive. I put the car in park but stay sitting there for a moment, just looking up at my house.

Do I believe Adrian? I trust my dad and Kyle and their judgment, but then again, I know when Adrian is lying. Would I be able to let go of what I have up here so soon if need be? I know at some point I need to leave Earth, but I've not even been up here for a month, and I have the threat of being exposed. I sigh and move it out of my mind; I don't need to think about it yet. I put on a smile and then get out of the car. I walk up to the door and throw it open.

"Honey, I'm home!" I shout.

"I've missed you so much. Never leave me again!" he says, charging into me, his arms wrapping themselves around me. I tap him on the back, laughing awkwardly.

"Okay, let me go now," I tell him. "It's getting awkward."

"No, it's not," he responds, not moving from his position. I take action and push him back. He joins me in laughing and moves back. His smile disappears when he sees my face.

"What happened?" he asks, no sign of the joke we shared moments ago as his face goes serious.

"Nothing," I tell him, forcing cheeriness into my voice.

"Scar, you can't lie to me."

Can you, though?

"I'm not," I reply, moving around him, meaning I don't have to look at him anymore.

"Did your dad find out?" he asks.

"No…Maybe…I don't know. They've made the search for you public, meaning you can't really go out without being found. Adrian…there must be proof if they are this desperate to find you. Are you sure that you have told me everything?" I ask, voicing my worries.

He nods, but that doesn't ease them. I look at him suspiciously for a second. Has he been lying to me the whole time?

I move on. "I'm going out. I'll be back later," I tell him, walking up the stairs. I am halfway up the stairs when I hear Adrian call my name. I wait for him to tell me something he forgot or kept from me.

"Scar, I know you don't believe me fully. I haven't given you a reason to, but I promise you that I will. I have always been, and will always be, loyal to you and your dad. You can trust me," he says sincerely.

I force a smile and nod, letting him know that I've acknowledged what he said. I continue up the rest of the stairs, heading to my room. I arrive in my closet and pick out a pair of shorts and a tank top, changing out of my clothes and into them. I pull my hair up to the top of my head, where I secure it in a messy bun. I grab a bag, stocking it with all the things I could possibly need and my phone. After pulling on a pair of trainers and slipping my sunglasses onto my nose, I walk back down the stairs. I find Adrian sitting in the living room, watching the TV again. I leave without saying goodbye.

***

Driving to Reid's, I blast the music on the radio, singing along to the ones I recognize and mumbling along to the rest. When I pull up outside the obvious gates, I lean out of the window, pressing the button on the box so I can enter. A buzz sounds, followed by a voice.

"State your name and reason for being here," a cold voice says.

He sounds like fun!

"Father Christmas, and I'm here to give you coal for being a bad boy," I reply in the same tone of voice, trying to hold in my laughter.

"Are you taking the piss?" he asks, getting angry.

"No, I'm taking all your presents," I say back, struggling to keep my laughter at bay.

"Okay, please leave, or we *will* make you," he threatens.

"I'd like to see you try. I'm just joking with you. You know a joke? They usually make you laugh," I say.

I get silence in response. *I was right—he's a bundle of joy!*

"You still there?" I ask, worried that he disconnected. In response, I get the same silence, but then it's followed by two words.

"Yes…Unfortunately."

"I'm Scar. You might know me…I'm the big guy's girlfriend," I explain.

"Come in," he says, returning to the cold voice.

"Great talking to you. I can't wait until the next time," I call out as I start to drive up to the house. I stop the car outside the front door, pushing the lever to put it in park. As I get out, I see that the grass is similar to the first time I came, scattered with people out enjoying the sun.

"Who's the guy that answers the gates?" I ask anyone who is listening and willing to answer.

"Why?" a girl asks, stopping on her way into the house. She wears a pair of shorts and a white crop top which contrasts against her mocha skin. Her eyes were dark, but her hair, however, was carrying shades of purple. It suits her.

"He needs to learn to take a joke."

She laughs, walking back down the steps to stop beside me.

"That's Clive for you," she tells me with a shrug. "I'm Bianca, by the way."

"I'm..." I start, going to introduce myself, but she beats me to it.

"Scar, I know. I was there yesterday. It'll be fun to have another girl who will give Reid a hard time. We can't let him get off lightly," she says with a wink.

"Do you know where he is?"

"I don't, but I don't have anything else better to do. I'll help you look," she says, walking back toward the house ahead of me. I follow behind her, a smirk on my lips. I like her already.

Chapter 26

Gang Leader Vs. Maze

As we walk around the house searching for Reid, we exchange facts about each other. I learn that she is nineteen and has been with the gang for as long as it has been around. We pause outside the stairs down to the gym, having too much fun to go down yet. Bianca has started telling me about some embarrassing moments in Reid's life, and I don't want them to stop yet.

"One day, about four years ago, there was a fair in town, and some of us decided that we wanted to go. Reid tagged along, and deep down, I knew he wanted to go as much as the rest of us. We arrived, went on a couple of rides, and were having a great time. At some point, Reid saw that they had a mirror maze, but this one was mostly clear panels. Reid, being Reid, decided that we should all go through to test our 'navigation skills.' I think this was just an excuse to show off. So, anyway, we all went in," she says, stepping forward and opening the door leading down to the gym.

As we start to descend the stairs, she continues with her story. "All of the gang went through with ease, and then it came to

Reid and me. We entered and started off at a fast pace, however, when we got to the middle, we got stuck. I'm not sure what happened next, but I think it was because we had our backs to each other, looking for the gap. I found it and continued on, thinking that Reid was behind me. I exited the maze and looked back to find that Reid was still stuck in the same place. He looked around to find me, confused, and when he found me, I could feel the embarrassment and anger coming off him from behind the many partitions of plastic. He was stuck there for about two minutes more, still trying to find the gap. He was the last one in the maze, and no one would go back through to help him, so we all just watched laughing."

I let out a loud laugh, imagining Reid stuck there. "To make it even worse, a girl who could have only been eight probably saw him struggling and decided to rub it in even more. She entered the maze, walked through it with ease, Reid trying to follow closely behind her, and exited walking off without looking back. However, at some point, Reid must have not seen where she went because he got lost again. He was so close to the exit but couldn't find the gap. At this point, I had tears streaming down my face. Reid was shown up by a girl twelve years younger. Eventually, the attendant saw what was happening." She stops as we get to the door of the gym, her laughter stopping her from talking.

Once she was calm, she continues, "And he walked into the maze from the exit, putting his hand through the gap Reid needed to go through. I could barely stand with how much I was laughing. It was his idea to show our 'navigational skills,' and he failed miserably as he walked out with a murderous look on his face. The attendant chuckled as well, with Reid getting madder before he stormed off—"

"And I remember after that telling you to never speak of it again," Reid says from behind us, his voice hard.

I try and stop my laughter but fail as I turn to look at Reid, not wanting to make it worse.

"Aw, was the big bad gang leader embarrassed?" I ask him in a baby voice.

"No," he responds, crossing his arms. I move back around, looking around the training room to find that it's empty apart from two people using the apparatus around the room. Reid's arms wrap around me from behind as he rests his chin on top of my hair.

"Are you going to allow me to kiss you today?" he mutters, squeezing his arms tighter around me.

"Hm…Maybe," I say as if I am thinking about it. I turn around in his arms, looking up at him. He leans down, hesitating as he gets closer like he is expecting me to pull back from him. When I don't do anything, he continues down. I mentally cross my fingers, hoping my dad didn't lie to me.

His lips reach mine without a cluck, not even a small one. I smile, kissing him back eagerly. I rest my arms on his shoulder, losing myself in the kiss, forgetting everything around me except Reid. As our lips begin to move faster and the kiss becomes more passionate, my hands going into Reid's hair, Bianca interrupts us, making us pull apart.

"Okay," she says, extending the vowel sound. "At least wait until you're alone to rip each other's clothes off. I don't want that vision imprinted in my mind for the rest of my life."

I detangle my fingers from his hair, moving back slightly from Reid, but he pulls me back to him by the hips, his lips going to my neck.

"We'll finish this later," he mumbles before placing a small kiss there. He lets go of me and pulls back completely. I turn to Bianca to find her looking at her phone.

"I should go, but come find me later?" she asks, aiming it at me.

"Of course," I tell her, smiling. She returns the smile.

"I'll tell you some more about Reid," she says with a wink.

Reid exclaims out at her, warning her not to.

"Later," Bianca calls over her shoulder as she starts back up the stairs. I can already tell that Bianca and I will be great friends; she reminds me of myself.

"You ready for your ass to be kicked?" I challenge Reid, walking backward to the mat in the middle of the room. He grins, moving after me.

"Don't you mean 'mine' when you said that?" he counters.

Dream on, Reid. Dream on. Even without the extra strength and speed I have, I could beat him. I've been trained my whole life by the best people in the universe; Athena was even one of my mentors for a short while. If he thinks he can beat the training given to me by the goddess of war strategy, then he has another thing coming.

Chapter 27

Don't Hold Back

Now both on the mat, we face each other. I throw my bag and sunglasses to the side, stretching my neck and other muscles, trying to loosen up.

"Shall we start with hand-to-hand combat?" Reid suggests as he shakes his arms out.

"Yeah, sure. Then we can move onto the weapons." I look at the wide array of weapons on the wall with a grin. Reid's eyebrows rise, but he doesn't object.

I wait for him to make the first move, but a minute has passed, and he still hasn't. I sigh, knowing that he's hesitant because I'm a girl. It's useful sometimes, but not right now when I want him to fight me. I swing my arm through the air a lot slower than I am used to, trying to connect with his face, but he moves back, evading.

When he steps toward me, his right hand moves forward in a weak punch. I chuckle, bringing my hand up to block it, swinging around, kicking him in the side much gentler than I do at home, not wanting to seriously injure him

"I guess I don't need to go easy on you then," he comments, following it with a quicker, stronger punch to my stomach. I bend over as if in pain, causing Reid to stop his assault and move toward me in concern, asking if I am alright in a worried tone.

I watch his feet, and when he's close enough, I flash him a victorious smile, hooking my leg around his, pulling it, making him fall to the ground. I fall with him, my legs going either side of his body. I lean down and whisper in his ear, "Looks like I don't need to go easy on you either. I guess I'll stop then."

His hands rest on my hips, a cheeky grin on his face. "I like this position."

"Hm?" I ask amused, leaning down for a kiss, but before I can make contact, he's flipped us, my hands now pinned under his, above my head.

I bring my head up quickly, head-butting him. He groans, his hands leaving my hands to go to his face as he falls backward. I slip out from under him, jumping to my feet. With a light kick to his chest, he falls back onto his back. I press my foot down, applying a small amount of pressure to keep him there.

"Give up yet?" I ask.

He struggles for a bit before eventually stopping. "Yeah," he sighs.

Triumphant, I take my foot off his chest, reaching down to help him up.

"Another round?" he asks, his eyes becoming determined.

"Of course, I'm just getting warmed up."

He doesn't give me time to prepare myself as he brings a leg up. I appreciate how fast and strong he is as I watch the leg moving toward me. When I realize that I am getting distracted with ogling him, I block his kick.

***

After two more rounds of me beating Reid, he has let all of the thoughts go out of his head about being gentle with me, not caring if he hurts me. I can see it in his eyes. He just wants to win one. It's extra embarrassing for him, as members have started to crowd around the mat, cheering us on. He doesn't want to lose to a girl; it would affect not only his ego but his credibility with the gang. Knowing this, I allow Reid to beat me in this round. I "accidentally" leave it too late to block a kick to my right side, causing me to "stumble" to the left. With the time it takes me to stumble, Reid is able to reach out and grab my left arm across his body, spinning me into his chest. His arm comes up to my throat, applying some pressure, his left arm holding my arm up against my chest, allowing him to hold onto them both. He pins me there for a second, causing cheers to erupt from the gang members at their leader winning a round. Reid kisses me on the cheek before he lets me go. I purse my lips and nod in approval, not expecting that.

"Time for weapons, I think," Reid says sweat pouring down his face and wetting his shirt, his ego reinstated. I wipe my forehead as I nod. It's a lot harder than I thought it would be, especially with me straining to keep my muscles at human capabilities.

I follow behind Reid, through the crowd, and to the weapon wall. Sparring against guards my whole life, I eventually got used to all different kinds of weapons, and I was able to beat them all at every weapon by the time I was ten. I would be able to beat Kyle on a good day, but I've still never beaten my dad.

I examine the array of weapons that Reid has, noting that some of them look more unused than others. I know Reid is handy with a knife from Meredith's scar, so I decide to see just how handy he is. Reid seems to be waiting for my decision before he chooses one himself. I exclude any weapon which is not a knife as I examine each knife closely. I reach out, pulling a knife with a five-and-half-inch blade off the wall. I flip it in my hands a couple of times, testing the weight in my hand. Once I am happy, I send a smug smile in Reid's direction.

He nods in approval, picking a knife off the wall also.

"Don't hold back," I taunt, skipping back to the mat. I turn on my heel, widening my stance. I tuck a strand of my hair which fell out of my bun behind my ear as I take in Reid opposite me.

He acts quickly, bringing the knife up and through the air. I dodge it, bringing my leg around as I move, trying to kick him or knock him over, but he catches it, pulling sharply.

I stumble onto the floor. Seeing that Reid is not waiting around, I quickly flip backward on my hands, so I am standing again, missing Reid's slash at me with the knife just in time.

I cock my head to the side and grin; he *is* good with a knife. I twirl the knife in my hands, so the knife is sticking up in my fist. I raise it, going to slam the end of the handle against his skull. His hand meets my wrist, squeezing it tightly. My grip loosens on the knife, sending it clattering to the ground. Reid kicks it to the side, bringing my hand around my back, twisting it at an angle. His knife rises, and he presses it against my neck.

"I think I won," he says smugly.

I relax, hoping to make him think that I am giving up. When it has the desired effect, getting Reid to pull the knife away from my neck and to loosen his grip on my arm, I don't hesitate. I take the opportunity, lifting my hands and flipping Reid over me.

He lands on the floor, the air getting knocked out of his chest. I see the knife and decide to give them a show. I go down into a cartwheel, grabbing the knife as I go, so when I am upright again, I am holding the knife over Reid. I lower down, pretending to go and stab him, stopping the knife so the tip is a millimeter away from his heart.

His shocked eyes meet mine. The room has gone deathly silent. Happy with my victory and making a point, I bring it up. Slowly, a small smile creeps onto his face. He motions with his hand, his eyes still on me.

"How can you deal with multiple attackers?" he asks.

I can sense it before it happens. A man from the side runs at me using another knife as his weapon. I lean down, giving a quick kiss to Reid, mumbling against his lips that he is really testing me. I spring to my feet, ready to face my attackers.

The man running at me lifts his knife to strike at me, but I block him with ease. I move to retaliate as I kick one of the other men running at me. I send a knee into the balls of the man in front of me as I turn to deal with the third attacker. As I turn, I haven't judged how close they are to me. As he keeps running and I step around, the momentum keeps him coming, causing the knife in his hand to sink into my stomach. A look of fear and shock slowly emerges onto the man's face as I cry out in pain. I look back at him with the same expression. How am I going to explain this to Reid and the others? It's going to heal much quicker than it would with any human. It won't heal straight away, as it was deep, but it will be healed in an hour. If I were human, I would be in serious danger. I fall backward, the knife slipping back out.

"You are a fucking idiot!" Reid seethes out as he runs up to me. I look around at the surrounding gang and see that Hunter and his friends are all near, watching me with worry and confliction on their face. Reid bends down, holding onto my legs and back as he straightens, so he is carrying me.

"I'm fine," I insist weakly.

"Everyone better move if they want to live," he yells dangerously.

They all move without argument. Reid strides out of the room, bounding up the stairs in seconds. I'll let him dress it with a bandage, and it can heal hidden, without him knowing how fast it has. I rest my head on Reid's chest as he runs.

"That was fun. We should do it again sometime," I mumble quietly.

Chapter 28

Is This Some Kind of Sick Joke?

Reid shoves the door to his office open, shifting us to allow us through the doorway. He places me gently on the couch, not stopping as he rushes through the only door I haven't seen behind. Through the small gap in the door, I am able to make out a bathroom.

Reid bends down, rifling through the cabinet, reappearing again with a first aid bag. He moves out of my line of sight, and I hear a tap running. Pulling the door closed forcefully behind him, Reid falls to his knees next to the couch, placing the glass of water and bag beside him. He reaches out and slowly, trying not to hurt me, pulls the bloody tank top up my body to reveal the slash in my stomach.

I breathe in a worried, shuddering breath when I see that the wound is slowly healing. *Just bandage it up and leave it*, I plead with Reid silently. Reid unzips the bag, grabbing a cloth, quickly dipping it in the water, turning back to me. He touches the cold water on my skin, trying to clear some of the blood away to see the full extent of the damage.

"You're crazy if you believe we are going to do that again," he murmurs, looking up at me.

I internally roll my eyes, but on the exterior, I keep my expression blank, not replying. He looks back down at my stomach, slowly working on wiping the blood away.

When he gets close the wound, I breathe in a sharp breath. His apologetic eyes rush up to meet mine whenever this happens. I take the time that it's taking him to clean me to observe him. His brows have a small wrinkle between them, which I want to reach out and smooth away, showing his concern and concentration. His blue eyes come up to meet mine when I look at them.

He smirks before looking back down at my stomach, only for a small frown to replace it. I follow his gaze and see that the wound has almost completely healed, leaving behind a surface cut about two inches long. Oh shit, it healed faster than I expected to.

"I told you it was fine. It didn't go in deep. It was just the angle." The wrinkles between his dark eyebrows deepen and multiply as he scrunches them up in confusion

"B-but I saw the knife. It had blood all over the blade. It went in all the way," he mutters more to himself than to me.

I close my eyes. I have two choices. One: to lie to him and keep him from my secret for longer, causing him to hate me for keeping it from him even more when he finds out. Or two: tell him the truth, risking him to hate me and all his memories of me being wiped again. It could also mean that I have to go back home to Hell, but that's all in the worst case. He could still react the same way he did when he first found out, with admiration and no hate or fear, but he's had his feelings about me at that time wiped from his memory by my dad. It was also in different circumstances; he still had the hormones raging through him from the bite.

I grab his head, pulling him closer to me. I lean forward so our lips are barely touching.

"Whatever I do or say next, please don't hate me," I plead in a whisper, and our lips rub. I don't allow him to answer; I claim his lips in a kiss. It starts off slowly, his soft, supple, rough lips moving over mine. Tingles shoot throughout my body, starting at my lips. Holding onto his neck, not wanting to let him go yet, I happily reciprocate Reid's movements which are getting faster and more passionate. He grunts as my tongue ventures into his mouth. He battles with me, stopping only to suck on my tongue. I let out all of my emotions into the kiss: how I feel about him, how I feel about the situation with Adrian and at home, and how I feel about what I am about to do.

Reid nips at my lip before he travels from my lips, over my face, down my jaw, and to my neck, placing small bites along the way. He searches until he can find my sweet spot. I let out a soft moan, and Reid grins against my neck and places another harder bite. He licks the tender place before pulling back, looking deeply into my eyes.

"I could never and will never hate you. I feel the total opposite actually. That is unless I find out that you're a cop or from a rival gang, then I will hate you for lying and gaining my trust. I don't trust easily, but you seem to be different," he says softly, his hand coming up to stroke my cheek.

I lean my head into his hand, taking a snapshot of this moment and his face, in case it never happens again.

"You still may hate me for what I am about to do," I tell him, looking away from his relaxed and happy face, not wanting the see the trust that is present disappear from them.

"I doubt it very much," he says, reaching out to me, but I move back and away from him. I concentrate for a moment, letting my horns and fangs extend, and feeling my face contorting.

I turn back to Reid, keeping my now red eyes off his blue ones, afraid to see his reaction. When he saw me the first time, it was at the very beginning when I didn't know him as much as I do now. Over the short amount of time that I have known him, I have grown to like him a lot, and if he can accept me for who I am, that would make it all the much better.

Reid blinks a couple of times to make sure he is clear on what he is seeing. Once he has confirmed it's actually happening, he backs away, his warm hand leaving my cheek, the comfort I was feeling from it as he talked also leaving me as well.

"Shit, shit, shit. Did you drug me?" he asks loudly.

"No," I reply with conviction as I try and reach for his hands.

"Then what the fuck is happening? Is this real?" he asks angrily, backing even further away, moving his hands out of my reach to his hair. He runs them through the damp hair repeatedly.

"Reid, you are not drugged or seeing things." I try to placate him.

His eyes meet mine for a moment, looking as if he's thinking something over. His hand goes to the back of his pants, pausing for a moment, almost as if he doesn't want to do it, before pulling the black gun out and aiming it at me. I don't give him any reaction. His finger hovers over the trigger, shaking.

"Is this some kind of sick joke? Did Meredith hire you to make me trust you and then stab me in the back by playing a big joke on me? I should shoot you right now," he spits out.

"You can shoot me. It wouldn't kill me," I tell him. His trigger finger twitches, but his hands are holding the gun weakly, meaning if he did pull it, it could be dangerous for him, and the bullet will not necessarily meet its target, and Reid knows this.

"I thought you wouldn't hate me," I point out getting angry. Why has he changed his opinion on me? He didn't react anything like this the first time. It's almost the total opposite. None of his prior emotions are present on his face.

"That's before you pull this." He waves the gun at me as he speaks.

"It's not a joke. It's real. I have nothing to do with Meredith. I hate that bitch. I was the one to give her the over scar for gods' sake!" I shout.

Reid looks taken aback for a moment before he recovers, shooting a glare in my direction

"I thought I could trust you! Get out. I don't want to see you ever again! You let me kiss you. I kissed a monster!"

I let my body fall back, feeling the hit from his words physically. That hurt, but it was the truth. No one has ever said it, but, of course, he would think I'm a monster, who wouldn't?

"Reid, just let me explain. I don't care if after that you want me to leave, but first, just let me explain..." I say my voice getting a lot quieter. He doesn't object, so I continue.

"You remember the first day we met and the men that you were with said that I was a demon?"

He nods his head slightly. At least he is listening and even responding.

"They weren't lying."

"What the fuck are you talking about? If you can, could you go back to the other face? You're fucking creepy," he says in disgust.

I let out a sad sigh but comply, changing back to my normal face.

"I'm saying that I am a demon," I respond.

"You're mad. Demons don't exist," he says, looking away from me.

I groan, knowing I will need to prove it further. I would have thought that my face would have been enough.

"The cut. You said that you saw the knife sink all the way in. It did. I just have a quicker healing process than any human. You know that it would have been life threatening to me if I was like you," I tell him, pulling the tank top up to show him my skin which is now fully healed.

His face slowly loses the disbelief, revealing that I am getting through to him.

"What's to stop me from telling everyone?" he asks.

"I don't think you'll want to deal with my dad when he's angry," I caution him.

"And why not?" he replies, raising an eyebrow in a challenge.

"Because he's Hades."

"The Greek god?" he asks with a snort.

"You won't remember, but when we had our date, I ended up biting you. I tried to wipe your memories, but it wouldn't work, so I had to take us down to the underworld, my actual home, and have my dad do it. He made it so you forgot what happened, but he also made it so whenever you went to kiss me that day, you would cluck like a chicken. That's why I wouldn't kiss you," I explain, smiling as I remember.

"I hated lying to you, but I was afraid if I told you again, I would get this reaction. I didn't know what the compulsion would do to you. I thought I would never have to tell you and if I did, it would be at a point where you couldn't be angry with me. But now that you know, you can't tell anyone. It could put both of us in danger," I beg with him as I lean toward him.

"I'm used to danger," he says, moving back and going to his feet.

"Reid, promise me you won't tell anyone," I say forcefully, hoping it would get my point across and he wouldn't have any other choice.

He strides to his desk, throwing the gun down there. His shoulders hunch as he grips onto the edge of the desk.

"Get out," he manages to say through gritted teeth.

"I'll know if you tell someone," I tell him. It would be easy to find out, as there would be an uproar from my dad and his siblings, as well as from people on Earth. I storm to the door, rushing out. I let the door slam behind me.

I should have just lied to him, but I couldn't keep it from him any longer. *It's no use now. I've lost him forever,* I think as I walk back, angrily to the entrance hall. I stride through the people who are quickly getting out of my way when they see my expression and make my way to the door, only to be stopped when I hear Bianca calling out.

"Hey, bitch, you didn't forget about me, did you?"

I turn with a sigh. "Sorry, I just…"

She crosses her arms, raising an eyebrow. "What happened?"

Wow, she's good.

"I think Reid and I just broke up," I respond with a frown.

"So *that* was why you were being so loud," she says.

My eyes widen. How much did she hear?

"What? You could hear us?" I ask her, panicking.

"We all could, but not the actual words. I, however, may have come down concerned about you, arriving to hear Reid freaking out, and decided to listen at the door."

"What did you hear?" I ask, my tone going higher, portraying my panic even more.

"Pretty much everything, although, I left when you were getting him to promise he wouldn't tell," she says with a shrug of her shoulders.

"What and you don't think I'm a freak? Reid sure did."

"Yeah, but that's just Reid for you. Reid is hard at trusting people. He'll come around soon enough; his ego will take over as he wants a girlfriend that is as evil as him. I personally think it's quite cool," she tells me, nudging me in the side.

I chuckle, relief washing over me. I now have a friend that I can be one hundred percent honest with.

"You won't tell anyone will you?" I ask.

She shakes her head. "It won't be any fun if you're killed or have to leave."

Just then, Reid walks into the entrance hall. I turn to him, waiting to see what he will be doing.

"I told you to get out," he snaps in my direction when he notices that I am still standing at the entrance.

"I have. You told me to get out of your office," I counter, crossing my arms.

"Get out of *my* house!" he shouts.

"Fine, I'm going!" I shout back. I spin, marching out of the house and to my car. I yank the door open, sliding down into it. I have turned the engine on and am about to pull away when the passenger door opens. I glance over and see Bianca has joined me.

"Nice car," she remarks.

I grin at her, speeding down the drive and out of the gate.

***

"So, how do you survive?" she asks.

"I usually survive off blood, as well as normal food. If I don't drink any blood, after about a week, my demon features will stay on my face until I do. The longer I go without, the more pain I feel. I never get to that point, as there are hundreds of souls I can feed on at home," I explain to her, glancing away from the road.

"So you're like a vampire if they exist?" she asks, fiddling with the radio.

I giggle. "Yeah, they do."

She stops and turns to look at me. "Shut up! Seriously?"

I nod, amused at her enthusiasm.

"Is it true that staking them can kill them?"

I look out of the corner of my eyes, hesitant on what information I give her. "Yes, but only with a certain type of rare wood, so don't rely on it."

"Does it kill you?"

"No."

"What does? You're immortal, right?"

I laugh, shaking my head at her question, silently telling her I'm not going to answer.

"Oh, come on, it's not like I'll be able to do it. You're probably much quicker than me."

I purse my lips and sigh. "Yes, I am. Decapitation," I say.

She looks pleased with me answering before moving onto something else.

"What about garlic for vampires?"

"Would you eat it raw? Also, have you smelt it? If it's bad for you, imagine it for someone with a heightened sense of smell." I chuckle, as I indicate to join the main road. I tap my fingers on the steering wheel, expecting another question from Bianca.

"Sunlight?"

"Myth spread by vampires when they were being hunted. It meant that they could go out and blend in without fear of being found out. However, the myth seems to be seen as true by many vampires, meaning that they stay away." I smile, remembering when my dad was teaching me about the different species and how he humorously recalled that time.

"Iron?"

"Myth. Blood has iron in it. All vampires and demons would be dead if iron were bad for us."

"Holy things?" she asks, pressing the button to put the roof down.

"Vampires and demons can go onto holy grounds, but when you have direct access to the gods, why would you need to? Holy water and crucifixes are other myths spread by vampires which were never passed down. If you're expecting something to hurt you, or do something, you are going to stay away and flinch when it happens to you," I explain.

"So can they, and you, turn others?" she probes, looking out of the side of the car innocently.

I look again at her out of the corner of my eyes. "Yeah...but I'm not turning you, if that's what you are asking," I tell her.

"I was just wondering," she says but looks slightly disappointed.

I hope she's not one of those people who are only friends with me because of what I am. I've had people in the past try and friend me because they want to become immortal. I return my gaze back to the road.

"Yeah...sure you were. Where are we going anyway?" I ask, leaning my elbow on the side of the car.

"I don't know. You tell me. I came and sat in your car. What were you going to do?" she asks.

"I was going to go back to my house," I answer.

"Fine then, let's go home. I can't wait to see it if your car is anything to go by," she says excitedly before reaching for the radio, turning it up, so we are blaring it out as we zoom down the road in the sunshine.

***

When the engine finally stops, she looks up through the windshield.

"I was right. Nice house," she comments. I get out, and she follows me up the drive and to the front door.

"I have a friend staying. He's harmless, I think, but he can be annoying," I warn her as I unlock the door.

"What is he?"

"A demon and he *was* a guard for my dad, so if he does act up, I'll be able to deal with him."

"Was?" Bianca asks, picking up on my use of words.

"Um…Yeah. It's a long story, and I'm not exactly sure, but he has been accused of something," I say, turning to her my hand still on the door of the now unlocked door.

"Do you think he did it?"

"I didn't, but now I'm not so sure," I respond honestly, thinking back to Kyle saying earlier that the search for Adrian is now public.

I enter the small entrance room, poking my head into the living room when I hear moans. I see that Adrian is sitting on the couch, drinking from a girl. I clear my throat to get his attention before walking in to allow Bianca in after me. Adrian looks up at us both, blood surrounding his mouth. I raise my eyebrow at him.

He looks down to my blood-soaked shirt and then up to Bianca, his eyes widening.

"She knows," I tell him.

"She knows?"

"Yes."

The girl sitting on my *white couch*, a wound still on her neck open, whimpers as she tugs on Adrian's arm, showing him to her neck. I roll my eyes at her desperateness.

He knows where your neck is. He's had plenty of experience and practice.

"The fun's over," I tell them.

Adrian shrugs the girl off, looking into her eyes to compel her to forget.

"Sorry about that. I didn't know he had someone," I murmur to Bianca as I watch the girl's eyes haze over and stand up. She walks past Bianca and I and out of my house. Adrian, now with a clean mouth, turns to us, more specifically Bianca.

"So, what's your name hot stuff?" he asks, smirking as he looks Bianca over.

"What's yours?" Bianca counters in a flirty voice.

"Adrian."

"OMG! Same!" she says with fake amazement.

Adrian stares at her for a minute dumbfounded before looking at me, silently asking me if she's okay. I burst out laughing at his face and the fact that he believed her even for a second.

"She's joking," I tell him.

"Yeah, I knew that," he grumbles, crossing his arms.

Bianca joins in with my laughter.

"Bianca. My name is Bianca," she supplies.

"Nice to meet you, Bianca. I hope I'll see a lot more of you," he says taking her hand and giving it a kiss. I pretend to gag.

"Where did you find the girl?" I ask when Adrian has straightened up.

"I went to a club searching for dinner, and she was there drunk and desperate. It was easy."

"You can't just go and find a girl. I have some blood in the house. I also told you not to leave the house."

"I'm free to do what I want," he replies, his voice getting an edge to it. I raise my eyebrows at him.

"Fine. If you want to be caught, be my guest. You are under my dad's command, so therefore under mine, meaning you will do what I say. That is unless my dad is right and I have been helping a traitor," I say, my voice getting harder with each word.

He sighs. "Sorry, I just want this all to be sorted out," he tells me.

"Just remember who you are under. Come on," I tell him before aiming the last bit at Bianca. I climb the stairs, Bianca following close behind.

Have I made the wrong decision about letting Adrian stay with me? Is my dad right? We're not going to sort it out unless he gives us answers, and he seems to be holding back some information. Why else would he run?

I decide to do something I should have done when Adrian first came to me. I get out my phone and send my dad a text.

You asked me to let you know if Adrian shows up. Well he has just now. He's in my living room currently, and will be here when you arrive.

I hope I've done the right thing.

Chapter 29

What Do You Think About Raising Ostriches?

I listen for the sound of my dad's arrival over the audio of a show that Bianca says that she is obsessed with. I've changed out of my bloody clothes and am now relaxing in something more comfortable. The commercials start to run as I hear a commotion start up downstairs.

"Stay here," I tell her as I get up off the bed and start toward the door.

"Aw, why?" she asks. I look over my shoulder to see that she is pouting.

"My dad will kill me if he knows I've told someone," I answer.

The pout stays on her lips, but she turns back to the TV not arguing it any further.

I run down the hallway to the stairs and then down them, not wanting to miss my dad. Coming off the last step, I see that Adrian is being held by guards and is working his best at breaking free from them. My dad is standing in front of him, his arms crossed over his chest. Hearing me, he looks up, shooting me a wink.

"Scar! Tell them," Adrian implores.

I press my lips together, avoiding his undoubtedly hurt expression when he realizes. It slowly starts to dawn on him that I was the one to tell them he was here, as he stops fighting for a second.

"You told them," he says.

I avoid his statement with a question.

"If you did nothing wrong, then why are you fighting?"

"You know what they are going to do to me. It's not going to help, everything will continue. I would never try and take over. You know me," he begs us.

Do I? Do I know him? Was our eighteen years of friendship just a ploy for him to get close to my dad and me?

"You don't have any proof, except for rumors. Are you just going to keep killing people until it stops?"

"Pretty much," my dad replies as he steps forward ready to leave.

Adrian shoots me a calculating look before he turns to my dad squaring his shoulders.

"Do you realize that you daughter allowed me to stay with her? Or did she forget to leave that out?"

I give Adrian my best glare as I hold back from strangling him.

"Exactly how long has he been staying here?" my dad aims at me, slight anger tainting his tone. I try to make an excuse, but my dad stops me.

"Don't answer that. We'll talk about this later," he says, bringing his hand up to pinch the bridge of his nose. I look around the room and see that the guards my dad brought up him have been watching our interaction uncomfortably.

"Take him, but don't kill him yet. I want to see or hear the proof before you do," I instruct them.

"I'm the devil, and I get to make the decisions," my dad replies shortly, trudging out the statement he likes to use whenever we are arguing.

"And I'm saying it doesn't only affect you," I reply in the same manner.

He sighs, knowing I'm right, but agrees to keep him alive. While I've got him here, I might as well see how he is getting on with finding answers to the problem I had with Reid on our date.

"Have you been able to find out anything about why I couldn't compel Reid the other day?"

"No, but I'm looking," he replies before teleporting everyone, apart from me, out of the room. I envy my dad with that power. Whereas I have to touch the people I want to teleport, my dad can pick and choose the people in the room to teleport. A perk of being a god I guess.

"Bye to you too, Dad," I mumble to the empty room before turning to go back up the stairs. However, my way is obstructed by Bianca who looks ready to leave.

"I have to go."

"Leaving so soon? I didn't scare you off, did I?" I joke although part of me is wondering if it's true.

"No, Reid's being an asshole and asked me to come back apparently for 'gang stuff.' He also 'instructed' me to stay away from you," she explains.

I scrunch my mouth up in anger. How dare he control who I see.

"I'll give you a lift," I offer. "Reid can't stop you from meeting me, we'll find a way."

"Thanks. Of course, we will. He'll get over it by next week," she says, following me back down the stairs and out to the car.

***

I lean out of the car, pressing the small button to talk to Clive. He answers with the same statement.

"State your name and reason for being here."

"It's Father Christmas again, and I've come back to give you your presents if you're a good boy," I answer.

I feel Bianca's curious gaze on me. I give her a grin, turning back to the talking box. I hear Clive let out a half sigh, half groan.

"Oh God, not you," he lets out.

"I won't give you your presents back if you continue to act like this. Were you expecting the tooth fairy? I believe that she is on vacation currently."

"Just enter," he says in despair.

Bianca giggles. "What did you do to him last time?"

"Told him I was going to take his presents. I don't think he was very happy with me," I tell her as I watch the gates open. I press down the accelerator, and we fly up the drive.

I halt outside the front door, allowing Bianca to leave the car.

"See you soon," she calls back into the car before closing her door. I don't move off just yet, staring out of the window in front of me.

Remembering how I felt when Bianca said that Reid called her back, I push my door open and get out of the car as well, deciding to confront Reid about it. Bianca has already entered the house and disappeared when I follow her lead.

Once in the entrance hall, I widen my hearing range to the whole house, trying to determine where he is. All the different sounds of the house hit me at once: moans of pleasure and pain, laughter, crying, and lastly, Reid's voice. I follow it, going by how loud it is at certain points, and finally, I stop outside a door with Reid on the other side talking to some of his members. I clutch the door handle, bursting in and saying the first thing that comes to mind: "What do you think about raising ostriches?"

That didn't happen. Instead, I say, "What the fuck?"

Reid looks up at me. I look around the room and find that we are in a small room with couches and a TV.

"Can I help you?" he asks as if I were a stranger. I get even madder at this. How can he go from the way we were to this—all because he found out I am not human?

"What the fuck allows you to control who I can see and when I can see them?"

"It may have something to do with me being the leader of one the most powerful gangs around, and one of your 'friends' is part of it," he answers, standing up from where he was sitting.

"Yeah, but it doesn't mean you have to be an asshole. You can be mad at me, but the people I hang out with is my choice, not yours," I say, getting louder.

He looks stunned for a minute before he recovers, anger replacing the astonishment. The people around the room are longingly looking at the door, which I am standing in front of, not knowing what to do, much like my dad's guards earlier.

"It's my gang, and I can control who they hang out with. I don't want them hanging out with someone like you," he says, jabbing his finger through the air toward me, his other hand clenching down by his side.

"I think they can make their own judgment," I counter.

"Well, *my* judgment wants you out of my house, and life. If I find you anywhere remotely near here again, I will personally be the one to kill you," he snarls.

I step toward him. "Really? Will you? You were the one to imply not even two hours ago that you loved me. I don't think you'd have the guts."

"I lied. So do you want to try me?"

I can't gather myself enough to focus on his heartbeat in time; all I can focus on are his words and the pain they're making me feel. *I lied. I lied.* They ring around my head, trying to make sense of them. I stay completely still as I stare at him before snapping out of it. I shove Reid in the chest.

"You're an asshole," I spit at him as I spin and storm out of the room, my face like thunder.

I get to my car, my movements furious as I open the door and start the car, wanting to get as far away from this house and Reid. The thing that I am most mad about is that if he called, telling me that he was sorry and didn't mean anything he said, I would go running back to him and I don't know why. I hold myself from lashing out, as I will easily dent my car and I don't want to do that. The only thing which will calm me is a drink of something more than alcohol. I need blood.

Chapter 30

Grant

As I drive, I get more and more annoyed with Reid and myself, so much so that I have to pull over afraid that I will crash the car. Before stepping out onto the sidewalk, hoping fresh air will help calm me as I search for someone to feed off, I check the mirror to see if I got so annoyed that my demon side took over. It hadn't, but I need to be careful.

Feeling the sunshine on my skin, I let my body relax. Now out of the heat of the moment, I regret the way I spoke to Reid. If he didn't trust me before, he won't now. I called him an asshole. I stop abruptly on the sidewalk. When did I start to care about other people's feelings and how I come across? *Earth must be making me softer*, I think as continue walking.

I sniff the air as I walk, trying to find some blood that I will enjoy. I pick up on a particularly pleasant one. I look around trying to find the source. The smell isn't moving, and it's getting stronger, so I am easily able to track them down. The source of the incredible smelling blood is a man.

His black, wavy hair looks as if he has been in the wind. I don't know if that look is intentional. His green eyes are watching over the people walking down the sidewalk as if he is waiting to meet someone. He is tanned and less built than Reid; he is also shorter at only a couple of inches taller than my 5'7".

As I am looking him over, I can see the same tattoo that Reid has (the skull attached to a scythe by a vine) on his wrist. A conspiratorial grin comes off my face. I can have a drink and feel like I am getting back at Reid at the same time. He never has to know. I saunter up to the man, stopping at his side to stroke my hand down his arm.

"What are you doing?" he asks as he looks down at me appreciatively.

"Just feeling what boyfriend material feels like," I flirt.

"What's your name, sugar?" he asks, his muscles bulging under my hand slightly.

I grin. "Scarlett, but you can call me Scar or whatever pet name you want," I tell him, leaning closer to him, looking up into his emerald eyes so it feels like what I am saying only applies to him. "What's yours?"

"Well, it's not stupid," he replies, a knowing smile coming onto his face.

"What?" I ask, dumbfounded.

He must recognize me from the meeting after the date.

"I was there," he responds. *Yep,* I think, *I was right.*

"What are you talking about?" I ask innocently, continuing to stroke his arm.

"I was there when Reid introduced you. I'm not stupid enough to sleep with the boss's girlfriend," he explains, knocking my hand off his arm.

"Ex," I correct, flashing him a quick smile through my disappointment.

"Well, whatever you are to him, I'm not going to get with you," he tells me, looking away and back to the crowd, walking down the sidewalk.

I go to turn and walk away, but I'm determined to get his blood, just to get a taste of the blood which smells so good. I turn back to him.

"One last thing, could you look into my eyes? I feel like there is something in it."

He complies, nodding his head, thinking that it will be harmless.

"During the course of this afternoon, you will forget who I am and afterward will forget everything that took place, okay?"

He nods before blinking and smiling down at me.

"Hi," I say as if we just met, returning my hand to his arm.

"Hi," he responds, his smile growing bigger. "What's your name?"

"Scarlett, but you can call me Scar or whatever pet name you want," I flirt, repeating myself.

"I like the sound of that," he comments.

"What's yours?" I ask, moving my hand to his chest.

"Grant," he says, his chest puffing slightly under my hand.

"Are you free?" I ask, curling my fingers slightly to stroke his chest. He looks around, thinking about it for a minute. I dig my fingernails into his flesh slightly, earning a grunt. He looks at his watch and then back to me.

"Yeah."

"Good," I say gladly, moving my hand back to his arm but gripping it tightly this time as I drag him down the sidewalk and in the direction of my car.

"Whoa, you have a strong grip." He notices as we weave through people sending us curious looks.

"Do I? Sorry, am I hurting you?" I ask, keeping my voice as if I know none the wiser, gripping his arm even tighter in my grip. He lets out a grunt of pain.

"No," he lies, wincing again when I tug on his arm.

He stumbles before stopping beside my car. I leave him and walk around the front of the car to the driver's side. I look over the top before disappearing into the car, seeing that Grant is looking down at my car in awe. As I wait for him to get in, I let the roof down. Once the roof will not fly off, I start the engine and pull out of my space.

***

I drive for a short while, the car silent. I hear Grant take a breath in, going to say something, as I see what I've been looking for. A deserted parking lot. I do a double check, looking around as I listen to see if I can find anyone in the vicinity.

When I am satisfied that we are alone, I turn off the road and park the car in the middle of the empty lot. The concrete is dirty and littered with trash of all kinds. A few cars look to be abandoned here, but apart from that, it's secluded, hidden by buildings on three sides. It's perfect; the road was quiet so no one would see what was going on.

"What are we doing here?" Grant asks suspiciously as he looks around the run-down space. I climb over the middle console, turning so I am straddling his lap. Not allowing him to react, I lean down and capture his lips in a kiss. He eagerly returns it, leaning up to me enthusiastically. The kiss is alright, but I don't get the feeling I do when I kiss Reid.

Stop! I can't carry on like this, comparing him to everyone I meet. If it's truly over, I need to forget about him.

I move from Grant's mouth to his neck, sucking and kissing the skin I find there. He lets out a groan, his hands falling to my ass and pulling it toward him. I let out a breath at the contact that it causes. I place a lick on his neck, tasting him for the first time.

Now for part two of my plan. I open my mouth and sink my fangs into his flesh, making sure that it doesn't feel pleasurable. He symbolizes the Grim Reapers at this moment, and I need to take my anger out with them on something. It just so happens to be Grant. His screams fill the air, making me glad that the roof is down. I drag the blood from his body into my own, wanting to taste the blood which I am sure will be exquisite.

However, as soon as the blood touches my tongue, it burns me. I swallow the mouthful, regretting it when it burns my throat. I try and stop the blood from entering my mouth, but it keeps flooding in, causing the burning to become worse. I begin to choke on it, my body trying to stop the blood from entering it. I pull back, holding my throat which is feeling like it is being ripped out. What on Earth is happening? I look up to Grant, hoping he will be able to give me answers to my questions.

"Oh, Scar, are you okay?" he asks, faking concern and sympathy. I don't even need my extra hearing to know he doesn't mean it, as his eyes are full of menace. I try to talk but am cut off by coughing racking through my body. I feel some liquid make its way up into my mouth with the coughs and see blood spraying out of my lips and onto Grant's shirt.

"Are you still hungry?" he asks.

I shake my head frantically as I try and back away. My back hits the dashboard, but Grant's grip on me keeps me in place. I struggle with him as he brings his wrist to my mouth, nicking his wrist on my fangs which are still out. I whimper when I feel the blood gushing into my mouth. I refuse to swallow it, wanting to spit it out, but Grant's wrist over my mouth, disallows me.

I try and hold it in my mouth for as long as I can, but I can feel the blood burning my whole mouth. I eventually swallow, the pain being unbearable. He keeps his wrist at my lips, making me gulp down even more of it. He eventually pulls his wrist away, allowing me to spit the blood in my mouth at him. I note that it's a bright red color, not blue like I expected from the burning sensation it caused.

He opens the passenger door, pushing me out onto the hard ground. I roll over, coughing racking through my body again. Blood dribbles out the side of my mouth as I continue to cough. When I have finally recovered and stopped, I fall onto my back, finding Grant standing over me.

"What in Hell's name are you?!" I ask him.

"That's a good question," he states as he reaches into his jacket pocket, pulling out the handle of a sword. I recognize it instantly as what my dad's guards carry. He must have contact with one of them if he has one. There is nowhere else he could have got it. He presses a button, and a blade slides out. He points the tip down at me on the floor.

"Let me enlighten you...Ask me what you want to know," he says, bringing the sword back up and swinging it through the air. His grip is weak, and the sword is wavering all over the place, telling me he's untrained and inexperienced with it.

I watch him cautiously. Although he is inexperienced and untrained, that doesn't make him any less dangerous. If anything, it makes him more. If he doesn't have control over it, it's more likely that an accident will happen. Hopefully, like with the sword, he won't have had any training in other departments, like in the act of interrogation. It could mean that he will let on more information than he intended.

"Why is your blood like that?"

"Well, we're not in the Vampire Diaries, so it's not vervain. Well, it's not actually any herb. That's at least what I was told. We're just made like this," he explains as if it were obvious.

I keep an ear on his heartbeat and hear that he is telling the truth. I was right; he just gave me more information than he intended. I only know what he's talking about from the things I hear when I come up with my dad. If he knows about a human book and TV show, it means more likely than not, that he was once human and turned into whatever he is. That's my next question.

"What are you?"

"I only know that I woke up and was like this."

I was right again; he was human at one point. My guess is someone is turning people without their knowledge. I wonder if this has anything to do with the revolution taking place in Hell.

"A man was standing over me and explained to me what I was—a special kind of demon. These were better than normal ones," he said. "We are stronger and faster. We appeal to other demons, and if they drink our blood, it's like acid, making them weaker. He then went on to say that he was putting together an army of revolutionists and new demons. Just before he left, he turned back to me, showing me a picture of you and a man, telling me if I were to see you or him, I were to kill you," he finishes, smiling evilly down at me still on the floor.

I guess by the other man he means my dad. This whole revolution is much worse that I could ever imagine. If someone, supposedly Adrian, is going around and creating a new species, then we are in trouble. Grant's sword skills aren't the only dangerous thing about him, his species being unknown is also a worrying factor.

"How? How were you created?"

"Pfft. I don't fucking know. I was unconscious," he says, flinging his hands out from his body. I subtly and slowly move my hand up until I am aiming it at him. I let fire fly out of my hand, hoping to bind him or even harm him slightly.

A dark chuckle leaves Grant's lips as he sidesteps the fire. I try and control the fire, moving it with him, but I miss him, lighting an abandoned car instead. Grant's head moves with the fire, watching it as it travels. Once the plume of fire has whooshes up from the car, his head snaps back to me on the floor.

"Didn't you know? Fire doesn't kill me," he says as if I were the stupid one.

"You know, your name should actually be stupid. You don't know who I am, do you?" I ask, my own chuckle leaving my lips.

"I don't really—" he starts.

I try and force my horns to grow, but pain stops them from appearing.

"I'm Hades', but you might know him as the Devil's, daughter," I tell him. A shocked look comes onto his face before he lets out a full belly laugh.

"Oh my God." He wheezes through his laughter. "I'm going to kill Hades' Daughter," he sings like it's the best thing in the world.

"Who?" I ask, needing a definite name.

"What are you talking about?" he asks, going back to confusion.

"Who created you and ordered my death? Do you know a name?"

"He gave me the name of Adrian, but I don't know if that's his real one."

I stiffen, not knowing what to think. On one hand, I don't think Adrian is stupid enough to use his real name, but on the other, he might just be smug or arrogant enough to want to have his name on the new creations. If the order is to kill me, I wouldn't be able to tell anyone that he was the creator and instigator. I decide to get some proof. I search for my phone and find it lying next to me, having fallen out of my pocket. I unlock it, talking as I go to make sure Grant knows what I am doing.

"Do you think you'll be able to recognize 'Adrian?'" I ask, putting together photos as a sort of technical line-up.

"I don't know..."

"Just try," I say, turning the phone so both of us can see it. I start with a photo that I took with Kyle.

"Nope," he says definitely. I move onto one that I took of Hunter.

"Nope," he says again with the same conviction. I flick to the next one, which I took with Adrian yesterday. This time, Grant is more hesitant on replying.

"I'm not sure, but maybe," he says. I breathe in sharply, going through the rest I put together. Reid, Leo, Liam, and Jake were all nos like with Kyle and Hunter.

"When were you turned?" I ask him, shoving my phone into my pocket, hoping to get more information I can go on.

"A couple days ago, I think. I don't know. It just feels like one long one," he admits.

"You don't sleep?"

"I thought you couldn't as a demon."

"Who told you that?" I ask.

"Films and books." I roll my eyes at him. He has a lot to learn.

"You can sleep. I can help you through the first couple of months. Just don't kill me," I tell him. He blinks as if he just remembered what he is here to do. I should have kept my mouth shut; the distraction was working perfectly.

"No. I'm fine thanks. You've sidetracked me for too long," he says, bringing the sword up and over his head. Remembering what I noticed earlier, I decide to make a run for it. He looks as if he's struggling with the sword already, and with the weight of it coming down, it will be even harder to control. I jump to my feet and run. I feel the air rushing past me, letting me know that I am going at my fastest, until I suddenly stumble and trip. Falling onto my hands and knees, I wheeze out a groan. What the fuck is in his blood? It doesn't take long for Grant to be by my side. He grabs me by the hair, pulling my head up, allowing him access to my neck.

"It's a shame. I bet you would have been a good fuck, judging by your kissing. I'm sorry it had to end so soon," he says as he brings the sword up in the air.

I'm going to die! I'm only eighteen. I'm not even one hundred yet. I squeeze my eyelids shut as I wait for the pain and then whatever happens after that. I hold my breath, bringing an image of Reid into my head. Even though currently we are not together, I want the person who made me the happiest to be the last thing I see.

Bang.

Chapter 31

Threats

My death isn't what I thought it would be like, I think as I feel Grant's grip of my head loosen before letting go. Was the bang my head being cut off? Ew. I wait for the blackness to overcome me. They say that the brain stays active after your death for a few seconds, and I hope that it doesn't feel like forever.

Bang. Another one? That's definitely not my head. I try to open my eyes and find that I can. That sounds like a…

I lift my head to find Reid standing across the parking lot with a gun pointed at Grant. The grip loosening on my hair was Grant falling away from me and onto the floor. Grant's just recovering as I let out a breath of relief. That was close.

I stagger to my feet, slowly feeling my strength coming back to me. I walk over to Grant and stomp on his wrist which is holding the sword. He lets out a cry of pain as I bend down to pick the sword which is now out of his grip. I grab his head, like he did to me, making him sit up.

"I don't know what the fuck you are, or if Adrian is the one behind this, but you don't nearly kill me and get away with it," I snarl down at him before swinging the sword around and chopping his head off.

His shocked expression stays on his face which I continue to hold as his body falls to the floor. I press the button on the handle, making the sword retract into the handle, as I step over the body of Grant. I drop his head near him before making my way up to Reid who is avoiding my gaze.

"What are you doing here?" I ask him, my hands going to my hips.

"I just saved your ass," he says angrily.

I force my mouth to stay closed as I take him in. He wants me to be grateful after he said that he lied about his feelings for me?

"I thought you didn't care about this ass," I counter.

"I don't."

"Then why save me?"

His jaw clenches as he looks away from me, not liking my logic.

"How did you find me and know I needed help? Are you following me? You want us to be over, Reid. Fine, we're over. That means you can't control and follow me. You said that you didn't want to see me again, and if you did you would…" I could continue on my rant, but Reid stops me.

"Is that meant to happen?" he asks, pointing behind me.

"What?" I snap, turning to see what he's looking at. I freeze with Reid when I see Grant's body, with no head, reaching for it.

"No," I breathe out.

Grant has reached his head and is moving back to his neck, and I am too shocked to do anything about it. The head meets the neck and starts to reattach itself. It's gruesome, but if I weren't worried about him killing me, I would marvel at it. Grant, now back with a head, stands up and rolls his head in a circle before his green eyes rest on where Reid and I are standing.

"Well, that was fun!" he exclaims. In a flash, he has me pinned up against the wall behind me by my neck. I struggle against his grip, but as he said earlier, he is stronger than me. His blood still being in my system doesn't help either.

"Oh look, it's the boyfriend...Why don't we have a little fun?" he suggests as he looks at Reid, moving his other hand to my shirt, trying to open it.

I struggle even more against him, trying to get his hands and him off me. Reid has begun to shoot Grant again, but other than a slight jolt of Grant's body, it has no effect. Grant's head falls to my neck, starting to kiss it as he continues to work on my shirt.

"Get the fuck off me," I seethe out. I feel a sharp pain in my neck before the pain is replaced by heavenly pleasure. The sparks originating at the bite place travel throughout my body. I stop struggling as the pleasure takes over, making me move my hands to Grant's head holding him there. I can get why humans like this so much if this is what a bite can feel like.

"Scar...Scar!" Reid's voice shouts, cutting through the fog. With the fog broken, it dissipates completely, and I can see clearly now. Grant still has his fangs in me, but I don't feel anything.

All my strength surges back through my body. I pull his hands off me, throwing him through the air. He lands a couple of feet away. I look to Reid who looks stunned as I bring my hand up to the bite on my neck. It feels open, and as if it isn't healing. Telling myself I'll worry about it later, I run up to Grant before he can get back up. Not knowing how to kill him, I give him an offer.

"I think we can make a deal. You be my inside man, and I will give you whatever you want. You want someone changing? I'll help you. I'll do whatever you want. Eternity is a long time. We both promise also not to kill each other, okay?" I extend my hand to him and wait.

If Adrian is the real creator, I want to know what is happening while he is not there. I may have an advantage that way. He looks at my hand, his eyes hardening. He reaches for my hand and shakes it firmly. As he goes to pull back, I grip it tighter and pull him closer to me.

"If you go back on the offer or tell the person in charge about our deal, I swear I will rip every fucking thing out of your body until I have killed you." I drop his hand. "Meet me back here in a week's time, and you can tell me what you have learned, along with what you want from me."

He nods, climbing to his feet. He gives me one last look before running out of the parking lot. I check to make sure that we are alone before rotating to look at Reid. He stares after Grant.

"Well, if it's just us, I'm going to leave too," he says, going in the direction of his car.

"Reid...wait," I call. He stops where he is, looking over his shoulder. "You can't just 'save my ass' and still believe that you don't love me...We need to talk about this. You can't just leave," I tell him.

"I can, and I am," he says, returning his eyes to his car and his destination.

I don't care anymore about how I felt about him and the fight. I want to show him how much *I* care about him and how thankful I am to him for saving me. I run up Reid, spinning him around. I don't let him have the chance to pull away as I let my lips cover his. Part of my mind is screaming at me to let him go, as he hurt me, but I ignore that part as I pour all my passion into my movements. Reid, however, stays unmoving. Once I am satisfied that I made my point, I move back and away from him. I stare into his blue eyes.

"You can lie to yourself for now, but once you have figured out that you are being a stupid asshole, you know where to find me. Thanks for saving me," I say before letting him go.

As soon as I have done so, I turn and walk to my car, letting him think about it. I bite my lip as I wait for that moment when he calls me back, which I have seen in a couple of movies when I have been on Earth, but that doesn't come. I get to my car without him saying anything.

I stare over the steering wheel, seeing that Reid still hasn't come back to his senses. I start the car with a sigh, turning the steering wheel to get out of here. I stop my actions, though, at my phone ringing. I put the car back into park and reach for it. I look down at the screen and see a number that I don't recognize. I answer it, bringing it up to my ear.

"The underworld. You do the crime, we torture you. You are speaking to Scar. How may I help you?" I speak in a formal tone.

"What? Was that meant to rhyme?" a voice I don't recognize answers. It's not even recognizable by gender or age. It's almost like a robot's, meaning the person is distorting the voice. I can tell, however, that I have caught them off guard.

"No, I was just stating a fact. If I wanted it to rhyme, I would have said something like: you perish, we eat you like relish," I tell them, earning a distorted, mechanical chuckle followed by a throat clearing. The phone goes silent. I wait for them to speak again, but a minute has passed and still nothing.

"Hello?" I ask, bringing the phone down from my ear to check that we were still connected. We are, so I return it to my ear.

"I'd watch your boyfriend if I were you..." the voice speaks again, but this time, in a more menacing tone.

"That was a change," I tell them, shocked at how different the tones are.

"I wasn't meant to say anything other than that. You caught me unawares."

I let out a giggle, only to realize the meaning of the message. I look quickly up and toward Reid to find him walking to his car on the road outside the parking lot. I narrow my eyes and search the parking lot for anything or anyone out of place.

"What? Are you trying to make me feel sad that he's walk—" I stop short. A fireball is flying through the air and aiming straight for Reid's car. I pull the handle on the car door, quickly trying to get out.

I spill out of the car but stay on my feet as I go running toward Reid, but I am too late. The fireball has made impact. Like earlier when I was trying to get Grant with my fire, the car explodes in a ball of fire. Reid flies backward at the force of the explosion.

"Oh shit! Why did you do that?" I shout, looking at the sky, wondering where it could have come from. Nothing is out of the ordinary.

"You and everyone you love aren't safe. We *will* take over hell, and you can't stop us," the menacing voice says again before hanging up.

"Fuck!" I scream, throwing my now silent phone to the floor. I run my hands through my hair and run to Reid's, hopefully, unconscious body. I drop down beside him, ignoring the pain in my knees.

His eyes are slammed shut. He is covered in scratches from the glass, and the smell of blood is strong which couldn't just be from the scratches. Blood is slowly pooling on the ground under his head. It must have hit the ground forcefully. I frantically listen for a heartbeat and hear the reassuring rhythmic thumping. I breathe out in relief, falling back onto my feet. I crawl to where I threw the phone. I pick it up, pushing the button to see if the cracked screen will light up. It does, and I immediately go to my contacts and to the only person on Earth that I trust to leave Reid with in this state. The phone only rings a couple of times before it is answered.

"Yes?" Kyle asks.

"I need you to look after Reid. I'm going home and getting some answers from Adrian. If he's the one behind all of this, he will pay with his life," I tell him through gritted teeth.

"Calm down. Where are you?" he asks.

***

I have been pacing around the parking lot ever since I told Kyle where I am. Reid is still on the floor and unconscious. His heartbeat is still going, but it's not as strong as it should be. I don't really want to give him any of my blood, especially after how he reacted to finding out about the real me; he could take it badly if I have to tell him. I'll just hope that his body will heal itself.

Kyle arrives five minutes after I called him, having run here. He looks around at the two alight cars and Reid, and then back to me and down to my neck which still hasn't healed. He must have something on his fangs.

"What happened? Are you okay?" he asks, his eyes trailing down to the blood on my clothes, which is partly mine and partly Grant's from me decapitating him.

"Adrian has made an army of special demons. They attacked me, caused an explosion, resulting in this," I explain, waving my hand around the parking lot, my anger evident.

"What?" he asks, looking confused and concerned.

"I'll tell you more about it later, but first, I need to go down and get answers from Adrian," I tell him heatedly.

"Okay, don't worry about Reid. I'll make sure he's okay," he assures me.

"Thanks, Kyle. I know you will. You've always been there for me and my dad," I tell him.

"You've both done so much for me. I can't imagine what my life would be like without you two," he says, giving me a reassuring smile. I give him a small smile back and then look down to Reid; it quickly falls again.

"You really care about him, don't you?" he asks.

"Yeah, but I think I blew it. He'll never come back to me."

Kyle's big, warm hand falls to my shoulder, rubbing it soothingly. "I'm sure everything will turn out okay," he consoles me. I shrug my shoulders as Kyle steps back from me, allowing me to teleport.

"Thanks again." I close my eyes and picture my room at home in Hell. *Adrian, I'm coming for you. You better have done everything you wanted to in your lifetime.*

Chapter 32

Demons' Torment

As soon as my feet hit the ground in Hell, I open my eyes and march out of my room, slamming the door behind me as I go. I feel the vibrations from the force as I open my mouth, putting all the anger, menace, and force into my shouts.

"Tell that fucking bastard that I'm coming for him!" For the second time in two minutes, the house shakes as a result of my anger.

As I make my way down the hallway, I hear a thumping making its way up the stairs. I meet the source of the noise, a very excited Tybalt, at the top of the stairs. My anger dissipates for a moment as I greet him. I didn't know how much I missed him until now. His whole body moves as I hold his head in my hands and place a kiss on the top of his head.

"Are you going to help me?" I ask him as I straighten back up, and Tybalt's excitement to see me lessens. Sensing that the reason for my visit is serious, he sits down almost as if standing to attention and looks at me expectantly. A small smile graces my lips as I move around him, but it quickly goes away when I focus back on why I came here. Stomping down the stairs, I ignore the congregation of guards at the bottom all looking up at me concerned and move past them to the hallway which leads down to my dad's study and my destination—the dungeons.

As we are already in Hell, and there's nothing worse than that, the dungeons are more of a place where we keep our prisoners. As expected, souls and humans are easier to torture, but with demons, it's a lot harder, as we can heal easily and have a higher pain threshold.

I pull the rotting wooden door open and look down the stone steps. Like the boats that take the souls from the Styx Lake, the wooden door is just made to look like that; it would take a lot to get it open when it's locked.

My dad's deep voice floats up through the darkness, and a smirk comes to my lips when I hear a grunt of pain after it. As we make our way down the steps and into the darkness, Tybalt starts to growl lowly, his hackles rising under my hand. I move in front of him and down the ancient steps.

When I look back up at him to see whether he is following, two red orbs stare back at me from the top of the stairs. He pads down the stairs when I motion him forward; he always gets nervous whenever we come down here. He knows that this is where we keep the stuff that can hurt our kind and senses that whenever he gets near the door, meaning he will avoid coming this way. Tybalt also understands that the reason for my anger is probably down here and feels the need to protect me, which I think is sweet.

As I walk past all the small cells, my eyes easily adjusting to the darkness, I realize that almost every one of them is full. Before I left for Earth, we were hardly using them. I peek in through the small window of one of the many doors either side of the corridor and see that a demon is sitting on the floor looking beaten and thirsty. I step back and ignore the drastic change in temperature down here and the shouts from the cells as I stride forward and toward the door which is ajar at the end.

We don't need to worry about the prisoners of this one getting out, as they are usually tied up and accompanied at all times. The door being open at all times is actually useful for us, as our philosophy is that listening to what is going on and possibly coming for you makes it all the worse. Welcome to the torture room.

Like the door leading down the dungeons, this one looks like it's going to fall off the hinges at any moment. I pause, listening to make sure that I have the prisoner I want—Adrian. I try and see if I can catch a scent, but the smell of damp dust and the other prisoners mix together and form a sort of barrier to me determining the individual scents. Instead, I rely on my ears.

"Tell me, damn it!"

Silence follows his demand, causing my dad to exclaim out in frustration. "We will get you to answer, Adrian," my dad murmurs.

This is all I need, and I bring my leg up to kick the door open. I only get a quick glimpse of the small room and the glowing plants in the corner because as soon as the door bangs against the wall, I am being lifted into the air by my neck.

Earlier when Grant said that there were no herbs or plants that were in his bloodstream, which he knows of, he was most likely telling the truth. However, a plant does exist out there that has the effects of Grant's blood. It's called daemoniorum tormentorum, which is Latin for "demons' torment." It was never officially "discovered" and named on Earth and hasn't existed there for millenniums, as my family all made sure that every plant was either destroyed or kept to produce for our own uses (mainly torture), meaning my dad was the one to name it.

I hear Tybalt let out a loud growl, ready to pounce on the person holding me.

I meet the eyes of one of my dad's guards who reacted to the intruder, raising an eyebrow.

"Good reaction time," I comment. "Although I could be killing you right now, if I wanted to," I say.

He sighs and rolls his eyes, dropping me to the floor. "Sir, your daughter is here."

I look to my dad as the guard speaks to him. He is paused mid-punch, holding Adrian by the neck. When he sees me, he flashes me a smile.

"Hi, sweetie," he says, his smile falling as his eyes go over my torn clothes, the wound which is slowly healing on my neck, and the glass in my hair. "What happened?" he asks, forgetting about his punching bag as he drops his hand.

"It's complicated. There has been a revelation," I explain as I look away from him and to Adrian who is tied to a chair with what smells like chains soaked in the Demons' Torment. His blonde hair is plastered to the side of his head by the blood. I see Tybalt's eyes are on the bright blue flowers in the corner, the blue petals glowing in the dim light. The flowers would be pretty if they weren't so dangerous.

Did Adrian order the attack from in here? Do we have a security breach? He looks concerned as he looks me over and maybe even angry. I inwardly scoff; he doesn't care about me; it's all an act. He's most likely angry at my survival and at Grant for not getting the job done.

"What are you doing *here*?" my dad asks.

"*To buy a unicorn.* What do you think?" I respond sarcastically. "I'm here to get answers." I see the guards exchange looks with my dad, but I ignore them as I clap my hands together.

"So, what do you think we should start with first? I'm thinking…" I start as I walk further into the room, getting cut off by my dad.

"You're not helping," he states seriously.

"Why not?"

"You both were once friends, and I don't think you would—"

"He's not my friend anymore, and you know me, dad. Once I'm crossed, I don't take it lightly," I say, looking at Adrian to drum my point home with him.

He needs to know our friendship is over. Eighteen years of great memories and friendship down the drain in one afternoon. The only way I can be here now, without breaking down in tears, is that I've learned to switch off my feelings to some extent.

My dad lets out a breath, putting his hands on his hips.

"I don't doubt that. I just…"

I interrupt him by pleading with him. "Please let me have some time with him. I don't want to have come down here for nothing. I need answers and justice for what they did to me."

"What did they do?"

"They tried to kill both Reid and me," I explain, looking at Adrian in disgust. His eyes widen as they look from me to my dad, fear creeping into them.

You better be scared. You may not even have eyes to show your fear when I'm done with you.

"What?" he manages, his voice weaker from his pain and the chains surrounding him, but underlying the pain is worry and shock.

"Shut up!" I snap at him as I turn to look at my dad again.

He closes his eyes and takes a couple of breaths before opening them again, his eyes holding concern but also understanding. "Fine, I have better things to be doing anyway, but you report every little thing he says. Promise?"

"I was going to lie to you, but I guess I have to tell you now," I tell him, a hand going to my hip and my head falling to the side. He shakes his head in exasperation as he turns to one of the guards standing in the corner, pointing at him.

"You," he says. "Stay here. The rest of you come with me."

I cross my arms as I watch the other guards leave the room after my dad, the door staying open a couple of inches behind them. I move around the chair in the middle of the room, slapping my hands down onto Adrian's bare shoulders. I move down so my mouth is by his ear.

"Let's get started, shall we?" I ask rhetorically, gripping his shoulders in my tightest grip. I let him go as I continue past the chair and to one of the walls, which, if I were to follow along, would lead to the dangerous plants in the corner. I press one of the stone protruding from the wall and am rewarded with the stones spinning back to reveal a wall of different torture implements. I grab a pair of the thick rubber gloves from where they are hanging, slapping the material against my wrists for effect as I put them on.

I recall the movie that Adrian had on when the cops were asking about Meredith. The scientist in it was doing the exact same thing. This turns the temperature of my anger from simmering to boiling. I spin and give Adrian my best sadistic grin, which even has the guard in the corner shifting away from me.

"Let's start off easy," I say as I walk to the chair again. I start to undo the chains and sling them through a loop on the ceiling. I pull it sharply, causing Adrian to be lifted violently from the chair, eliciting a cry from his lips, his toes scraping the floor. I stand in front of him, my fingers intertwined as my arms hang by my sides.

"What do you know about the revolution?"

He doesn't reply instantly, his chest heaving with his rapid breaths. I hear him swallow before he answers hoarsely.

"Not a lot. I only know that someone is gathering supporters and bringing new demons back with them from Earth."

I listen closely to his heartbeat, which is already fast from the torture, and look at his eyes, wanting to see if he's lying to me. I sigh, acting disappointed.

"Come on, Adrian. You know better than that," I say, keeping the false disappointment and adding false disbelief at his actions. "Don't lie to me. You know more than what you just told me."

I stroll back to the wall of torture devices and pick out one of the tamer ones—a gun. I take the cartridge out and start to fill them with bullets laced in the Demons' Torment. I slam the cartridge back into the gun and return to Adrian.

"We're going to play a little game. Every time that I hear a lie, a bullet will be fired into your body. That sounds fun, right?"

Adrian changes the way he is hanging slightly but doesn't say anything. I shrug and start to walk in a circle around him.

"What do you know about what happened today?" I ask.

"Nothing," he answers shortly.

I wait to see if there are any signs that it was a lie, but nothing happens to make me believe it is. They must have decided without his knowledge. I relax slightly, glad that we don't have to worry about him controlling everything from his cell.

"Are you the ones creating the new demons?" I fire off another question, not giving him any time to relax.

"No. I've been trying to find out who is and how," he mumbles.

I stop and narrow my eyes. This is not any fun after all; the cartridge of bullets is still full.

"How did you first find out about what is going on? More specifically, how did you find out about the revolution and plan to take over Hell?"

"From other demons talking," he states truthfully.

"About starting it?" I ask.

"No." When he says this, his heartbeat rises. Almost straight after him saying it, I lift the gun and pull the trigger. He lets out a cry, twisting away from me and the gun. Things are starting to look up.

"Tell me the truth, Adrian. You were once my friend. I deserve to know why you want to hurt me!" I shout at him.

He hangs his head but not in shame, more out of tiredness. "*If* I was the one behind all of this, then how is what you're doing to me now any different? You're hurting me," he points out.

I lift my gun, not looking at him, and pull the trigger again causing another shout of pain.

"I told you the truth. You can't say I'm lying because you don't like what I said."

"I shot you because what you said isn't the truth. The two things are totally different. The pain I'm causing will help me get answers. We can stop this right now if you just tell me the truth. So, answer the damn question!"

"I was there," he admits. I lower the gun slightly as I wait for him to say more. "But I said no to joining and tried to stop others."

"Who else was there? I need names or descriptions," I demand.

"I—I don't remember," he pleads. I shake my head and pull the trigger again. "Please, Scar—"

"Don't you dare say my name like that!" I shout angrily as I pull the trigger again. My eyes go to Tybalt in the corner who is lying comfortably watching me from where his head is resting on his paws. I purse my lips, contemplating whether Adrian will be more compliant when he is on the other end of what Tybalt can do. I let out a whistle, getting Tybalt's attention, causing his head to lift up.

"Threaten," I command, and with that one word, the loving, adorable dog is replaced by a vicious killing machine. He jumps up from his spot and stalks toward where Adrian is hanging, his canines bared, his snarls and growls filling the room.

I know if I were in Adrian's position, I would need a new set of underwear. I notice, however, Tybalt is holding back, and I realize I have been as well. I could have gone straight for the worse tools and forced his answers out. Instead, I've given him a chance to go without any pain. We both, deep down, still see him as the friend we used to know.

"As you well know, with one word, he can rip you apart. Now, do you want to give me the answer I want?"

"If I tell you, I'll be killed," he cries out in panic.

"And if you don't, you'll be killed anyway. So make up your mind. Either I kill you after you are tortured, or they can kill you."

He closes his eyes as he moves yet again, trying to find a comfortable position. I am about to open my mouth to encourage him, but he stops me when he begins to list off six names. I don't recognize them all, only a few I know to be guards.

"Okay, Tybalt, lie down," I instruct. The growls immediately stop, and he returns to the loving animal as he moves back to his prior position. "Is that it?"

He nods. I pull the trigger.

I ignore his attempts at getting me to believe him, shouting over them as I make my way back to the wall.

"Don't fucking lie to me. Who else was there?"

When I can walk no further, I look back at Adrian and see that he's shaking his head, silently telling me he's not going to say anymore. I clench my jaw as I look back to the wall and swap the gun for a knife. I flip it over in my hand as I watch Adrian. He continues to shake his head, his eyes imploring me to leave it. With one last flip of the knife, I lift it and throw it into Adrian's shoulder.

"Hold that for me," I say as I make my way back in front of him. I cross my arms. I believe him when he says that he's not part of the revolution, and this gives me relief that he didn't betray me. However, I do not feel guilty for everything that is happening or what I did. He has information about who is behind this whole thing, and he kept it to himself. I need to know everything he does, and that means getting him to talk, and the only way I can get him to tell me the things he doesn't want me to know is by making it the better of two options. At the end of the day, everything I do to him will heal.

Well, maybe. I step closer to him and pull the knife from where it is lodged in his shoulder.

"You saw what I can do with a knife," I say to Adrian, referring to when I gave Meredith the scar. "So, are you going to give up the names?"

His face goes white, but he doesn't say anything.

"Okay," I say, stepping back from him again. I look to the guard in the corner, who is still standing as far away from me as he can without making it look like he's actively avoiding me. "Would you go and get a barrel and fill it with water?" I ask.

He nods without any hesitation and leaves the room.

The guard returns a minute later, pulling behind him what I requested. I thank him and position the barrel where I want it before I move to the corner holding the Demons Torment. I pick a couple of the flowers and return to the barrel, dropping them into the water. The solution dissolves the flowers, and the clear liquid is replaced by a bright blue, glowing one.

I dip the blade of the knife into the concoction to halt the healing process in Adrian and move to stand in front of Adrian again. I lift the knife to Adrian's face, pressing it against his cheek. Adrian hisses with pain as the scent of burning flesh fills the air. I flick the knife so only small scratches mark his skin. I ignore the confusion that Adrian watches me with as I move over his face.

Once I am happy with the result, I take the chains out from the loop and grab him by the arm tightly to stop him falling. The guard moves to his other side, now wearing gloves also. Together we drag Adrian toward the acid-like potion. Adrian, now putting two and two together, starts to struggle as we get closer. He already knew what I was doing with the barrel, but he didn't understand the cuts on his face. I kick him in the back of the knees so he falls to the floor.

"One last chance. Are you sure that those names are this important to keep a secret? Because like you said, once I start something, I can't be stopped until I'm satisfied."

He closes his eyes as if thinking about it but still doesn't say anything. I move my hand to the back of his head and push his face down toward the liquid. I pause just above to see if he'll give in, but when he doesn't, I continue down. The stinging from the Demons' Torment will be even worse with the tiny cuts all over his face. The liquid starts to bubble, and Adrian struggles against our hold but doesn't budge an inch. I go to let him up, but then I remember what happened to Reid and keep him there for a minute longer. He's protecting whoever are the last names and the ones responsible.

When I eventually pull him out of the liquid, his face is marred by burnt flesh. I let him fall, and Adrian turns onto his side wheezing. He coughs, and blood dribbles down his chin and onto his chest.

"Know the last names yet?"

"It's only one," he replies, his voice almost gone completely. "The last name is…" he starts but stops. Through the burns, I can see that he doesn't want to say it and is upset. I swallow, suddenly nervous.

"Who?"

"Kyle," he mutters, his eyes closed as if it physically pained him to say it. It might have, as the Demons' Torment most likely got into his mouth. "He was the one leading it all."

I am stunned into silence. The person I trusted the most to have nothing to do with it, the person who has been by my side my whole life. All of a sudden, all the questions I had going around my head about Adrian transfer to Kyle. Why would he want to hurt my dad and me? He sees us as family. A pain begins to form in my chest, and all the emotions I feel break through the barrier that was holding back all the emotions from leaking out.

"You're lying!" I scream at Adrian as I fall down on top of him, using all of my strength with each punch I land on him. "I know it isn't him. He's been on Earth with me. I even showed that demon a photo of him. He showed no recognition." I try to convince myself, not wanting to believe what he said. But I have to, his heart stayed at the exact same rate, his breathing didn't change—he was telling the truth. No one is that good of a liar.

"It started way before you left, and as for the demon, he may not have met him." What he says makes perfect sense, but the thought of what it means causes tears to start streaming down my face. "I didn't want to tell you because I knew you would become upset and angry," Adrian continues.

"You're fucking lying!" I scream in my devil voice unintentionally.

Kyle helped me; he wouldn't want to kill me. I fall back off Adrian, anger coursing through my veins. My horns make an appearance, and I know that the anger has caused my inner demon to come out. I stand up and begin to pace around the room, needing to get rid of some of the anger. I let out a loud grunt and turn, punching a dent in the wall. The stone crumbles around my hand, and I ignore the pain on my knuckles. I trusted Kyle. I trusted him with my life. My mind zooms back over every good time we had together. *Both of us laughing as we hide from my dad, watching as he is at the receiving end of one of our pranks; him teaching me how to fight; our rebellious trips up to Earth without my dad knowing; Kyle helping me when I nearly killed the guy at the party; when he joked with me about Mr. Ward.* I even kissed him! Were all those good memories all lies? Was he using me and plotting the right time to turn around and stab me in the back?

Reid. I left Reid with him.

He hadn't hurt me yet, but I have given him the ammunition to. Maybe he was just waiting for the right time, like now. Kyle knows how much I care about Reid. I told him how he means the world to me. I have to get back. I try to teleport out of the room, forgetting about the spell which doesn't allow anyone in or out if they don't go through the door.

"He's free to go," I tell the guard as I move to go out of the room.

"Are you sure?" he challenges.

"Yes, I'm fucking sure!" I shout, turning back to look at him.

"Shouldn't you ask your father?"

"Yes, she should," my dad's deep voice says from behind me as he stands in the door.

I turn to see his arms are crossed, and his serious stare is moving over the room. He lingers on the dent on the wall, Adrian on the floor, and then my face.

"What happened in here?" he asks.

I don't answer.

"Scar, have you been crying?" I look away from him; I hardly ever cry.

"Someone better tell me what happened, *right now!*" he demands.

"I know the leader's name," I scoff.

"Who?"

"Kyle," I spit out, finding it harder than I thought to say his name. I see anger flash in my dad's eyes before it's replaced by sadness. I look to Tybalt in the corner and see that he even looks sad. He watches me push past my dad and move furiously past all the cells.

"Where do you think you're going?" my dad calls after me.

"Back to Earth. I left Reid with that fucking traitor," I say. I rush up the stairs and as soon as I am out of the field of the spell, I teleport.

***

I appear in my house, still running. I stop abruptly and listen to see if there are any movements. I hear a faint heartbeat and shallow breathing of someone, but nothing else. I smell the air to find that both Kyle and Reid have been here recently. I yank the gloves off my hands, throwing them to the floor.

"Kyle?" I taunt. I get no reply. I frantically start to search the house for either Kyle or Reid, hoping that the heartbeat I can hear is from Reid and not Kyle. I don't know what I would do if he were here.

I barge through the door to my room and stop when I see an unconscious Reid in the middle of the bed. Rushing over to Reid, I check him over for any new injuries. Luckily, it looks like nothing has changed. I sniff him, checking that he has no other blood in his system, but all I can smell is the scent of Reid. I give a sigh of relief as I fall onto the edge of the bed. A crinkling sound lets me know I am sitting on something. I shift and pull the piece of paper out from under me and recognize Kyle's handwriting.

I had to go, but I'm certain that he will be OK and there is nothing seriously wrong with him.

However, it wouldn't hurt to give him some of your blood, as he has lost a lot of his own. I would have done it, but I thought that you would prefer to do it.

K x

I scoff, crumpling the piece of paper in my hand. That doesn't sound like a note from someone who wants to kill me. He even took into consideration my feelings about him giving Reid blood. He helped where he could have caused me more harm. I shake the thoughts from my mind. I don't have to deal with him yet. How am I going to react to him at school tomorrow?

I throw the ball of paper into the trash and lay back on the bed, listening to Reid's heartbeat. It's exactly as I left him, not as strong as it should be. He's not gotten any better. I hate to admit it, but Kyle's right, the healing qualities in my blood will help Reid. I sit up, allowing my fangs to extend, and bite into the flesh on my wrist. I quickly move the wound, before it can heal, to Reid's mouth. I push it between his lips, and instinctively, he swallows the liquid in his mouth.

Once he has the taste for my blood, which appeals to the drinker as a result of the Ichor in it, he gulps it down, all the while unconscious. Not being subdued by pleasure, I am able to feel the sensation of the blood being pulled out of my body, which is a weird one but not entirely unpleasant. When I hear his heartbeat become stronger, and I think that he has had enough, I pull my arm back and away from him, watching as the wound seals itself back up before my eyes. I lie back down and wait for Reid to open his eyes.

***

A couple of minutes have gone by, and I am starting to worry because he still hasn't opened his eyes. I am just leaning over him, getting ready to shake him, when he sits up with a start, causing me to scoot back in shock. He stops when he doesn't recognize the room, his eyes flying around it.

"Who are you?" he asks when his eyes come to rest on me.

"What? You don't remember me?" I ask, concerned that maybe I didn't give him enough of my blood. His eyes look curious for a moment longer before the amusement wipes everything away. He lets out a loud laugh before he stops and lifts a hand to his head.

"Fuck! What happened? Why do I feel like I've been hit by a truck?" he asks, his eyes scrunching in pain.

I roll my eyes. "Not funny," I tell him before going on to explain what happened. "Your car exploded, causing you to hit your head when you went flying back."

"What did you give me?" he asks when his hand explores his head and finds no wound.

I bite my lip, hesitant on replying. "Some of my blood," I tell him, gauging his reaction before I continue. When he looks freaked out, I quickly give him a reason. "It has healing properties and won't do you any harm. It will be present in your veins for six days before it goes." I press my lips together as I wait for his reaction. He calms down considerably and even looks thankful.

"You saved my life?"

I nod.

"Yeah, you did save me, so I thought it was only fair. I know that you probably…"

He stops me from talking with his lips. I sigh into the kiss. I need this now more than ever, knowing that I'm not alone and that our relationship prospects didn't end when he found out about the real me. Every couple fights before making up again, and I just wish this is one of those moments. My hands move up and into Reid's brown hair. I run my fingers through the longer strands as push my body forward so that there is no space between us. Both of our lips move over each other's as if they were made to do just that. I close my eyes, moving my body against his, causing tingles of pleasure to course through my body. I let out a moan. This stops Reid's lips from moving any longer, and he pulls back. I follow him, trying to keep the contact.

"Scar...Stop."

"Why?" I ask, moving my focus from his lips to his neck. I lick from his chin up to his ear, placing a small bite on his earlobe. He grunts.

"Because I'm not ready to do that with you. I can still see the monster when I look at you," he admits.

I freeze. "What?" I ask angrily. He's such a hypocrite! "You were the one to kiss me."

"I know. I still need some space, but I couldn't go any longer without kissing you, especially after you saved my life."

I back up and clamber off him. "Fine," I start loudly. "If you want space, have it! Leave! But don't kiss me and then say you still see the monster, because you wouldn't have done it if you did," I say, pointing at the door and then him.

He leans forward, trying to pull me closer. I step back, my arms going across my chest.

"Scar..." he implores.

"No, Reid. Either you want space, or you don't. Make up your mind."

He looks guilty as he pushes himself off the bed. As he walks past me, I look away from him. The smell of his blood and mine mixed together has me weak at the knees, but I stay strong. He pulls the door to the bedroom open, but I stop him before he can exit.

"If you were to drink the blood of six people while my blood is still in your system, and then die, you would be like me. Just something to think about," I tell him. I don't know why I said that. Do I want him to do it and be like me? He couldn't think I was a monster if he was the same, but would he regret it? Do I want him to know how easy it is to change from human to demon?

Reid looks back at me but doesn't say anything as he continues out of the room.

I plop down onto the bed. My emotions have been all over the place today. I've wanted to kill almost everyone—Adrian, Kyle, and Reid—for being a pain in the ass. Let's hope tomorrow and the rest of my time on Earth will be better.

Chapter 33

I Love You, Scarlett Hades

The next morning, when I wake up, the house is eerily silent. I realize that for the first time in my life, I have felt what it's like to lose someone. I never experienced it with my mom, as I was only young when she either left or died. I still don't know what happened to her. She could still be out in the world for all I know.

The feeling is awful. I feel as if an elastic band is wrapped around my heart while someone repeatedly punches me in the stomach.

I turn onto my side and see that there is an hour before I need to be at school. I roll onto my back and look up at the high ceiling. I know that I have to see Kyle today; that's if he even shows up.

I grudgingly drag myself from my bed and scuffle toward the closet. I go for the closest things, not caring if how I look today. I put them on after doing a drawn-out version of my morning routine.

I don't want to see what today has in store for me, I think as I walk down the stairs. I glance at the couch, half expecting to see a tired Adrian sitting there watching TV, but he's not. The house feels empty without him. I spent just over two weeks in this house alone and felt fine, but all of a sudden, the house feels like it's barren without another person in it. Not wanting to stay in the house any longer, I continue to the kitchen, drinking down a bag of blood before moving around the house and collecting my supplies for school.

I drive around for a while, without any particular destination. Once I need to get off the bike, I finally make my way to the school.

When I pull into the parking lot, I find that it is empty apart from a couple of cars. I park the bike and stroll toward the entrance. I pull the door open and find the hallway is empty—none of my dad's guards here yet—and almost silent.

My ears pick up a sound, but I can't put my finger on it. As I walk down the hall, the click of my heels echoing around me, I try and pinpoint where the sound is coming from. I determine that it's coming from a store cupboard, my nose wrinkling in disgust when I realize what the sound is. The sound of muffled moans and grunts sounds out of place in this building, and that was probably why it took me a while to work it out. I try and block out some of the sounds, feeling sick at hearing it, but when it only gets louder, I decide to do something about it.

I stride to the door and pull it open without any warning. I chuckle at the sight I am greeted with. Mr. Ward has his pants down by his ankles and is buried deep inside of Tiffany who is bent over toward the door, her skirt up and exposing her bare ass. Tiffany looks up with an annoyed grunt when Mr. Ward stops pounding into her, only to blush and let out a yelp when she sees me. Mr. Ward starts to pull out, and before I can get scarred for life, I grin at them, stepping back and away from the door.

Once I am out of view of the doorway, I run the fastest I can toward the principal's office. She is just sitting down in her desk chair when I push the door open. She looks up, her shoulders falling slightly when she sees it's me. *Nice to see you too!*

"What are you doing here this early, Ms. Hades?" She sighs.

"Mr. Ward and Tiffany are fucking in the store cupboard near the entrance," I tell her bluntly and matter-of-factly before leaving her sitting there, shocked at the situation and my crass language. There's no use in beating around the bush.

Going back out into the main hallway, I walk out to the tree where Hunter and I had the cigarette on my first day. I fall down to the ground at the base of the trunk, my hands going over the dry leaves on the floor around me. I pick a handful up before letting them fall again, watching as they float back down. I pick one up, examining it as I hold it in both of my hands in front of me. I light it from the flames coming out of my fingertips and watch as it disintegrates, the embers falling to the floor. I scoff as I pick up another leaf. It's just like mine and Kyle's relationship—been around for long time but easily destroyed.

I continue to set the leaves alight for a minute before a shadow above me has me jumping and abruptly stopping, shoving my hands in the pockets of my jeans. If they saw me lighting the leaves, hopefully, they'll assume I was using a lighter.

I see Hunter standing there, dark glasses over his eyes. He shoves his hand into his jeans, his other going into his jacket, pulling out a pack of cigarettes and a lighter. He smirks and falls down beside me, silently tilting the open pack toward me. I take one and hold it out for him to light. I bring it to my lips and breathe in the warm smoke, getting flashes of my last visit down to Hell. I exhale up into the air, adding to the white wisps contrasting with the blue sky.

"How's the knife wound?" he asks, looking at me.

I clear my throat, remembering how Reid reacted. I don't want Hunter to do the same.

"Reid overreacted," I start truthfully. "It was more of a scratch. The angle made it look like the knife went in deep."

"That's good. I noticed that Reid was acting strangely yesterday, anyway," he comments, bringing his own cigarette up.

"How so?"

"Just little things. Once he came back from following you, it was like he was on his period. He was grumpier than usual and kept going to the kitchen to grab something to eat. He would blow up at insignificant things and was complaining of a headache."

I look at Hunter out of the corner of my eyes. After everything I have learned about the new demons and about how they are undetectable, I am wary of what I say around everyone. He could be working for Kyle for all I know; he wouldn't be the first person I thought to be a friend to betray me. Does he know that he's describing the side effects of having demon blood in the human body?

I shrug.

"He's probably just annoyed at me," I say, watching as the principal pulls the door to the store cupboard open. I pull my phone out and see that it's only been about five minutes since I found them and told the principal. By the looks of the principal's face, Tiffany and Mr. Ward continued after I left. I hold back a gag.

"What happened?" Hunter asks, bringing my attention back to him.

"Hm?"

"What happened between you and Reid for him to be annoyed at you?"

"Oh, we had a fight. He then was being a hypocrite. He said he wanted space and I gave it to him, only for *him* to kiss me, and afterward saying he still needed the space. And that only happened all in one day," I explain, rubbing a hand over my face.

"What did you two fight about?" he asks yet again.

"What's with all the questions?" I snap, harsher than I intended. What is this—an interrogation? I sigh and throw the cigarette to the floor, moving my foot to step on it. "Sorry, I found out that a close friend died yesterday, along with everything else that happened." He may as well have when I heard Kyle's name leave Adrian's lips. The Kyle I know has died.

"I'm sorry," Hunter says gently.

"It's not your fault. It's not like you were to one kill him. Right?" I half joke. I still don't know if he has anything to do with it.

He chuckles. "I haven't killed anyone recently," he says, nudging my arm.

I force a laugh as I examine him.

"So, where are Liam, Leo, and Jake?" I ask, wanting to change the topic off me. If Hunter were with Kyle, then most likely all of them would be.

"They're on gang business," he tells me, looking down the corridor at the principal still talking to Mr. Ward and Tiffany who seem to still be in the closet. His answers seem to be kept short and vague on purpose.

"I thought you would all work together. Why aren't you with them?" I keep my gaze on him as he answers, noticing how he shifts. He could just be uncomfortable, but my paranoid mind immediately jumps to his guilt. *He's innocent until proven guilty,* I tell myself. Hunter hasn't shown any signs of knowing anything out of the ordinary, and Reid could have just asked Hunter to keep secrets regarding what the others are up to, or he might not know himself.

"We usually do. I didn't feel like it today," he says, smiling at me, his eyes soft.

The sounds of sirens making their way closer to the school reach my ears, which causes me to let out a laugh. I guess I won't be seeing Mr. Ward around here anymore. I hear Hunter asking me what's so funny, but it doesn't register as the door to the main building opens, and Kyle's big figure steps through. All thoughts fly out of my mind as the anger takes over. I jump to my feet, causing Hunter to push his sunglasses up his head as he looks up.

"Where are you going?"

"I—uh—I need to talk to Kyle,"

"The new teacher?" he asks, confusion clear. With that one sentence, my paranoia is abolished completely; he wouldn't be able to fake that confusion. At least I don't have to worry about Hunter when I confront Kyle.

"Yeah. Wait here," I instruct him as I pull the door to the building open. I watch as Kyle walks up the stairs and toward his classroom.

At the door closing, Mr. Ward looks up from where he is standing with Tiffany, both fully dressed, along with the principal. His eyes narrow into a glare, causing a smirk to touch my lips. As I walk past him to the stairs, I mutter low enough for him to only hear, "Have a nice time in jail. You can replace Tiffany with a much larger and manlier version." I don't get to see his reaction as I continue past him and up the stairs to the second floor.

I storm down the empty corridor and to room 217. I look in and see that Kyle is standing above his desk, sifting through some papers. He reaches into his bag, and this is when I throw the door open and walk in. His head flies up, his eyes watching me as I walk into the room swinging my arms. I give him a smile.

"What are you doing?" I ask innocently. He pauses, looking as if he's trying to gauge something. He knows what I was doing last night and that Adrian knows about him, but what he doesn't know is whether Adrian told me about him.

"I am trying to find my lesson plan for today," he says.

I nod slightly in acknowledgment as I walk in front of his desk. His stare never leaves me as he watches my every move. I turn to face him, slamming my hands down onto the top of the desk. A small crack in the surface forms, but I watch as Kyle doesn't look surprised at my actions.

"So, as you know, after a try at mine and Reid's life, I went down and had an interesting conversation with Adrian. I thought you might like to know what he said. Why don't you sit down?" I suggest, resting on my hands.

"I think I would..."

"Sit down!" I shout with force on each word.

He reluctantly falls into his chair.

"You know," I start as I pace in front of him. "There were some extraordinary things that came out of Adrian's mouth, such as his blood, him attending the first meeting of the revolution, an army of a new kind of demons being made, special demons if you would, and a couple of names I recognized. But the most extraordinary thing for me was when I heard your name come out of his lips as the one leading it all. Crazy, right?" I finish as if it were ridiculous and impossible because that's how I felt when I heard it.

Kyle slowly stands back up, walking around the desk and toward me.

"Scar..." he starts, trying to placate me, but I stop him with a punch to his face. His head whips to the side with the unexpected hit.

"I should know how to punch after all you taught me," I tell him eerily calm, punching him again. I thought I would be screaming at him. He allows the punches but shows that he could have easily stopped me whenever he felt like it because his hand shoots out and closes around my fist, holding it there between us.

"How fucking dare you! I thought we were family!" I scream at him, going to hit his chest with my other hand, but, again, he stops me. His grip is tight as he looks me in the eyes.

"Don't make me hurt you," he says in a tone of voice I have never heard come from his lips. Menace. Pure and utter menace.

"Et tu, Kyle?" I ask, scoffing.

I pull my hands forcefully back as I bring my leg up, going to kick him in the side, but as soon as my hands are out of his, he grabs onto my leg mid-air. He swings me around, almost like the hammer throw, and I go sailing through the air like a ragdoll. I finally stop when I hit the wall, sliding down it. I fall to a crumpled mess on the floor, taking only a minute before I spring back to my feet.

I'm surprised to find Kyle is still standing where I left him, watching me. I take the chance to rush at him, knocking the desks out of the way as I go, but Kyle's hand stops me again by going around my neck, lifting me, so my feet are dangling. My hand comes up to his wrist, trying to alleviate the pressure. He's holding me far enough away from his body that I am unable to wrap my own hand around his neck. He's silent as he pulls the glass of water on his desk closer to him. He digs his hand into his pocket, pulling out a squashed blue flower.

I instantly recognize it as Demons' Torment. Does he carry the flower around in his pocket wherever he goes, or did he have it because he knew I was going to confront him? I notice that he is touching the plant without it affecting him. He drops the flower into the water, much like I did with the barrel that I tortured Adrian with. He picks the glass up. I struggle against him, knowing I should be able to wriggle free, but he's stronger than I remember.

"I'll give you a choice. You either drink this, or you can watch Reid become a demon."

My eyes widen. I can't believe he would just flip like he did and do this after everything we've been through. Reid would hate me for the rest of our lives, which would be forever if he were turned into a demon involuntarily. I would regret choosing that decision for the rest of my life; I close my eyes and put my hand out.

He passes me the glass, and I wipe my thumb up and down the side, waiting for a moment. I can't make it this easy for him. Do I want to risk it though? I bring it up to my lips, pressing it to my lip. When he looks like he's least expecting it, I bring it back down and throw the liquid over him. I should have known when I saw that he wasn't wearing any gloves, that it wouldn't affect him, but all reason went out of the window.

Kyle grins evilly, letting out a sardonic chuckle. He pulls me close enough so I can see, and smell, the sheen of liquid covering his face. He licks his lips, and before I know what is happening, his lips are on mine, transferring the Demons' Torment onto my own.

I struggle, a muffled scream erupting out of me as he pushes his tongue through my lips. He touches almost everywhere in my mouth with it, and I feel the bile starting to rise in my throat. Just as I'm going to throw up into his mouth, Kyle throws me away from him and back into the wall, but this time, I don't get back up as a result of the Demons' Torment weakening me too much. I hear the door open and then Kyle leaving. I try to shout after him, but it comes out hoarse, almost indiscernible, and my voice catches before I can complete the sentence.

"Stay away from R..." I start to cough and roll over, spitting out the blood that has made its way into my mouth. Once the coughing has stopped, I hear footsteps coming down the still empty corridor outside. I look up as the door opens, expecting to see Kyle has returned, but instead, I see a very concerned Hunter.

"What the fuck happened in here? I heard shouting, and I when I arrived up here to see what was happening, Kyle rushed out of the room at an inhuman speed and sent me flying. He hurt you, didn't he?"

I pull in a wheezing breath and wince as the Demons' Torment is pulled down my airways.

"Do you see anyone else?" I ask rhetorically.

He shakes his head as he starts to pick through the overturned desks, picking a few up. He looms above me as he moves the desks to make a space around me. Once he is able to, he crouches down beside me, pushing a piece of my hair out of my eyes. His chocolate eyes move over me, becoming more frantic and worried as he sees more.

"Why do you look like you've been burnt, and why is there blood? Tell me what he did to you. I promise he's not going to get away with it," he promises, his tone like his expression.

I push myself up further, leaning back against the wall for support. I look up and see that the wall is cracking from where I hit it both times.

"I'll be okay," I assure him.

"You look like shit," he comments as his hand comes up to touch my lips. I pull back, hissing in pain.

"Thanks. You too," I respond sarcastically.

"What happened?" he asks again, his face still serious.

What do I do? I don't want Hunter to hate me like Reid did, but how do I explain Kyle running out of here faster than any human ever could? I could just forget about it, but I'm sure Hunter has hundreds of possibilities going through his head, and it'll be better for him to hear it from me. At least that way I can control what he knows and how he finds out, so it won't be through him going home and deciding to look up on the internet what he saw today. He would get back false results, mainly about superheroes, but if he were to find something on demons, not all the information is correct. We are usually all painted with the same brush—chaos-inducing, fear-striking, heartless monsters who only come out at night.

For a moment, I reconsider letting him do that. It's highly unlikely that he would put two and two together and get four; all the information about superheroes would confuse him, and he would never get to the correct answer. But the big part of me that wants the reassurance that Bianca gave me—that in fact, I'm not a monster and I have a chance of people knowing me and not being freaked out—has me telling Hunter the truth. The worst that could happen would be that he stops talking to me like Reid did and I am taken from Earth by my dad for letting too many people know about the real me.

"Do you remember when you came over before my date with Reid?"

"Of course," he tells me, nodding. "But what has this got to do with what just happened?"

I ignore his question and continue.

"And what you asked me—the joke?"

This takes him a bit longer to remember before he nods hesitantly. I can see that he's already starting to work out exactly what I'm telling him.

"Well, I was telling the truth when I told you I was the 'or something,'" I tell him, biting my lip as I wait for his reaction. I expect him to stand up, point at me, and yell that I'm a monster, but it never comes, only curious confusion.

"What do you mean?"

"I'm a demon of sorts. You could say goddess."

"Goddess?" he asks.

"Yeah, Hades, the god of the underworld, is my father," I tell him, wincing again as I bring in a shuddering breath. He slowly nods, trying to process everything that I just told him.

"How do I know that you're not just crazy?" he asks, moving from crouching to sitting on the floor, his legs stretched out in front of him. At least he hasn't said he doesn't believe me.

Like with Reid, I let my demon side take over, allowing him to see my fangs, distorted face, red eyes, and most importantly, my horns. He jumps slightly, pushing himself away from me, but he doesn't scream or shout. There is no fear on his face, just surprise. I feel hope rush through me; not everyone is going to react like Reid.

"So, why did Kyle hurt you? Is he like you?" he asks, moving back toward me, his legs crossing.

At the knowledge of a human who is not involved in any way knowing the true me and not judging, I let everything that has happened come rushing out. I explain what really happened with Meredith and what happened when I told Reid. As I go on, I see him becoming more comfortable around me. He sits there, his jacket on the floor beside him, and listens without interrupting. I didn't know I needed that until right now.

When I get to how I found out about Kyle and the revolution from Adrian, a wet substance begins to run down my cheeks. I quickly lift a hand and wipe it away, worried that the Demons' Torment is causing blood to come out of my eyes. A clear droplet sits on the top of my finger. I'm crying, again? Wiping the tears away, I carry on telling him what happened today when I confronted him.

"I don't know what to do now. I've never been in a situation like this before. The only thing that has come close is when a single demon decides to rebel. I can deal with that, but this..." I feel the tears trying to resurface.

"I can't say that I know what you're going through, or have been through anything remotely similar, but I do know this: you are strong, and you *can* get through this."

"So, you don't think I'm a monster?"

"I knew there was something different about you from day one, albeit, I didn't expect this, but it doesn't change who you are. I know you've been yourself, and this," he says, motioning to my face where my demon features are still present, "is only a face. What matters is what's inside. I know you're not a monster because your human side is stronger. You would have killed me already if the demon side of you was who you were."

I let out a small sob which has Hunter bringing his hand up to my cheek, wiping away the tears. My face changing back to normal, I hold my breath as I watch him curiously. I forget the pain which is caused by my sharp intake of breath as I feel his stay hand on my cheek, his rough fingers moving. My heart is beating faster, as I see his brown eyes are gentle and caring. Hunter clears his throat, bringing his hand down from my cheek and looking away from me.

"Sorry."

What is he apologizing for?

"It's alright," I mutter, as a comfortable tension fills the room.

"Are you feeling better?" he asks, standing up and brushing the dust off his jeans, his back to me.

"I'll be fine. We should try and put the room back to the way it was before everyone arrives," I say, skirting around the subject of how I'm feeling as Hunter turns to look at me.

Emotionally, I feel like a small weight has been lifted away from the rest on my shoulders. Physically, I feel like those weights are real with my lips, throat, and mouth screaming at me in complaint every time I take a breath in. I push myself to my feet and go to take a step forward when my knees buckle. I go falling toward the floor, my hands flying out to the sides, trying to grip onto something to keep myself up. It's affected me more than I thought, and as a result, I didn't expect to be this weak. Hunter's hands find my armpits, holding me up.

"Whoa," Hunter exclaims.

I lean against his chest, pushing myself up, so I am standing straight.

"I just need to get home. I'll be okay after that," I tell him, trying to step away from him.

"You're not driving anywhere like this. I'll drive you. Why do you need to go home?"

"I need to get some blood. It will help me get my strength back up and will kickstart the healing process," I tell him.

He contemplates something for a moment before speaking quietly.

"You can have some of mine."

"No, you don't have to do that," I insist.

"I want to if it means you'll feel better."

I press my lips together, studying his face for any signs of hesitancy. He looks determined and sincere and is showing no fear. It will be pleasurable for him and me. Do I want to get that intimate with him?

"Okay," I finally agree.

I get a glimpse of nerves as he closes his eyes, looking like he's bracing for pain.

I hold onto his shoulders as I allow my fangs to extend again. Hunter opens his eyes, and the fear is replaced by admiration. I lean into his neck, not wanting to look at his face anymore. I let the tip of my fangs touch his neck, pushing against the skin, and I hear a gasp come from Hunter. I breathe out and then let my fangs sink in. His hands run down my body and to my waist, pulling my body closer. I grip tightly onto his shoulders as his sweet and intoxicating blood touches my senses. He grunts as I gulp the liquid down, trying to get even closer to him.

I smile when I notice the bulge in his pants, how I am affecting him. The more blood I take, the more I feel stronger; I no longer feel the pain of being thrown into the wall, and the blood going into my mouth and down my throat soothes the burn from the Demons' Torment. Even though I know I can pull away, I don't want to.

If I could, I would want to stay this way forever, but eventually, I would drain Hunter, and that would be no fun. The thought of if Reid found out and how it would cause him to become more distant as his trust was broken again has me pulling back from Hunter. I lick the holes that my fangs made and go to step back, but Hunter's hands on my hips stop me. I lift my eyes to meet his and see lust.

"You're beautiful. You know that, right?" he says, dazed from the bite. He brings one of his hands up to my cheek. Not giving me any time to think, he leans forward and captures my lips in a kiss. I don't know what makes me do it, but I return it with the same vigor. My earlier thoughts about Reid go out of the window; technically, we're not together. What he doesn't know won't hurt him.

I wrap my arms around Hunter's neck as his hand on my cheek moves to the back of my neck. His lips are soft as they open, allowing his tongue to run across the seam of my lips. He walks me back until I feel my back hit the wall, and Hunter's hard body presses into me. This is the only time I want to be stuck between a rock and a hard place.

I moan as I let my head fall back, giving us both a breather. I could continue, but Hunter is human and can't hold his breath as long as me. Hunter's mouth doesn't leave me as his mouth moves over my face and down my throat. I gasp when he places his own bite there.

I rub my hands over his shoulders and down his chest, stopping at the hem of his shirt, tugging it up marginally so I can get my hands under it. Hunter continues to attack my neck as I drag my nails down his muscles. He grunts, pulling back and dragging the shirt up his body and over his head. I trail my finger lightly over his chest, watching them go over the ridges of muscle and up onto his tribal tattoo on his right shoulder, continuing onto his chest.

Hunter's hand comes to my chin, lifting my face up so he can go back to kissing me. This time, the kiss is gentle and slow. Hunter lifts me up, and I wrap my legs around his waist. I move against him, enjoying the friction, a distant ringing starting up.

It takes me a moment to conclude it's my phone. I ignore it, not wanting to stop. If they really need me, they can call again. Sure enough, when the ringing stops, it starts up again moments later. I ignore it again, but when it stops and starts again, I groan and pull back from Hunter.

I keep one hand on Hunter's shoulder as I grab my phone from my pocket. I look down at the screen, seeing that Reid is the one trying to get my attention. A short spurt of panic runs through me, thinking Reid knows what Hunter and I were doing, but I quickly push it away. There is no way that it's possible. I look at Hunter, biting my lip as I feel guilty for what I'm about to do. I need to be sure that Reid will never find out. If Reid is calling, he must have realized how stupid he's being.

"You can't tell Reid what just happened. It's not going to happen again. I just needed a distraction," I tell him, trying to convince myself at the same time.

Hunter drops me abruptly, hurt obvious on his face. He clenches his jaw, his back to me as he grabs up his shirt, putting it on. He clutches the jacket in his hand as he begins to pick his way through the mess to the floor.

"Yeah, it was just the hormones from the bite. It would have never happened otherwise," he tells me. Was it true? Would I have still kissed him and him me if we both weren't affected by the bite? A stab of pain hits me in the chest as if my heart has just been ripped out. I have to check that it hasn't, as the pain is so real. Was everything he said a lie?

He pulls the door open, striding out of the room, his exit being made final by the slam of the door behind him. I stand there a minute, staring at him. I clear my throat as I look down at the still ringing phone and answer it, bringing it up to my ear.

"I need your help," Reid announces straight away, sounding scared. I bet something rarely scares him.

"Where are you?" I ask hurriedly as I make my way out of the room, every bad situation running through my mind. Has Kyle got to him? Has he been hurt? I forget about the mess I'm leaving behind as I run at the fastest normal pace that I can. I hear Reid tell me he's at his house, and I tell him I'll be there shortly.

I don't see Hunter as I make my way out of the building, and the guilt returns. I didn't mean what I said; I was just surprised by the feelings I felt toward him. When Reid and I were having problems, I went to two of his gang members. If Reid didn't trust me before, he definitely wouldn't now. He's shown me that he doesn't trust easily. The betrayal would probably be worse than him finding out I'm not human. I push all of the thoughts and guilt about what happened with Hunter out of my mind as I rush out to my bike, ignoring the students who are slowly arriving.

***

I skid to a halt outside of Reid's gates ten minutes later. I lean and press the button on the box so I can gain approval to come in. When I hear the speaker crackle, letting me know that the mic has been activated, I talk.

"Hello, how are you today?"

"Oh God! It's you again," the guarder of the gates, Clive, mutters.

I hear a bang. Either he dropped his head onto the table, or he shot himself.

"Hello?" I ask.

I earn a grunt in response. He's still alive, thankfully.

"There's no need to be rude. I only asked how you were."

"Just go in," he pleads like last time.

I chuckle as the gates slowly slide open, allowing me to pull through and zoom up the drive. I jump off the bike, putting the kickstand down before I go running up the steps toward the entrance. I am about to pull the door open when a shout stops me. I turn to find Bianca lying back on the grass on the other side of the drive, sunbathing.

"Hey, bitch, what are you doing here?" She stands up and walks toward me. I meet her halfway, going back down the steps.

"The almighty one called me," I tell her.

She smirks. "Yeah? He's been acting pretty strangely today," she comments.

"He might be like that for about a week, but he'll be fine. He's had demon blood, and his body is telling him to have human blood," I say. I see hundreds of questions going through her mind, but I stop her by changing the subject. "Do you know where he is?"

"I think he's down in the training room," she tells me. I thank her, feeling glad that he's home, before running back up the stairs.

"Okay, I'll just wait here then," she calls after me.

I laugh. "That'd be great. See you later," I call back to her over my shoulder as I go through the door. I walk through the hall and down the stairs to the training room. I try and forget that the last time I was down here it didn't end well as I see Reid waiting for me outside the closed door.

"So, have you decided that you've had enough space now? You ready for me to be around you, or are you going to say you need more space?" I ask, coming to a stop in front of him.

He nods as he talks.

"Yes, I'm sorry. You're not a monster," he says.

I raise my eyebrows at him. "Really?" I ask sarcastically.

He looks apologetic as he exhales loudly. "It was just a shock to see the person you love and trusted the most to change into a demon," he admits.

My breath catches at his words, and I try not to get too hopeful.

"Love?" I ask, thinking it was just a slip of the tongue. He doesn't hesitate as he steps closer, his hands going to mine.

"Yes. I love you, Scarlett Hades."

No one has ever said that to me before. Well, my dad tells me, but to have someone who isn't family say it with the emotions that were in Reid's voice is new to me. I feel a smidge of guilt, but I ignore it as Reid leans forward. He stops, looking at my face for permission, and what he sees there has him leaning further and placing a soft kiss on my lips. I let a small smile come to my lips. However, I try to keep it as minimal as possible. I don't want to go straight back to the way we were because he's said he's sorry. I need to be sure; I don't want to be hurt again by him changing his mind. I've survived without a man for this long, but as soon as I am up on Earth, it all changes. I shouldn't need or want to rely on anyone to make me happy or be there for me.

"Why did you call me here? Were you just lying to me so I would come?" I ask.

At my words, Reid's face visibly pales.

"No. I really do need your help," he says, pushing the door to the training room open.

The smell of blood hits me, and if I hadn't eaten already, I'm sure Reid would be pinned to the wall as I feed off him. I look around the room as I enter and see that it looks like a massacre has happened. Four bodies are scattered around the room, blood pooling around them. I pick through them, listening to see if they have a heartbeat. They don't. I hold my breath as I turn back to Reid who has closed the door and locked it.

"Did you do this?" I ask.

His eyes flick around the room, and I know that my blood inside him is telling him that he's thirsty and that seems to be scaring him. I move back to him, gripping his face between my hands so he looks at me, getting his attention away from the mess.

"Yes," he starts off shakily. "I was at the punching bag when one of them cut themselves. It smelled amazing, and when I went to help him clean up, I went into a sort of frenzy. I attacked him, and then it just didn't stop. I had fangs, and the blood was like nectar," he rambles, sounding panicked.

I smile at him reassuringly. "It's going to be okay. The demon blood in you took over your body," I tell him.

Reid begins to grab his hair in fists. I move my hands from his face to his hands, bringing them down. I stroke the back of his hands comfortingly, discreetly smelling him. His blood is mixed with four other scents from the people he attacked, as well as my own.

"They're all dead, which makes things easier."

"Okay," he says, putting his gang leader face on. "What do we do next? Am I going to turn into a demon like you?"

I shake my head as I step back from him, happy that he's back in control.

"No. You'll be fine. Like I said after I gave the blood to you, you need to drink the blood of six people. I'll deal with the bodies," I tell him, lifting the closest of the men onto my shoulder with ease.

"Scar, I am so sorry," he says.

"Don't worry, Reid. We'll talk about it later. I'll be back in a minute," I say, picking up the other three bodies.

I close my eyes and teleport out of the training room, making sure that I end up in a different country, in a wooded area. If they were to find them, they should have a hard time trying to identify what happened to the bodies or who they were, but if they were to, it wouldn't be traced back to Florida. I look around, seeing if anyone is near, and when I see that I am alone, I drop the bodies. I set them alight before I teleport back to the training room in Florida and Reid. I notice that my clothes are ruined with everything that happened today, making me glad that I just threw some random clothes on and didn't wear anything nice.

"It's dealt with," I tell him.

He looks upset and has started to pace the room. "Why am I like this? I can usually deal with something like this," he groans.

"It's the demon blood again. Your emotions will be heightened for the remainder of the five days," I explain.

An alarm begins to blare throughout the room and the house. I throw my hands over my ears, not expecting the onslaught of sound on my sensitive hearing. Reid automatically runs to the door, unlocking it. A sea of people enters the room and runs to the weapons. They ignore the blood splattered around the room, only focused on getting to their destination.

"What's happening?" I shout over the noise of the alarm and people shouting to each other.

"We're getting attacked!" Reid responds without stopping his movements to the weapons, equipping himself with some.

"You're not going," I call to him as I run up beside him.

"Yes, I am. It's my gang under attack, and you can't stop me from defending it," he replies.

I watch him for a moment. There is nothing I can do to stop him. He's going to do it anyway. I groan, grabbing a knife from the collection. I don't need it, but it could be handy. I run after Reid, following him up the stairs. I'm not going to let him leave my sight. A fight equals blood, and he can't control himself yet.

Chapter 34

Disappearing Act

The entrance hall is almost silent when we come out into it. The alarm stopped pretty quickly after it started. It's hard to believe that there are people on their way to the house, wanting to harm and kill everyone inside.

"What are we fighting? Ghosts?" I ask, trying to lighten the tense mood somewhat.

"Well, have you angered them lately?" he shoots back.

I purse my lips as I look at him. Touché.

"Ha ha. Very funny," I tell him dryly. "So, who are we fighting, Mr. I-know-it-all?"

"I don't know," he admits before calling a passing tall, thin girl over. "Diniya!"

She stops and turns, walking toward us, her big, golden eyes flicking toward me. She shows me her teeth in a smile, and I wink at her. Pushing her reddish hair behind her shoulder, she answers Reid. "What?"

"What do you know about what's happening?" Reid asks her.

"I wasn't the one to pull it this time if you're insinuating that," she replies, her hand going to her hip. I hold back a laugh.

"Good—well, bad, but..." he stumbles over his words.

I shake my head. I've never seen him be affected like this, not even with Meredith. My blood must be a part of it, or is it that he can't handle everyone like he makes out?

"I think what Reid is trying to ask is if you know who is attacking?" I intervene, curious to the answer as well. Is it Kyle? I'm going to be on edge every time there is something wrong, imagining it's going to be Kyle behind it.

"When the alarm was raised, I heard rumors of a sighting of Fallen Angels outside the gates before the gates started to get rammed. Everyone outside is trying to keep them back, but they're slowly making their way closer," she tells us.

I sigh in relief as Reid nods as if he expected this.

"How many?" he asks, his eyes on the closed doors. Now that I'm focusing on it, I can hear shouts and banging outside. The doors open, and everyone immediately gets into a stance of them being ready to attack, but they relax when they see it's not a hostile person.

"Fifty tops," Diniya tells Reid.

He nods, thinking it over. When I see that Reid isn't going to say anything, I thank her for him. She smiles again before running off into the house, going to secure it ready for if Meredith succeeds in entering the house.

"So, what's your call?" I ask, turning to Reid.

He ponders it a moment, looking around. I can see the thoughts going across his face. He's worried for his members, about their safety, but he's also worried about how he's going to stop the enemy from entering. There is one last loud bang from outside before gunshots start to sound. It looks like Meredith and her gang has decided for him. Reid takes his eyes off the door and turns to me, his hands reaching for mine. He squeezes them, looking intently at my face.

"Be careful, please," he implores.

"You forget. It takes a lot more than a bullet to kill me," I tell him quietly.

"Still, be careful," he says, stroking my hair back from my face.

"You too."

He leans down and brushes his lips gently over mine. "I missed being able to do that," he murmurs before stepping back and looking back to the floor.

"Then why take so long to get over who I am?" I mutter, not intending for him to hear, but he does, as I feel him stiffen beside me.

He is saved from responding by the door flying open. As soon as the person is visible, the knife I picked up is sinking into the person's chest. There is a stunned silence for a moment, as everyone in the hall looks to me where my hand is outstretched having just thrown it. Then gunshots quickly follow. The room becomes a hive of activity as people face off against each other, guns raised, and more people struggle with each other over their weapons. Reid steps forward as the smell of the blood starts to fill the room. I hold his arm tightly, stopping him from attacking the closest person.

"Breathe through your mouth. It'll help," I offer, as I get him to do it with me. He follows my instructions, visibly relaxing.

"You lost your only weapon," he tells me, facing me full on. "Here take this." He tries to push a gun into my hand, but I don't take it.

"I haven't." He looks confused, but I wink at him. "Perks of being a goddess," I tell him, raising my fingers and waggling them, fire dancing on the end.

He lets out a breathy chuckle before nodding as if to say good luck. He turns and walks off to help his members. I quickly lose him in the scuffle happening around me. I try and follow, wanting to keep the promise to myself that I wouldn't let him out of my sight. As I walk, I look at the surrounding fight. This is not going to end well; Styx Lake is going to be inundated with people. Some of the scuffles I see happening draw my attention. Has Kyle added people into the gang, or are they all working for Kyle disguised as Fallen Angels? I hear someone running up behind me, and without stopping my thinking, I turn, raising my leg, kicking the man in the side. He goes flying through the air, crashing into the wall.

I need to find a way of determining how I can sense these new demons. Grant said that they appeal to demons more, but I can't rely on that. I have no feeling from them; usually, I can sense anything that is not of this world.

Another man runs up to me, knife raised, and I focus my attention on the fight happening around me. I forgot about watching Reid; he could be attacking people right now for all I know. Before the man can strike, I grab him by the neck, snapping it easily. With his head at an odd angle, I drop him to the floor. I hear a shot fire, and I dodge out of the way. I watch as the bullet moves slowly past me, as I use my adapted sight. I see Reid fighting a man who quickly goes down. I can tell Reid is struggling because as soon as the man goes down with a slash to his neck, Reid bends down, ready to drink the blood pouring out of him. I rush forward, weaving through the people, grabbing his arm and pulling him with me to the closest wall, pushing him against it.

"You need to calm down. Anger is not going to help your bloodlust," I tell him forcefully when I see that he is furious.

"I am calm," he insists, going to pull out of my grip. I pull him back, so he's looking at me.

"Reid, I'm serious. Calm yourself down," I order, putting the tone I use with demons at home into my voice. Yet another person creeps up on me from behind, and I spin to deal with them.

"Did you never get told it's rude to interrupt people when they are having a conversation?" I ask as I let my fingernails grow. I clutch his throat, my hand going around his windpipe. His eyes widen as they look at me. I pull my hand out, cutting his air supply. The blood sprays like a fountain out of his neck, and luckily, we are at such an angle that the blood misses Reid completely. The man, now with a hole in his neck, slumps to the floor, and I kick him further away so Reid can't get to him.

I wipe my hand on my pants as I look back to Reid. His eyes are wide and full of hunger. I bring my non-bloody hand up and across his cheek, bringing his attention to the pain rather than the hunger.

"Think of anything else. I don't care but just calm down." He pulls me closer and gives me a deep kiss. Pulling back, he looks much better.

"I'm calmer now," he smirks with a wink. I smile and watch as he walks back into the fight. I turn and start to follow him again when I feel a hand on my shoulder. Without thinking, I flip her over my shoulder, following her to the floor. I straddle her and lift my hand, only to pause when I see a surprised Bianca under me. I sit back, stopping completely the descent of my hand down to her chest.

"Whoa, it's only me. I should have known not to creep up on you though," she says as I get off her and pull her up.

"Have you seen where that bitch that interrupted my sunbathing is?" she asks.

I look around and shake my head.

"Sorry, not seen her."

Bianca harrumphs in disappointment, pursing her lips.

"I'll let you know if I find her," she promises as she starts to walk away.

"Have you got a spare gun?" I call after her.

She laughs as she turns back to me. "Of course," she says, reaching for the back of her shorts with the hand which is not holding a gun. She passes me the one she retrieved before waving at me. I notice someone making their way closer to us, so I lift the gun and shoot a bullet right between his eyes over Bianca's shoulder.

"Well, I'm going to find the bitch. Have fun," she jovially says as if we were just playing a game of paintball. I guess you get used to gun fights if you're in a gang. I take out the magazine of the gun and see that it's full apart from the one that had just been shot.

The next time I look up, Bianca is skipping into the dwindling fight, shooting people around her.

A sharp pain in my shoulder has me wincing and looking around for the perpetrator. The bullet tears through my shoulder before it continues out of my body. At least I don't have to worry about removing it later. I notice that one of the last men standing has his gun pointed at me.

Before he can pull the trigger again, I am running toward him, knocking the gun from his loose hands. It skids toward the entrance, and I follow it with my eyes, watching it as it moves past bodies lying on the floor. The fight is winding down with the remaining Fallen Angels retreating. The bodies surrounding us are mostly members of the attacking party. However, I am sad for Reid to see that some are his own members. The man in front of me sees that I am distracted and uses it to kick me in the side. Stumbling, I stay on my feet as I lift the gun and shoot the man in the forehead. He falls to the floor with the rest of the wounded and dead. The fight seemed like it was over before it really begun.

The chaos and confusion slowly die down, and I begin to search for Reid, finding him tending to a knife wound on his arm. I start toward him, only to get intercepted by Bianca who is pouting.

"I watched everyone leave, and I couldn't find Meredith. To be honest, it was too easy for it be Fallen Angels," she lets me know as she walks with me. I bite my lip to stop myself from mentioning Kyle's name. I don't want to drag her into it, as Reid will have a way of finding out from her, and it could only end up with us all being worse off.

"Maybe she wanted to use it to scare you all and knew to keep away," I suggest.

She shrugs, looking outside. "I'm going to continue my sunbathing while I can," she tells me. "I've had enough stress for today." She winks at me before she walks out of the house.

I chuckle at her laid-back attitude. You would never think that she was just in a bloody fight to the death.

I tap Reid on the shoulder as I step up behind him.

"How are you doing?" I ask him, hoping he'll catch that I mean his thirst.

"I feel like I'm dehydrated," he replies, swallowing after.

"It's the quantity. To your body, you are dehydrated, as it can smell all the blood that it wants, but you're stopping it from having it."

"Is it this hard and painful for you all the time?" he asks, sounding strained.

"No. I've grown up learning to control it. The only time that I can say that I feel like you are now is when I feel strong emotions. My control over the bloodlust usually slips then. It usually doesn't help when there are large quantities, such as now, and my throat does feel a little dry, but I've had enough blood today to keep me in check," I clarify, looking away from him when I remember who gave me the blood and what happened after. A remorseful expression takes over his face as he continues to look at me.

"I'm sorry about calling you a monster. You're far from it."

"You already said that," I point out, clearing my throat as I feel the atmosphere change.

"I know, but I just wanted you to know I mean it," he tells me sincerely. Wanting to make sure I won't fall for him to only break my heart, I listen to his and the steady rhythm of it.

"I believe you. How's the arm?" I ask, looking at it, thankful for the distraction.

"It's just a scratch, nothing major." His eyes cloud over when they fall onto my shoulder and to where the guy shot me.

"What about you?" he asks concerned, as he pushes my hair back and away from it.

I look down and see that there is a bloody hole which I know will heal by the end of the day. He turns me, looking down at the shoulder again from the back, pulling the hair up. I hear a hiss as Reid sucks a breath through his teeth.

"Who did this to you?" he asks angrily.

I turn back to him and shrug it off, wincing slightly at the movement.

"It's fine. It'll heal in a couple of hours, like the knife wound did," I tell him as I pull out of his grip which is getting tighter, unintentionally, as his anger grows. He scans the room. "And I don't think I would be able to pick him out, anyway," I lie.

His eyes zoom back to me. The crystal blue color has darkened considerably. He clenches his jaw as he grits his words out. "Tell me which one."

"It's not going to help anything. He's dead. I shot him in the head," I tell him. Surveying the room again, now looking for people with bullet wounds to the head, Reid zeroes in on the man.

"Was it him?" he demands.

Surprised at Reid finding the man, I press my lips together, giving him the answer. Satisfied, he grunts as storms past me, looking ready to murder someone. The man is lucky that he's already dead. He stops over the dead man, pulling his gun out and emptying the rounds into his body.

I see when the smell hits him, as he looks like he was physically hit by it. He leans down, his finger poking at one of the wounds which has blood pooling there. As quick as a bolt of lightning, I am beside Reid, pulling his hand away from where it was going up to his lips, holding it in a grip which makes him unable to move it. I back up, watching as his eyes flick to all of the blood as we move. I grab the back of his neck, so he is looking at me as I wipe the blood away from his hand.

"Calm. Down," I grit out yet again.

His face is stone, letting me know that his anger is still bubbling under the surface.

"He hurt you."

"I'll live, but you won't if you keep going like this. You'll be a demon before you know it." What I told him is not technically true; he would have to die for it to affect him. He could have six people's blood in his body, and when the six days are up, he would be fine, but I don't want to risk it with Kyle's threat hanging in the air.

"Don't you want me to be like you?" he asks, backing away from me, slightly hurt.

"Only twenty-four hours ago, you thought I was a monster." I raise my eyebrows at him. "So, no. You would change for all of the wrong reasons. It's not like you would only do it for a week, and if you didn't like it, change back. This is for *eternity*, Reid," I stress to him.

He grumbles something under his breath, leaving me to assist his gang with moving the injured and dead. I groan at Reid before I go to help as well. I see Diniya dragging a body toward the entrance, and I go to help her with it. I lift up the legs as Diniya studies my face before looking at Reid.

"What's wrong with him?" she asks as we work together on moving out of the house and to the growing pile of bodies.

"He's being a hypocritical, stubborn idiot. So, nothing," I joke.

She laughs as we drop the body. I walk back into the entrance hall with Diniya by my side. I look around and marvel at how it feels like the fight never happened. The only difference would be the bullet holes, blood, and bodies.

I see that Reid is talking to one of the members by the staircase. Diniya leaves me, walking to help someone else. I cross my arms as I watch him. I might have been a bit harsh with him. I am just about to apologize when a movement out of the corner of my eye and shouts of terror catches my attention.

I look over and see one of the "corpses" sitting up, lifting their arm to point the gun in his hand at Reid. Not caring about the people surrounding me and what they will think, I lift my own hand and shoot a ball of fire at the man. Hopefully, it will distract him enough to get him to lower the gun. When the—what I assume to be—demon moves out of the way, still aiming his gun, I am torn. Do I go to the demon to stop him, or go to Reid to try and save him?

What happened next seems to be in slow motion and makes my mind up for me. As soon as I hear the loud bang, I run toward Reid, racing the bullet to the destination. If I can just get there and knock him out of the way, it will be okay. I am in reaching distance when I see the bullet enter Reid's chest, where his heart is, and he slumps to the floor. I catch him, kneeling down to keep the blood in him as long as possible. I block out the screams as I lay his head on my lap, holding it. If I can just keep the blood in him, maybe the demon blood can heal him enough that he doesn't have to die. However, I am aware that he doesn't have nearly enough of my blood to save him fully.

"Reid...Reid...Stay with me," I choke out, around the tears. I cover the wound, bringing my hand to my lips, biting it so I can get him some of my blood. I move it back down and to his lips, but Reid's heart is getting weaker, and the blood isn't getting into him nearly fast enough. My emotions being heightened means that my demon side is stronger and has the wound healing from my bite faster than usual. I bring my now healed wrist to my mouth again. I can't lose him. I've already lost one person too many with Kyle. At his name, I ponder what would have happened if I had chosen the other option and just drank the Demons' Torment. Would Reid still be alive?

He coughs, and I see blood start to trickle down his chin. I see my tears start to drop onto his face as I smell the blood in his body. There are four different scents in his blood, other than mine and Reid's. He doesn't have enough blood to turn him into a demon. I don't want to see him become a soul yet.

"I love you," he starts weakly. "I want you to know that."

"Bianca!" I scream loudly. She's the only one around who knows about me and can possibly help. I need someone to reassure me. I turn back to Reid. "I love you too. Please don't leave me yet. I don't want you to. We were…" I stop when I hear his heartbeat start to drop before suddenly stopping. I cry out and begin to shake him, wanting it to be a joke and for him, or me, to wake up. I thought I would have more time and that my blood would keep him alive longer.

"No. No. No. Please! Dad! Zeus! Do something! I hate you! Why couldn't you stop this!" I shout, looking around for the person who took him from me. He's disappeared. I see Bianca running through the front door, but I ignore her as I lean down to place a kiss on Reid's still lips. I feel more tears fall when they don't respond.

"I'll get you back," I murmur the promise against his lips. I fall back and away from him, my head going to my hands, running my fingers through my hair.

"Oh my God," I hear Bianca breathe out as she takes in the scene. I look up to see her checking for a pulse.

"He's not dead," I convince her and myself.

"He has no pulse. That usually means that they are," she tells me gently, noting how upset I am.

"I'm going to get him back. He's not been sorted yet," I tell her determinedly, shoving the tears off my face. I ignore the curious looks I am getting from the people who have crowded around us.

"Can you do that?" she asks.

"I don't know, but I'll try," I tell her. I don't care about anyone finding out, or what happens, as long as I get Reid back.

I close my eyes, the image of Styx Lake in my mind.

***

My feet hitting the soft ground causes my eyes to fly open, and I begin to look at every face in each line. I go back over them again and again, looking at the new people, and when I am sure that everyone has been seen, I move to the closest demon and demand for their tablet. I look at the last half an hour to see if I can find Reid's name, finding it weird that he's not here. I want to see with my own eyes Reid's name with the hundreds of others. I don't want it to seem like he's the only one that's died, and that would be the case if I were to search his name. I move through the thousands of names, looking at each one. I finally find his name— Reid Brice. It says that he has died but not been sorted yet. Getting even more confused, because I'm sure that he's not here, I pass the tablet back to the guard. Maybe he slipped through, but that's never happened. Reid's one of a kind though. I hear the boat making its way back to the dock, and I greet it at the end. They are usually good at remembering everyone who has gone through, and they should remember someone like Reid. I ask the demon who jumps off the boat if she has seen Reid, describing him.

"No, sorry, Scar," she apologizes. I'm getting more and more befuddled. What's happened to him? He can't have left any other way; the gates don't let any souls through.

"Dad!" I shout so if he's in Hell he can hear. All the souls turn to look at me, but my determination on finding Reid has me focusing on my dad's reply.

"What?" he whines, causing the ground to rumble with the volume.

"I need your help!" I shout back.

"Ugh. Fine," he relents as he appears beside me. "What is it?"

"Reid died," I state, forcing down the tears.

"Oh, I liked McDonald's boy," he says, disappointed. "If you're asking if I can bring him back to life: one, I can't do that. Ask your uncle. And two, I wouldn't if I could." I don't register what he's telling me enough to ask why he wouldn't bring Reid back to life.

"You have no one to bring back. He's gone."

"That's impossible," he says.

Yeah, like I don't already know that, Dad.

"That's why I need your opinion. The tablet said he was dead but not sorted, and he's not down here," I explain.

He produces a tablet out of thin air and starts it up.

"What's his full name?" I supply it for my dad, who then types it in. His eyebrows draw together when he gets the result.

"See," I agree with him.

"Are you sure he's dead? It says here that he's not dead and never has been," my dad says as he moves the tablet so I can see what he's talking about. *No results found.* I check how my dad spelled it, but it was all correct.

"How—no. I saw him die right in front of me. He's dead! His name was there," I say, getting angry.

"Okay," he agrees before turning to a passing soul. "Are there good asylums on Earth?"

I punch him in the arm, angry at him mocking me instead of trying to believe me.

"I'm not mad! I didn't imagine the whole fight!" I hold myself back from yelling as I cross my arms. He nods, obviously not believing me.

"Okay, have some blood. You look a bit peaky," he comments before walking away.

I groan throwing my hands up into the air. Wondering if I did imagine it, or if Reid wasn't actually dead when I left, I teleport back to the gang house.

I look around and see that the entrance hall is empty. My head starts to hurt as I notice that all the blood has disappeared and there is no sign of the fight ever happening. I know earlier I said that I wasn't obvious, but this is taking the piss. There are no signs of it happening, not even bullet holes. I run out of the front door and see Bianca lying on the grass, sunbathing, where she was when I first arrived, and no sign of the pile of bodies which was growing when I left. I slowly walk up to her.

"How did you get it all cleared up?" I ask.

"Hm? I didn't hear you arrive. What do you mean? Aren't you meant to be with Reid?" she asks as she leans up on her elbows.

"The remains of the fight," I tell her, feeling stupid as a result of everyone not believing me.

"What are you talking about? Did Reid and you fight on your date?" she asks, pushing her sunglasses up onto her head.

"The fight, where Reid died..." I prompt.

"What? Reid died? What did you two do on your date?" she panics.

I look at her, feeling extremely confused.

"I did not imagine that whole fucking fight!" I exclaim in anger.

She shrugs her shoulders. "I'm sorry, but I don't remember anything. Maybe you should get some sleep," she suggests.

I let out another loud groan. What is with everyone?

I stomp towards my bike and speed toward my home.

***

I arrive in my drive to see that my door is open. I approach cautiously, smelling the air.

Kyle!

I ready myself to attack him if he is still there and enter the house. I listen and hear nothing, only my own heartbeat. He must have come and left without staying long as the scent is not strong. The scent of blood is stronger. Dread fills my veins, imagining the worst, that it's Reid's. The smell, however, is too sour to be his. Relief makes me continue forward to find out where the smell is coming from. I walk into the kitchen, grabbing a bag of blood to see if maybe my dad was right. Maybe the Demons' Torment was still in my system.

I sip the liquid as I go to walk back out, but the smell of the blood is strongest here and an arrow painted with it on the wall has me stopping. I follow the direction of the arrow and see that it is pointing to a cupboard. I creep closer, opening the door slowly, feeling fearfully curious. The head of the man I saw kill Reid is lying at my feet. Attached to his head with a pin is a note. I rip it off and read it, my fear replaced with rage.

Do you doubt yourself yet? Maybe this will help.

Wondering where lover boy is? I can help with that as well. He's with me, and very mad.

See you on the battle field.

With love,

K x

Kyle! That bastard! He was behind it and now has Reid. Kyle somehow made everyone believe I was mad. I am going to find him, and when I do, I will kill Kyle the longest and most painful way I can think of. If he wants a war, then I'll give him one—one that he won't win.

THE END

Can't get enough of Scarlett and Reid? Make sure you sign up for the author's blog to find out more about them!

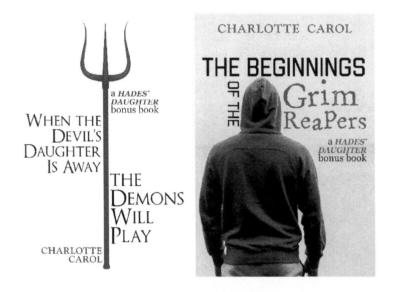

Get these two bonus chapters and more freebies when you sign up at author's account on charlotte-carol.awesomeauthors.org!

Here is a sample from another story you may enjoy:

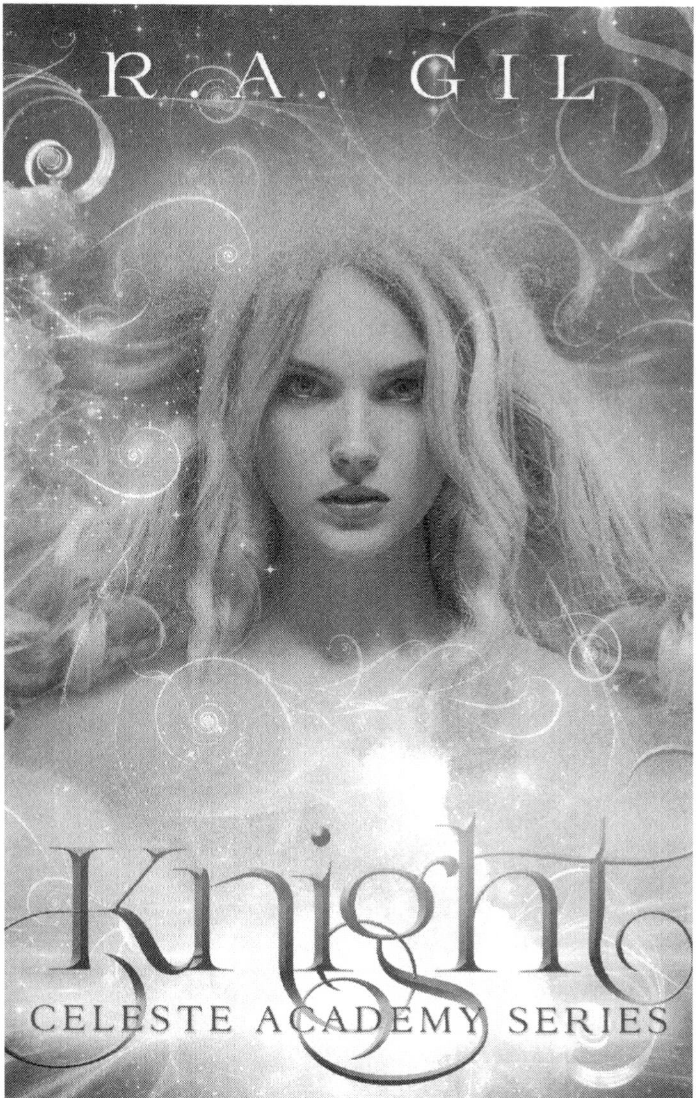
R. A. GIL
Knight
CELESTE ACADEMY SERIES

Prologue

"This is the first time in a while the gates will open," said Lord Aeron as he watched the woman approach the rippling image of monstrous towers—structures of glaring titans and prideful giants that pierced the skies. "I see a lot has changed, but they remain the same."

The woman, Seraphina, looked on with a flash of apprehension. Her fingers curled around the weapon sheathed by her side as she reached out with her other hand and touched what felt like silk and water—the boundary that separated this world from theirs. A strong force nipped her skin, pulling her in like a lover beckoning. It felt warm yet forceful in a way, as though eager for an embrace.

Seraphina stepped back, withdrawing her hand from the portal as she swallowed and breathed nervously. "How do I return after this mission is done?"

"Return to the same place you came out of, and all will be well. The gates are weak, so it should be no trouble for you." His hands were laced at the curve of his spine. "You will know where the portal is. Earth lacks the power pressure Valemnia possesses. The energy will be evident to those who can sense it." A crease gathered between his brows as he eyed the city before them. A small sigh escaped his lips—so subtle it felt like a mere breath.

Seraphina nodded. She straightened her spine as she stepped forward, her hand subconsciously reaching for the cravat around her neck, tugging on its length as though doing so would appease her nerves.

Aeron stood back. "Remember: do not return unless necessary. We cannot afford opening the gates all the time. You will not be able to use your element while there, so you must rely solely on your skills to fight."

"I know." She nodded, branding his words in her mind and letting it echo a few more times to make sure she didn't forget.

Mustering courage with a huge intake of breath, she determinedly jumped forward, breaking through the fragile silk that was the boundary, tearing through the space and forcing herself on foreign soil.

It gave in, parting for her but mending itself once she'd gone through. It rippled, and she appeared on the other side, walking on the pavement on the streets of Boston.

She turned and looked over her shoulder. In place of where her world had been was nothing but a wall.

Chapter 1

On a Summer Saturday

The peaceful morning of a summer Saturday was shattered when Valeriana Kerrigan found an alternative use for the railings. A smooth glide was not much work. She had perfect execution without much grace. Unfortunately, her landing was more of a crash. And she had the hem of her jeans to blame; it caught on the ornate metalwork and tugged her back gruffly, causing her to lose balance and land on the paneled floor of their living room.

She landed with a loud thud. To top it all off, her duffel bag hit her in the face like salt to an open wound.

"Valery!" a loud voice reverberated, packing all the threat in one go.

"I know!" she exclaimed, shuffling in the direction of the dining room. "Coffee," she muttered. "I need my coffee. Mom, why didn't you wake me?"

"I tried," replied Lily, her brown eyes peeking past the frame of her reading glasses. "Have you been sliding again?" she asked.

The lights were turned off, and the windows were wide open to welcome sunlight. Valeriana's mother and her thirteen-year-old younger brother were already at the table. Jareth was squeezing out the bottle of maple syrup over his pancakes while Lily was preoccupied with the newspaper. Her eyes were on the coffee, even so. There was already a cup on her end, so she spent the next few moments brewing.

"I was in a hurry."

Her mother shook her head and sighed in defeat. "How many times has that happened? You never learn."

Valeriana shrugged. She stirred the steaming beverage as she moved to take her seat, setting down her cup on the table. Gathering her honey golden locks in a high ponytail, she pulled on the scrunchie around her wrist and snapped it in place.

"What time is Xandra's flight?" Lily inquired.

"I don't know. I heard it was twelve something in the afternoon," Valeriana said. "I'm supposed to meet her at ten."

Jareth was still not done with the maple syrup. Valeriana eyed the pooling juices on his plate and frowned.

"You're not aiming for diabetes, are you?" she told him, hitting his arm as she wrenched off the bottle from his grip and safely placed it out of his reach. "Enough of that."

Jareth made a noise of irritation. "What's it to you? It's not your body." He rubbed his arm and mussed his ginger brown hair. He then resumed nibbling on his food while hiding his grass green eyes behind squinted lids.

Valeriana snubbed him and tossed a pancake onto her plate while sipping her coffee. She then took a lump of butter and dumped it over her share, sparing the syrup a glance before ignoring it altogether. Jareth was eyeing her with contempt the entire time.

"If I'm too into sugar, you're too into butter." He huffed. "That's why you're fat, pig."

Valeriana bit her lip and leaned over to smack his arm one more time. "I dare you to say that again. You do not call a girl fat. I am definitely not fat!"

She watched her brother wince. Considering he had fish bellywhite skin, it was sure to leave a mark.

She had just the right build and the ideal weight. She might have extra deposits on some parts that made her feel insecure, but she definitely wasn't fat. Just a healthy teenager her age too lazy to go to the gym.

"Keep telling that to yourself," Jareth told her.

"Goddamn—"

"Language," their mother cut in. "Just focus on eating, you two. Stop fighting."

He stuck his tongue out at her, shoving the dripping slice of pancake into his mouth.

"Immature," she said, cutting off a small piece and chewing on it. She suddenly lost her appetite.

"And you think you aren't?" he mumbled through a full mouth.

"Stop it, Jareth. Valery, the longer you argue with your brother, the longer you'll stay," their mother said, a hint of a smile on her lips.

"Mm-hmm," she hummed, stuffing her mouth and swallowing incessantly. She reached for her coffee and drank, washing down the food she almost had stuck in her throat. With a clean plate and an empty mug before her, she stood from her seat and began heading out.

She waved. "I'm off! Bye, people!"

Valeriana kissed the tip of her fingers and brushed them on the portrait of a man on the wall just beside the door frame, flipping back her hair and admiring his image for a moment with her azure eyes.

"Bye, Dad."

If you enjoyed this sample then look for
Knight.

Introducing the Characters Magazine App

Download the app to get the free issues of interviews from famous fiction characters and find your next favorite book!

iTunes: bit.ly/CharactersApple
Google Play: bit.ly/CharactersAndroid

Acknowledgements

First of all, I would like to thank everyone who has been there for me through the last few years; you were the ones that made this book happen!

There are a number of exceptional people I would like to thank:

- My parents—for giving me my fingers and brain that allowed me to write this book, and for their constant support.
- My clucking mad brother, Oliver—for giving me the inspiration for all the silliness in this book and always making me smile.
- Gemma—for always being there for me!
- Calvin—for helping me, and my family, fight the demons. I wouldn't be where I am in life without him.
- Rae—for teaching me English well!
- Mel—for being my fabulous hairdresser and friend.
- My publishers—for believing in me and my book, and making my dream possible. I wouldn't be here doing these acknowledgements if it wasn't for them.

And thank you to all of you who have taken the time to read this book, whether it be when it was online or now. I wouldn't be achieving my dream without you!

Author's Note

Hey there!

Thank you so much for reading *Hades' Daughter*! I can't express how grateful I am for reading something that was once just a thought inside my head.

I'd love to hear from you! Please feel free to email me at charlotte-carol@awesomeauthors.org and sign up at charlotte-carol.awesomeauthors.org for freebies!

One last thing: I'd love to hear your thoughts on the book. Please leave a review on Amazon or Goodreads because I just love reading your comments and getting to know YOU!

Whether that review is good or bad, I'd still love to hear it!

Can't wait to hear from you!

Charlotte Carol

About the Author

I love to write, usually different types of romance. I like to think that I am a friendly, funny, and happy person. You will most likely find me reading, writing, eating chocolate, or going an adventure somewhere (some of them at the same time!).